NEW PEWS FOR SUNDAY

By Stephen E. Scott

Prologue

The Reverend John Rowlands walked casually along the right hand side aisle towards the highly polished light oak communion rail, which spanned the front of his church, turned left as he reached the front row of plastic seating, walked to the left hand aisle and ambled back towards the open front doors of his church as he waited for the first delivery of the new pews. He ran his fingers along his grey flecked, black, goaty beard and then through the sides of his black wavy hair just over his ears to the back of his neck; his mind flitting as he reflected over the previous twenty months of fund raising, events, coffee evenings, where the focus had been on saving enough money in order to buy the new seating.

He stopped in the vestibule rather than going out into the fresh October morning as he caught sight of his reflection in the glass of the two closed inner doors which led into the church. His black rimmed glasses obscured some of his image slightly as he studied himself and realised they needed a good clean. The bottom of his black jumper removed the marks off the lenses.

It was one of those moments, a moment when anyone with time on their hands, with no time to do anything else of any importance, looks at themselves and thinks about their life, a rushed moment when their life, which should be considered as the most important thing to anyone, is given some fleeting, reflective thought.

Like many, like most, he had a good life. He was not rich but like eighty percent of the population in Britain, he was comfortable, no unnecessary worries. His family were loving with the usual sibling fractiousness between his three children Paul, Rebecca and Rachel.

His reflection told him he had aged to forty two but that didn't bother him. John looked at himself and felt blessed, grateful for his life. He turned sideways and looked at his five foot ten body. His stomach was still relatively flat despite his liking for real ale, wine, in fact most alcohol, a residual vice in some of his congregation's pious eyes, left over from his rugby days before his calling. He didn't look at it like that. Life was too short and you had to make the most and the best of

your life as it could end tomorrow and it was down to you, to stay in control of things.

John was not your conventional minister or the TV's general portrayal of a cup of tea, with a Welsh cake or a glass of sherry minister, calling on little old ladies for an hour's chat, although he enjoyed those type of visits as well. He liked rugby still and most sports. Meals had wine. Some church meetings unconventionally spilled over into a pub with his gentle encouragement, where the more open minded committee and church council members might socialise with him in a more casual atmosphere, relaxed by his openness. Some people thought him a bit too forthright and individual, that he should be there for them and should do what they wanted or proposed. John was far from a shrinking violet and had a way about him that engaged people, made them and their suggestions feel important, even if he didn't end up agreeing with them or doing what they wanted.

The vestibule along with four shelves of regimented red bound hymn books, a rough bristled welcome mat flanked by two black umbrella and coat stands; had the customary picture of Jesus surrounded by children and other pictures of saints and martyrs, which were there well before he came to this church five years ago. He wondered how they could have been so resolute in their faith when they had to stand up for their beliefs, the influence that God must have exerted on their lives and looked at himself again in the glass and spoke to his reflection. "Could you do what they did?" He paused and

thought about his answer. Was his faith, his courage as strong as theirs?

"God forbid I ever have to do anything like that," he said quizzically back to himself but God is not the only force that can exert influence and John's thinking had not in those brief moments of self examination considered there were alternatives. He continued to look at his reflection and jumped backwards as the glass in the door suddenly misted up along its length, as if it had been filled with smoke, robbing it of its transparency and his reflection.

"Good grief! What on earth?" He put his hands instinctively up to the glass, momentarily reacting as if it was going to fall out of the frame, cautious to stop it. John glanced around the vestibule to look for the cause. The glass covering the other pictures hanging on the walls had misted over as well, obscuring the subjects underneath.

Above the background of the general street noise, he heard the sound of a lorry's air breaks pulling up outside of the church

brakes

gates. John stood back still dumbfounded at the now opaque glazing all around the vestibule. His head shook with disbelief until he gathered his surprise and controlled his shaking head and just gazed, transfixed by the glass. Logically, illogically, he didn't know but thought innocently to himself, "I'll sort that out later," not knowing what the "that" might be. He turned his attention and thoughts to getting this delivery organised and meeting the men bringing the

new pews.

John turned to walk down to the lorry and was stopped by the sound of the door glazing cracking. John swirled around and watched open mouthed as the cracks turned into a crescendo of shattering glass. For a few seconds he stared, amazed at the pile of shards, his mind blank to any explanation as to why they would just disintegrate on their own for no apparent reason. He was, like everyone else would have been at that moment, oblivious to the thought, the concept that "something", some force or influence other than God would have been within his church. There would be a logical explanation for it happening but finding it would take John some time to discover and test his determination, his faith, even his own belief in himself.

Nothing happens for no reason.

Dedication.

This is my first book and comes from an idea I had years and years ago. My love and thanks to Shan and Samantha for not only their belief in me but also for the help they gave me, when I needed it, with the things I couldn't do in order to get it published.

Special Thanks

My thanks to my life long friend Martin who posed and put up with me one Saturday afternoon for the back cover and to Michael Dearden, who modified the original photos to make them into the book cover.

CHAPTER 1

"He's pointing the way!"
"What?"
"He's pointing the way."
Andrew had a lost expression, not catching on to what Paul was saying. Paul could see this. "God struth". He pointed, slightly frustrated to a shaft of light coming through a break in the overhanging rain clouds.

The beam did seem to ominously point the way to the church where they were heading with the first delivery of the new pews their carpentry firm had made, as it fell on and around the building. The accidents that had happened during the pews production had been forgotten in the main and been put down to "one of those things" but they were the only accidents that had ever occurred during the production of anything either of them could remember, if they had given them a second thought; apart from the customary splinter.

Andrew's attention however, was more interested in the way the light was catching the twitching of the black PVC mac worn by a blond woman walking past the entrance gates. They were still about a hundred yards away so he couldn't really appreciate the curve of her hips underneath the coat though he concentrated hard on looking at her.

"See what I mean!" Paul still attempting to get Andrew to understand his joke."Oh yeah, I'm with you now, we wouldn't have found it without HIS help!"

The church that they were going to was about two hundred

years old, built in the days when congregations were large, when everyone went to church on Sunday, when fire and brimstone sermons ruled the pulpit. It was big, built out of blue pendant stone with a welsh slate roof and sandstone inlaid bricks around the arched stain glassed windows and doorways. The beauty of the stained glass was hidden to the most extent by ugly iron shutters that had been fitted during the Second World War and had been refitted when the windows suffered more vandalism during the seventies than anything they had been exposed to by the Luftwaffe. The shutters were opened on a Sunday to light up the church and the windows that remained still caught people's attention.

When it was first built it stood alone and the large grey steeple would have pointed its presence against the backdrop of empty sky and mountains, a symbol of faith, drawing its congregation every Sunday. Now, other larger buildings had been built close to it and with two hundred years of urbanisation, it stood in the middle of the town and with everything that had been built around it; it had lost its domination. It was on the main street with a relatively high wall in the same grey stone, about five foot high, with sandstone capped pillars about a foot and a half taller. In between the pillars which stood about ten feet apart were black, rust bubbled, wrought iron railings which took the boundary up to 8 foot from pavement level. There were five stone steps, fourteen foot wide between the two gate pillars and their two foot depth were weather and foot worn and lead worshippers slowly and gracefully up to the forecourt outside of the two hand carved, arched solid oak doors with brass handles.

The roof ledges on each corner were home to hand carved creatures, crouching and straining to look down on mere mortals but the erosion they had suffered, gave them a far more sinister appearance than had been intended by the sculptor.

Paul looked for the space that was supposed to have been

coned off for their arrival. Andrew was still more interested in the twitching PVC mac and now as they drew closer, he could see the curve of the blonde's hips and buttocks as the below knee length coat pulled in tight mid way down her thighs.

"There's something about black." Andrew said, who was now beginning to visualise more than the mac revealed.

"You had better clean your thoughts up before going in there!" Paul motioned with his head as he pulled along side the space made for their parking; only it was too small.

"What do they thing we'll be bringing, a bloody moped!" The space was there but about fifteen feet too short for the 7.5 ton delivery wagon they were driving.

Paul looked at the gap, the front and back of the lorry overlapping the gap in the parked cars.

"Get out and see if you can get something shifted," Paul told Andrew.

"Where?"

"I don't care but I can't park here and we're not parking elsewhere and carrying the things, they're too flipping heavy."

Andrew did what he was asked, not knowing quite what he was going to do. "I'll tow one of these cars away with my teeth then, shall I?" as he jumped down into the road, "just get one of them shifted." He muttered sarcastically to himself, "just pick one up and stick it in my pocket, yeah no problem."

He stopped on the road and looked at the parked cars either end of the space, he looked around, hoping to see someone who looked like they were coming back to a car. There was no one that fitted that description.

"Holy shit!" He blurted out as he felt a hand on his shoulder and a voice saying, "you the delivery boys?"

He turned around at the same time as his reaction to face the minister, his brain taking a snap shot of his first impression, dog collar, black shirt, V necked black jumper, black rimed glasses and closely cut blackish beard and smile. The minister's face changed slightly to a disapproving countenance and slipped back to its full smile within a second or so.

"Sorry Father, you scared the crap out of me then!" Andrew realised what he just said, remembering his opening comment. Inside he felt his stomach cringe a bit and then felt his face was doing the same.

"I'm not a Father, I'm a minister, a Methodist minister to be precise, I'm John Rowlands." He held out his hand and the smile remained.

Andrew grabbed his hand, pulling him towards the pavement as he did. "Any chance we can move one of these cars?" He didn't hold out much hope.

"I'll move mine, I put it there because we didn't have enough cones, they keep getting stolen, causes a problem for weddings and things so I got here early this morning."

It was still only 9.10 "That must have been early, I thought vicars only worked on a Sunday," Andrew jokingly mocked, trying to gloss over his earlier faux pas and then thinking, "I bet everyone says that to a minister," on seeing the ministers smile freeze slightly when he said it. His stomach churned again.

Rev. Rowlands jumped into the first blue Ford Focus in the line of parked cars behind the lorry, put down the passenger window and shouted, "guide me out please."

Andrew watched and waived him out when the traffic allowed and watch him park on the other side of the road and then jog back across the road to the back of the lorry which Andrew was now guiding back into the elongated parking space. As Andrew motioned Paul backwards, the lorry lurched towards him, narrowly missing him as he reacted by jumping to one side. Andrew stared at Paul's face reflecting in the driver's door mirror. "You dick!" He shouted, thinking Paul was testing him.

Paul jumped out onto the pavement, oblivious to Andrew shouting at him from the pavement or the fact that the lorry had momentarily shot back while he was reversing. "See there is a God! That wasn't so hard was it?" Andrew still stared at his mate. Paul caught his look, "what?"

The minister appear from behind the lorry, following Andrew. "Glad to hear it or I'd be out of a job. I'm John Rowlands." The hand and smile both extending to Paul.

"Hi Father." Paul said.

"He's a minister," Andrew corrected. "Same thing isn't it," looking at The Reverend at the same time as shaking his hand.

"It's close enough." John had heard all the computations and jokes over the years and realised that in general, people always felt they should behave differently around a clergyman, acting more awkwardly than normal and more awkwardly when trying to "act proper" when he was wearing his dog collar.

"Is it only the two of you?, will the two of you be enough?"

"We should be fine, we've got enough room at the back to get them out."

Paul, six foot two, thirty two years old with blond wavy hair, had been heavy labouring all his working life. He had been glad to get this job four years ago at Williams' Carpentry and had learnt a lot about using the saws, joints, the properties of timber from Mr. Williams who was a friend of his mother's from their school days. He didn't approach any physical situation with any concern.

Andrew was twenty seven and had joined Williams' when he left school at sixteen. He had been lucky. Unemployment in the area had been high for years but he had always been polite and on the one occasion when he went with his dad to the timber yard for something his dad wanted, had been found looking into one of the cutting sheds by "this older guy" who started talking to him. The "older guy" as Andrew still recalls affectionately was Mr Williams and Mr Williams was quite impressed by the teenage boy who as he said "spoke to me without his knuckles dragging along the floor."

Mr Williams was looking to take on a "general cleaner, come tidy upper" as he put it, as they had just got quite a big job and he didn't want to take the skilled guys off production. Andrew was just in the right place at the right time and he was well liked and had gone out in later years, representing Mr. Williams when he had been too busy or he thought the opportunity to develop Andrew had presented itself on smaller quotations.

At five foot eight, curly brown hair and brown eyes, a keen gym goer and rugby player, he was muscular and chunky with an enviable V shaped torso; equally as strong as Paul but thought a little bit more. Still, with a bit of thought, the unloading of the first twelve out of twenty seven pews should be straight forward enough and he looked at the unloading as a bit of extra gym work.

The brown roller shutter rattled loudly as it opened up revealing the lightly stained oak pews inside, lined up six abreast with the second six supported by racking and ropes lifting their one end higher than the backs of the first six, which were placed further to the front of the lorry. There was a waft of wood polish and the faintest lavender fragrance from the inside of the lorry as the roller door opened, presenting the pews.

It had taken more than two people to put them into the lorry, four in total with one on the fork lift and the other three guiding, placing and tying off ropes so that they were secure from falling or moving to any degree while being transported.

Taking them out would be easier as the weight was going downward and one man could release the ropes while the other held the pew, ready for the manoeuvring from the back of the lorry using sheer brute force and the small wheeled trolley where possible.

"If we get these first six down and onto the bit by the front door, we can take them in afterwards." Andrew agreed and he jumped into the lorry, positioning himself to lift the first pew off the rack.

The first six came down with no problem, just muscular effort from the two men. They knew how to work with each other and both respected the strength of the other, knowing that with warning, one could hold the pew from falling while the other repositioned himself ready for the next manoeuvre.

"Are you sure I can't help?" Rev Rowlands asked.

"No we're fine", Paul said, "open the front doors Vic," talking to THE Minister as if it was his first name and best buddies!

Rev Rowlands was relieved, "They do look heavy!"

At forty two years old, married with three children and a dog, he tried to stay fit, a long left over conditioning from his youth and twenties of playing rugby. John did a lot of walking and rambling but never seemed to get time to "go to the gym." He did try to keep muscle on his five foot ten frame but while doing the odd work out, he knew that if they had said yes, he would have found the pews significantly heavy. He was happy to open the front doors!

The light wind lifted and rearranged his black wavy hair as he stood watching Andrew and Paul, interested at how they went about the unloading, wiping some smears off his black framed glasses as he leant against the boundary wall of the church.

The first six pews were lined up outside of the front doors. The sun had broken through within this last forty minutes and was glistening on the highly polished stained and varnished timber.

The grain in the wood swirled and knotted, twisting and rotated into patterns, emphasised by the varnishing, embellished and brought to life by the sunlight.

Rev. R just looked along each of them the fronts, the backs, admiring the natural beauty.

Unconsciously, he rubbed his close cropped greying, black goaty style beard, his fingers and thumb rubbing along both side his jaw line up to his ears.

"Pleased?"

"They are lovely," he responded, his smile even wider than when he first put his hand on Andrew's shoulder. His green eyes were vivid with an excited sparkle. Andrew was drawn to looking directly at him, this minister's eyes exuding eagerness and interest.

They had only just met but Andrew felt almost mesmerised by his aura. John pervaded calmness and interest, his eyes drew people in when they talked to him. Whether he was in dog collar or anything else, he had something which made people feel at ease and interesting, that they and their lives or fuddy duddy concerns were important. John loved people and the sociability of his calling and had learnt a long time ago that eye contact mattered. It created a bond and made people feel special and for him, it wasn't a trick or psychological con but a heart felt enthusiasm for being alive and for the opportunity to meet people over and over again or to make new contacts and to enjoy the presence of others.

"Are they all from the same tree do you know?"

"Good God no." Andrew instantly wishing he had picked another expression as he felt a lesser cringe on his face. Rev R didn't notice. "We've used timber from six trees altogether. They're from the same area but there wouldn't have been enough to do all the seats and the backs, cos they're ten feet long. They're nice aren't they!"

"Beautiful. Do you fancy a cup of tea before you start unloading the next six?"

"Yeah great. Two sugars and one, we'll have a look at where they are going to go."

Andrew looked inside the open front doors at the variety of chairs replacing the old pews which his company had removed when they got the order for the replacements. They had matched up the styling perfectly with the originals and had destroyed those affected by dry rot.

The £37,000 was a tidy price he thought for British oak, the removal, fashioning and fitting of new pews and he was aware of the fund raising the church had carried out as he looked at the New Pews red and white triangle tabulator made by the Sunday School and coloured in each week at the front of the church.

"Tea!" Rev. R and Paul both arrived by his side from different directions.

They all stopped sipping as they watched the same PVC mack from earlier, walk past the other way, the coat now open, catching a glimpse of a shapely leg through a split in the knee length kilt below. Andrew looked up at the woman's face as Rev R shouted to her. "The new seats are here Barbara!"

Barbara turned, the light from the sun catching and coaxing

sexiness out of the fabric.

"That's great," waiving her arms over her head as she carried on walking, turning back to face the way she was going but giving Andrew and Paul at least, enough time to see the face of an admittedly very spritely sixty five year old, heavily made up, with bright blue eye shadow and bright red lips.

"Always the same Barbara!" stated Rev R. "A child of the sixties. Always in the same mack but a heart of gold."

Paul look sideways at Andrew. "There's something about black!"

CHAPTER 2

Andrew walked down the steps to the back of the lorry and looked in at the next six pews. He noticed an odd mark of the first pew on the left hand side. If he didn't know any better, he would've thought it was dried out blood. It looked black. It looked a lot darker than the rest of the grain. He jumped up onto the floor of the lorry and was extending his legs to their full length to be standing tall at the back of the platform and suddenly felt a nauseating sharpness down his right shin.

His right foot had slipped off the platform and his leg caught on the steel edge which formed the end of the floor. He then felt the same steel edge hammer into his groin, following along the length of his penis, his full body weight crushing down into the concentrated area giving him the instant feeling that he was about to vomit the cup of tea straight back out. Every inch of this edge made an impression into the soft flaccid skin and then radiated outwards to his testicles. He spun off the edge cutting into his groin, aware of his leg and then the tarmac of the road against his arms and back.

He felt winded but the overwhelming pain between his legs had him hold himself as he wondered how he was in the road. He felt Paul and John Rowlands come towards him, not so much hearing them because the only sense he was aware of was a spinning like agony in his head, his eyes shut, chocking back the liquid contents of his stomach, his ears hearing a muffled conglomerate of all the sounds around, not able to distinguish any one particular noise, more a wall of white noise filling the capacity of his hearing.

He writhed and rolled, jerking as his hands held himself firmer, trying to relieve the pain. His penis felt massive, swollen instantly by the impact of all his body weight, crushing against the steel edge of the floor.

Andrew became slightly aware of two sets of hands on his body, his head, his back but he couldn't really feel them. There was the hint of sensation that he was being lift to his feet, this more from the elastic stretching feeling that cut into his privates. He looked down and through the spinning, whirling feeling that was still filling his head, expected to see blood. Andrew thought he must have amputated his penis. He had been kicked in sport before but this felt far, far worse.

His hands held himself tighter, with a bit of conscience thought stringing sense and the situation together. His fingers parted, there was no blood. He could feel himself, just. The numbness to touch being swamped by the pulsating pressure that emanated from his groin and filling his throat.

"Are you ok? Andrew.....are you ok?" Paul's voice seemed to come from outside the bubble where Andrew was. The volume of Paul's voice increased with his concern but it sounded no louder to Andrew. He was aware he was standing but not on his own. The pressure of his own weight standing even with help, increased the pain, like a sharp scalding razor blade along his swelling member.

"Let's get him to where he can sit down." John's voice didn't really make it into Andrew's bubble either, he just had a sensation of being lifted from around his waist and from pressure around his shoulders.

The firmness of the newly unloaded pews standing outside the church door seemed for a second to offer relief as he was lowered onto the cool varnished seat, its slippery surface allowing Andrew to move forward after being placed down. He tried to regain that eased feeling, by moving himself gently forward and back but that wasn't to be found, just the heavy throbbing of his testicles followed by the cutting, grating sensation that was still dominating his attention to his groin.

Andrew looked at his right leg, evidence that it was cut behind the jeans.

He bent over trying to find more relief but the weight of his chest and stomach increased the pounding. He lent back, it felt like someone was cutting through him.

The cold towel on the back of his neck broke the bubble.

"Drink this," a glass of water held to his nose, John holding the towel and messaging his neck through the cool towel with his other hand.

Andrew took a sip but thought it might be straight back out. He poured the glass over his head, water running down inside his T shirt, its coldness easing his groin pain as it tracked down to his waist and the damp cooling affect going on down beyond his belt.

He wished he had poured the glass straight into his trousers. Why hadn't he thought of that. "Dick" he thought. Yes just that, he thought of the irony of his thought!

"Jesus Christ you muppet. What the hell are you doing?" Paul's voice was really clear now.

Andrew looked up at him still feeling that relentless throbbing but at least he could move now without creating a whole range of other new pains to contend with. He looked at him with an expression of disbelief and despair at Paul 's choice of words and the thought,
"did he really mean to do that?"

He looked at the minister, "sorry, thank you, sorry."

"Sit here for a bit," John said still massaging Andrew's neck, "I'll get you some more water." John left the towel draped around his neck and went off for another glass of water, not sure what Andrew was apologising for, it was just a clumsy but painful accident.

He became aware of the towel moving as Paul took over the neck rubbing.

"If you think that's going to get you out of your half of lifting the benches, I'll kick you in the nuts as well."

"You're all heart." Andrew breathed out a long pain relieving breath and thought it might be a good time to stop holding his groin.

After about twenty minutes of hanging around, a trip by Paul to the pasty shop, (Andrew didn't want one strangely or so Paul thought !) and Andrew had recovered enough to start to continue with the unloading. He was more conscience of his leg than anything else now and this time used the tail lift to get up to the lorry load floor.

He went straight for the first pew on the left to look at the mark. It really looked like dry blood but black and under the varnish. It was a stain about eight inches in diameter on the outside edge of the back rest, where there was a fancy bit of carpentry, forming the side of the seat.

Andrew started thinking that perhaps it's not one to install. " What do you think about this?" he called to Paul.

"What?" Paul looked from around Andrew's right hand side.

"This." He motioned to the mark and Paul's hand followed Andrews like a fly past of planes, rubbing his hand over the side of the pew after Andrew's.

"What? It's just dust or something, there's nothing."

Andrew looked, no mark. "Is it on your hand?"

"There's nothing there." Paul motioned to the pew and turned his right palm over to demonstrate, "look nothing", the pew and his hand showed no mark, just interesting, swirls and grain and a clear palm.

"It was there, I'm sure." Andrew was insistent but a confused tone dominated his comment.

"Well there is nothing there now, so lets get on with it."

Andrew pondered as he edged his way to the far end of the pew, getting ready to push or lift it, depending on what Paul said. The tail gate was up, ready to take whatever needed to be lowered to the floor. They went to lift.

"Are you lifting?"

"Of course I am." "Are your nuts hurting?" "A bit, what do you expect but I can still lift this."

Andrew felt a pulsing, cutting then aching feeling in his groins as he exerted to lift the seat.

"We'll lift, on three....one, two, three.......Jesus this is heavy." Paul strained far more than with the first six, "bring it to me." Paul shuffled backward towards the tail gate.

Once on the tailgate he moved to the right, feeding his end out over the pavement so that Andrew could bring his end on the tailgate, its length laying across the width of the platform. Andrew shuffled his end on. "This feels like it's made out of lead, it weights a frigging ton". His groin started to pulse again with his effort. He gritted his teeth to hide the returning pain from Paul.

He put his end down and pressed the green down button.

The tailgate started to move slowly downwards and then

"slam" it just dropped to the road. The two boys feeling that they had hit an air pocket on a plane, the impact of the tailgate hitting the floor, jarring Andrew's leg and groin; too soon and another reminder of earlier, Paul letting out a "F F F" but nothing else came from his mouth, his mouth grimaced as he bent over trying to lift his end of the pew off his foot, as it had bounce up and off the tailgate. Both felt their breath and been forced from their lungs into the heads, the shock on impact to the floor initiating momentary dizziness.

Paul despite his size couldn't lift his end. "Give me a poxy hand with this," he said through clenched teeth.

Luckily the steel reinforced boots that they had to wear took the pain and certainly all of the would be damage to his left foot, though he was aware of the weight. Andrew went down to Paul's end and between them, they strained to lift the end off Paul's foot.

They just looked at each other with an expression which said "how is this one any different?"

"You ok?" "Yeah fine," Paul replied, looking at his left foot and then the pew.

"Are you boys ok?, any problems?, can I help?" Rev R stood at the top of the five steps, with expectation on his face.

"You can help with this one," Paul said, "it must be a real dense piece of wood, it weighs a god damn ton."

Andrew went to look at him but just gave up. Paul was oblivious to being subtle or respectful. What came out of his mouth was sent there by his brain, without question or analysis, that's what it was, as he saw it at that time.

"Grab this end with me Father, Andy can pull and we'll lift. This ones a right cow."

Andy did wonder at this point if his choice of words was deliberate or just a happy accident; it could have been worse.

"Padre, get over on my right, on three lift our end up and push towards Andy..... One, two, three". The groaning effort was obvious. John instantly thought as he strained that those opportunities to go to the gym and the things which seemed to get in the way, were now just excuses.

As they lifted, with Paul taking most of the weight, the pew made its own way to the right hand wall of the entrance gates and as they pulled and pushed it towards the church, it seemed to twist itself ninety degrees to the right. "Hold it, hold it". Andy shouted. "I am, we are, hold it Vic, I've got it, lift the bloody thing."

John put what extra effort he had into lifting his end, trying to obey Paul, trying to help.

The pew stopped, resting against the right hand wall of the steps, the top edge of the back rest leaning against the stone work but at least it was, all bar five feet, up the steps and on the paved area in front of the arched doors.

The three panted in different degrees, looking at the pew. The sun was now quite bright and caught the varnished grain as with the other pews.

Reverend John Rowland's saw within the grain a lion head and mane on the right hand end of the pew as he sat on the fourth step, taking deep breaths.

Paul looked at the back of the back rest and wished he had a can of petrol to set light to the bloody block of wood.

Andy, now feeling the strain on his leg and groin again, looked along the seating section and now rubbing himself, gently this time, to ease the pulsing; saw beautiful swirls and faces, ears and noses, heads and hair, as he looked along the ten foot length.

"You all ready for the next five?" Paul interrupted their recovery, we got to go back and get the next two lots yet, as well as start to screw them to the floor."

"Stay there Rev, in case we need another hand, appreciate your help if they're all like the last one."

John nodded and hoped the next five would be a lot easier.

In the main they were. The next four came off and went to the paved area without the slightest problem. They left the first really heavy one where they had put it and carried the next four up the left hand side of the steps, leaving them all outside of the main front doors.

"Is the kettle on again Rev?" Paul asked, "gagging for a cuppa!, It's been about an hour now."

Rev J hadn't done too much in terms of help since the heavy pew but had spoken to a lot of people who were passing and looking at what was going on. Not everyone he spoke to attended church, neither this one or the Catholic Church up the road but within the community, lots of people knew each other and what was going on.

"They look posh seats for shining your ass on," joked Malcolm who owned the fish and chip shop opposite. Not a church goer, more an atheist with his fingers crossed if truth be known, quick to pass comment but quick to apologise; just in case.

"The carpentry company have done a really good job," John shouted back across the road, "come and have a look. There must be one with your name on!"

Malcolm waited for a gap in the traffic and sprinted his rotund little body, clothed in kitchen whites, the eight strides across the road to where John was standing at the bottom of the steps.

"Oops, sorry boys," as he realised he just ended his run half way up the steps and behind the back of Andrew who was walking backwards up the steps with the last pew.

Perhaps the unexpected hindered loss in momentum, his earlier injuries, Malcolm's hand on his back, Paul's, "shove the thing up the steps" approach, all had their part to play; as Andy found himself falling over backwards as he stepped backwards up the steps, with the last pew.

Malcolm had moved over to the right of the steps and had almost within the same instant started talking to John about the look of the pew leaning against the wall. Within a few seconds, he was running his hand, caressingly around the side end panel, feeling its smoothness, the chiseled and hand sanded edges and was about to say to John, "what a lovely job," when his thought was replaced by the searing agony of his right wrist being snapped as the pew slipped like a temperamental guillotine that had released itself to complete its drop, catching his hand and wrist between the bottom of right hand end side panel and the top of the fourth step.

As he cried out and looked up he saw Andrew completing his fall over the side panel of another pew on the area in front of the oak entrance doors; catching and then clutching his lower back which caught the top of the edge, as he got pushed over, when Paul stumbled up the last two steps.

The sixth pew dropped to the floor, leaving Andy's grip as he went backwards over the waiting pew. Paul on slipping when Andy dropped the pew, caught the end of the arm rest with his lower lip and jaw, splitting open his lower lip and catching his right hand between the bottom of the pew and the top step, cutting all his knuckles on his right hand that had been underneath the pew's end for leverage.

"Good God boys, is this the first time you've done this?" Rev

John shouted, partly out of surprise and partly out of panic. He had his left hand on the heavy pew, not trying to lift it off Malcolm's wrist but aware he was trying to lift it all the same. He looked at Andrew, who was behind him and just about coming to rest from his tumble over the pew. He saw Paul, blood coming from his bottom lip or teeth, dripping onto the chest of his blue pullover; he didn't know from where exactly and he became aware of Malcolm swearing about the pew and yelping in pain, as the pew wedged his hand and wrist between its leg and the third step where its slide had been stopped by jamming against Mal's body and the right hand wall of the steps.

It seemed an age as John stood there, looking at the three casualties, one after the other, not knowing which one to help first but predominantly trying to lift the pew off Malcolm's wrist.

Andrew regained his feet, helped by Paul up on his way to the other end of the pew, blood dripping between his teeth and down his chin.

Paul looked for a tissue or something in his pocket but only had a five pound note and a lottery ticket which he hadn't got around to checking. He used the lottery ticket, it probably had more worth as a wipe than a chance to win seven million he thought but put it back in his pocket after trying to wipe most of the blood away.

It wasn't very absorbent and just spread the blood across his face. He didn't realise this as he went to help Andrew and the Reverend to pick up the fallen end of the pew, off Malcolm's wrist.

"I'll sue you ass holes or this bloody church for this; if I can't work and I lose business because of you lot." His podgy, chip tasting face was bright red with anger and pain and his redness extended onto his scalp which was covered with grey, short cropped hair. The two boys tried to lift the end of the pew up and away from the step but they were straining. Only when Rev John gave the third set of arms and hands did the pew lift and they were able to give it one final lift and push so that both ends were on the court yard area in front of the entry doors.

"I'll take you to hospital now Mal."

"No it's ok, I'll get my son to do it. We'll sort this out later." Malcolm shouted back as he held his wrist with his left hand and lower arm, crossing the road at the same time. His face was red with anger and pain and these were equally evident on the back of his head and neck as he walked away across the road towards his chip shop.

"I am so sorry. I don't know what happened, this has never happened before!" Andrew looked at both John and Paul as he apologised, directing his conversation to The Minister who was sitting, embarrassed and angry on the top step.

"Yeah Father, Andy's right, we're sorry mate. I've been delivering for four years and never scratched anything!"

"I'm not a Father. Call me John, Rev or Vic, I don't mind but I'm not a bloody Father." John used his left hand that had been on the top of the pews backrest to pull himself up as he corrected Paul. "You need to clean yourself up. Go out the back and wash your face."

Paul got up and walked in through the front doors. He didn't know where he was going exactly and didn't want to ask the Rev J in case he got another telling off.

"I thought vicars were supposed to be forgiving," he thought to himself, "bloody hypocrites."

"My face is bloody bleeding because of your stupid wooden seats and it's my fault!" He found the toilets without any effort and turned on the hot tap.

"Bloody typical......cold, every church I've ever been in, no hot water in the taps. What's the point of having a hot water tap with no hot water."

The cold water stung the open cut on his lip and he spent the next ten minutes cleaning up and stopping the bleeding.

Outside, Andrew was still on the receiving end of one angry minister, who had found comfort with his back leaning against the heavy pew.

"Look Reverend Rowlands, Paul is right, I'm sorry. We've done deliveries like this loads of times; not to a church necessarily but large wooden structures and stuff, with no problem."

"For the moment, just get the pews inside and get the next lot up here."

Reverend John calmed down a bit as he moved the mixture of chairs out of their temporary positions for church services. He watched as the two slightly self conscience men brought in the pews one by one, laying some of them in the gaps that he had made, some in regimented lines in the isle to the left of the church; all waiting for final lining up and securing to the floor.

Both of them looked at the final pew which had caused the problems as far as they were concerned though they didn't know why. Why was it so unusually heavy? It was no longer than the others.

They looked at each other as if to say, "we're not going to be beaten by this piece of wood" and both looked at each other, along the seating length, at each other and then lifted the offending oak seat and then put it down again as they got to within five feet of the entrance doors.

Whether they were tired or demoralised but they both looked at each other panting in disbelief. Yes these things are heavy but not for the two of us together. Both their thoughts said the same and their unspoken expressions to each other confirmed what the other had thought.

"One more go or I'll put an axe throughout the frigging thing." Paul had lost his limited patience with this inanimate adversary.

"It's going through these poxy doors if it's the last thing I do, after three."

"Stuff three.....one, I'm not giving it any chance." Andrew picked up his end and then Paul did the same....just. Both ends didn't lift very high off the ground, certainly not as high as the other eleven;

Andrew responded to his "one" call to action and propelled himself backwards, confident that Paul would be following through, lifting and pushing at the other end.

Andrew stepped backwards inside the threshold of the main doors and felt victorious........ for a moment. He heard Rev John call from the back as he opened The Vestry door. "How we doing now?" and as he opened that door, the through draft, caused the two front entrance doors to slam forward, trying to shut but Paul had not yet got over the threshold.

The left hand door caught Paul in the face, causing significantly more facial damage than the earlier split lip, while the right hand door caught his fingers between the edge of the door and the base of the pew which he was holding. The effect of both was to knock Paul back out of the doorway causing him to drop his end of the pew.

Andrew fell backwards slightly with the change in weight ratio but regained himself in a second or so and managed to pull in the last few inches of the pew to the inside of the church vestibule, dragging it over the hessian welcome mat and onto the rich blue carpet.

He rushed forward to see how Paul was and on opening the now closed doors, saw Paul trying to clutch his now noticeably swelling face with his bleeding right hand that had been caught by the door. Andrew paused and looked at his friend but it looked like his hand was not responding to his intentions to hold his head as a result of the impact of the other door.

Reverend John came rushing up to the front doors. "Now what's happened?" He sounded exasperated.

Andrew stood still almost to embarrassed to speak, cringing inside at the thought of another explanation. He concentrated on the deep blue carpet that covered the vestibule floor, the coarse rush mat on top for wiping your feet and the umbrella stand. He started to count the red covered hymn books lined up in the five foot tall, open wooden shelving that stood on either side of the vestibule, both adjacent to the entrances of the two main side isles that lead into the church. Even the notice board looked inviting to convey his interest at his surroundings, which he hoped would deflect this now highly agitated minister from asking more questions. Andrew hoped he had become invisible to scrutiny.

He hadn't.

CHAPTER 3

By the time they got back to the timber yard for the next of the two pick ups, Rev J had been onto Mr Williams to tell him of events.

He was concerned about the accidents and wanted to know their side of the events. In fairness, Rev John did not complain about the pews only his concern for their competence.

Mr Williams in return reassured John Rowlands of their competence but still wanted to hear their account.

"It's got to be more than that."

"Honest that's exactly what happened."Andrew said, after Mr Williams' initial disbelief.

"How can one seat be heavier than the rest? There all made to the same size and specification." Mr. Williams was not looking for the answer to his rhetorical question, more making a final point.

"Do you feel ok to go back?" He asked both. Both nodded an "uuhh" not feeling like talking too much.

"Go and get a quick cup while I get twelve more on with some of the other boys and you may want to change your jumper, you've got blood on it. Are you both sure you are ok?"

"Yeah we're fine." Andrew answered for both of them as they walk away from Mr. Williams and then splitting off from each other, Andrew to the kettle and Paul to the locker room.

Mr. Williams climbed athletically for his sixty plus age onto the seat of the fork lift where the machine had been left last night and glided to where the remaining fifteen pews were lined up, calling to Peter and Mike on his way.

Jeff the oldest of his employees who had started as an apprentice and now a trained turner and joiner, with thirty five years of experience called to ask if he want him to help as well.

Mr. Williams gestured for him to stay at the band saw by waiving his hand and pointing to the timber he was cutting and the pile of birch planks that needed to be cut for veneering MDF board, for a cabinet they were making for a local restaurant.

Peter tail gated himself into the back of the lorry, ready to guide in the first of the pews as they had done the previous night. The tail gate appeared to operate normally and neither Paul or Andrew had remembered to tell anyone about the tail gate dropping earlier when they had got back to the yard or during their bosses questioning.

"Let's hope these go in without the same problem as last night."

Mr Williams was about to ask what Peter meant but gave up speaking as the band saw screamed, slicing through the birch wood Jeff had started to feed through.

Peter was going to elaborate as he could see from Williams' expression and body language of lifting himself off the seat, that he had started to ask what had happened. Peter decided not to bother to compete with the band saw but would tell him later how one of the pews must have got caught by a breeze or gust of wind or something, as it was being loaded. The pew had been made to spin in the harness suspending it from the forks, which normally allowed the loaders to rotate the pew length away with the lorry and made loading easy.

The harness went around the first three seats and were loaded as per normal, with the three men shouting and gesticulating to each other to compensate for the lost words that were swamped by the screaming band saw.

The right hand prong twitched at the retaining bolt as the third pew was placed against the second. In fact the prong had moved a little with every pew after the twisting and swinging of the previous night.

The band saw stopped as Mr. Williams shouted instructions which were now disproportionately loud to Mike, to lash up the harness on the fourth pew.

Andrew was back with his tea and had climbed more cautiously into the rear of the lorry to give a hand when wanted.

The straps took the strain as another oak seat was lifted. Mr Williams felt a little shudder with the weight and then turned gently to the left, letting the back of the truck swing to the right and towards the remaining eleven seats which lay in lines. This had been a good job to get he thought to himself and while he had only taken £5,000 deposit with the rest due on completion, he knew his money was safe; well if you couldn't trust a church, there was no chance. He wondered if this morning mishaps would have any repercussions.

"Naa!" He thought, the only damage done was to Paul and Andy and then he remembered the chip shop owner. "Was he the sort of bloke to sue?" He started to think of the "sue them culture" in the country, "no win no fee". Perhaps he had better go up with the next delivery. Hopefully, this Malcolm will say it was his fault, he shouldn't have been touching the seat, he should have seen it was resting against the wall.

"Look out. WOOOOWWE." Peter and Mike shouted out to the fork lift as the band saw started up again. Mr Williams saw Mike waving his arms, paddling them to the right as he ran towards him, as if trying to push the truck in the opposite direction. He caught sight of Peter standing on the lip of the loading floor of the lorry, hanging onto the right hand edge with his left hand, waving his right at him.

His thoughts about his going out on the next trip changed to produce a startled expression. He felt the truck strike something as it jolted from the back end. Rotating his head and torso, his green overalls popping open the second and third button down, he saw the first pew fall over and heard the dead thud of the oak back rest as it hit the floor under the noise of the screeching band saw.

Luckily, the pew missed the next one lined up against it, as if it had caught it with the added force of being knocked over, it would have toppled over the second pew and possibly a third and fourth; although they were symmetrically designed, they were designed to be bolted to the floor as their length, height to weight ratio made them unbalanced if moved out of true.

He looked at Jeff who was the only one oblivious to the thud, his ear guards streaming out the harshness of the saw and any awareness of other sounds around him when the saw was running. Mr Williams stopped the truck from moving, looking down at the fallen pew. He could not see any damage, well not from that distance at least.

The harnessed seat swung towards the lorry, a reaction to the jolt and the sharpness of the fork lift stopping. Peter watched the pew bite at him, straining in its bondage, reminding him of a crocodile he'd seen on T.V. coming out of the river, taught and full of aggression to grab a drinking antelope. He moved his head back and pulled himself back into the hollow of the lorry, watching the end of this now animate wood sweep past the back end of the lorry.

Peter saw the grains and had time to appreciate the life that the back of the seat seemed to have as it came to a stop, ready to pendulum back.

The left hand harness broke, the frayed edges giving a false statement as to its relatively new condition. The pew had already started its return, twisting and now jumping onto the cargo floor of the lorry, its momentum rolling and causing it to flip, start and then change its mind as to its summersault and then skagging across the floor as it aimed itself to the far side of the lorry where Peter suddenly thought he had been as close as he had wanted to be to this pew, the oak seeking vengeance for what they had done to it.

The right side of the pew, still supported by the unbroken harness kinked and jarred as the seat did its acrobatics in the lorry. Mr Williams instinctively tried to reverse the fork lift back away from the lorry not because he saw it and its movement towards Peter, it was all too quick but he had become aware of the broken strap. As the fork lift lurched its two to three feet back away from the lorry, it yanked the still tethered end with it, as if trying to control a rearing head strong stallion pulling at the bridle. The combined affect broke the bonding on the harness and this right hand side thundered to the floor, the weight of the top end still sweeping inside of the lorry, with the edge of the lorry floor acting like a fulcrum. The now bottom end of the pew spun, looking for a smooth circumference around which to rotate but the difference in the seat to the back rest measurements caused the ten foot crocodile to kick and buck. Its bottom end slipped away from the lorry, lowering the height inside, with the final weight jarring the right side panel and its carpentry into Peter's chest.

Andrew watched, rigid in disbelief for the three or four seconds the pew sought its target. He put down his half drunk cup of tea in the same movements as going to Peter's aid. He grabbed the top end of the pew, to restrain it, to stop it from moving. As he held it he saw Peter's greyed face surprised, almost disbelieving, his right hand up to his chest, his left somewhere between still holding on to the inside of the lorry and somewhere else, the final destination undecided. It hovered, moving from side to side with short indifferent movements. Andrew could see there was no blood, which was a good thing so he thought but was still concerned for the man who had given him most of his direct training.

Andrew looked at Peter and in that instant saw a frightened ghost in his complexion, the shock of the impact ageing him by twenty years so he looked seventy, his centrally bald head flanked by jet black hair had lost its usual redness, his brown eyes looked in pain through his brown framed glasses, his normal five foot six frame appearing to have shrunk.

He hesitated to say anything, almost out of respect, thinking that Peter would already know what needed to be known. Peter was still trying to get his breath, still holding his chest which now didn't have the oak against it, it was now a leaning pinnacle supported by the edge of the lorry's floor.

Mr. Williams jumped down off his seat and within ten steps was looking up at Peter and now Andy from the tail gate which was on the floor.

"Where did it catch you, are you alright, are you alright?" His impatience, concern and the volume of his questions increasing in the two seconds he took to ask the questions.

Peter gasped his first breath after being struck by the oak seat. He knew its weight had done some damage and while he looked down at his chest, he really hoped he would not see any blood. There was no blood, that was good, but he had sensed a crack as his adversary had stuck him.

The second breath probably confirmed the first with a sharp, knife like cutting feeling to his lungs and chest. He tried to take that second, really deep breath, so that he didn't feel like he was drowning. Peter needed to fill his lungs when he was standing on the inside of the lorry rather than feeling he was twenty foot under the surface of some water.

He had broken ribs. The sharp, agonising cutting feeling confirmed his first thought, broken ribs!. How many broken ribs?, which meant he couldn't work, couldn't move, couldn't even breathe to the most degree. He felt his legs slip and his back slide down the side of the lorry. He felt one of Andrew's hands support him in his decent to sitting on the floor of the lorry, his knees up to his chest.

Mr. Williams stood there almost transfixed, waiting for a sign, unaware that Paul had come out of the locker room with new T shirt and had made his way up to the back of the lorry. Paul looked at the erect pew, standing like some sort of gladiator over its defeated opponent slouched in the corner; looked at Peter and then Andrew who was now kneeling, holding Peters shoulders and then around at the general area, not putting the location of Mike who was still basically standing in front of the fork lift and then Jeff, who was still feeding birch timber through the band saw; as some sort of accident site.

"What's happened?" he asked.

There was no instant response. "What's happened?" he shouted to anyone, looking first at Mr. Williams and then to Andy, his words getting lost to the supremacy of volume, generated by the band saw.

Both Andy and the boss were aware of what he must have been asking but the band saw dominated everyone's senses, its screeching filling their ears, its efficiency swamping their brains from cohesive thoughts to create an answer.

They were all unaware of Chip the factory Staffy, running in from the outside yard and grabbing part of the broken harness, thinking it some kind of snake or pulling game and then thrashing it around in his teeth, the lose and longer end flipping and writhing, as he demonstrated the strength of his jaws.

Jeff's attention was drawn to Chip, having caught a glimpse of the flicking end. "What have you got?"not thinking it was part of the harness. As he turned more towards Chip, he saw the three men looking into the lorry but could not see why.

He finished feeding the length of birch through the saw and turned it off, taking his ear guards off, laying them on the approach area to the blade, leaving the two pieces of birch still just beyond the silent blade.

Mr. Williams told him the events as they got Peter into Jeff's car, ready for the hospital.

The four remaining men stood looking at Jeff's car leave and then at the courtyard, all of them not looking at anything specific until they heard the flicking and knocking of the securing buckle on the harness, the now cobra that Chip had to defeat; having seen the one end uncoil to where he could reach it, from where Jeff had put it ten minutes before.

He shook his head, growling, the broken harness some four foot long, sometimes reacting along its length, sometimes only within the first two feet, depending on his energy.

Mr. Williams grabbed the harness out of his dogs mouth and recoiled it, putting it more squarely onto the feeder platform of the band saw, Chip sitting, waiting for an end to tempt him as it had done before.

"Let's get these things away from here." He called to the other men as they all walked back to where the fork lift and lorry stood, the fourth pew still with its top end inside the lorry, its lower end just on the tail lift.

Mike and Paul climbed into the lorry, both taking hold of the pew on its higher most end, waiting for Mr. Williams and Andy to lift the lower end so that it eased down into the length of the lorry. As they lifted Andy felt a bruised and aching feeling down in his groin, the effort of bending and then lifting the pew, telling him he was not at his best.

The pew tilted into the lorry, the two men inside, guiding its height on to the lorry's floor and then dragging to its transport position. They looked at it quickly. "There are a few marks on this one." Paul motioned with his finger to a few spots on the pew, but didn't do a close examination, thinking more of the next seat to get in.

By the time they had loaded the remaining pews, man handling each one onto the tail lift, shunting one end out over the edge as they rotated it, Paul supporting the protruding end from the floor as Mr. Williams and Mike turned and pulled it; then with lifting the second row of pews onto supporting trestles, they all felt shattered and it was now 3 pm.

Mr. Williams knew it was too late to do the run back to the church and phoned Rev Rowlands to explain, though leaving out the accident detail to Peter, just that there had been a delay and loading had taken longer. He asked about the chip shop owner, hoping in a sense not to get a reply or comment. Rev Rowlands hadn't heard any news so the "don't know at the moment," was quite a welcome relief. That would be a problem for tomorrow.

"Do any of you fancy a pint? we'll finish for today. Can you ring Jeff on your mobile and see how Peter is."

Mike phoned on the way to the pub, as they all drove separately around to their local, the usual Friday, late afternoon start of the weekend local. Jeff did not answer the phone. It was probably switched off if he was still at the hospital.

CHAPTER 4

John Rowlands finished doing the administration jobs that had been waiting around for a few weeks for him to look at. This was not the part of being a Minister he enjoyed, though to be fair, there were a few congregation members that did the bulk of this aspect, leaving him to visiting, counselling, weddings, funerals and of course Sunday, the only day a minister works!

It was an hour ago that Mr. Williams had phoned him. A disappointment not to have the remaining pews delivered but they had waited six months, since the old ones were removed and had made do with chairs from the family room, some from members' homes, plastic garden ones mostly; some from the concert room. It had been easier to leave these in place than to keep bringing chairs in and out of the church every time there was a need to have them somewhere else in the building, when they were needed for mother and toddlers or the dinner club.

John wandered into the church not bothering to turn the light on. It was dim inside, the early October nights drawing in quickly and despite the fact that it had been a mainly sunny day and a mild October in general, there was little light coming in through the narrow arched stained windows.

He looked at what now appeared to be the debris of chairs that had been shifted out of their lines when the two had brought in the new pews earlier. The mish mosh of styles and sizes had been the cause of a lot of amusement and source of togetherness and inspiration. It was the bonding of people, their oneness in times of hardship: not that there was much hardship sitting on differently styled chairs but the tradition of support to others from within the church, to look for the best in a situation, to think the best of, rather than the worst of.

John had used the differences in the chairs for a few sermons over the last six months, using these differences in one sermon, to emphasise the same about people despite their variations.

He sat down on the nearest pew, it wobbled slightly as he leaned back. John leant forward to compensate, resting his elbows on his knees, a slight panic in his movements as he eventually rested his close shaven greying bearded chin in the palms of his hands. These eleven pews were lined up together within the two wide side isles, their width increased in parts by the absence of pews. Only the one had been placed out of regiment, virtually dragged into the church with one last effort after all the incidents it had been involved in the day before. He looked at it, thinking of the problem the boys had and Malcolm's wrist. He had meant to go over earlier but had been waiting for Andrew and Paul to come back until he received Mr. Williams phone call. He'll call on the way home to find out Mal's condition.

His mind started thinking through the fund raising process over the last year as he looked at the four and a half lines of carved and shaped oaks, visualising how many trees would have been used, how the trees had been cut, how old the oak was. He wondered if the congregation would appreciate the new pews on Sunday when they saw them for the first time at 11am service. Had this been the best way to spend £37,000? What else could have been done with the money? There was so much hardship, perhaps they should have stuck to the miss matched chairs and enjoyed the banter and jokes they had created, using the money else where but then £37,000 wasn't £370,000 was it!. A church needs pews to be a church not green

and brown plastic B and Q patio furniture.

He stared at the back of the excluded seat, the tall back rising to about two and a half feet above the seat, not that he was measuring it but it seemed right, just the right height for a lot of people to let the back of the head or neck rest on during sermons.

The dimming light altered the impression of what he thought he could see, the lightness of the stain now appearing so much darker with no light to give life to the grains. He looked and looked, lost in these thoughts about these sermons and these new pews, the worth of them, the gloominess making the pews and the green and brown seats more now like silhouettes, only the white chairs standing out, higgledy piggledy within the church.

That's a new way of talking about the light he thought, using the chairs yet again for inspiration. But what's the point? His expression now more one of annoyance and impatience.

"John, John," he got to his feet, startled by the voice interrupting his day dream, causing the pew to rock backwards as the change in his weight leaving the seat and the back of his right leg pushed against the front edge, tested the imbalance in its dimensions to the distribution of weight throughout the ten foot seat. He turned around to catch the top of the backrest so that it didn't topple backwards but the weight had started to move, helped by the left end leg traversing a carpet trimming end, allowing for a more rocking capability than if it had been on a flat floor and bolted as intended. He could feel it pull on his lower back as the weight tipped slowly away from him. John jumped to his right, swivelling his right hip even further outwards to avoid the left hand end of the pew, not taking his hands off the back as he did so. He adjusted his hand grip to one more associated to pushing than pulling but he was not far enough behind to be effective in pushing the pew back upright. John just strained for a few seconds as the seat momentarily stopped its backward direction, teasing him with the thought that he had been successful. The pulling on his back returned and he realised he needed to get behind the seat to stop it from toppling over as it may hit one of the others. The thought of having to pay for damaged seats even before they were fitted went through his mind. What would the council say? Would he have to pay? All that fund raising!

He felt the weight move sharply away from him. He thought, rather than felt that he must have now pushed too hard and was about to jump back the other way to stop it falling when he heard the same woman's voice. Turning to its direction, he saw Elaine his wife standing there at the far end of the pew, her right thigh and her two hands firmly on and against the back.

John put his hands on the side end to steady the pew, which was now back in the upright position and not moving and it reassured him.

"Are you ready to come home?" Elaine didn't even make reference to the tipping seat, whether she could see or had thought about the situation and the possible domino affect, John didn't know, he was just glad that she, someone had been there and in the right position to do what was needed at that moment in time.

"What do you think of them?" He gestured to the rows of seats.

"Well they look fine I'm sure if I could see them. Why are you in the dark, have you been in here long on your own, are they all here?, there doesn't look enough!, is there some sort of problem?, what's wrong with that one?, why is it over there on its own?"

Elaine's series of questions seemed to sum up John's whole day, once he could be bothered to go through the whole story.

"I'll tell you now, lets go to the chip shop. I need to speak to

Malcolm!"

Elaine helped him turn out the lights in the other rooms of the church where he had been working and they made their way over to the chip shop opposite.

Malcolm was at home, his wrist secured, broken and apparently not too happy.

CHAPTER 5

Mr. Williams drove Mike and Paul to the church, Andy was left at the yard with Jeff, having turned up for work intending to go back to St Andrews but very conscious of the bruising he now had in his groin and on the inside of the tops of his legs as well as the bruise which was all down his right shin.

He had gone to rugby training, got changed but even the warm up was too strenuous so helped with the training of the under nineteen's but running had been out of the question.

In the showers afterwards, he faced a torrent of jokes as the team members and other players found it immensely funny at the story he had to tell about six times, to bring various players and friends up to date on his day, after being asked what had happened to him, over and over again. Andy could see the funny side but still hurt when he laughed.

Mike was happy for a day out of the yard. A ships carpenter by trade since leaving school at sixteen, as his father used to be a steward on the P and O cruise line and had put his son forward to P and O. He was a gregarious character, full of chat, stories and quick wit, most of the stories involving cruising around the world when he was young and single. The years had been kind to him. Now forty six, his hair was still fair, no grey and he always looked to have a slight suntan even in the winter, darkening significantly during the summer. His slim build was honed and he looked after himself. Mike enjoyed the jokes about him looking in his late twenties, that he "was just a lad, a Dorian Grey". The job with P and O had turned out to be fantastic as it took him from ship to ship, not just woodwork but also general maintenance while at sea and he had learnt a lot, so now there wasn't too much he couldn't turn his hand to. He put his youthfulness down to the lack of stress and the enjoyment he had got from the cruise line.

Mr. Williams was silent during the journey for the most part, anticipating what sort or reaction and reception he would face from Malcolm in particular. His conversation with John Rowlands had been amiable enough and didn't envisage any issue between the two of them. He thought about Peter and his four cracked ribs and sternum. Peter would be off work for a good number of weeks and probably milk the situation for weeks, no months.

Peter was a nice enough guy, certainly a good worker and good at his job. At fifty three, he had worked for the council for twenty years and had taken redundancy seven years ago, a good severance cheque and early pension as part of the deal but had got bored after about two years. Pleasant enough as he was, Mr. Williams never felt he was committed to the job despite his interest in training Andrew and that's why he now thought he might take a bit more advantage of the situation in the long term.

Williams' thoughts blocked out Mike, who probably talked about something all the way from the yard but driving and his concerns had stopped his ears from working properly. It was Paul's belly laugh that brought his awareness back into the cab, as Paul shifted about in the middle seat, his arms and shoulders pushing against him, his right leg almost in the way of the gear stick. Mike should have sat in the middle he thought now; didn't think when they got in the lorry, the three men were not the usual combination.

It was raining when they arrived outside St. Andrews and they saw the main doors ajar as they pulled passed the parking

space made by Reverend J., using some of the soon to be redundant plastic chairs.

John came down the steps in game keeper style rain coat with matching hat, the rain at that moment torrential and went to the drivers window.

"Wait for this to pass, I'll make some teas, or coffee if any of you prefer."

"Three teas are fine Vic, thanks." Paul responded first. Mr. Williams gave him a similar glance as Andy had done yesterday at "Vic." Paul was unaware as he shuffled about on the seat as he tried to put his hand under it, to get the three coats out he had rammed there at the yard.

"Three?" John questioned, stepping back to try and gain a higher visual perspective into the cab. He then realised the driver was Mr. Williams. "Nice to see you again." He gestured a friendly wave and displayed a little surprise, as they had not seen each other for five months and there was no mention of him coming with this delivery during the phone conversation yesterday.

The rain did ease off but never stopped so unloading was slower than normal as the pews became slippery when they became wet, the varnished surfaces almost impossible to grip with any tension, despite all three men's grip being strong from years of tool handling and lifting, etc.

This time they carried each pew up and into the church so that they didn't leave them standing outside longer than needs be and they continued to line them up with the other eleven or in the entrance porch, width ways, as the porch was only about eight foot in depth. Passers by stopped occasionally to watch the manoeuvring. They didn't approach the troublesome pew with any different approach to all those they had taken out yesterday and its exit out of the lorry was more well behaved that its entry.

As they carried it up the steps to the church doors, the rain quadrupled in volume, water now running down the length of the pew like some sort of one sided water feature. Where as before the rain drops had stayed separate they now merged together, transferring their form. The water as it increased in capacity, cascaded off the lower end of the seat, the pew being carried upright, Paul at the top end, walking backwards, the other two lifting and pushing the dead weight. Their combined awareness of how wet this pew was, made them impatient, trying to lift, pull and push and lift with now, added agitation. They got to the church doors, Paul at the threshold, the other two still standing on the fourth step, all three were adjusting their grips, trying to squeeze the part of the wood they were trying to hold so hard as if to force the wood to become dry underneath their hands so that they could hold it without slipping. The seat had a stream of water rushing up and down its length, running against the bottom of the back rest, oscillating, as the level changed, the three men concerned about getting into the dry but having to snatch at gripping or cupping the back, side, leg or seat.

"Tip it!" Mike shouted, "tip the water off."

All three rotated the pew to allow the stream to change direction and cascade as a short lived waterfall over the lip of the seat. The change in weight distribution and his wet hand left Mike's grip with nothing in it, just wet hands.

Mr. Williams now was the only one holding the weight at the bottom of the pew. He slipped at the added burden, trying to find extra strength to compensate for Mike leaving the equation. His stumble hindered Mike's attempt to regain his grip. Paul imagined crushing the parts of the pew together as if by doing so it became easier to handle, as he attempted to inject extra effort from the top end, rotating it back to a more upright position as he did so. This rotation caught Mr Williams off guard and he felt his slippery grip slide along the wood, the wet varnish robbing his hands of the little tension they had on it. He scooped at the pew, trying to stop his end from smashing down on to the court yard and steps. He was in Mike's way, who's fingertips only made contact with the pew, Paul's extra effort taking the target an extra six inches away from his reach. Mr. Williams right foot twisted on Mike's left as their joint momentum to catch and hold this indifferent object found them beginning to entangle themselves with each other, only separating into two men again when the pew, now escaping even Paul' s grasp, landed right end leg down of the third step, its now downward weight increasing its ability to ski down the steps.

"I've got it, I've got it," Paul shouted. He had recovered enough from the pew being dropped at the other end, forcing him to let go, that when his end kicked up, he managed to get his left forearm around to the inside of the end panel and his right hand onto the back and outside of the left leg.

Mr. Williams got up off his knees and caught hold of Mike's coat on the left shoulder, to hoist him up. Mike appreciated the help and got up shaking his right hand.

"Ow, ow ow." He looked at his boss and then put his right hand under the inside of his left elbow, clamping down the arm to try and take away the pain.

"The bloody thing landed on my fingers. Shit that hurt!" Mike was almost jigging in a mock dance.

"You two alright? shouted Paul. "Yes. Fine."

"Time for a pasty I think," added Paul. Mr Williams looked despairingly at the floor at his ill timed hunger.

Mike lifted up his left arm, prompted by Mr. Williams who had seen red mixed in with the rain falling down the drape of Mike's blue wind cheater, the diluted mixture swirling together and separating in interweaving streams, looking like an unfinished cordial being mixed. Neither thought they would see parts of Mike's small and right ring fingers missing.

"Oh God." His boss was the first to react. Mike looked at his hand as if it wasn't his, not believing he didn't have a full set of fingers.

"Stand there Mike, now! we've got to get this moved." Mr William's meant so they could find his fingers as the pew was in the way. Mike thought he meant that they had to finish moving the pew before any concern for him. He clamped his hand back under his arm, the pain and realisation coming to his awareness together. He looked at his boss with venom, his misunderstanding making him angry, affecting his usual high opinion and regard for Mr. Williams.

"Move it, get this inside the doors, get it out of the way." Rev John appeared from behind Paul having come out of a side door. "Reverend give us a hand now, we need help now!Get this thing inside with us." The urgency burst through Mr. Williams voice.

John followed Mr. Williams orders, trying to help by gripping the underside of the seat, his face pressed up against the back of the backrest, his close shaven beard pushing against the wood like a worn brillow pad, sliding on the wet timber as he tried to lift the pew.

Whether he was any extra help he wasn't sure but they did get the pew through the porch and into the church and almost threw it against the solitary troublemaker from the day before. The two naughty boys in the corner.

Mr. Williams was embarrassed by the fact The Minister was there as he went out the door and towards the steps to where he hoped to find the fingers.

"Reverend, not to be rude, any chance of some teas, we're all soaked through". He tried to look casual and appealing at the same time, gesticulating to inside the church, hoping the minister would follow the line of his gesture, which would get him away from the steps and front door and the missing fingers.

Mr. Williams walked to the point he had dropped the pew, looking down on the floor through the rain and into the water splashing and running down the steps, while trying not to show John what he was doing.

Mike was still out in the rain, kneeling on one knee, a little to the left of where he had done his pain dance and he to was looking, hoping in a sense that he wouldn't find them as that would mean that were still on his hand.

Mr. Williams looked at him, still clenching his right hand under his left arm, his face blank of pain now, blank of any real expression. He recognised Mike was in shock and they needed to find his fingers.

"How many sugars for all of you, I can't quite remember."

"How irritating a question at this moment," Mr. Williams thought, "just go and make the bloody tea, please go away."

A little of his irritation came out when he said to John, "no just make three cups, we'll be in now, just dropped something."

As soon as he said it, he realised he should have said something else.

"What have you dropped Martin?" The Minister now just about the come back out of the door and into the rain again.

"Don't worry, we'll find it." Martin Williams turned full circle, walking back up two steps as he said it, wanting his walking back towards the Minister to influence him to turn the other way and leave. He was aware of the Ministers concern. John had used his first name. They had been on first name terms when first discussing what was wanted for the church. Martin could hear it in his voice.

He completed his rotation on the top step. and started to walk back down. "Please go and make the tea," he realised he'd said this under his breath rather than keep it in his mind.

"Sorry what?, I didn't catch what you said. What have you lost?" John thinking that's what Martin had said, the quietness of the comment actually bringing Rev John closer to coming out of the door than going to make the tea.

Martin rotated back up the steps, his eyes sweeping the floor, trying to use whatever movements he was having to make to scan for those fingers, trying to remain nonchalant.

His turn brought Mike into his rotating field of view, still in the same kneeling position. He hoped that The Reverend would just think he was looking for something rather than kneeling because he lost something.

Martin was now back on the top step, still turning. "It's ok John honest, we'll find it." He hoped his use of John's first name would reassure him that they were more interested in tea than in any urgency in finding what they were looking for.

Martin was now walking back down the steps, his eyes scanning, probing for tell tale signs of blood or the ends of Mike's fingers within the water and through the rain. He looked further down the steps wondering if they had been washed down within the waterfall affect that covered most of these steps.

"Give me a break." His thought was stopped.

"What's up Vic?, what's happening? A cuppa would be good if that's alright with you." Paul eased himself past The Minister who has just about in the doorway, to come out from inside the church and onto the paved area outside.

"They've lost something."

"What have you lost? We'll help you find it won't we Vic."

This turned Martin back up the stairs. "Oh God could this get any worse?" His eyes widened, his eye brows lifted. His eyes flicked to the right. These expressions and gesture aimed at Paul, mentally willing him to know they were looking for Mike's fingers, hoping Paul would see his meaning and what he wanted him to do in his face and that it wouldn't go beyond and convey any other thought to Rev J, other than to go and make the tea.

"Come on Vic, the quicker we can find it, the quicker we can all be inside. Have you got biscuits by the way?"

"Noooo" Martin thought, "can't you see what I'm telling you. Why can't you use your brain rather than your mouth. Surely you can see what I'm telling you. This can't get any worse."

Paul had reversed slightly back into the doorway as he put his left hand on John's shoulder, as if to ease both himself and John out and to join the search.

"NO." Martin's increasing internal stress beginning to emerge in his voice now as we'll as his face.

He listened to his own abruptness, "no" the second one was calmer, "he hasn't got a coat on. Honestly, John, we're fine. You go and make the tea. Paul's here as well, we're fine." Martin tried to say it with the reassurance and sincerity of a doctor to a patient. He kept his voice slower and gentler.

"You're the lucky one Vic, it's still pissing down!"

God, he's going to have to have a word with Paul.

Martin turned around for the third time and started to make his way down the few steps, slightly more relaxed than seconds before, as he saw John starting to turn away and on his way to make that tea.

"John, John." Martins downward viewing was altered from the steps, to see a woman under an umbrella with a black and white border collie dog pulling on its lead, standing just inside the gate at the bottom step.

"How's it going?" Martin couldn't quite see her face because of the umbrella.

He glanced over his right shoulder at John, who had stopped leaving again and was now in the process of leaning towards the open door. "Please, please go and make the tea. Who's this woman now, go away." Mr. Williams mind was willing John to leave and this woman to do the same. He started to think he knew her, vaguely. And the dog!. This was John's wife. He now remembered these other two components to his family. Martin had met Elaine once when he visited The Manse and the dog had been there as well. "Please go away." His thoughts repeated themselves.

His recollection was stopped,

"What a lovely dog. I love dogs, always wanted one but the wife says about the mess." Paul had been speaking primarily to John who was now more or less by his side just outside the door, not expecting it to be anything to do with John.

Paul had started to make his way towards the dog. "Come here boy, is it a boy?" he shouted down to the woman.

"No, she's a bitch." John called after Paul, the dog and Elaine making their way up the steps. Paul looked back at the Reverend with a "how do you know" expression.

John could see the question. "She's our dog!"

Paul caught on for once "This is the misses is it Vic?"

Paul politely held out his hand to greet Mrs. Rowlands then

realising she would find it difficult to shake hands, her one hand holding her umbrella, the other the lead.

Martin stood watching, unable to find the appropriate time to say hello between his frantic eye search of the steps, his thoughts on Paul, Mike beginning to stand up out of well brought up politeness, to say hello to The Ministers Wife.

Martin couldn't see as much of the steps now as before. The dog scampered up and down them excitedly on his lead, on seeing John inside the church doorway, at Paul leaning down to fuss her, Elaine trying to hold her on her lead, the rain still torrential, Mike now standing and about to extend his hand to introduce himself, almost robot fashion.

Mrs. Rowlands dropped her umbrella with the mixture of the excited dog and her natural response to the two approaching men, one walking down the steps towards her, his hand outstretched either for her or their dog; the other silent, still faced, both she thought with the intention of shaking her hand.

The falling umbrella struck the dog on her back, causing her to jump and also momentarily, stop her lapping at the water coming over the edge of the steps.

All three men went to pick up the brolly, Martin using the opportunity to come down around Mrs. Rowlands to the bottom of the steps, to see if the missing fingers were lower than he had thought, washed down by the rain.

The dog went back to gobbling at the puddles within the old, worn, wide uneven steps.

Paul and Mike redirected their right hands now to trying to clutch the bobbling, turning umbrella, Paul the more animated of the two, Mike still trance like, their two hands catching hold on the rim of the fabric in different places.

Martin thought he caught a glimpse of a finger. The dog was still moving around, the umbrella still bouncing, turning on the steps, helped in its erratic gyrations by getting caught up within the dogs frantic paws.

He moved crouching towards what he thought was one of the fingers, his face being slapped by the dogs wet, wagging tail, the smell of wet fur instantly hitting in nose; his glasses being knocked off by the movement, trying to avoid Mrs. Rowlands feet as he went under all the activity above him.

"I'll get your glasses boss." At last something helpful from Paul, he thought, Paul coming down another step to swish his hand around, feeling for the glasses on the parts of the steps he couldn't see, the puddles within the worn steps possibly hiding any small body parts.

Paul saw Mike now had hold of the light blue umbrella, which he thought had been all blue when he saw it first as he came down the steps and when he was grabbing for it. It now had red swirls. Mike held the umbrella out for Mrs. Rowlands to take hold of the handle, dangling it with his remaining fingers, blood running down and across the diameter of the fabric as he held onto the canopy.

Mrs. Rowlands looked at Mike, smiled and looked at the changing colour of her umbrella, wondering how?. She followed the stream of colour up to Mike's outstretched hand. Her smiled disappeared, her mind now analysing the situation.

"John quick, call an ambulance. He's been hurt!" John could tell from this ex nurse's tone and the fact he had been on the receiving end of it, occasionally; to do what his wife said and now.

He disappeared inside the church.

"I've got them boss." Paul held out the glasses to Mr. Williams.

As he opened his hand, he saw what looked like the end of a chip shop sausage which he must have scooped up with the glasses.

"Yuucchh, why don't people put their muck in the bloody bins. There's one on the post there, ten frigging feet away."

Paul aimed the sausage at the bin. "In one, even in the rain, the boys got it!"

Mr. Williams took the glasses off Paul, still thinking to himself about his ability to miss the bigger picture.

"Do us a favour Paul, go and make us all a cup of tea."

"Yeah sure thing."

Mrs. Rowlands had walked Mike up through the front doors. Paul slapped him on the back as he caught up with them then ruffling the dogs fur on her back. The dog turned its head to look up at Paul and stopped licking at the blood that was mixed within the rainwater, dripping down Mike's coat.

"You were quicker than me with that umbrella you little bugger. He's quick isn't he?"

Martin got the "sausage" out of the rubbish bin and went down on his hands and knees to look for the second finger.

CHAPTER 6

The Reverend wanted to know what had happened. Martin told him the facts and John's face told the story of what he thought, more so about not being told and asked to make tea.

His wife had found a blanket and a bandage.

Martin had found the top part of Mike's little finger and had both of them in his pocket wrapped in kitchen roll. The large bandage around Mike's hand slowly turned red as they waited for the ambulance.

Martin hated being in the position to ask the already annoyed Reverend if he could possibly help, if they needed it of course, to get the last few pews in from the lorry.

The Reverend reluctantly agreed saying that, "he probably wasn't as strong as the rest of them but if he could help, if was needed that is, he would, as the job had to be done."

"What's wrong with your hand?" Martin had seen him rubbing and squeezing his right palm and fingers.

"I've got splinters I think from that last pew. I'll get them out later, don't want them to turn septic."

A bit of an over reaction Martin thought, he had thousands during his thirty nine years in the timber business, not one had gone bad, really bad that is, just get them out and get on with it. He didn't mention these thoughts to the Reverend.

The remaining pews were a struggle, for Martin especially. At sixty two and a fit sixty two, the weight with just Paul for him, was very hard work but he really, really didn't want to ask The Minister, especially as he had splinters.

The paramedics had taken Mike, his fingers and told Martin to call the hospital first before turning up to take him home that night, in case they were going to keep him in. Martin thought this amazing; to think the hospital might send him home after an operation to rejoin his fingers.

Mike had gone, still in a daze, without saying anything to anyone, just a smile to Elaine.

It was 2.30 now. "Fancy some chips boss? I'm hanging." His question stopped Martin's thoughts instantly.

With this mornings events, Martin had forgotten about the chip shop owner. He dropped his head, another problem just waiting for him. He reluctantly agreed, suggesting a sandwich or pasty from the bakers shop instead, as if not going to the chip shop would get rid of Malcolm and his broken wrist.

Paul wanted chips and curry sauce.

As if to rub salt into the wounds, Paul came back with three bags wrapped up, an extra for John, who was still there. "Thought this might go the right way. I was talking to the bloke who hurt himself yesterday when we were here. He said he would come over after the dinner time rush."

Martin didn't want to hear that, nor had he wanted to hear how Paul had said "I said to him, that was bad luck you getting hurt yesterday. One of our boys had his fingers chopped off today, when the boss dropped the pew."

Martin ground his back teeth together, wondering if he should take this chip break to start to talk to Paul about some things.

He looked at Paul stuffing four chips at once into the curry sauce and then his mouth, clearly enjoying his food and  thought, "now is not the time."

CHAPTER 7

The two carpenters got to the point within the church, where they had moved some of the pews into their final positions waiting to be bolted to the floor.

Martin's back was aching now, being thirty years or so older than Paul showed after a long, hard day.

Reverend John came in with Malcolm. Martin had thought he had got away with this meeting, at least for today. It was now 4.45 and when 3.30 had come and gone, he thought, hoped, Malcolm would have been too busy to come and see him.

They found themselves standing behind the first of the two segregated pews, looking over the back rest to John and Malcolm, who took up standing behind the second pew, rather than walk around and be face to face. It felt like Parliament.

Martin leant on the back of yesterday's offender, his stance stout, arms shoulder width apart. He smiled at the other two men and waited to see what attitude came out with who ever spoke first. He hoped that by smiling, the attitude from both would be softer.

"This is the bloke from the chippy," Paul stating the obvious. Martin looked at him. Perhaps he should have had that talk with him or at least started it when they were eating "this bloke's chips."

He saw an opening appear, not due to any planning by Paul.

"You do nice chips I have to say. They tasted really fresh and the piece of fish I had, well it was gorgeous."

The compliment took Malcolm away from his purpose of coming over. "The secret's in the oil. I use a mixture, always have and keep it fresh. Some people use the oil for too long, affects the taste of the chips, I..."

Malcolm stopped himself. He would talk more than needs be on his chips as he was proud of his business and his chips. He had won some awards when he was younger and had been the town's favourite chippy for more or less the twenty years he owned the business. Most people in the town knew Malcolm, MAL 'S as people referred to it, even though it was called The Maris Frier and had been before his time. The logo was a ship cut out of potatoes with chips for masts and a flat fish as a sail. On buying the business, he thought changing the name would spoil the continuity of the business and the logo made him smile. It was so bad and dated, it was brilliant.

Everyone thought they knew MAL and he had the trick of making you think he gave you a few more chips than anyone else and that made his customers feel special. Mal would be talking to all the people in the queue the whole time they were in the shop. Going to MAL's wasn't just to buy chips, it was to some of the older, single or bereaved people, an experience, a place where someone made them feel that day was a better day.

Both he and the Reverend did the same sort of thing in their own ways. They were there for people. The Minister having the edge in social standing : Mal having the edge in his perceived accessibility as he was open from 11.30 am to 12.00 midnight, being there ninety five percent of the time; for pensioners to late night scoffers after a night of beer and drink.

His right wrist, now secured in a bright pink cast; he asked for it to make it a talking point, was now side by side with his left, both holding onto the backrest of their chosen pew, mirroring Martin's stance, like two determined bulldogs leaning forward on their front legs about to pounce but both smiling, for the moment.

John stood silent after Paul's announced introduction, rubbing his fingers, his right ones especially with his fingers of his left hand, as if coaxing the skin to move along the bones would push out the splinters from inside.

"Have you got them out yet?"

"No, not all of them." He answered Martin with a little shake of his head and a slight dismayed expression.

"Try soaking your hands in hot water to make them soft, that often helps."

"Just get a bloody big needle Vic and dig the bug....bu....them out. Then have a whiskey. That's what I do when they are really deep."

"Thank you Paul. I might try that."

Martin appreciated the attempt at the restraint Paul had used in giving his advice.

Martin continued with a casual, concerned approach. "How's your wrist?"

"I'll live, it hurts and I've been told to rest it, not much chance of that really, not doing what I have to do six days a week."

Martin found his gaze being drawn to the patterns and formations at the top of the back rest where Mal had his hands as he listened. He loved wood, its grain, its versatility. He eased his grip on his own support, aware he had tensed his hold slightly during Mal's response. What was he going to say next? His first answer had told him he already works six days.

Martin tried to keep the conversation's tone light, concerned but without apology.

"How did you manage to do it?" Martin looked back at the polished wood after asking this question. This would be the crunch.

He started to see curly hair in the grain and then looked back up at Mal. His eyes were drawn back to the wood, the curly hair was still there and now a cheek, the hint of an eyebrow. Wood can do that, a bit like clouds, only clouds move and change their shapes.

"I didn't do it, your boys dropped it on my hand." He said it as a statement of fact, no aggression.

Martin casually lifted his gaze as if to convey he had been looking at Mal all the time, admittedly from a different angle but always looking at him as he spoke, still keeping the image of this face in the lower part of his periphery vision.

"I know they didn't drop it Mal, it was already leaning against the side, they'd already put it down earlier, so they could not have dropped it."

The curly hair moved, a trick of not looking directly at it but now the eye?. This face, hinted at within the grain, it looks like ....

"How did he know my name is Mal? The Reverend didn't say anything when we came in.

Perhaps the tall guy heard some one say it when he was in getting chips, no there were only three other people in at that time. Did I say my name when we came in, ...no", Mal's thoughts were interrupted and his attention taken to Paul.

"That's right, isn't it Vic! You were there. It was this heavy bugger." Paul put his left hand onto the top of the back rest, his tone almost congratulatory, his hand stroking the top, feeling its smoothness.

Reverend John was cautious how he agreed to this fact. He was there but not to take sides, appreciating why Mal may want to talk to the men who had been delivering the pews but tending to agree; it was just bad luck that the pew moved when Mal was looking at it, as the two men were certainly not holding it at the moment it fell on his hand.

His caution made him hesitate.

"Tell him Vic." Paul's prompt slightly irritated him and so did "Vic" now. He was still rubbing his right fingers, feeling the sharp, pricking sensation, the lingering acuteness of the wood shards inside his hand.

He "ummed" to start his answer, looking at Mal apologetically, aiming to convey, there was nothing else he could say other than the truth.

He hesitated further as he sniffed the unexpected scent of lavender.

"It was very unfortunate really. Perhaps I should have thought as the boys were in the middle of unloading. Perhaps we were in the way at the time but no, they didn't drop it."

He saw Mal's body shift slightly at this confirmation.

"I don't really know what I can do to be honest Mal. It is as The Reverend says. I know it's no consolation but it was just unfortunate, just an accident, it wasn't anyone fault." Martin saw John's comments as another opportunity to put over the absence of any liability on their part, purposely using The Ministers title rather than his first name, to add authority to John's view of the accident.

Martin remained looking at the formation of the image in the woodwork, keeping his head lowered in a deliberately submissive gesture as he said it, so as not to antagonise Mal; becoming more engaged with the wood than his opposition.

"Just seems you have too many accidents to me, your boys fingers this afternoon, the lad who got hurt yesterday and the one on Monday!" There's was still no aggression, just increasing eagerness to get over his point.

"What one on Monday and how did he know about Peter yesterday?" His look questioning Paul who now had both hands on top of the backrest, the three men now all in the same bull dog stance.

"What happened Monday I don't know about?" frustration in his voice now that there was something else that could be used to imply more incompetence and of course, The Minister had to be there, listening to this. Martin felt himself grip the backrest harder, waiting for Paul to say something, hopefully tactfully, mindful of the affect opening his mouth could have given this circumstances.

"It was nothing really, something about the fork lift and loading these things. Peter was telling us as we were leaving yesterday, I wasn't listening to him really, I wanted to get away to get here." He stopped there.

"You must know more than that!" Martin wondered then why he asked Paul for more information, considering he didn't want anything else that could be brought into the discussion.

"Something broke or went on the fork lift, one of the pews slipped or swung I think and it caught Jeff on the arm. He's ok."

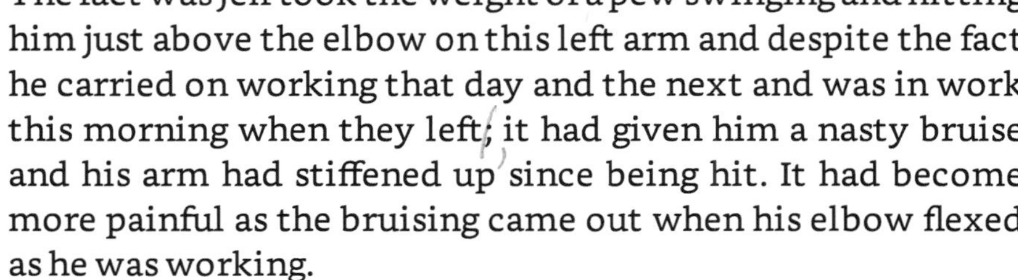

The fact was Jeff took the weight of a pew swinging and hitting him just above the elbow on this left arm and despite the fact he carried on working that day and the next and was in work this morning when they left; it had given him a nasty bruise and his arm had stiffened up since being hit. It had become more painful as the bruising came out when his elbow flexed as he was working.

"See another accident and you don't even know about that one. What sort of place do you run?" As Mal said this, Martin was cursing himself for asking Paul for more information.

He could see John's face, his expression changing from one of non judgmental interest at the discussion between himself and Mal, to one of growing despair on hearing of another accident with his expensive pews.

"How many ribs did that lad break yesterday, three?, four?"

"Who has told him that? Why can't his boys keep his business to themselves, not go blabbing everything that has happened and when to everyone." Martin's thoughts felt angry. He looked deep into the wood and the picture his eyes had drawn from the grain. It must have been Paul who told him, Mike had been hurt, Paul went to the chip shop, Paul doesn't think when he opens his mouth, it had to be Paul.

He looked at Paul, Martin's grip still tight on the back rest. His face reflecting his thoughts as he looked up at him.

Paul must have sensed the accusations from Martin's expression, his very large hands squeezing the backrest, vice like, his arms strained taught, as if he was going to try and lift the pew.

"What?" Paul asked questioningly, puzzled almost as to what he was asking. There was some confusion in his mind.

Martin didn't say any of these thoughts out loud to answer Paul's question. His eyes looked over and through the two men opposite and back to this conjured image. It was still there, now familiar.

He was thinking about asking Mal, how he knew these things but at the same time didn't want to, as he thought it would give Mal an opportunity to be more critical, more condemning.

"Look, you've got enough problems on your plate at the moment and I can see you've got a lot to do."

Mal's voice was calm, strangely sympathetic, a tone he recognised but hadn't heard in this way for a long time. He felt a rise in nostalgic emotion.

John saw it too, on Martins face. He was grateful, sad and relieved at the same time.

Mal turned his body to leave, restricted as he still held onto the top of the pew as he did so. "I'm sorry about your wife Martin. She was a lovely woman. Just too young!"

Martin's face froze as he stared bewildered at what Mal had just said, his eyes glazing over within a second of hearing his reference to his wife.

CHAPTER 8

Paul phoned the hospital to ask about Mike. Martin had asked him to. He seemed a bit preoccupied with something.

Mike was going to be kept in for a day or so and the hospital had asked if they or his wife could bring things in for him.

Paul said he would go to Mike's house to tell his wife and Martin agreed, thankful not to have to face another problem that day. It would still be there tomorrow, now with a possible injury claim, two men off work, a job to finish and a stranger he had only just met, being sorry about his dead wife.

How did he know?. Had he known his wife? Had they met before so he could have known through that and had he forgotten that he had met Mal from before?

Martin didn't remember him but it preoccupied his thoughts on the journey home and back to the church the following day, to bolt the pews to the floor.

Mike's wife had gone hysterical when Paul told her about his accident. He tried to explain that they had phoned her house a couple times but didn't get any answer.

His explanation didn't help her uncontrollable crying when in answer to her question, "why didn't you phone my mobile?" Paul said, "we asked him your number but he couldn't speak, must have been in shock!"....that increased her crying.

Paul had tried to reassure her that he was going to be ok.

"Martin was down on his hands and knees looking for his fingers in the driving rain." He thought this sign of Martin's determination to find her husband's fingers would have calmed her down a bit, "he even found the one I threw in the bin cos I thought it was a sausage!"

Her blond shoulder length hair was swishing in anger as her head flicked to look at him with even more disbelief and anger as his "reassurance" failed to calm her.

"How could you think Mike's finger was a sausage?" She screamed at him.

"Because there's a chip shop opposite." Paul's logic escaped Hazel.

Paul offered to drive Hazel to the hospital with Mike's things but she preferred to ring her Mum for her to go with her.

Hazel was still crying but without the vigour of earlier when Paul left, just before her mum arrived.

"Don't worry," was his last comment, "the ambulance man put his fingers into ice so that they could stitch them back on. They've done the operation. They told me that when I rang them on the way here."

He felt sure that her reduction in crying was down to what he had said to her.

CHAPTER 9

The Reverend's fingers were still hurting that night. He had tried hot water as Martin suggested, tried a needle, squeezing, working the skin. Elaine had tried using her nurse's experience but in the end his fingers and palm were hurting too much.

"They'll work themselves out!" He had a whiskey. His hand still hurt but at least he enjoyed the whiskey, Jamesons.

John wasn't one of these Ministers that preached and believed drink was evil. Moderation!Enjoy everything on God's earth but in moderation. That didn't extend to drugs. He was dead against drugs and had preached against them and been involved with drug rehabilitation over the years. The area had a high drug use and there had been a number of raids on local houses selling and growing cannabis over the last ten years.

People blamed the high unemployment in the area as a major factor contributing to the use of drugs. Nothing to do. No where to go. Kids on the streets, no future, no jobs, just drugs, drink or sex as their only ambition.

Looking for the positive in each situation was not always easy but it was the way he lived his life and believed Christians, in fact the way everyone should live.

John was in general a patient man, even before becoming a minister. You could get him worked up, more excited than angry, which can on occasions be difficult to distinguish.

The second glass of whiskey tasted as good as the first. Better in fact on this occasion as it lessened the gnawing sensations in his right hand. He closed his green eyes, their sparkle lost, tired from the day.

"I can't believe the problems or accidents those guys have had with the new pews," he said his thoughts out aloud so that Elaine could hear but wasn't really looking for an answer.

His right hand draped over the arm of the brown leather chair. Their dog Lucy, licked his hand a few times. "Don't Lucy, go and sit down." John pointed lethargically to her rug in the corner of the room.

Lucy obeyed and gave a small snarl.

"Did you growl at me? Go to your rug."

Elaine looked in from the kitchen, surprised by the reactions of both.

CHAPTER 10

The final bolting of the pews to the floor was left to Paul and Martin, who turned up at the church separately but within ten minutes of each other. Paul had driven the lorry to Mike and Hazel's house after dropping Martin back to the yard last night and had driven directly from home to the church to finish the job, the last three pews unloaded without any incident and very little discussion.

Martin had picked up all the necessary bolts and tools and they were now in his car.

John's overall demeanour on arrival was less intimidating than the feeling Martin had got from him the previous day.

Mal had left calmly, he was able to tell John that Peter, who John had never met anyway, was going to be ok but would be off work for about a month, to let the fractured ribs heal and that Mike had an emergency operation on his fingers last night and looked to be fine but it was too early to tell definitely at this stage, if he would have feeling or use of those two fingers.

Martin felt that if he persuaded Paul not to have chips again that day and that they could bolt all the pews in place, they would be finished that day and would have also avoided Mal and the possibility of more discussions about his accident.

They lifted and fitted the first four of the five front rows of pews into place; shuffling them, nudging them with their hips and thighs, tugging and pulling, lining them up where possible to the existing holes that had secured the old ones to the floor.

Some holes had to be drilled out with new plugs inserted so that they would swallow and bite on the bolt as it was ratcheted into the floor.

Reverend John came in a couple of times during the morning, twice with tea and once with Eric Morgan, a stout senior member of the Church Council, Head of The Sunday School, to look at progress. Each time John came in, the happier he looked as he saw the rows of polished pews multiply, filling the spaces, making the inside of his church look like a church again rather than the remnants of a make do barbecue.

Now in the next stage of fitting, the remaining pews were inserted, one here, two there, some side by side, some in front with a new one behind; unlike the first five centre rows, which were all new.

This took extra time and these insertions confirmed the accuracy of their formation, each pew placed into its space, waiting to be secured to the floor, all bar the two from the day before, which were still placed to one side of the church.

They felt as if they were getting heavier as the day went on, Martin still aching a bit from yesterday. He had not planned to do the fitting himself but that's what happens when it's your business.

They had forgotten about the segregated two and the incidents they had be responsible for until they selected them to insert into the spaces in the centre isle, six and seven rows back.

On going to the first of the pews, they found themselves straining and puffing more than any other so far that morning when trying to manoeuvre it into its proposed position. They guided it along the gap between the back of the fourth row and the start of the sixth row, the gap where the fifth row would finally be secured.

"I think we did this the wrong way. We should have put the odd ones in first and then fitted these front five rows from the back, working towards the front! That way we would have had more room, we wouldn't have been crouching down between two pews!" Martin looked bemused as he gave his belated analysis to Paul on how he now felt they should have gone about fitting this section of the new pews to the floor.

"Good God, I don't understand how this is so heavy! Is it me? it must be my age boy!" Martin made light of his straining.

Paul put extra effort into the operation to try and compensate for his older boss.

First one end went in, then the other, the first end coming back out. They changed ends, Paul jumping over one of the old secured pews to go to the back of this trouble maker, Martin walking down the length of the row and into the space in the row in front, so he could stand back slightly to get an overall view of the problem. As one end aligned the other refused to comply. They switched positions at the ends of this pew again and again, the smallest of adjustments to its bolting position seeming to create a greater refusal at the other end. They looked along its length, was it warped? They brought in an eight foot level to lay against its edges. The level showed nothing but uniformity.

"I can't bloody believe this! What in God's name is stopping it?" Paul felt frustrated. The more effort and strength he mustered to help Martin, the more the pew seemed to fight back.

Paul looked up to the ceiling of the church, heavenwards and gave a mock tirade, first pointing at the crucifix on the front wall and then to the sky. "Don't you want these bloody seats fitted. They've been nothing but trouble since we started. I've had a guts full of this. Can we stop for dinner? We can come back to this one later?" He looked at Martin.

Martin rested his forearms across the top of the back rest and agreed with Paul, "Dinner."

"You get the tea, I'll go for the chips. The curry sauce is bloody lovely."

Martin gave Paul a £20 note and asked for fish instead of curry. He couldn't be bothered to suggest an alternative and at that moment couldn't really care if Mal said any more or not.

Paul brought Reverend John some chips whether he wanted them or not and all three sat in the kitchen, the atmosphere between them relaxed and jovial.

"Right this is the way we'll do it." Martin sounded positive and determined as they walked back into the church. "We'll forget that one for now and come back to it later. It always seems better and easier that way. We'll fix that one." He pointed to the second reluctant pew.

"Jesus sodding Christ." Twenty minutes of the same confrontation and argument and the second pew remained unbolted. Martin's frustration now overtook his calmness. "I used to fight against my mother taking me into the dentist like this. I'd grab on to anything; walls, bushes, flowers, the door frame, seats."

"Let's try switching them." Paul could see Martin's frustration. They didn't work often together despite the fact Paul worked for Martin but Martin was clearly getting uncharacteristically stressed by these last two pews.

Martin looked unconvinced at Paul's suggestion and emphasised his response. "They are all the same. The saws were set up for the same specs and they went through as one batch!"

This confirmed Paul's awareness of Martin's stress. In the time he had worked for him he had never seen him with "an attitude" only preciseness to solving a situation, reflecting his skill and training to his work. He was never curt to his employees and when it transpired they may have done something wrong or badly, Martin had always approached the admonishment with fact and with humour but everyone knew when they had been told off and everyone always seemed to want to try to resolve the situation, even if it meant working longer than normal, including Peter.

"OK, let's try it." Martin sounded totally unconvinced as they switched the pews between the spaces waiting for them in the sixth and seventh rows.

They started on the main offender, now in front in the sixth row, looking at each other with their expressions confirming they were not going to be defeated.

"Let's put one of the bolts into one end and tighten it right up after putting the others in at the other, we'll put the middle ones in at the end." Martin's instructions did not require discussion, Paul nodded at he knelt down inserting the bolt through the hole of the securing bracket that had been fitted to each pew at the yard.

The first went in with no resistance, Paul tightening it to three quarter tension. He stayed kneeling, his arms resting on the seat of the pew, holding his ratchet while he watched Martin line up the other end to the hole and to the old secured pew next to it. He thought that the pews they had brought might have been better installed if the old, darkened ones had been moved around so that was not a mismatched in age, a change of colour here and there as you looked along the rows. They had matched up the colour varnishing and staining well, as best they could, given that the old pews had aged and changed shades after two hundred years of use but the irregularities in uniformity would not have been something he would like to live with. Despite his failings, he liked consistency, things to be the same.

He belched, the semi digested flavour of chips and curry sauce filling the back of his throat and his nose with the burning sensation of spice.

His eyes compared the lines of his supporter as he leant, stretching along its length, the smoothness of the varnish letting his forearms glide along, almost massaging the wood. At the end of his stretch, he let go of the ratchet, carefully releasing it, placing it at the end of his fingertips on to seat, caring, lovingly not to mark the stain. Paul, pulled himself back along his original path, sliding his hands and fingers over the seat, their pressure on the wood giving him extra support, his lower back pulling his large body frame into an erect kneeling position by the side of the pew. His hands changed position his right going to the top edge of the backrest, his left to the front edge of the seat. He pushed himself, slowly, the pressure increasing on his knees as his body moved further away from upright. His eyes penetrated the varnish as his face came closer to the surface of the seat. He enjoyed the life the wood gave back to him, rotations, undulations, changes in shade. His chest pressed against the the edge of the seat. He felt his breathing, his chest expansion being pushed against the immovability of the wood beneath him, causing his body to rise slightly. Paul pulled himself back, whipping the start of his return motion, his large, strong hands altering their pressure to the rear of his palms, his fingertips lightly touching on the wood's surface. He returned to his upright kneeling position, satisfied by his efforts, his inspection.

"There are a few dents on this bugger!" Paul disturbed Martin's entanglement with the bolt. "You've brought the fillers and wax; have you?"

"Yes, but worry about that later. Come and give this a shove for me."

Paul went around to the back of the pew, nudging and pulling; his thighs, hips and groin area making various contact with the back of the pew as he moved it forward, his shoulders, arms and lower back, pulling the pew back towards him during his adjustments.

He thought of Ann.

Martin was beginning to screw his first bolt through, the first bracket reluctantly lining up to the existing hole in the floor. "It may have been better to fix these brackets onto the floor first and then the pew to the bracket."

Paul listened to the comment while he continued to leave his lower half pressed against the backrest, marshalling it to stay where he had encouraged it finally with small, trusting gestures of his hips and pelvis.

His thoughts went back to Ann as he looked down at Martin who seemed to be having trouble tighten this bolt, his shoulder and head movements not fluid but jagged, snatched.

Paul's hands were now exploring this area of the pew expecting to find it different from earlier.

"Do you want me to do that and you start working on these dents, there's a few more here."

"Aaww!" Martin gave out a small yelp, "no, I'm fine now, the socket head kept slipping off. Don't worry about the dents. When we've finished they won't know they are there. I'll do the last bolt here, you go back and do the second on your end."

Paul walked back along the length of the pew and the row, his hand limp over the top edge, flowing from the new pew to the old one that stood adjacent, the change in surface apparent to his touch.

He remembered Ann's hair, tussled was the best way to describe it, blond? or golden?

Paul screwed in his second bolt and shuffled around to the centre supporting leg to bolt his side to the floor, Martin already being there, working his bolt on the opposite side, their heads almost bumping as they mirrored each others movements. When they finished within seconds of each other, Paul first, he saw the tissue Martin had wrapped around his right index finger which he had cut against the front edge of the leg, when the ratchet slipped.

They both knelt, their backs to the alter, hands still holding their ratchets, their palms leaning on the front of the seat.

"Why was it so difficult earlier?", Paul shaking his head while he was getting up, "that one now." He pointed with the ratchet to the second pew behind. They approached it from either end as if to stop it from making a getaway, herding it to remain in position. Ann came to mind again. Paul stopped himself from speaking as Martin bent down to look at the pew and its alignment.

It was lighter than the last one, possibly heavier than some but they both knew, definitely lighter than the last. They were able to "hip" it into position. Martin's older ratchet broke, as he was putting the final torque onto the second bolt, his right hand rocketing forward and catching the same wound, this time on the edge at the rear of the leg.

Paul heard his pain this time. Martin had been more aware of this slip and its outcome than the first, holding his finger and clamping it between fingers of his left hand, to neutralise the throbbing. He got another tissue out of his pocket, wrapping it around the first. He pulled some black insulating tape out of his trouser pocket and bound it around the tissue, pulling the end off with his teeth.

They both lent again on the pew, relieved.

"How old was Ann when she died?" Martin looked shocked, stunned, his mouth opened, not to answer but to take breath.

He couldn't believe Paul had asked that, now, in a church.

He had never met his wife. She had died eight years ago, four years before Paul had come to work for him.

The other men at the yard who had known her, never mentioned her and never suggested that wives came out on their Christmas do. That had stopped the year she died, February, so by the time that first Christmas came, when Martin asked Jeff to book five places at The Bombay Brasserie; they knew that part of things would never be the same.

Ann had been lively, vivacious even, interested in her husband, his business, his men and families. She had made the effort to look at the small record files in the office, their home addresses, find out their birthdays, their wives birthdays at Christmas do's and the occasional, impromptu curry or barbecue and had made the effort to buy flowers or wine, just something to show they, Martin and her, appreciated not only the men but the family that worked for Martin. She would almost bound into the yard, smiling, waving, lifting everyone up to a happier state, her golden curly hair bouncing, flowing, natural.

Ann had been two years younger than Martin but fifty two was no age to die. Stomach cancer.

Paul looked inquisitively at his boss, no expression of remorse, just expectation at getting his answer. He saw his boss' face grey; the colour, even added to by his recent exertion and injury, drained.

Paul felt slightly sick. He didn't know why, he felt bloated.

"Come on, let's get on with this." Martin was a little curt, which was very curt by comparison to his usual manner. "This job is already a day behind and there's been too much happening. Let's just get it finished and get out of here and paid for."

Martin had emphasised the "here" in what he had just said. There was a feeling of aggression and anger in the words.

The remaining pews bolted in place without any issue but the two men worked in silence, Paul conscience that he must have upset Martin but not knowing to what degree; he was only aware that Martin had been married but was told by Jeff when he started working for Martin, she died four years previously. He hadn't given their relationship any thought since that day.

Martin worked with a sullenness until the last bolt was secured.

He looked indifferent at Paul. "I'll do the repairs to those two there. Just check all the others if you would. They should be alright. It was only these two that got dropped wasn't it?"

"Far as I know, I'll look now." Paul checked, all the other pews were undamaged.

"You go Paul, I won't be long here." His voice trailed off, as if the effort of talking was just too much.

CHAPTER 11

John was nudged from behind by Paul as he stood by the office photocopier, the sound of the machine covering Paul's entrance.

The Reverend was thinking about his sermon for Sunday, new start, integrating the old and the new, racial harmony, different beliefs and religions; all revolving around the new seating.

The coffee jumped out over the top of the cup as John flicked the cup as a reaction to Paul's nudge.

"See you Vic. Thanks for the tea. Enjoy the seats."

"You've finished?" John asked with excitement, as he put his cup down and flicked the splashes of coffee off his sleeve.

"Almost, Martin's just finishing, about another hour but I'm off, just wanted to say thanks for the hospitality."

Paul left John walking to the church entry via the vestry door, the next room on from the office; on his way to have a quick look and Martin.

Martin had the wood filler, wax block and various other items he used for rectifying small areas of damage. He was kneeling on the first pew, looking again at the back of the seat Mal had been holding onto during their discussion yesterday. It was not deliberate, although his earlier sullenness had developed into sadness and remorse, his mind now not being able to stop thinking about his lovely Ann at one level while still fundamentally thinking and concentrating on these small repairs.

They were lucky really. The knocks these pews had taken had only cause minor dents and scraps. Nothing had split. Oak was strong, his favourite wood. He had lots of oak furniture in his own home and Ann had appreciated its beauty as well.

He used the edge of a fine chisel to score a key into the wood. He started the process, looking down at the various fillers and waxes. Working on the backrest of this pew, his eyes saw over the top edge he was working on and beyond to the second pew. There was no image as he had seen yesterday. There were three or four areas of damage to the top edge and the front edge of the seat, some more obvious than others but Martin was quite prepared to build up and mould the waxes and filler matching in the contours of the back rest especially as it was more sculptured than the front edge of the seat which had a straight, sharp edge.

His eyes went back to the second pew still no image, just grain, sweeping along its length. His mind went to Ann again as he worked the wax, reminding him of the massages and kneading the back of her neck that she enjoyed so much, not just after they found out about the cancer but one of those things she loved having Martin do: more so though after she had the diagnosis. He had strong, hard hands from years of manual work and she loved the feel of them when he rubbed her skin.

As these memories grew, his efforts with the waxes and fillers became more vigorous, pressing hard into the wood, aiming to build up the damaged area quicker so he get away from this place sooner.

Martin didn't know if it was his imagination. He stared over the back of his patient, looking down at the seat of the pew behind but the grain looked different. The long lines of variation were still there, varnished, segregated yet as one and he could now see more vague patterns within the main grain, faint lines, hinted twists with another agenda, drawing him into their illusion.

He could see what looked like a wisp of feather, a plume. There was a darker more definite shape though still faint by comparison to the top layers, a small thin oblong to the right and underneath hints of circles, some complete with the full circumference, some parts on others missing, then reappearing further around the circle.

His chisel cut off the excess filler. He put this on an old piece of ply, ready to use again. He rubbed the repairs with fine glass paper.

Martin worked another area a couple of feet further to the left, his eyes still drawn to the right, now seeing the suggestion from a different angle. From here the oblong looked like a finger, some other faint almost invisible flicks within the varnish creating a mirage of fingers, a hand?.

His thoughts saw Ann and combined the six months after she was diagnosed into minutes. The formation, his love for wood, for Ann, not letting him look away.

The day she came home from the doctors after getting the results, Ann came back with a bottle of Krug champagne. "£170, are you nuts." He still regretted his initial reaction even to this day.

Her explanation had Martin in tears. He, they, had not expected the answer to why she had been feeling sick, loss of appetite, bloated tummy to be... final.

Ann had held him so tight that evening, their whole courtship and marriage condensed into her one long hug. Ann had consoled HIM at his forth coming loss, his tears streaming down his face, onto her neck, mingling with her hair. She had not cried, she had been strong, resolute almost that they were going to be happy. The Champagne was something she had always wanted to try but the price was very extravagant. They drank and liked champagne, not regularly but Krug was special and Ann loved it. She said it was the sign that they were going to celebrate the last six months together, this was their excuse for doing the things that they had talked about, as "one day". They should thank God that they were to have six months together.

Thank God ! ? Martin never could reconcile this.

Martin thought of the rides and parks in Florida. People had said you didn't need children to go to Disney and the three weeks they were there had been fun from start to finish, Ann laughing and teasing Martin all through the holiday. He had forgotten she was ill and her illness didn't show to any great extent or she kept it from him. He felt guilty now at the recollection that he had forgotten during that holiday she was going to die, their enjoyment together overshadowing the future.

The opera at La Scala was breathtaking, its performance uplifting, the four day trip Ann had arranged was sophisticated, five star all the way. She had worn a neon blue evening gown and her hair up with diamanté clips. They joked that you couldn't tell the difference to the real ones rich people's were wearing. Ann could. Martin remembered her every gesture during that night, his beautiful wife exuding life, her enthralment with the music. He had not played opera since.

As the six month drew the energy out of Ann, the amount of time they spent together remained constant almost continuous, Martin only very occasionally going into work, his mind staying on his wife; the support and understanding of his employees, tender, emotional, especially within the last month when they were asking about her and finding out she had made her own funeral arrangements on one of the occasional full days Martin had been at the yard. That way, he told them, she said I wouldn't have to worry about anything. He hadn't been able to hold back his tears, Jeff, Mike, Andy all putting their hands on his shoulders for manly support but transforming to a circular huddle filled with compassion.

The trips grew less and the time sitting together grew more. They looked back through photographs from their wedding day, their holidays, birthdays, family occasions, both remembering different things the photograph brought out of their combined memory.

"Tell me about our cottage," Ann would say. They had always wanted a cottage in Pembrokeshire with a sea view. One of their favourite things was to look at the sea together, walk along the long beaches. Martin would hold his wife and describe how their cottage would look, what they would have inside; big squishy red cushions on a big squishy four seater red settee, the sort of settee that swallows you within its softness, big enough for them both to sit end to end to each other and to cuddle under a fleecy blanket with a glass of wine in front of a log fire.

Their cottage would have had a large kitchen come dining room overlooking the sea, large enough so six friends could come and stay and would have four bedrooms. Martin used to embellish and protract on occasions, his descriptions of the wooden furniture he would have made, to bait her. He would talk about the chairs and oak Welsh dresser as if they were real and he would watch tauntingly as Ann's eagerness to get to the best bits grew.

His descriptions and imagination may change some details but the cushions and fire always had to be in the story.

"Tell me about the cushions and the fire," Ann would ask, when Martin deliberately left them out of his story, teasing her, prompting her. He would describe their colour, how they would feel as they folded around them when they sat down. "The cushions will always feel warm from the fire, we'll feel their warmth and softness on our necks as they fold around us. The fire will be blazing with the wood I brought from the yard and we can toast marsh mallows.....for me....not you.......cos you won't want to get fat" and he would cuddle or squeeze her thin waist depending on how they were sitting.

In what turned out to be their last week, he had found a cottage with a sea view looking across a short semi circular beach. The pink walled cottage had a gravel path leading up to it and the best thing was the wooden french windows in the dining room that opened onto a decked patio. Although it was February, there had been a few sunny afternoons when they had gone for a short walk or just sat there, in thick jumpers, hat and gloves but that had been magical, the salt air, the waves, perfect.

On the Thursday afternoon, the sun was shining and Ann had said to sit out on the patio. She had asked Martin to get the bottle of Krug she had sneaked into the fridge. They sat, hugged together on a rattan two seater outdoor settee, only moving so that Martin could top up their glasses. Halfway through the second glass, Ann had turned her head to kiss him, her blond hair blowing across his and her face, their kiss meeting with locks of her hair caught between their lips. She tasted of champagne and Ann. Martin could taste and smell her now as he rubbed on the pews. Ann turned back to look at the view after giving Martin a second pecky kiss on the lips.

"The bubbles still go up my nose," she giggled slightly......................" Make sure you finish the bottle darling." She sat back into their hug and gripped his arms. Ann didn't reach for her champagne after that.

Martin did finish the champagne, trying not to disturb Ann or their position as he leant for the bottle. He, they, sat there for hours. He left her glass, still quarter full.

He kissed the back of her head, his face burying deep into her curls, "I love you my Ann, I love you my Ann," with every kiss. He could smell again her hair and feel the dampness his crying had created, the saltiness of his tears mixed with the salt sea air, his grief wetting the back of Ann's head and neck.

As Martin repaired the pew, his tears splashed straight from his eyes onto the polished oak seat. His memory of that February afternoon dragged his heart and insides out of his body and he felt his strength collapse, his hands slipped into gripping the edges of the seat and backrest to try and stop his complete demolition into an empty man.

Their courtship and marriage emerged to his conscious recollection, each special thing over their twenty five years together pulling on his heart, the strain of trying to keep each one in his mind before the next took over, made him grip even harder to the pew as if it had become his best friend. His head lay against the seat pushing in a pump action of increasing and decreasing pressure, created by the shuddering his shoulders gave to his upper body as he lost himself within his resurrected grief.

The funeral Ann had arranged wasn't conventional but wasn't lavish.

The single white horse she asked for with black plume head dress pulled a small carriage with her coffin. The flowers on it were simple, daffodils. Ann had loved yellow. So happy and bright. Ann had been yellow.

The gathering of mourners packed the church and the graveside. The men and their families were there and so many from the church where Ann and Martin had gone. Martin had not been able to see the faces of most as he stood by the grave side during the committal, just parts of heads and faces.

He had found it difficult to come to terms with, keep self occupied by working to the extent that he had the detail of those days, pushing them to where they could not upset him.

The image of these fingers, the oblong were now dominant, leading his mind to Ann. His face was wet. His nose was dripping. He could not stop his shoulders from shaking despite now holding on with both hands to the top of the pew. There was a small chisel wedged between the fingers on his right hand and the top edge of the back rest. His chest heaving, gasping for air as his crying expelled the breath from his lungs, as the momentum of his crying increased.

Reverend John came into the church to look at the end result but found Martin hunched, chisel still in his right hand, the tip acting like a spring as Martins forehead repeatedly pressed down on it, trying to stop his mind from remembering.

"Martin!" John rushed into the row, grabbing the chisel with his right hand and Martin's chest, just below his Adams Apple, with his left hand, pulling his body and head away from the chisel.

"Martin, what are you doing, what's wrong?"

Martin didn't answer, he couldn't. His crying had increased beyond sobbing to wailing, loud exuding screams of breath filled with the anger and emotion associated to loss and despair, now rekindled after eight lonely years.

John managed to ease the chisel out of Martin's hand putting it to one side on the pew, small drops of blood dripping onto the varnish.

"Martin, come on, come on." His words forceful and reassuring. "Ann wouldn't want to see you like this. She is with Our Lord now, she's at peace and happy."

The mention of Ann's name, these assumptions had Martin whirl around, forcing John backwards.

"What do you know about Ann? How can you tell me she is happy?"

Martin's mind exploded with a venom of thoughts, his anger unleashed. He clenched his fists, his arms ridged, the muscles and tendons straining in his neck, the thin slices in the skin of his forehead, forcing blood out. Martin had so many thoughts about God and his involvement in his life, that not one of them materialised into words. They stayed latent, boiling on the tip of his tongue.

John felt Martin's weight increase, aware of the exertion of emotion and now the relapse as he helped Martin out of the church and into the vestry.

John didn't mention Ann but felt he knew what Martin would have said if he hadn't subsided. He had heard grief and anger so many times, the unfairness of life, God's lack of compassion, his inept judgement on who should live or die.

CHAPTER 12

"Bloody hell Vic, didn't expect to see you again. "Paul's greeting had Reverend John whirl around in his chair. John gathered his surprise.

"How's Martin?"

"He's not in work today, Jeff said he rang in this morning, that's why we are here." He pointed to Andy who was leaning on the office door frame. "We just got some little scratches to sort out and we'll be done. I thought Martin would have done them before going home yesterday. Did he get stuck or something or what?"

John was vague about the answer not wanting to give too much information in case that lead to future embarrassment for Martin. He knew how workmen could be, ragging and goading each other but this might be a bit too sensitive.

He had cleaned Martin's forehead up, the cuts looking worse than they were, when the blood was being forced out while Martin was emotional, but looking very thin and redeemable; no need for stitches once the blood had been wiped away.

Martin had apologised over and over again for not finishing the touching up and had driven himself home.

"Go and get some chips....and a curry sauce for me," Paul asked Andy, throwing Andy a five pound note. "Want some Vic?"

"Oh no thanks, not three days running."

"We'll get on then. Can I stick the kettle on so we can have a cuppa with our chips. We won't eat them in the church, promise."

"Yes that's fine." John couldn't but help liking Paul. What you saw was what you got.

The two men finished their dinner and went into the church. They stopped and stood by the alter rail, partly looking to see where they should go and partly to look at the church itself. The shutters were open on most of the stained glass windows and there were hints of colour within the sunbeams that made their way towards the rows of pews. Andy turned the light on and the sunbeams faded for the most part within the now illuminated church.

The deep blue of the carpet gave a strong contrast to the overall browns of the wooden seating and floors. The first floor galleries had dark oak hand rails running all the way around the front edge and the walling underneath the rails which closed off the gallery, had been painted in a light power blue.

Paul noticed that some of the walling was flaking off or cracking. Parts were showing white underneath and he wondered what sort of materials had been used. His pondering was interrupted. "There's the repair stuff". Andy said pointing to the materials waiting, where Martin had been the afternoon before.

"It's only these two to do, all the others are fine," Paul put his hand on the front pew, "you go around and do that one."

Paul could see where Martin had finished and the areas left to do and picked up the materials as if he had started the job initially.

Andy marked out the areas on the rear pew with chalk and started going through the process of repair.

He sat down more through the process than Paul, the initial

coolness of the wood giving soothing relief to his still bruised groin and upper legs. He slid himself along the seat every now and then, the new cold section of seating appearing to cool the bruising affect he was so conscious of.

Paul remained standing, his large frame not suited to a squatting and looking backwards position, so he leaned over, standing on the floor, his left knee occasionally resting on the seat of the pew. Paul finished first. He didn't bother to touch up the marks underneath as he took the view that they couldn't be seen unless you were kneeling on the floor looking up, under the seat.

He went around to Andy's isle with the intention of attending to the marked areas of the pew, so that the job was finished quicker. The two remaining marks were so close together that the men were in each others way. Andy agreed that Paul should leave him to it, leaving Andy in the church on his own.

Andy sat down on a new section of seat, now cold again, that temporary soothing effect giving relief, then fading.

He finished the last but one area and slid back along the seat to view it, his right leg lying along the the seat, his left on the floor, his left hand on the backrest of the pew in front. Andy started to feel nauseous and bloated.

"Bet it's the curry sauce," he thought to himself.

CHAPTER 13

Sunday, 10.30 am and the doors were open, the two greeting parishioners waiting to welcome the congregation for morning service, the pre service prayers taken in the vestry by The Reverend John Rowlands.

Lots of the church goers liked to always sit in the same seats or at least in the same pew.

Services had not been quite so conventional over the last six months, given the obvious mix of old pews and patio furniture, yet despite the fact that there were still enough seating positions on the old pews, certain people still sat in the patio chairs, even if it meant complaining about their back in the process, or that the chair was too wobbly.

There was an air of expectation regarding the new pews. At long last after all the fund raising and discussions, the consultation and quotes, the new pews had been fitted. The church was now back to normal.

This morning The Reverend John was also on the door, with the intention of enjoying the fulfilment he felt, the expectation the people in the congregation felt and hopefully, the satisfaction of a good service, its message and the appreciation of the new pews.

John wondered if the people he knew who had sat in the patio furniture would go to the same position and now sit in the new seats or would they swap their position for another, perhaps preferring an old pew instead.

In general, most people sat where they sat when the plastic chairs were there. Only a few, Mrs Mortimer, Mr. and Mrs. Evans and John Jenkins, JJ as he was known, sat first in the new pews to the sides and rear of the church and then moved.

Mrs. Mortimer having shuffled her seventy two year old bottom along one of the new pews at the rear, felt that it was just too hard and decided to try one of the other new ones closer to the front, although she preferred to be at the back of the church. That position allowed her to be one of the first to leave after the service and to congratulate which ever minister or lay preacher had been there that day on what a good service it had been.

"It's important to be positive, give encouragement," she would always say and while not the oldest in the church, she felt her age gave her the prerogative to give the younger preachers her support.

She flumped down on the pew Martin had worked on, its seat welcoming. This was so much comfier than the last one. She undid her green woollen overcoat so she could sit comfortably, adjusting the matching green felt hat with wide brim, which had slipped down in front of her eyes slightly, as she bounced herself up and down during her adjustments. Her permed, light whispy blond coloured hair refusing to move, held firm by a generous coating of hairspray.

"Sorry dears, it's far easier to do it now than during the sermon, get myself comfy that is, would you like a polo?" How's married life? Is he treating you well dear? Remember feed your man well. Always treat her well young man, you won't find another like her, she's a gem. How's your parents Haley? I haven't seen your mother or your father come to think of it for a couple of weeks now, are they both well? What do you think of the new pews? I tried one at the back, ooh I thought, too hard for me. We'll have to get some cushions on this one if I'm going to sit in this one next week, mind you, you'd think with all my padding I wouldn't need cushions."

She fumbled for her tube of polos in her right coat pocket, her wrist getting caught in the pocket as her coat folded when she sat down. She tugged at her own fist as if it were nothing to do with her own body. She stood up, her hand came out with the polos, offering them as she spoke. She patted her right hip to put identity to her padding.

Further along that pew sat Haley and Alister Langley, newly weds back in June. Both had been church members for years, Alister swapping to St Andrews when he and his parents had moved to the area twelve years ago, Haley since she was born.

Mrs. Mortimer had been her Sunday school teacher at one point, Girls Brigade officer for many a year until she had felt she had gotten too old to carry on doing those sort of things.

Haley had always really liked Mrs. Mortimer and she thought a lot of Haley. Twenty one though, she thought, was too young to get married; especially in this day and age, it had been different in her day, she had been nineteen when she married Frank.

Haley took the polo, passing the first to Alister. Alister smiled his thanks. He had come to like Mrs. M, as he referred to and addressed her. My God, can that woman talk he used to say to Haley, when he first met her. It was the amount of talking that had been the barrier to him getting to like her. Alister had initially thought that anyone who talked that much, asked so many questions and didn't wait for any answers, wasn't interested in anyone else, only themselves.

Mrs. M. was certainly interested in things. She may have felt that she had gotten too old for some of the church activities but her interest and opinions were still heard.

"You look very nice dear, you've curled your hair, it looks

lovely, it frames your face." Mrs M touched Haley's left arm approvingly. Haley smiled demurely, fingering some of the longer black curls that draped around either side of her face, her brown eyes fluttered a few times in response to her compliment. She glanced towards Alister, her red glossed lips smiling.

"There you are see. I said you looked stunning with your hair like that." She squeezed Alister's hand accepting his confirmation as she had hesitated at curling it, especially for church: she had wondered if it looked too partyish. She was a little self conscious about herself and Alister tried to increase her confidence by encouraging her to make more decisions on her own, without always asking him for his opinion.

Alister felt very lucky at having a wife who looked like Haley. She had a gorgeous figure and olive skin and her face he thought, was beautiful, high cheek bones and natural full lips with distinct edges. He was five inches taller at five foot eleven and certainly didn't consider himself as anything to look at by comparison. He didn't really like his blond to ginger wavy hair but Haley loved his dark brown eyes and he had a square chin with a small dimple. Her private nick name for him was Spartacus, after Kirk Douglas who had the same sort of dimple.

Mrs. M turned to say hello to Mr and Mrs Evans when they sat in the new pew behind her and then JJ when she heard him sit down.

She, Haley and Alister, glanced around as people came in either down the right or left isle, watching their selection process of where to sit or their determination to sit where some one was already sat, "in their place" in one of the new pews.

They watched as virtually everyone looked at and touched the pews with seeming approval. Their reactions made Mrs. M think that she had not looked at the pew she was sitting in.

She moved her hips and bottom to the right and left exposing the seat her bottom was covering, sliding easily on the varnished surface.

The grain was deep, an area of darker wood within the overall colour of the pew. She felt a little shiver. Best keep my coat on, she thought to herself. The church was a large, high ceiling church, with minstrel galleries at the rear and along three quarters of its sides and it took ages to warm up. These were rarely used, certainly not for Sunday service.

Mrs. Mortimer settled herself, her bottom back to its original position on the seat.

JJ and the Evans' watched her, their eyes now being drawn to the back of her head and hat. JJ started looking at the rear of her pew.

"Look at that!, can you see that?" He lent over to his right slightly to tap Mr. Evans on the forearm. "Can you see that woman's face in the wood?"

Mr Evans looked to pacify JJ. They didn't always see eye to eye so it was odd that they found themselves siting so close to each other. He and his wife had initially sat in a new pew on the right of the church while JJ had sat closer initially to the front but both decided to move and had arrived at this pew at the same time from the opposite direction. Neither were not going to sit down and move again because of the other.

"No, no, I can't see any face." Mike Evans response was irritated as he looked at the backrest.

"You can't see it? Look, there! There's her mouth, the eyes, this bit's her nose." JJ's fingers drew the shape of the features as his right index finger followed the shapes in the grain.

"It's a piece of wood. There's no face." Mr. Evans now more irritated by JJ's insistence.

"Ohh, I can see her. This bit could be her hair and this line here could be the front of her neck." Elizabeth Evans, Liz as everyone knew her by, leaned around her husband to trace the incomplete portrait that JJ was illustrating, their fingers almost touching.

"There's no face there." Mr. Evans now extremely irritated by his wife and her connection with not just the wood but with JJ.

The two smiled at each other, aware now that they were both annoying Mr. Evans. "What shall we call her?" Liz asked JJ and then looking at her husband, knowing this would wind him up more, giving a name to a unseen face, completely irrational in his opinion.

"Beth" JJ said, winking at LIz.

Mr. Evans shuffled on his seat, pursing his lips, twitching them, his nostrils flaring as he tugged on his dark blue suit jacket to establish his importance, smoothed both sides of his closely cut light brown hair and adjusted his steel rimmed glasses. He was far from amused. Liz and JJ had known each other since they were seven and forty years later they still had a special relationship, a strong friendship and this rubbed the wrong way on times with her husband.

John Rowlands went up the stairs to the pulpit, a big uncontainable smile on his face. The church was full for this Sunday service. He looked around at, he estimated a hundred and twenty five in the congregation.

JJ looked back to the rear of the pew in front, to have another look at Beth but the grain had now hidden the face that he saw so clearly seconds ago. He leant forward with the intention of motioning to Liz, for her to look for her name sake. JJ had deliberately chosen a connotation of Elizabeth, as homage to his friend and as a red rag to Mr. Evans.

Reverend John started speaking. JJ sat back and abandoned his intention.

"What do you think of the new pews?" He wasn't expecting to get everyone shouting the answer in unison just the expected muttering of approval he heard.

His intention today was to preach on acceptance, the mixing of the old with the new and the opportunity of accepting and adopting new ideas brought into a person's life.

He gripped the two sides of the open bible that lay on the pulpits lectern and he felt a sharp pain radiate from his right palm and middle finger, combining to remind him of his wood wounds. He had not been able to get these out and these two last intruding shards had made these parts of his hand tender.

John's mind jumped back to the occasion earlier in the week, the accidents, the sacrifices that people had made to get these pews to the church.

It hadn't occurred to John to tell the congregation of the accidents, merely to give thanks for the new seats and to acknowledge the efforts made in raising the money and to those people who with their skill, had made the pews.

John started his welcome.

......" and now that everyone's efforts and personal contributions can be seen or at least sat on, I think it's important for you all to know that one of the carpenters had two fingers severed when one of the pews slipped and his hand got caught between the leg of the pew and the steps outside. It was very unfortunate and he was in a state of shock. You could see the bones in his fingers but from what my wife could see, through the blood that is, was that the bones were not cut cleanly, like a guillotine but had signs of being crushed and then being broken off. Elaine ......" As he said her name and glanced over to look at her, he became instantly aware from her expression that something was wrong.

John had continued to smile when telling the congregation about this particular event but his smile was different. Elaine could see this, whether the congregation could see the difference, she hoped not as there had been signs of glee in eyes, an enjoyment almost at the misfortune and within the re telling of the accident.

Elaine's face was a mixture of anger and astonishment, her eyes boring into John, her head giving the slightest of shakes, her lower jaw protruding, twitching, mouthing as if she received an electric shock; warning him not to say anymore. She had leaned forward on the pew she was sitting in, trying to look as if she was not involved with any communication with her husband, not to bring what she was saying and doing to the attention of any other person.

John stopped in mid sentence, thinking what could she be trying to say to him. His approach within services was not ridged and old fashioned but traditional with warm, varying, some times off the cuff interaction and unplanned anecdotes, as if he was having a conversation with you rather than preaching "to you or at you." People had even shouted out answers to rhetorical questions when he had asked them as they had become so involved in what he was talking about. It wouldn't have been out of place for her to gesture more visually, given the way his services were conducted and the sometimes unexpected involvement of some listeners.

John looked down at the bible, his telling of the accident returning to his memory and the realisation what Elaine was trying to do.

"Our first hymn 365, Thyne be the Glory." He felt relieved that this was something to change the pace at this point, to deflect from his opening comments. "What was I thinking?, I bet someone will say something at the end of the service when they leave. I bet it will be.... who?" He thought. "I know, Mr. Evans, he's never happier than when finding fault? That's what poxy accountants do, nit pick." He looked down at the bible to say thank you as the introduction for the hymn started and the congregation stood up. There were a few drops of blood at the bottom of the right hand page, where the palm of his right hand had been resting.

The congregation gathered themselves, taking their surprised and confused thoughts about John's opening comments and turned their attention to keeping up, with the tune of the first hymn.

Following a few more hymns and prayers of thanks, Mrs. Mortimer and the rest of the congregation settled themselves for the twenty to thirty minute sermon. This service had been a bit different, a hymn service with six hymns with themes of acceptance and celebration. She was glad now of a long sit down. Standing up and down aggregated the knee replacement she had five years earlier.

Judging by the hymn and prayers so far, The Minister's sermon would be celebratory as well. "Why is he fidgeting with his hands?", she thought.

She offered another polo to Haley and Alister who accepted, breaking their hand holding to do so. "That was lovely to see," she thought, "not many young people in church these days, nice to see young love."

The polo seemed to settle the sick feeling she had in the back of her throat. Mrs. M straightened her back so that its full length and her shoulders were pressed against the upright back rest. There was no support in these pews for your lower back and she had been told by her parents this was the way to sit in a pew, don't slouch.

She folded her hands across her lap and looked down to the right of her at the piece of exposed seat between her and Haley.

"That looked different," she thought and then thought no more about it but she still kept looking at the seat as she heard John start his sermon.

Haley became conscious of her red short skirt and legs, although she was wearing thick black tights and black knee length flat heeled boots, she thought Mrs. M might be assessing her, looking at her legs.

She was not. Mrs. M was transfixed by the shapes she saw in the wood. Her eyes squinted through her glasses to concentrate more on the forms she thought she could see? John's voice was in the background, the sermon of acceptance in its early stages.

"They really are beautiful pews. I wonder if they all have these sort of patterns in." She thought to herself as she looked back up at John in the pulpit.

"A young woman lived in a small village which was close to a large wood or forest. Her parents had died a few years earlier so she was left in the house on her own. The woman unfortunately to some had a mental disorder. She was prone to out bursts. On some occasions when she went into the village to do some shopping, she would sense people looking at her, sometimes pointing, all of which didn't help with her trying to control her out bursts.

On one occasion when she was in town, one of the older women and she, went through the doorway of the same shop at the same time, she coming out the older woman going in. The older woman thought she had the right to be allowed to go through the door first, simply based on the fact that she was older.

The older woman was impatient and looked down on the younger woman and because of her condition, pushed the young woman out of her way, the young woman catching her arm in reaction to stop herself from being pushed over.

The young woman screamed at the older woman's rudeness, cursing at her, clawing at her face, catching the older woman's cheek, scramming it, taking some of the older woman's skin under her fingernails as she did, drawing blood in the process. Her blond hair seemed to envelop her head and body as its waist length volume whipped and twisted as she tussled with the older woman.

When the young woman got home she removed the skin which she found under her nails and put it in a small earthen ware pot.

The older woman's husband was so angry when he saw his wife's face and after he had listened to her side of the story went to the young woman's house with the intention of beating her.

When he first saw the young woman who was at the back of her house picking some herbs that were growing there; she was so attractive that his initial intention changed.

The husband was a big man and he was able to hold her down. He rubbed his huge hands up and down the length of her body and legs, first one side and then the other. As he stretched out, the pressure on his knees increased and when he reach his full stretch, his lower back pulled him back so that he ended up kneeling upright by her side. He repeated the move. His eyes enjoyed the life her body gave him. Her eyes penetrated his."

Haley became aware of Mrs. M rubbing both her arms with her hands, her arms folded across her 40D chest in a hugging manner. She thought Mrs. M must be feeling cold. Mrs. M was still looking down at the seat, Haley realised she wasn't looking at her at all but she was transfixed to looking at the seat.

Haley squeezed Alister's hand and indicated for him to look at her. Alister leant forward slightly and looked around Haley.

Haley became aware of Mrs. M's movement, she seemed restless and uncomfortable as she was not sitting still. Mrs. M started undulating herself on the seat, moving gently back and forth, from front to back and then side to side. They both watched for about thirty seconds and the sermon slipped into the back of their concentration as Mrs. M became their focus. She started to breathe funny, deeper.

"Do you think she is alright, is she having a heart attack or something." Haley whispered to Alister.

They both looked at her. She was oblivious to them.

"Perhaps the seat is just too hard for her."

Haley caught sight out of the corner of her left eye of the Evans' moving their heads from side to side, trying to compensate for Mrs. M as they tried to look past her at The Minister.

Alister could just about see from the angle he had from sitting in the row in front that Mr. Evans had a very similar annoyed or irritated look to the one he had earlier with JJ. They did not know why she was bobbing around so much. They just wished that she would keep still so they could see The Minister.

Haley looked back at her old Sunday School teacher. It didn't look like she was having a heart attack. She was smiling. Her breathing was now deep and panting. It could be a heart attack, she was sweating a bit.

Mrs. M had stopped rubbing her arms and was now gripping the front edge of the seat with both hands. She had stopped moving but her cuddly, granny body looked coiled, ready to spring. Her hat had slipped down the front of her forehead as a result of all her rocking, its wide brim adding to the obstruction of their view of The Minister for Mr. and Mrs. Evans.

Haley could see the tension in her arms from the fact that they were straight and quivering, her wrinkled hands, vice like on the seats edge, her knuckles had gone white with the strength her grip was exerting.

Haley shook Alister's left knee to regain his attention "Look she must be having some sort of attack." She was really now quite concerned.

Alister leaned forward again to look around Haley. It looked to him as if she was now pulling herself down onto the seat, trying to force her bottom to have the greatest amount of contact and tension with the wood as possible.

"Mrs. M are you alright?" Haley whispered so as not to be heard outside of their pew, "are you ok?"

Mr and Mrs. Evans now had their attention drawn to Haley's voice. Mrs Evans leaned forward and towards Haley, her both hands resting on the back of Mrs. M's pew, now between the two. She was looking around from Mrs. M's right hand side. She could see the small beads of sweat on her right temple and on her right cheek. She wore very little makeup, just a little foundation powder. For seventy two, her skin was still very smooth, with very few wrinkles.

"Mrs Mortimer," she said softy, "are you alright, is there something we can do?"

There was no response. Mrs. Mortimer had stopped biting her lips which had now parted slightly and she was making little squeaking noises that seemed to come out of the top of her nose.

Alister and Haley began to giggle at her noises, both feeling really guilty at laughing when they were becoming more concerned that she was in the middle of some sort of seizure or ..... something.

Haley took a deep breath in, trying to stifle her giggles but at the same time her nose snorted a pig like snort, louder than Mrs. M's squeaking. This made Alister giggle louder. He put his hand up to his mouth, his face now turning red as he tried to control his sniggers; which encouraged Haley to giggle even louder and more than before.

Alister clamped his hand over his mouth, lowering his head so that he could not be seen to be laughing, or so he hoped. The tears started to well up in his eyes. "Oh God, don't make me laugh here, not now. Please stop her from squeaking." His thoughts turned to prayer as he thought them. His shoulders started to rock as he desperately tried to control his giggling, the tears now streaming out of his eyes.

Haley tried to shush him by pinching his left leg, just above the knee. "Shut up, it's not funny," she said but by now she was gripping the seat in front, her head lowered so that it was below the back of the top edge of the pew, hiding; while still looking at Mrs. M who was squeaking with more frequency, her mouth now wider than before and her panting, short, shallow, frequent and now urgent.

"Mrs. M ......please tell me.......that you are ok." Her suppressed giggles punctuated her question. She could hear Alister, his head almost between his knees now, pleading, praying out aloud but very, very quietly, to himself really, "please make her stop squeaking at least, don't let her be having a heart attack but make her stop squeaking."

He started making the same "eek, eek" imitating Mrs. M so this would make Haley giggle more. He tried to control himself so that it would only be Haley who would be caught giggling, by him naughtily trying to make her laugh more. "Please stop Mrs. MMMMouse from squeeeeeeking" he whispered to Haley out of the side of his mouth. He was wiping his eyes with the palm of his hand pushing into his eye sockets, trying to stop the tears. Haley bit her bottom lip gently in an effort to control herself.

Reverend John had started to notice the small huddle that was forming in the right hand pews of the centre section, just past the half way point. It was more noticeable as the activity was emphasised by the fact that there were two brand new pews at this point, one in front of each other. All the other pews immediately around these were older, darker with age.

He could see the brim of a green hat leaning towards him like a satellite dish. It had been moving oddly a little earlier and had caught his eye while he was speaking. John was beginning to catch the sound of little whispers and giggles. The acoustics in these old churches were marvellous he had always thought, considering they were built without any modern technology.

JJ was also leaning forward now from Mrs. M's left hand side. Mrs. M's mind was still involved with the young woman and this deviant husband.

JJ looked at Liz Evans and then at Haley. As the older lady, she was exercising more control but even so the smallest of smiles came to her lips as she leant forward and asked if everything was alright.

All JJ heard was Mrs. M's squeaking and then giggles from further over from the pew in front coming from Haley and Alister. He wondered what on earth was happening as he had been sitting with his head bowed, in an attempt to disguise his dozing.

He too, now slid himself forward, his knees and chest against the front pew and put his right hand on her left shoulder and gave it a quick squeeze, then shake. "Beryl, what's wrong?"

He and the others involved expected for some reason that Beryl Mortimer would answer even though she had ignored the same question from the others sitting around her.

Beryl's face had now coloured. JJ saw the trickle lines of perspiration on the side of her face, her foundation powder now water marked; the affect subtle but it reminded him of the veining in Carrara marble.

He could see that her eyes were tightly shut. He moved his right hand to hold the rear of the body of her green hat, his intention, to adjust it so that it sat more squarely on her head.

Beryl was rigid, the top of her nose and throat were now producing, louder, short yelps, taking over from her squeaks. It didn't look to any of the five people now all leaning in towards her, all concerned; that she was breathing in, just out, yelping.

Mr. Evans looked at his wife, beginning to feel a little embarrassed that he was caught up unintentionally in this ill timed predicament. He could see The Minister's glances towards this huddle and then back to his notes, his sermon continuing, his eyes flicking around to other parts of the congregation keeping other listeners engaged but more often looking back in their direction.

JJ lifted Beryl's hat.

Beryl exploded onto her feet, her hands adding to her propulsion off her seat, then clamping onto the back of the pew in front, like she was going to use this momentum to vault over into the next row of seating.

"THANK GOD" she shouted. Her voice though strong and loud, tailed off to sound more hushed and relieved on the "GOD".

JJ was left holding her hat in his right hand.

"Thank God indeed Mrs. Mortimer. I'm glad you feel like that as well." The Reverend John felt a sense of achievement at her agreement to the point he had just made in his sermon.

"So do I Reverend!"

Beryl sat back down, her face still redder than on her arrival to church. She adjusted her seating position, feeling her hair and then looking down in the pew followed by turning to Mrs. Evans and finally to take her missing hat off JJ.

JJ asked his partly disheveled friend as she took the hat from him, her face still smiling. "Beryl, are sure you're ok?"

"You bet Hun!" She wasn't aware of the increased mumbling going around the pews. She took the hat from him put it on the seat next to her, turned back to him, pinched his left cheek with her right index finger and thumb, turned back, adjusted her clothing and picked her hat up and rammed it down on top of her head. Berly's mind was now filled with sexual memories of Frank, a cruel subversive trick, reminding her of passion long past and missed, rekindled to torment her and renew her grief.

Haley and Alister sat back into the pew, holding each others right and left hands respectively, both just managing to hold their giggles as giggles and not to develop into full blown laughs.

"She should change her medication," Mr. Evans whispered to his wife. She elbowed him with her left elbow.

JJ slid back, his right hand giving Beryl's left shoulder a similar squeeze and touch as earlier, as he did so, reassuring himself that she was fine and as thanks for her friendly pinch.

Beryl gave his hand a passing tap with her left hand as it left her shoulder. She wiped the tears from her eyes.

She turned her head back to look at the same section of wood within the seat next to her.

CHAPTER 14

"The young woman lay on the floor and watched the husband leave. She shouted curses after him, vowing to avenge what he had done. Her eyes blazed with anger, their bright blue almost turquoise colour appearing to glow from the rage she felt.

The husband ignored her ranting, putting it down to the stories about her ravings he had heard. As big a man as he was, wasn't concerned about what he considered, empty threats from some twenty year old girl.

The girl gathered herself together, finishing her selection of the herbs and plants she had started to pick before the husband's arrival and took them back into her house, mixing them with the woman's skin and dried blood that she had removed from under her finger nails.

She boiled them, mumbling to herself the same words over and over.

When the husband got home, he didn't say what he had done despite the victorious feeling it gave him. He told his wife that the young woman would never bother her again and that next time she knew that he would kill her.

The following morning the two of them woke up, her husband recoiling in disgust and fear as he looked at his wife's face and then her arms, legs and body, which were now all covered with scabs and scars as if she had become riddled with the pox".

Mrs. Mortimer looked at the seat more and more intently. There were strokes in the grain which looked to her like a tree with some sort of shape in front of it. The shape appeared to keep moving as opposed to being part of the tree itself.

She could feel for this young woman.

In the pew behind, JJ again saw a image of a woman's head within the wood, directly behind where Beryl was sitting and it looked identical to what he saw before the start of the service.

He stared at the image, not able to come to terms in is own mind why it was there now and not before. The wood grain was constant, why couldn't he see the same things all the time. The knot in the wood was shielded on its right side by a series of almost equi - distance parallel swirls, that swept down past the knot, then vanishing at different lengths or points into another formation within the grain. The knot seemed to follow him. He moved his head from side to side and then back to front and the centre of this knot just appeared to follow his attempted evasion.

JJ felt uneasy but didn't know why.

"The older woman shouted at her husband. "What did you do to her? You told me you were going there to beat her. You told me you were going to kill her but you didn't, what did you do?"

The older woman had now become hysterical and had run out of the house. She could only see the marks on her hands, body and legs but these were enough to send her running without looking or thought.

Her husband ran to the young woman's house, now full of anger and conflicting remorse and he hammered on her door. She opened the door to him, without fear, knowing that it was him. She looked at the husband who on this occasion, had forgotten his strength and size. He looked at her and he remembered how her eyes penetrated into his the day before, defiant almost psychotic.

The husband now pleaded with this young woman to help him as he loved his wife. She made him agree that he must do exactly what she asked him to do in order that she could help her.

They walked casually but quickly into the wood and she tied the now willing but desperate husband to a tree, his back to the bark and his arms stretched down either side behind him, holding the trunk of the tree between his arms. As he stood there expectantly, he looked around at the primroses and the beauty of the wood around him. The smells of the trees, grass, flowers surrounded him within the gentle warm breeze even though it was relatively early on that June summer morning. He felt a strange affinity to the young girl, based perversely on his actions from the day before and this delusion and his desperation clouded his judgement and his trust."

Mrs. M saw the tree more clearly as her intensity increased, believing everything that was now entering her mind. "This doesn't seem to fit with the rest of the service!" She thought to herself, "we'll see!"

JJ could see other aspects to the left of this knot. The wood seemed to sneer. He could see lines develop where they were hidden. Lips formed, emerging through concentration or imagination.

"The husband now that he was tied up, now that he had submitted, again asked the young woman what she wanted him to do, so she would help his wife.

The young woman told him to be calm, not to worry but that he must let her do what she was doing, so that she could help his wife.

She finished tying the ropes which went around the back of the tree, binding the husband's ankles so that his legs and feet would not have the opportunity to move forward, nor would they be able to kick out at her. As the husband stood there, spread eagled to this tree, he became more concerned that he had been foolishly trusting when pleading with her to help his wife.

She looked at the husband, her smiling, calm expression now changed to vengeful, a second look in her eye playful and wicked.

The husband started pulling on the ropes as his anxiety increased, the bark of the tree pressing into his back as he strained to pull his hands and arms forward. The tension on the ropes increased, every muscle in his face pumped with blood, exerting his effort and concentration to break the ropes. The young woman had tied his restraints well. The coarseness of the bindings became sharp, abrasive with his repeated and increasing efforts to break free, cutting into his wrists. The opening wounds being encouraged to expand by his pulling and twisting, the course ropes nicking pieces of skin, enlarging the cuts.

The young woman started dancing in front of him, first smooth, flowing movements. She now held a lavender blossom in her left hand. Her arms moved like waves spreading out across a pond, undulating, bending, flexing, the end of her movements flowing to the last flick of her finger tips. Her legs and feet apart, swaying, shifting weight between the two, Her hips swayed, filling first one side of the rough brown sacking cloth she was wearing and then the other. Her right thigh lifting, bending her leg, weaving and pirouetting, all the time her eyes fixed on his. After one pirouette, another, her left leg, copying her right, her rotation reversed, each alternate sequence ending with a dip of her body, her knees bending then flexing back to their full length.

With each spin her spotting focus remained his eyes. The intensity of her stare and its direction increasing as she finished each spin, the implication that no matter what she did, he would remain her target.

The young woman's hair whipped around, the differences in length exaggerated by the poorness of its hacked cut. The longer lengths reached to just above her waist, the shorter lengths to her shoulder blades, when brushed, as one, when disturbed, chaotic.

The husband weakened in his struggle, his mind telling him that his efforts would fail, his will convincing him that he would break free, his eyes transfixed to hers; not even the lashing blond hair, tangling across her face obscuring her features, stopped her stare from reaching his soul.

He started to plead with her to let him free, promising that he would do whatever it took to make amends and for her to help his wife.

"How does it feel not to be able to move?, the ropes, the tree are stronger than you."

She did not want an answer, her question playing with his growing fear.

Her dancing continued, its repetition changing to take her out of his view, first to her being to the right side and then behind the tree, its bulk blocking any chance of him seeing where she was, no matter how much he tried to turn to see, his thick neck straining in the process, the tree obstructed his vision and his uneasiness grew.

Mrs. Mortimer watched the story unfold. She could see the young woman had something in her hand, an occasional flash of light as she danced in the sun. The Reverend John, his words outside of her hearing.

The moving object in front of the tree stopped, the husband had given up struggling. Mrs. M could feel sudden, sharp agonising pains in her left fingers. She gripped them with her right, rubbing the aching fingers. It was unusual for her arthritis to hurt that much and without any build up, no warning. She made a low "uh" sound, deep from the back of her throat. She jolted as she did so. Those around her, sensed her move and all thought she had caught herself dropping off to sleep.

Mr. Evans lent to his wife, "Make sure we don't sit behind her again."

JJ also slid himself forward and looked over Beryl's right

shoulder. She was breathing normally this time and her eyes were open; that was a good sign. He slid himself back, his eyes going back to the wood grain. He rubbed his hands either side of his greying light brown hair.

Haley caught Mrs. M's eye as her head jolted, her concern instantly returning to the level it had been earlier. She saw Mrs. M give her a wink with her right eye, confirming she was fine.

The knot in the wood now looked like an open mouth, more than the eye JJ had envisaged when he first stared at the imperfection in the grain's flow. Its edges looked irregular, giving the impression that the mouth was straining.

"The husband screamed, his eyes shut tight at first during his initial cry, opening wide as he gasped to take a breath in order that he could scream again, agony showing on his eyelids as his eyes narrowed. He felt vomit in his throat, rising from his stomach, the smell filling his nostrils from inside before it would fill his mouth. His breath gave momentary relief, the searing sensation of pain from his left hand wained slightly as his body and brain had to concentrate on this more basic bodily function. He felt the edge of something hard slip under the little finger on his left hand. His mind wasn't able to analyse his understanding of what was against his finger. It just didn't develop. He clenched his teeth, making his mouth as small as it would go, the opposite to its first reaction. The vomit now emerged through his teeth, still clamped top to bottom row, trying to restrain his cries of pain. He could not stop the exodus of his stomach. His mouth now open with his bottom jaw protruding, his chin pointing out, the skin being pulled taught as his body sought respite.

His left hand felt like it was on fire, sharp, acute, pulsing sensations coming along his arm and smashing into his brain, making his head reel.

The restrained husband unconsciously used his pain, to again strain on the ropes, this combination with the cuts on his wrist adding to the overall pain he was experiencing from that area of his body.

He felt a hard edge turn against another of his fingers sensing a move from a wider surface to a very narrow edge, was it sharp, was it supposed to be sharp?. His finger sent sensations to his brain but his thoughts couldn't catch up.

His finger eventually felt a second edge. The young woman paused, her excitement rising laced with revenge, as she squeezed the handles closer together, watching and enjoying seeing his second finger turn first white from the pressure, the skin compacting at the point of contact.

The husband felt his skin give in, its surface parting, slowly, reluctantly and then his awareness that the bone in his finger was being touched directly by these thin unyielding assailants. He felt the slow, protracted, biting affect repeat on his finger, a dullness of touch, not sharp or quick. The finger wouldn't move. His mind, his reaction and now his awareness was shouting at his finger to move but it refused. It lay between the edges chewing at it, their rusty, blunted blades making hard work of his second finger.

He tried to pull his hand away but the bindings limited the flexibility of his wrist to pull the palm of his hand and his fingers away from the tree bark and the jaws of the shearing cutters. As he pulled his left hand and arm desperately away from the blades, trying to escape from their gnawing, the opposite reaction was occurring on the other side of the tree. His right hand and arm both combining to pull on his right shoulder, his escape efforts on one side adding to his pain on the other.

The young woman struggled to cut through this finger's bone, the first small finger being easy as well as a surprise. The old shears, their bluntness, the stiffness of movement around the handles fulcrum, all contributed to her gripping the handles with two hands, shaking with effort to try and cut through. The psychotic evil had returned to her eyes, their blue irises illuminated from the revenge she felt within, her temper growing with these shears and their combined inability to cut through.

The husband was screaming, now with added awareness and anger, his face crimson with effort and rage, the veins in his neck and temples pulsing, their size increased to double the normal, blue with pressure.

The amalgamation of her weakness, the effort she was trying to exert to get the jaws to bite through and his jerking, desperate attempts to move his hand and finger exposed more and more of the bone as if they were both working together in trying to peel the top of his finger off the bone beneath.

The husband's cries increased in volume, his normally deep voice, scaling up an octave, his pitch harsh. He felt the twisting, yanking, pulling on his finger pass, the shears finally closing together, his second finger now at the base of the tree, nestling in between the exposed roots that broke the surface of the ground.

He gritted his teeth, cheeks puffing, pumping, taking in air quickly, sucking it through the gaps and spaces on each side of his mouth, between his teeth and the inside of his cheek. His eyelids clamped shut, his forehead furrowing into irregular folds. The sweat was dripping off his nose, his eyebrow, his chin from his efforts to break the ropes and to block out the agony. His black, unkept straight hair, wet from his perspiration was stuck to wherever it touched his face or neck.

The young woman danced around to stand in front of him, this time with a mixture of arrogance and tiredness, her movements deliberate but short, quick. They had lost the initial energy and fluidity. She stood in front of him, her hair disheveled. The shears had been the only thing she could secretly catch hold off when they had left the house, the plan of revenge that had formed in her mind for the husband being modified when he had turned up earlier than envisaged. They had not been the perfect choice but the only choice for what she quickly planned to do, given his arrival. Now things were different. He was weakened, in pain, the strength in one of his violating hands at least almost eliminated but he was where she had always wanted him, tied to this tree.

She looked down at the scuff marks on the ground where his feet had moved during her first attack. They had been restricted from doing anything other than the front of each foot jerking from side to side in reaction.

He was now leaning forward, slumped as much as the ropes would let him, his shoulders taking the strain of his mostly unsupported weight, his legs more dangling than standing.

There were marks on the tree from where the ropes had rubbed during his struggle, more so to the rear of where he was now hanging. She could see where pieces of bark had been caught or broken off as the rope jarred against its surface, the jaggedness of the wood catching on his bindings.

She regained her energy. Her eyes looking at her slumped victim.

The young woman, altered her swaying, hip twitching to a slow rotation turning to her right, her face smiling, her eyes intent on the husband but almost sympathetic. She rotated slowly completing her first three hundred and sixty turn, to stand straight in front of the husband. She started to hum, enjoying feeling the breeze in her hair and the cooling affect it had on her skin, chilling the perspiration on her body as it passed through the weave of her clothing. There was a strong smell of lavender in the breeze.

She turned a second time in the same direction, rotating on the ball of her right foot, kicking her left leg out to give momentum to complete the turn. On finishing the rotation, she faced him again. This time her eyes were staring, manic, her mouth sneering; it was like he was looking at a different person. She started to dance again, the rotation had stopped. The same previous, initial energy returning as a result of her first victory.

Her hair whipped and flicked again as she thrashed her head about with a frantic pendulum motion, her body possessed by its own irrational rhythm; her shoulders and then waist, dipping towards and then away from the husband.

She kicked her right foot, altering the next rotation to her left, the dipping and whipping motion lessening, as this slower turn went through the degrees, transforming into a turn with a more fluid action, her left foot her pivot, her right foot taking small steps by comparison to her previous sweeping pirouettes.

She faced him again, her expression and dance warm and soft, her arms and hips now swaying gently, drawing him to look at her, his mind now seeing another woman. He relaxed, misguided by her change of demeanour.

She spun back the other way, escalating her energy and aggression, facing him as she stopped, her eyes blazing hate. The husband recoiled back, his head thudding into the tree truck behind him, his eyes wide with surprise then fear, as her gaze held him frozen, compelling him to look back at her. She spat at him, her saliva running down off his forehead.

The husband was now tense again, his legs finding the energy to help him stand back up, catching his back on the bark as he straightened himself, adding some more cuts to his already torn skin. The young woman started to sing, her words first indistinguishable. There was a gruffness to her song, no melody, just growled lyrics from her throat "two sides, two sides, we have two sides"

As his mind deciphered these sounds and he realised what she was saying, her voice became sweeter, lighter, the melody forming, a chant, her dancing dissolving back to a fluid tease, a rhythmic undulation in her hips, alluring. He looked back to her turquoise blue eyes, they had reverted back to sympathy and his anxiousness about what she was going to do, how he was going to break free, subsided. Her expression had changed completely, she smiled, the sort of smile that melts a man's heart, that makes a man feel spe-

cial, secure, loved, he relaxed. As he slumped forward again, the tension from his body weight being taken at his shoulders, he was going to ask for her forgiveness again, to appeal to this angel, this alluring, beautiful, sensual woman; her smile conveying compassion. He took in a breath to speak.

The two blades of the four inch shears stabbed through to the back of his eye balls simultaneously. The vitreous humour fluid sprayed out like a mountain water spring. Its purity being contaminated by the blood that joined it from his eyes and the gashes on both sides of his nose that had been partly sliced, partly gouged by the open, blunt blades as they'd passed on the way to their intended targets.

His scream filled her mind and body with elation. She followed through with her thrust, forcing his head back against the trunk, feeling the resistance from the blades, their inability from penetrating any deeper into the confines of his skull, a mixture of the blades length and their widest part jamming against the bones that formed his eyes sockets, their tips searching for his brain inside.

Every particle in his body shuddered at the strain of having to combat the most violent, agonising pain he had ever felt in his whole life. There was the remnants of the smell of rusty metal filtering through his nose to his brain; the blades of the shears, their coating of brown, golden, green corrosive deposit, which had hindered their ability to move easily when cutting through his fingers, now sending another, different message through another overwhelmed sense.

His whole head erupted with searing, hot electrical impulses and brain crushing pounding as the release of the pressurised eye vessels ruptured when the points of the blades cut through his brown irises and cornea.

His remaining fingers clenched, pumping more blood out of the holes where his finger and his finger tip should have been.

Had his mind been capable of analysis he would have realised that he had urinated and dirtied himself at the same time, the pain now eliminating any control his mind used to exercise on his bodily functions.

This resistance on the shears, enveloped her, inspiring her to push a second thrust without extracting the blades, his head banging again against the tree behind.

She stood holding the shears, stretching slightly to reach up to his height, smiling; the last expression he had seen.

The young woman turned and walked back to her father's tool shed at the side of her house, her arms floating, feeling the breeze against them, cooling, refreshing.

The husband screams would have been heard around the wood, if there had been anyone to hear but the house was isolated at most, remote at least; a reason why he had felt so safe yesterday.

The blood poured out of his mouth from the burst blood vessels in his throat, their exertion for help or pity at their extreme.

He found it difficult to breathe. The shock paralysing his body's natural responses. The taste of his own life filling his mouth, his body shaking, quivering, convulsing, his stomach retching to find anything to regurgitate as his torso jerked on the ropes like a demented marionette.

Blood covered his face from his eyes, nose, mouth; down his neck, through his clothing and on his chest. His eyelids tried to close as a reflex action but they were stopped from doing so by the empaled blades.

He passed out, his body and mind unable to regulate, as a result of the destruction to their natural control.

He slumped, twitching and unconscious. The shears slid out of the slits they had made, shaken lose by his head's involuntary convulsions, falling to the ground and bouncing off another tree root to rest next to his two fingers.

CHAPTER 15

Mrs. Mortimer was concerned by all this and started to rock from side to side uncomfortably. What was the Reverend John Rowlands thinking. She looked up from staring at the seat. He was still rubbing his right hand, more vigorously she thought than earlier and he looked calm, undisturbed. Was he more callous than she could imagine, so at ease with all of this?

She felt more uncomfortable as she continued to look, her concentration on him blotting out the sound of his voice, her thoughts dominating her mind. She was determined to have a word with him when the service was over on her way out.

"Here she goes again." Mr. Evans pushed his right shoulder into his wife's as he noticed Mrs. M's rocking, to emphasise her movements.

Mrs Evans said nothing and just cleared her throat as a sign of rebuke.

Mrs. M noticed Alister's hand was resting on the inside of Haley's right thigh, while still holding hands through the sermon.

Her eyes went back to the pew. Unconsciously she adjusted her seating position, stretching her right arm out, so that it lay along the top of the pew's back rest, leaning her body towards Haley, her head bowed again, looking at the seating area between them.

"This real was a lovely pew," she thought to herself. "The company had done a beautiful job." She loved the grain, its swirls and twists. The grain of a tree tells you how old the tree was, or so she remembered being told!

She returned her concentration to this unbelievable scenario, determined to try and find the good, the meaning in it.

The grain held her attention as it had done before. Her eyes traced the lines, the changes in shade. She saw the hint of a heart shaped knot, small and faint, almost behind the top layers of grain.

She rubbed her eyes from under her glasses hoping that this would make the image clearer.

"The young woman meandered back from her father's tool shed, sometimes carrying, sometimes dragging the wood axe her father had used, its weight too heavy for her to carry the two hundred yards to the tree, without altering the way in which she carried it.

She put the axe down in front of the husband, momentarily disappointed that he was still unconscious and didn't see her next, her more affective tool. The shears had been blunt.

An hour passed while she sat on the ground looking up at her victim as he hung unconscious; making daisy chains to pass the time, sometimes humming to herself, sometimes singing "we have two sides", over and over.

The husband's hearing was the first sense to return to his awareness. The sound of her singing creeping in through his ears, his brain, his mind eventually realising the sound was singing. At first it seemed distant but as his consciousness started to return, he recognised it from somewhere.

The smell of blood and its taste returned in that order when he became aware of his breathing, followed by traces of vomit, the smell and taste of which had been subsequently diluted by blood.

The feeling of pain returned, his brain now processing the origins of these nerve signals, establishing his awareness of the parts of his body that were sending throbbing, searing, agonising impulses.

His fingers moved, then his hands; realisation he couldn't move. He couldn't move his legs but as he tried, he felt himself rise and then became aware of the aching feeling in his shoulders as he straightened up slightly. Her singing was now more distinctive.

His memory had a sudden rush, the ropes, a finger, no two fingers, his eyes, oh God his eyes.

He lifted his head to establish the direction of this singing, his total awareness of all his remaining senses focusing on the loss of the fifth, his mind was now over run with sensations resulting in panic. His large body jerked, his strength being sent to his limbs from his inner most core. His arms tried to pull forward but their flex was restrained. His forearms and elbows and lastly his shoulders all sending the messages of restraint.

His cry at regaining consciousness was filled with anxiety, fear, the regained knowledge of what had happened and why.

The young woman listened to the sounds he was now making, enjoying hearing the terror, the fear, the pain that was in his cry. Her body absorbed his fear. She thrived on his panic, her feeling of exhilaration escalating into rapture as she bent down and picked up the end of the axe's handle, its head still on the ground.

She leant forward until her face was two inches from his. The smell of his bodily fluids intoxicated her. His appearance gave her satisfaction. Her excitement couldn't be contained and it was released through her manic giggling laughter, her whole face smiling, her eyes gleeful, flashing.

"What's next my lover?" Her question calm, direct, threatening.

His face pointed to hers, blood filled lifeless eye sockets, where his eyes should have been. He could smell her, the same smell as yesterday, heathery. He tried to speak, to plead but his mind was too occupied with pain, his release: his woeful, long, breathy whimper reaching a crescendo with an agonised squawk as he took in breath.

Her singing filled his ears, he could hear nothing else but sensed she'd moved away from the proximity of his face. The strength of her heather smell disappearing but lingering, confirmed by the direction of her voice moving to his right hand side and then from behind him, at the rear of the trunk. He tried to decide if the smell was heather or lavender, this momentary concentration for his brain, a diversion to his senses and his agony.

He felt the rope move as she pushed at it with the end of the handle, then felt a repeated action, a tapping?, then a heavier vibration through the trunk, then still.

His mind told him she was going to cut it, going to release him.

He felt the tree thud with the impact of the axe's blade. It didn't feel like it was behind him, more to the right side. His arms and hands still didn't move when he tried to move them forward, the rope still tight as his binding.

The young woman was going to have another go as she'd missed the rope the first time. Her efforts to release the blade from the bark could be felt, the smallest of vibration as she pulled on the handle, back and for, the tree unlike his eyes, refusing to let the impacted blade from leaving the slit it had made.

He could hear her efforts, small grunts, intermixed with heavier breathing and the same song, the same words, over and over again.

There was a lull; silence, her singing had stopped and he felt her concentration and waited, his own pain in those moments of anticipation, suspended. All he could initially think of was being set free, that she had her revenge.

His mind jumped to the future. "What am I going to do? Oh god my eyes, my eyes, I'm blind, my wife, my hand," every thought compounding the rising, returning panic the previous thought created.

He felt a second thud against the tree.

He went to move his hands and arms. The right one moved forward away from the tree, he was free!

His left side failed to move in the same way, he slumped down onto his right knee able to do so by his newly granted freedom. It seemed an eternity. His movements drained, slow, his consciousness blurred, out of focus.

His left hand and arm still pulled back at the shoulder, towards the rear of the tree where she was standing, singing again; refused to move. He could not understand why. She had cut the rope? He would have to try and untie the knot at his left wrist. The binding on his right ankle pulled and scored with the strain from him kneeling down on his right knee.

He felt himself fumbling with the rope. The young woman watched as he tried to untie the knot, her giggling and then laughter increased the more effort he put in.

The husband couldn't understand why he could not feel the knot, the rope even. His body had twisted around enough he thought to the left of the tree for his right hand to be able to feel his left wrist, his lower arm even.

His left forearm and wrist felt the heat from a warm fluid ,run along the top of his forearm first and then down to his left wrist, mixing into the twinning and fabric of the rope.

The young woman's laughter was hysterical, demonic. She tore his right hand and wrist out of the loops she had made around it, when first tying him up with the rope.

She pushed it in his face, the palm of his hand covering his mouth and lower part of his nose, his own fingers and thumb folding across his forehead and cheeks.

He went to grab it instinctively. His brain telling him to catch hold of it with his hand and to move whatever this thing was off his face. His brain did not receive the sensation of his fingers moving, gripping this thing. It just felt......nothing!

The stump of his right arm kept moving, searching and eventually pressing against the back of his own hand. The young woman let go of his hand and his momentum continued to press the bleeding part of his forearm against his disembodied hand, holding it to his face, the awareness and anaesthetic of its amputation growing and diminishing at the same instant."

Mrs. M had had enough. What is this man thinking of. She had never got up and walked out of church before but this could be a first but if she did that she thought, she would not be able to speak to him after the service. How much further is this going to go? She decided it better to wait until the end but this had better get better or she was going to have a few things to say this This Minister.

She gripped the top of the pew, her arm still stretched along its length, unaware that she had been "tutting" under her breath.

"The husband screamed again but the burst blood vessels and blood in his throat robbed its volume. The pressure of his stump against his hand slackening, allowing it to drop and for the flow of blood out of the end of his arm to increase. The hand dropped to the floor. The strength disappeared from his legs, his left knee crumbling, his thighs, thick as they were went limp, he could not exert enough will or strength to stand.

His stomach was now convulsing, there was nothing left for him to vomit. The muscles in his lower body straining to expel something.

As he floundered around on the ground, stumbling on one knee then the next, his left arm pulling on his shoulder, his stump trying to find contact with the ground but his senses unable to cope, unable to calculate and then compensate for the change in the length of his arm missing the ground as he blindly, frantically tried to put it down to gain control of his own writhing body as he repeatedly fell off balance. The jaggedness of the erupted tree roots caught the rawness of his open nerves and bone as he fell or tried to push himself back onto his knees. His eyes, now bleeding tears of blood, his head exploding with known and new unknown sensations, agony, pain, bewilderment. His demise had reached its peak and the conscious thought that death would be a relief came to his mind.

The young woman bent over slightly and put her right hand on the left side of his face, the warmth of her touch, its pressure providing the control his mind was looking for. His writhing stopped, directed by her hand, its pressure increasing on his left cheek as if she was pushing a dogs head into the ground to exert mastership.

"What next my lover?" Her voice calm and threatening as before. "We need to be quick, I've got a cow to milk!"

This almost seemed a relief. He could not see any way out of this situation and his will had resigned itself to death.

He made one last attempt to pull his left arm free but the two nails she had hammered through the rope into the trunk held firm.

He felt her standing in front of him as he was now slouched, grovelling on the ground.

He heard her exertion as she lifted the axe, her aim this time more accurate as she imbedded the blade into the trunk, cutting his last two fingers and thumb off, a diagonal cut from his wrist to his missing ring finger.

Nothing came out of his mouth. No sound, no breath....nothing. His senses were on shut down and his will had left him.

His face encompassed every sinew, every muscle. His features became lost within the distortion of his skin, his eye sockets streaming, trails of optical nerves leaving the eye sockets and matted onto the top of his lower eye lids, one long nerve reach his right cheek, having been drawn out by the shears when they had slid out and dropped to the floor.

He looked up in her direction but without his eyes he had no expres-

sion, just bloodied lifeless holes. He hung there, kneeling, his left arm still tied to with the rope, suspended by his shoulder.

The young woman left him and went to milk her cow, singing...............

The young woman returned an hour later carrying a small pale and kindling wood from the house.

He was still slumped in the same position as when she had left, his breathing gruff, irregular, full of effort.

She put the kindling wood down between his feet, a small mound about the size of a pumpkin.

He could smell the warm milk as she lifted the pale to his mouth. It tasted creamy, thick but curdling. He could not drink much. Its richness made him feel sick as he drank. He tried to resist her tipping any more into his mouth.

She held his nose with her left hand and held the pale under her right arm as she forced his head back, tipping more milk into his mouth, most of it being spat out or spilling out the side of his mouth as he tried to spit it out or close his lips, his final act of defiance.

She put the pale down and collected more wood debris, pilling it on top of the kindling until it stood over his head height when he was kneeling.

"What next my lover?" Her tone exactly the same as the two earlier occasions when she asked this question.

He didn't answer, he couldn't. His mind was so in shock that normal responses were now beyond him.

The young woman was not looking for a normal response. She wanted total retribution. She wanted the donation of his soul as *his final act of penitence.*

He heard a grating, scrapping sound. It made no sense. He knew he wasn't able to function properly now. It wasn't consistent, there were gaps, spaces in the sound. He doubted what he heard and wasn't sure if he heard anything.

The head of the axe dragged across the floor, lifting momentarily as it bounced over the exposed tree roots.

Her shoulders dropped, relaxing as she dropped the handle, its weight breaking the connection with her body as she let go of the handle, it bounced twice as it hit a root.

She lent down to him, her hair touching his face, his senses smelt something familiar, heather or lavender, his brain still working out the conundrum. His lips moved but there was now no thought behind their movement. Somewhere deep in his mind he wanted to die as he couldn't control his faculties so that they worked together.

Her right hand touched the left side of his face again, its pressure increasing as she encouraged him to become conscious of where he was, what she was doing; what was happening. She took her hand away from his face and took some leaves and herbs out of her right hand pocket in her dress and then ground them together between the palms of her hands, their combined aroma sweet, musky. She held it under his nose, his reaction jerked his head back and away but she followed it, cupping her hand over his nose and mouth so that he had no option but to breathe in the scents. Small particles of the mixture became inhaled up his nose, despite his attempts to move away from her hand with his stump.

They permeated through his nostrils, through his sinuses. He could feel his head clearing, it wasn't pleasant. The top of his eye lids began to burn. His ears started to pulse. He started to taste the vomit again and the smell of blood through the lavender he had eventually named as the smell that dominated his nasal passages. He tried to wipe the smell away, the stump of his right arm prod-

ding against the bottom of his nose, like he was using a blunt stick; the bone and his stump acute in its touch, radiating fire up his arm into his shoulder and onward to his brain.

His senses came flooding back in a rush of agony and the first thought his mind had was of death and to ask for it.

"What next my lover?" The words now took his panic to another level. His breathing increased in speed from short agitated breaths to gasping shallow gulps, neither taking in the volume of air his lungs needed to fill his chest.

Her both hands now came to cup his face, his cheeks in the palms of her hands. He now felt the pressure of her squeezing his face and head and her lifting him to his feet. His legs were now receiving impulses from his brain to keep him standing but without strength. His whole body felt like it had lost its supporting skeleton inside. He was now aware of where he was and what had happened. His eyes, his hands, their absence, his entire being now devoid of his previous strength, just a jelly like effigy of his former self.

She kicked his left leg at his knee, forcing him to stumble and open up his stance; her hands still cradling his face for support, giving the extra strength his body was lacking.

He now stood, slouched at the shoulders, his feet apart, his left arm still tied and pulled back behind him; her concoction having cleared his awareness. He wanted to run but his legs did not feel as if they would respond but then his recollection of his remaining bondage.

He started to twitch, attempting to pull his left arm and hand away from the rope that tied him to the tree. The pressure she exerted on his face increased, controlling his movements. She took her hands away and his panic increased. Her singing returned, the same words, same sounds but lacking any melody; only threat.

He heard her grunt as she lifted the axe, its total weight an effort for what she had in mind.

Her breathing showed signs of effort as she manoeuvred the axe, it lost its smoothness and regularity. His hearing focused where his sight should have looked, on her nose, her mouth, the sounds of her breathing in and out, the changing sounds of her respiration as it became influenced by her efforts with the axe, her throat emitting soft grunting.

Her breathing stopped.

He could feel her concentration. His breathing stopped, his head rocked slowly from side to side, listening. He felt ......"

Haley squeezed Alister's hand, the fingers in his left hand crushed where they joined his palm, the bones in his palm being forced to try and form a pyramid, rolling inside the skin. He winced in surprise at her grip and looked bewildered at his wife.

"Owe, what's wrong?" He asked with urgency and concern, his voice trying to project to her but to no one else in the church. He said it again, this time more breathy, more subdued in volume but still with its original urgency and concern.

"Look!....look!", her chin and eyes were motioning down. His eyes looked downwards, leaving her face and tried to follow where she was looking. He didn't know what he was trying to see, what she wanted him to see.

"What?, what is it?"

Her eyes were full of tears, the first of which had started to run down her left cheek. She had let go of his hand. He felt relief and now more able to concentrate on his wife than his hand. She was folding her coat across her chest, her eyes targeting above her arms as they folded across her breasts. Her eyes were anxious and wide, her pupils within her dark, rich brown eyes large and intense.

"Are you alright, Haley, what's wrong?"

He looked at her arms. What could be wrong with her arms? "What's wrong with your arms?" She turned and looked at him with a womanly expression that said, "why don't you know what I'm talking about? Why is this so difficult?.....it's obvious!"

"What? Tell me." His confusion increased.

Her look didn't change. He was none the wiser. She wondered for the very first time why he didn't know what she was talking about, especially now.

He looked at her, straight into her eyes, those beautiful brown eyes that now had the, "you don't understand me look"..... mixed with anxiety.

She pulled open her short black coat very discreetly, exposing the the curve of her chest. He looked, a furtive look considering he was in church. Her blouse where her nipples stretched the fabric to its extremity, looked a different shade of white, it looked stained, wet. He noticed an odour, not her perfume but a milky smell.

"What's happening?"

"I don't know. This shouldn't happen now, it's months until the baby is due."

Alister put his right hand on to her stomach. "Is the baby coming?" There was no logic to his question, it was reaction.

"Noooo." She whispered through clenched teeth and straight, tight lips emphasising her response with her eyes, her expression changing to one of disbelief. Her mind thinking, "what's going on in your head?" Haley willed him to move his hand away from her stomach, not to draw attention to her and her predicament. Her eyes remained wide open, looking at him, giving him the instructions she wanted him to follow.

It didn't work. Alister looked at her still bewildered. He moved his right hand from her stomach, his brown leather jacket creaked as he moved his arm and then hesitated as he looked at her, his face asking if he had done the right thing and then put it back on her left breast, inside her coat, before her expression changed.

Haley grabbed his hand hard with her left hand, pulling it downwards off her breast and back onto her lap. She saw his face wince again from the pressure of her grip. Her eyes now told him he had done the wrong thing. Haley ground her front teeth together, her bottom set grinding into the back off her upper teeth, her words now growled out from the back of her throat, her lips not moving, her cheeks and jaw tense.

"What are you doing, are you stupid?"

Alister didn't think this was quite fair, he was only concerned for his wife. He looked hurt.

"Your boob is wet! Why? Are you alright?" Alister rubbed his moist palm with his left hand, his fingers starting the motion, gliding across the palm, wiping the wet feeling away, his left palm stopping with his right when it made full contact.

"I know it's wet, they both are. I don't know why." Haley growled out her answers, her lips still not moving but her voice now had a frightened edge.

"What do want to do, do you want to go out?" Alister asked her, his whisper now more concerned and urgent, reflecting her fright, his own tone anxious.

"We can't, not in the middle of the service."

"Of course we can". Alister grabbed Haley's right hand and started to pull her gently but with purpose. She pulled her hand out of his, twisting her wrist to break his grip, her movements sharp and contained so as not to draw attention to them. She folded her arms and jacket over her chest.

"No, stay there."

"Haley this is stupid, let's go."

Both their heads were bowed as they made their exchanges, getting lower as each sentence was spoken, both trying to become smaller and less noticeable.

John Rowlands had become aware of the odd movements he could see from the pulpit as he came close to the end of his sermon. This had not been the easiest of services he thought as he continued to speak. What was going on with those two. From in the pulpit their sounds had risen to his attention. He couldn't hear the conversation just hissed, growled muffles but he felt something was not right. He continued to rub the palm of his right hand. This splinter had really become an annoyance now and the wound had become red a day ago and was staying red, become more sore, partly from his attempts to get it out and from the increasing infection.

John became conscience of the fact he was rubbing his hand and that he had been rubbing it throughout his sermon; he hadn't really realised that his rubbing had been continually from the start until now, his attention now drawn to the young married couple.

"Are you two alright?" Haley jumped, her posture changing instantly from being hunched forward to her back making contact to the backrest, the question from Mrs. Evans behind bringing her out of her own world, at this moment contained within the church pew with Alister, her self consciousness hidden immediately under her polite, "Yes fine."

Mr and Mrs. Evans had been aware of the whispered exchanges, again they had not been able to hear the conversation but their movements and talk had been a little distracting for their concentration on the sermon.

"The husband felt the heavy metal head of the axe, the pinnacle of its blade, its shaped cutting edge slicing into the top of his right thigh. Both his arms went to reach for his leg, his scream, its initial volume and agony subsiding to a pitiful whimper, his remaining strength leaving him.

The stump on his right arm pressed against the flap of flesh that hung off the top of his right thigh. He could only feel the sensation of the flap being pressed back to the hole where it had come from on his bleeding leg. He slumped back to the floor, his knees catching on the roots, his balance stumbling, his bondage providing stability to his left side, the stump of his right arm providing nerve burning support when he stooped in his oblivion to put his blood caked bone on the ground.

He could hear her singing in between her heavy breathing, the pause in which, if he had been fully aware, indicated her next effort.

The young woman gave every last ounce of effort and concentration to her next avenging blow.

The head of the axe lay on the floor. She gripped the handle, her right hand below her left.

"I told you I would help your wife!"

His head twitched on hearing her voice. She could see by the open, silent lip expression that he did not understand what was happening.

"I told you I would help your wife," her tone was constant and reassuring.

Somehow strangely her words got through to his brain. "How?"

"You are the first part lover. I needed to cleanse you first so that I could help your wife as you asked me to. You shouldn't have done what you did, it wasn't nice. Why did you and your wife treat me so

badly. You didn't know me." She asked the question with a calm innocent tone.

His mind went to the previous day, to his former victory over this young woman and now for the first time, serious regret entered his mind. He opened his mouth indicating he wanted to speak.

The young woman was not looking for an answer but she now had his attention again.

"What next my lover?"

His mind raced. What more could she do.

She rubbed the palms of her hands together, the herbs being ground together again, releasing their mind clearing odour. She held them under his nose. She smiled, to herself.

The husband's mind was clear again and he felt every fibre of his body sending pain to his mind. His head pulsed, his legs shaking

as he knelt in front of the tree, the nerves and their electricity criss crossing between his limbs and his brain.

The axe made its final cut, the blow direct and controlled by her refocused total concentration. He heard the silence after her last deep breath. He heard the effort in her sigh as she lifted the axe high up over her head and then her feet shuffle against the grass and roots as she stood over him. What little energy he had was used to hold his stump up above his head to shield the blow he expected to receive to his head. This once large, powerful man shuffled around on his knees, their movement slight. He knelt erect as his remaining strength would allow, his thighs apart, blood still pumping out from her first slice of his thigh.

He heard the "whoo" of the blade of the axe as it moved through the air towards him, his scream in anticipation of it cutting into his skull, his arm held up in front of his forehead in an attempt to fend off the axe.

The young woman adjusted her stance as she swung the axe, step-

ping forward with her left foot, swinging the blade from high over her head, with a downward swing to her right, the weight helping with her effort, combining to make the momentum deadly in its speed. She angled the upward swing by twisting her body to her right, the blade now moving as fast as her effort and its weight would allow.

The focus in her eyes was intense. There was only one target in her mind and her eyes did not leave it. She used every bit of her strength and concentration to continue her revenge.

Both knees jumped off the ground abruptly as the axe thudded into his groin, the blade which she had sharpened before bringing it out, cut through the rough sacking cloth that covered his abdomen and legs, splitting his penis in two, its end fully separated and just held to his scrotum and testicles by skin, the cut finishing where the blade finished, clean, sharp.

She giggled at first and then burst into uncontrollable laughter as she pulled the axe away and out of his groin in a way that would have resembled Arthur pulling Excaliber from the stone, holding the axe across the width of her hips with both hands, looking down on her adversary.

His screams grew louder with each scream as they left his blood filled throat, sprays of saliva and streams of spitting blood splattering on the ground in front of him and this invigorated her. Her blood and heart pumping, his agony enriched her senses. She stood over him, soaking in, absorbing his pain, relishing the blood patterns on her dress and skin. She valued each drop of blood he had bled at her hands, each scream, each cry, his pleading, eyeless expression of pity brought her over whelming joy and satisfaction.
Her body trembled with excitement, escalating to shaking, her laughing taking hold of her head then shoulders, rocking, shuddering with ecstasy, bending her over as it reached her belly, her stomach muscles tensing and aching with the effort to keep a balance of her breathing to her laughing. She held onto the axe, placing the

head onto the ground, holding the shaft vertical as a support.

She stood there for a few minutes, her laughing filling his ears, mixing with the agony of all his other feelings that cried for an end to come.

The young woman laughed until she felt sick but a pleasant happy feeling of sickness which she swallowed and took a deep breath to regain control of her hysteria.

He had slumped back, his back now resting against the tree.

She had stopped laughing but her enjoyment had not disappeared as she look down at him.

There were traces of splattered blood on the kindling wood she had put down earlier on the ground in front of him. She used her right foot and then her hands to push the kindling wood up to his crumpled body, tucking the wood into the gaps between his feet and legs as they lay, his right splayed along the floor, arched slightly at the knee, blood still oozing from his thigh and groin; his left leg fully bent at the knee, his foot flat on the ground.

He could smell the wood. He could feel the pressure of the wood being pushed, compacted into the gaps and crevices his body formed with the tree but his other pains took president; what she was doing with the wood meant and felt little by comparison.

The husband was now so weak through loss of blood and pain that the smell of smoke as it started to take a hold of the wood made little impact on his reasoning. He recognised the smell but couldn't put a name to it. The smoke started to increase, its density and colour changing from grey to black, the wisps becoming billows of swirling black acrid fog, chocking, suffocating, every plume directed to his nostrils, making its way into his lungs, clogging his air sacs and trachea.

He started to cough, the effort forcing more blood out of his wounds. The fire took a hold of his clothing, first smouldering on the parts that were soaked in blood, his expelled bodily life keeping him alive for longer as it tried to suppress the fire from igniting his clothes.

She waited for him to start screaming but it didn't happen. The smoke was choking the last bit of life from him. She could see he was going to pass out. He heard her say for the last time in a tone full of threat before he passed into unconsciousness "What next my lover?.... Your wife."

He tried to fight at hearing these last words in his fading consciousness, his mind disappearing.

The smoke had done him a favour. It had robed him of his last senses, his unconsciousness sparing him the pain of each lick of flame as it burnt his clothing, following the contours of his arms, his legs; the flames eager to engulf his whole body. His unkept long matted black hair igniting, becoming a crimson halo, the hairs on his body sparking and flared with flame and then the skin on his face, limbs and torso, bubbling, charing black, blistering, blood burning as the fire ate its available fuel, his existence.

She sat there watching, her legs crossed into the lotus position, making a daisy chain from the few daisies that were close to the oak tree, a feeling of disappointment beginning to come across her emotions. He had not felt her last act of revenge. She felt indignant.

He had passed out, robbing her of her last bit of satisfaction. She would have to remember that for the next time, for his wife.

His body burned congealing to the bark of the tree as the young woman watched, taking in every detail of his departure from being a human being to a burnt corpse.

The heat of his body felt good as the evening started to lose the heat of the sun, It penetrated into very sinew and pore of hers, warming her through, devouring his essence. His odour filled her nose, a smell she had not experienced before and this exited her. She breathed deeply, enjoying each breath and the combined smell of burnt bark and him.

She dropped the daisy chain on his head after sitting there for about an hour, watching the last charrings cool on his corpse. The tree hadn't suffered much damage, just scorching where his back and bottom had been leaning against the bottom of its trunk, a black, blood like stain, colouring the bark.

She walked back to her house, dragging the axe, its sound becoming silent in those moments when it bounced off the ground as it hit whatever obstacle the wood had on its floor."

Our final hymn 386. Mrs. M gathered herself as his announcement brought her back.

What sort of sermon was this. This was absolutely outrageous. Mrs. Mortimer had given The Minister a fair chance by listening to the whole sermon, without leaving and this is what he is preaching; revenge, murder, torture, to make whatever point he was trying to make, this was beyond acceptable and he was going to find out that she was not happy about this at all.

CHAPTER 16

As soon as Reverend Rowlands finished the benediction, Mrs. Mortimer was on her feet and bee lined the porch to wait for The Minister.

John Rowlands walked up the left hand aisle of the church to the porch and the front door. He smiled at members of the congregation, looking a bit longer at Haley and Alister, noting that Mrs. M was no longer in the seat next to them. His smile changed to a sigh as it dawned on him that she would be there waiting to speak to him on his service and sermon, in particular.

He saw Haley pulling her jacket tight and he felt his hand burn as he walked past their row of pews. As he arrived in the porch, his face smiling as he saw Mrs. M.

Despite her weekly advice and comments, he knew and felt her heart was in the right place; so what was she going to say to him this week. John felt he had delivered his planned and rehearsed sermon on acceptance, well. He held his hand out for the customary handshake, she slapped the back of it with her left hand, the impact stinging and jarring his right hand.

They looked at each other, both with surprise, she at her slapping The Minister on his left arm, he at the fact she had slapped him. John gathered his composure first. "What was that for?" He didn't feel any anger, his mind just jumped from thought to thought. What did he say, had he forgotten something, anything in connection with Mrs. M?, he couldn't think of anything.

Mrs. M scolded him like a little boy. "You should be ashamed of yourself!" John's face stayed surprised, his mind still trying to find a reason for her reaction.

"I have never heard a sermon like that in my life, what are you thinking of?"

"Thank you very much!"

"Thank you? ....thank you?, since when does a woman mutilating a man and burning him on a tree coming from a teaching in the bible?"

John did think to point out that "Our Lord was abused, and then nailed to a tree," in his defence as he looked at her. His surprised expression incorporated hints of concern and a flick of disgust.

Haley and Alister caught his eye as they tried to leave the church with the minimum of attention, Haley's jacket done up and her arms casually folded across her chest so as to give the impression that nothing was wrong.

"You two alright?" Haley blushed as she smiled back, waving her right hand with her elbow locked against her body, protecting her embarrassment.

"Yes fine."

Alister smiled as he put his both hands on her shoulders, reinforcing their attempt to convey that everything was normal.

"See you soon." John watched them leave, gently taking hold of Mrs. M's hands at the same time to continue their conversation and to find out what she was talking about.

As he gathered her fingers within his, he felt the wound on his right palm burn. His face winced within his concentrated look into her eyes as he asked her what had he done to upset her.

She was still huffy, indignant at his ignorance, her hat wobbling on top of her head as it vibrated from side to side, short sharp movements, the veins in her neck indicating the energy of her displeasure and her determination to convey this to The Reverend John Rowlands before she went home for Sunday dinner.

"Reverend John, you must know!", she said firmly, her eyes directly to his.

He could feel her response to his gentle, pastural grip, her fingers twitching within his, first sharply but softening as the grip lasted, the twitches becoming reciprocal in contact, her thumbs outside of his hold, touching his cupping fingers from underneath.

John continued to look at her, deep into her eyes, purposely to convey his concern.

"No, I'm sorry I don't know,....what?"

She now was returning the hand holding, her thumbs putting pressure onto his fingers.

"I'll repeat myself then, shall I! I don't think sermons on mutilation and revenge and in the way you said it are right. I've never heard a sermon like that in all my years at church and I'm sorry John, that was disgraceful, you disappoint me I'm

sorry to say, I,.......I feel disturbed and you should to if you think like that."

The Reverend's face was about eighteen inches from Mrs. M's now as he had unknowingly leant in towards her as she spoke her mind. He could smell heather or lavender as he thought and thought it strange for Mrs. M. She may be an older lady but he didn't remember her ever smelling like this before, in fact she smelt often like his wife, as she wore the same perfume on times, DKNY and he knew this from the Christmas and birthday instructions he had received from Elaine about her surprise present.

His eyes were totally focused on hers, his mind trying to work out what she was talking about. John's lips were slightly apart, their shape changing between an open, small questioning smile to slightly pursed, confused and back again, in unison with his brain as it analysed her feelings by comparison to his sermon.

He had not mentioned any woman or anything vaguely like mutilation in any part of it. John knew this without thinking but in the few seconds of Beryl expressing herself, he had gone back through it, almost questioning himself.

John could feel her thumbs pressing more firmly on the underside of his fingers. Her eyes had become still, her pupils had darkened within her brown eyes, their focus directly back to his pupils. John felt slightly uneasy.

They almost cracked heads together as the scorching, cutting sensation, ripped through his groin, his grip on Beryl's fingers crushing them together with his reaction to this unexpected pain as he pulled her downwards and towards him, his hands going to grab himself.

Beryl's face crumpled, becoming significantly wrinkled as she tried to cope with her own expected shock.

John let go of her hands as he continued his movement down to his groin, his body bending in two, his hands trying to clutch himself, the two sides of his purple stole swinging like wings as he wielded around, to turn his back on Beryl, the thick material of his cassock acting as a temporary barrier, stopping his hands.

Beryl had stumbled forward, after the initial tug by John had caught her unaware and pulled her off balance, her body unable to react as quick as a younger person. As John turned and fell to his knees, Beryl lost her legs, their strength not enough to hold her standing and she buckled at the knee, falling forward onto John's back, pushing him forward, flat onto his chest, his face scraping across the course welcome mat that covered the width of the entrance doorway into the vestibule, his hands and arms of no use as they had now reached his searing pain.

Beryl found herself lying flat across The Minister's back, weighing him to the floor. John's hands and arms were under his body, his face smarting and scuffed red from the entrance mat, his teeth clenched, the exclamation of pain grunted from the top of his throat where it joined his mouth.

"Oh my goodness, oh my god! John, I'm so sorry, I'm so sorry, what a stupid old woman I am." Beryl was completely flustered and embarrassed at falling on The Minister. Although she had felt him pull her hands, everything happened so quickly that she thought it was her fault that they were now in a pile in the entrance of the church. She tried to get herself off his back, her hands trying to find contact with the floor, trying to reach around and over his back, her finger tips just touching the mat, her feet and legs flaying around, kicking and struggling, breast stroke kicks, her bright red face almost totally engulfed by the brim of her hat.

John would have been glad of the distraction if he had been more aware of Beryl on top of him, as it hid his own predicament.

He held himself, his shoulders hunched, his hands together between his legs, the weight of Beryl on his back adding to the pressure on his lower back and pelvis, his right palm now felt like it was on fire, burning, throbbing, his black cassock draped off his body, folding itself onto the floor; the overall impression, a big black bat being taken by an old green frog.

"Beryl, are you alright? Give me your hand. What are you

doing, jumping on my husband. If I didn't know you better, I'd think you were getting frisky."

Beryl felt Elaine's hands grip her arms underneath her arm pits to lift her off her husband.

"Elaine, I'm so sorry. What must you think! My legs must have given way, I don't know how, I don't know what to say, what a stupid, stupid old woman I am. I'm so sorry."

Elaine pulled her backwards, her old nurse training and experience on lifting patients coming in handy, her technique bringing the bulk of Beryl's body off John, getting her feet onto the floor so that she could start to put pressure through her legs to stand up.

By now there were twelve other members of the congregation who had entered the vestibule, all wondering what on earth had happened as they saw Mrs. Mortimer in her green coat and hat on top of The Minister.

Beryl felt six to eight other hands grip hold of arms, her body being lifted off The Minister, her feet through everyone's help now firmly on the floor, her legs not so sure. They were now genuinely weak, her self consciousness and embarrassment obvious on her face and their combined affects running through her body.

"What happened?"

"Are you alright?"

"Beryl what's wrong? Come and sit down."

"Someone get some water."

"Someone help John."

"John are you ok?"

There seemed to be a barrage of questions and concern coming from the other worshippers.

As Beryl was moved away to the left of the collapse scene, her fellow church members holding her up, their arms around her, giving her support; the other members were helping John to his feet; his holding of his groin, they put down to Beryl falling on top of him. None of the congregation were going to make reference to his stance or ask The Reverend anything relating to his groin.

John stood up, with their help and put a pained smile on his face as he looked around at the members of his congregation who were helping him and Beryl.

"Thank you, thank you all. Phew. I don't know what happened there," he said with an embarrassed and artificial laughter. "I must have fainted or something!" John was trying to put the event down to him, something other than the pain in his groin which he was now able to disguise as its intensity was fading. He had stopped holding himself and Elaine had noticed this or rather had noticed the fact that he had gone to hold himself before he ended up on the floor with Beryl on top of him, as she had come from the side aisles to the vestibule.

"Beryl I'm so sorry. Did I hurt you? I'll take you home in the car, just let me finish here."

Beryl, with Elaine still with her arms around her, giving her what she thought was extra support, moved towards John. Elaine had her right hand outstretched to slip it around the back of his neck, her love transmitted through her tender touch, her awareness of his embarrassment. Beryl mirrored her actions, her left hand extended, touching his right cheek, her fingers, then her palm sliding around the whole of the right side of his face, cupping it, exchanging warmth between the two different parts of their being; their eyes again fixed on each other, John with a quick glance and smile towards Elaine, thanks in his eyes to his wife and Beryl with a fixed eye to eye look with John.

"Yes I'm fine Reverend, I'm so, so sorry, that's the curse of getting old, you can't do the things you used to be able to do; my old legs, they just gave way."

The small crowd of people who were leaving the church had grown, most unaware of the event in the entrance. They saw Mrs. Mortimer giving The Minister what looked like a squeeze on his cheek.

Elaine laughed again, hugging Beryl with her left arm which was around her waist. "I'd better keep my eye on you with my husband, you little hussy."

"Oh I don't think you have anything to worry about there my dear, not with an old girl like me." Her eyes were smiling with a lively twinkle as she looked straight at Elaine, her gaze incorporating an intensity.

Elaine smiled and laughed back at her comment. "What do you think John?", her hand undulating on the back of his neck.

Beryl mirrored Elaine's action again, her face smiling with a wide lipped smile, supported with a fixed, intense eyeballing straight to John's pupils as she turned her look away from the wife and towards the husband, her hands still embracing her minister cheek.

Mrs. M's focus was direct as she looked at The Minister. "Yes what do you think John? ....What next my lover?" Her eyes sparkled with devilment as she asked the question, a strange lilt in her voice.

CHAPTER 17

Alister and Haley arrived home without stopping anywhere. Haley ran upstairs, took her jacket and blouse off and looked down at her breasts within her white lacy bra, the cups discoloured by her leaking milk.

"I don't understand this, this shouldn't happen now! Why did it have to be in church! Do you think people saw, do you think the minister saw?" Haley tumbled out her questions to Alister in a flow of distress, her tears now beginning to break through her earlier self control.

"No one saw, you had your jacket on, don't worry." He hugged his wife. "Not even Mrs. M knew and she was sitting next to us." He hugged and squeezed his wife reassuringly, kissing her on her neck as he did.

"How.....how is this happening?" He hesitated at asking the question, not wanting to hear anything he didn't like or understand, not wanting to embarrass or upset Haley more than she already was.

"I don't know." Her voice indicated panic. She had left his hug and was walking around the bedroom looking at herself from different reflections, twisting and rotating her body, in the wall mirror then the dressing table mirror and through the en suite door and her reflection in the bathroom mirror, trying to convince herself that no one could see her damp blouse, looking at herself from different angles, to reassure herself that no one would have been able to see her pre birth breasts giving milk.

She remembered that within the last forty five minutes, when she was sitting in church, she had felt a strange sensation. Mixed in between her attention to the sermon, Mrs. M's squeaking, her biological quandary and Alister's attention, she had felt a feeling, a feeling.....of dominance. When Alister had been lost as to what was happening, what she wanted, behind her embarrassment was frustration and the need to feel in control and to control Alister. She had not felt like this before.

Haley was not a yes girl or wife to Alister. Their relationship had been built on friendship first, from years of knowing each other in church, followed by love. They talked through things as best friends, joking and teasing each other and their liking for each other had held back the relationship developing with a romantic connection.

"I'm going to ring mum, this can't be right," her voice continued to convey distress; she was still bouncing from her reflection in one mirror and then to the next, comparing the angles of what she saw now to the sequence of events in the church and what and who may have seen what, from where ever they had been sitting.

Alister listened to Haley relate what had happened in church, repeatedly asking as she paused in the story, "was this right?", her voice escalating as the her story progressed, Alister was aware that her mother had not said anything that noticeably calmed her.

Alister took up a small glass of white wine to Haley who had just come out of the shower, with the thought that it would relax her as she hadn't touched any alcohol since she found out she was expecting. She looked a little calmer and he hesitated as he asked her if she was "alright?" and "what did your mother say?" He hoped her answer would help him to understand and would reassure him.

"She didn't know why it happened. You're not supposed to start producing milk until after the baby is born apparently, which is what I thought. Do you think things will be alright? Do you think the baby will be alright?"

"I'm sure she'll be fine, you'll be fine." He cuddled her in her blue bath towel with his left arm, still holding the wine glass in his right hand. He kissed her on her right cheek, his lips pressed firmly and lingered for five or six seconds, conveying his concern and his love to Haley.

She took the wine and pushed her cheek back against his lips.

Haley felt clean now and the cold wine brought her mind back from the church to their bedroom.

She looked at Alister, raised her glass and took her second sip of wine, which turned into a slowly poured stream into her mouth, Haley relishing its chill and flavour, sucking in air over the top of the wine so that it bubbled on the tip of her tongue, the oakiness and butter from the heavy Chardonnay filling her mouth, the pleasure of its taste had been absent since she suspected she was expecting; her eyes fixed on Alister's from over the top of the wine glass.

The blue towel dropped on the white carpet after Haley yanked it off her body. Her left arm went around Alister's back and she pulled his body into hers as she turned to be face to face with her husband.

He looked at her first with surprise, which turned on his face after a few seconds to excitement and expectation.

"Well, Hal....". His words of encouragement were stopped within his mouth as Haley clamped her lips over his. Her kiss started as a warm mouth massaging kiss, her lips chewing sensually on his and then her kiss turned into a chilled tight lipped purse as she blew the Chardonnay into his mouth: the transfer of her wine another, new surprise which found Alister not knowing what to do, whether to take it into his mouth and then swallow it or to reciprocate and to blow it back into Haley's mouth.

His surprise with Haley and then his indecision, allowed the wine to run out of his mouth and down his and Haley's chin and then onto the top of her breasts which were plumped by the pressure of her squeeze of her body into his, her left arm still around the small of his back.

Haley didn't seemed to mind. She released her hold on his back, her left hand coming around to his face as she took a step back with her left foot.

She raised her right leg and put the ball of her foot into Alister's stomach and pushed him backwards onto their bed, her foot following him so that it rested on him as he lay there looking at Haley as she lent forward and over slightly looking down on him.

He looked in shock and his excitement was obvious. They looked at each other for a few seconds and then she slipped her foot to the right of his body and then jumped up onto him, her left thigh slipping down to the other side of his chest.

Haley sat on his abdomen aware of how he was feeling and caressed his left cheek with her right hand "What next my lover?"

CHAPTER 18

The young woman skipped back into the forest the following morning, picking up daisies to make a chain as she went, enjoying the mid morning sunshine, the feel of moss under her feet and between her toes; the smell of flowers, grass, trees, heather and the faint reminiscent smell of smoke and burnt corpse.

She placed the daisy chain on the charred head of her victim. Her smile was filled with satisfaction as she reminisced on the day before.

"I'd better make use of these bones," she said out aloud to herself, "yes you'd better," she turned and looked in the opposite direction, turning in a sense to look at herself asking the question.

The bone of the husband"s left upper arm crumbled slightly as she gripped it with her right hand, snapping it easily away from his shoulder joint, his whole left arm blackened and ridged within its fragility.

"You are going to powder down nicely my stinking lover." She looked with a scowl at the head of the skeleton, talking as if he could still hear her.

The remainder of the skeleton virtually collapsed into a pile of black, powdered bones, the air above his remains filling with charcoal dust. She breathed in, smelling his particles as they passed thought her nose. She loved the feeling that the last evidence of his existence was under her control. She chose to breath in and smell his legacy, a legacy she would now powder for her concoctions.

She gathered the bundle of bones into a manageable pile, like fire-

wood and carried them back in her black apron, looking down at the limbs and ribs as she walked back to her house. "Not much left when all said and done," she thought to herself.

Back at her house the young woman folded her apron around the bones and then hammered them with a small hammer from her fathers shed. She left the skull to one side.

The broken up pieces she then put into a large wooden bucket and then used the pestle to further grind them into a powder, something which took her the rest of the day to complete but as she looked at the earthenware jar full of his ground ash, she felt delighted by her efforts of the last two days.

The young woman started to think about what she was going to do next..... to complete her whole feeling of satisfaction.

The wooden chair creaked as she sat down and as she put her elbows onto the table, that creaked as well. The blackened skull starred back at her from the other side of the table. "Time to see your wife."

CHAPTER 19

"What do you think was wrong with Beryl Mortimer today?"

"I have no idea. She was going on to me about torture and mutilation, that I shouldn't be preaching that sort of thing in my sermons."

Elaine started the conversation, casually, belatedly. She had not said anything relating to the service on the way back home in the car but now at home, she thought she needed to talk to John.

"What? You didn't mention anything of the sort....during your sermon."

"I know that, so do you, so does everyone else in the church today and when she fell on me....well!.... but I must admit while I felt stupid, I did feel sorry for her; it's horrible getting old. How long before dinner?" John took a full mouthful of the white wine Elaine had poured for him and he let it move around his mouth, enjoying the sensation of the liquid and the small swallows he took, relishing the flavour and analysing each event as he had seen them with each swallow. He didn't come to any conclusions.

"Dinner won't be long but I'm more concerned about you talking about how those men got hurt during the week at the start of the service. What was in YOUR mind. You were positively enjoying talking about their injuries. Your eyes made you look looked like Satan himself."

"Don't be so stupid." John was indignant and slightly self conscious.

"I'm not being stupid. I've never seen you like that. John what were you thinking?"

"I...I....I don't know. I wasn't thinking anything as far as I know. I was just telling everyone about their efforts."

"Telling everyone! You looked like you were relishing it."

"I wasn't relishing anything you nagging bitch." John exploded out of character, his eyes angry outside of his control. "Why are you going on about it?" He jumped forward out of the chair, his face reddened with aggression and he moved toward Elaine as if nothing or anything would stop him from putting his face directly to hers.

"John! John!" Elaine jumped back with unknown fear, a new emotion between her and her husband, her eyes wide with surprise and fright. "What are you doing?", she felt her lower back push against the oven, the heat from the roasting joint and the sauce pans converging around her body, adding to her unease.

John took the rest of the wine in his glass into his mouth in one go, sucking air into his mouth, his top two front teeth just touching his bottom lip, his lips slightly apart, the flavour of the wine coming through as the air enhanced it by forming bubbles on his tongue, the affect pushing his mind harder with aggression.

"What time is dinner ready mum?" Rachel as their seven year old and youngest daughter had been sent into the kitchen by the other two children to ask. Her arrival stopped the altercation instantly, John turning to her with a big smile. "It won't be long, mum's just finishing it off now. Go tell them ten minutes."

Rachel left, her black waist length hair bouncing as she

skipped back into the lounge to Paul and Rebecca. "Dad says ten minutes." Rachel shouted with a singing voice from the hall, on her way into the lounge.

"That smells lovely as usual." John kissed his wife on her left cheek. "Do you want a drop more wine? No service tonight, there's a Lay Preacher tonight, so I think a bit of relaxation and unholy indulgence this afternoon Hun." John poured another glass and put another two bottles off the wine rack into the fridge and then topped Elaine's glass even though she had only taken a sip and had shaken her head nervously to decline the top up.

John sat down on one of the pine kitchen chairs and looked at Elaine, his smile to Rachel who had left the kitchen remaining as he then looked again at Elaine.

"Come on then, we've told them ten minutes," his smiled continued, natural and unforced; no hint of the man that had seconds earlier borne down on Elaine.

Elaine looked flustered and wiped her face with both hands, turning to face the cooker as she did, gripping the horizontal door handles as she concentrated on her thoughts about John.

"He's never been like that, never!" She thought to herself.

Sunday dinner conversation between the two parents and three children was as normal but there was less direct conversation between the two parents, or at least from Elaine to John, not that the children noticed. They told mum and dad what they did in Sunday School and Paul their oldest at seventeen asked about the service and sermon and all four of them were in fits of uncontrollable laughter when it came to the part when John told them how Mrs. M's legs had given way and she had falling forward onto him and they had ended up lying on the floor in the vestibule.

Dinner ended and John asked the children to help mum with

the washing up, something he always did as it showed his appreciation for the work she did in making the Sunday dinner the special meal of the week. He opened the third bottle of wine, a Chilean Sauvignon Blanc, different from the first two Australian Oaked Chardonnays and he sat himself down in the brown leather arm chair in the lounge, another big glass on the mahogany occasional table to his right.

He looked around at their lounge. The only thing that was relatively new was their brown leather three piece suite and while the one three seater, one two seater settee and his chair fitted nicely into the large rear lounge of The Manse, it showed up the age of the green, thirty year old patterned Axminster carpet and the faded yellow curtains that were beginning to thin from washing. "I think I'll decorate this before Christmas," he thought to himself. He sat looking more closely at the green and yellow dominated, small flowered pattern wall paper which now he looked, he could see, was beginning to rise at the joins in places. Only the furniture including the mahogany coffee table in the centre of the room, the two occasional tables and the low level side board where they kept a lot of board games in the door compartments at either end of the centre four draw section looked worth keeping and they had brought the wooden furniture from their last placement. He took another large sip of wine and savoured its taste as much as he had done with the first before dinner. John put his head back into the leather and looked around the room again, this time without any further thoughts.

"Is dad alright? He always does the washing up with you, why are we doing it?" Rebecca asked puzzled. At fifteen she was used to helping around the house but this "wasn't normal for dad" and even she noticed the third bottle of wine go into the lounge.

Elaine hugged her shoulders and told her that, "he was probably a bit tired, as a lot had happened this week."

When they all went into the lounge about twenty minutes later, Elaine and the two eldest noticed half the third bottle had gone, the empty wine glass and then blood on John's right hand and trousers.

"What's happened, where's the blood from?" Rebecca noticed the letter opener slightly hidden by the bottle of wine on the table, its blade with blood smears on it. Her father didn't answer. His face was fixed with an intense stare at the bleeding gouge in his right hand as he squeezed the muscle at the bottom of his thumb from different angles, trying to force the splinters that had been in his hand since he helped carry the pews into the church, to come out. His imagination saw them appear like pips from a halved lemon being squeezed, emerging through the yellow flesh but his eyes saw just swells of blood, oozing from his squeezing no matter how much his mind was willing to see the splinters rise out through his blood, they remained embedded.

Rachel jumped up on her dad's lap, half on his legs and half on the left arm of the chair.
"Dad .....uuugggg, there's a hole in your hand!"

"Get off me you stupid girl, you'll get blood all over your dress and I'll have to find more money to buy you another one. I'm a minister not a bloody bank."

Rachel's smiling and concerned face collapsed into a composition of scrunched up eyes, and big protruding bottom lip, her eyelids unable to hold back the tsunami of tears that burst instantly she heard her dad speak to her as he did. Her bottom lip vibrated, reacting uncontrollably to the upset she felt in her little heart, her feeling that her dad had stopped loving her at that very moment.

Elaine grabbed Rachel, sweeping her off John in one movement and up into her arms and towards the door of the lounge.

"Come on darling, don't be upset, dad's not feeling too good, his hand is hurting him, let's leave him alone. Come on, we can go and watch Aladdin in Becky's room can't we." Her eyes changed from disbelieving anger to a look of compassion and then for sisterly support to Rebecca as she changed her focus on her two daughters they all left the lounge. Rebecca put down the pink nail polish she was using to paint her nails and whipped her head around to watch her mum carrying Rachel out of the room, feeling that she was being instructed by Elaine's tone, that she had better follow them. She swept her long blond hair back from across her face, taking care not to smudge the still wet nail polish on her left hand and un curled herself from the smaller settee. Rebecca smiled awkwardly at John as she left the room, the slight build up of a tear in her blues eyes not noticed by John. "See you later dad."

John carried on squeezing his hand as he gave a slight glance up towards the lounge door. "See you later, love you all." Elaine thought she detected a hint of sadness, within his overall tone of emotional indifference.

CHAPTER 20

"Evening Reverend, on your own tonight?"

"Assessing the lay preacher." John smiled at Mr Evans as he walked in, trying to be discrete, dressed in normal clothes, brown cords and brown jacket with beige shirt; his head a little muzzy still from the afternoon of wine and just wanting to get into the church with the minimum of attention and sit down, to be lost in the congregation, before the lay preacher spotted him.

Most of the evening congregation were there and most had sat to the centre of the church so John felt drawn to mix in so as to hide himself as best he could. Sitting out to the side would make him stand out so he sat, hidden within the crowd as the Lay Preacher shouldn't where ever possible, be distracted by seeing an assessing minister in the congregation.

John didn't realise it but he ended up sitting in one of the new pews, the one behind where Mrs. M had sat that morning.

As the Lay Preacher started her service, John took a deep breath in a last bid attempt to clear his head as the walk from home had failed to perform the miracle he was hoping for as he walked to his church.

He took out a little note book and made comments and observation on the progress of her service, mostly positive, with some constructive criticism in his eyes for her future benefit.

John did what he hated most about "sermon time" which was he began to doze slightly as he settled down for twenty to thirty minutes. He fought hard against the slumber feeling that came over him, squeezing his knees, gripping the edge of the pew, taking deep breaths.

He ended up leaning forward, his head bowed to hide his eyes as he fought to keep them open, the wine relentless in taking his concentration.

His mind went to his service of that day and now the comparison he was making to his thoughts when in the pulpit to now being sat in a pew, having to listen. He urged his mind to concentrate for this sermon, the earlier bits of her service far easier to assess as they were short and sharp, the cohesion from one prayer to the next hymn easy for John to analyse but now for twenty minutes, he needed to concentrate.

The Lay Preacher Patricia Williams started her sermon, gripping the side of the Bible on the lectern to steady her slight nerves.

She was not new to lay preaching but was aware that she was due to be assessed and as she hadn't spotted a minister in the last few of her services, knew that this one or the next was going to be where a minister turned up for her assessment.

John started listening to her speaking. At first he thought she was too quiet, too self aware, self conscious rather than self confident. He looked at her light blue jacket and skirt. John thought it lively but he wasn't there to assess her fashion sense. However she did look very fresh and presentable.

As he listened to her talking, he started to look at the back of the pew where Mrs. M had sat and started wondering back to his service. His legs were stretched out in front of him, the edges of his feet resting against the centre leg, making a connection between the two troublesome pews, their history forgotten in the present by John.

John made a conscious effort to look casual as he sat with a small note book and little pen he had borrowed from Rachel's pencil case, resting on his lap, so that he could record the odd word which would prompt his memory for his assessment. He kept his head down, deliberately looking at the back of the pew in front so as not to draw the attention of the Lay Preacher to his face and so that it didn't alternate between looking at her and then down to his note book, as once spotted, she would then become aware of his scrutiny.

His eyes unknowingly became transfixed to the back of the pew, a recollection of admiring the wood's beauty came to mind and then he took a second, deeper look at the grain, prompted by this thought. The wound on his right hand throbbed more and there was a faint trace of blood through the thin gauze dressing he had quickly wrapped around his hand before coming out.

John swapped the note book into the fingers of his right hand so the he could put gentle pressure with his left on the wound in a small attempt to urge it to seal and not bleed.

The smell of Mrs. Mortimer filtered into his nose, the smell and perfume distinct as it had been that morning when she lay on top of him. Then there was another smell but he couldn't instantly name it, although he recognised it. John took a slow deep sniff with the aim of identifying it. He smelt the new wood in front and what he was sitting on, the varnish, Mrs Evans' perfume from where she was sitting to his right, the same place as that morning.

Curly hair, an eye, leading to a cheek bone formed in his vision, his eyes now totally engaged with the grain. The definition and emphasis of its shading changed as he stared at the pew, the Lay Preachers voice become a soft mumble in his ears as the pew stealthily took over his attention.

The beauty of the young woman was evident as she walked into town, her curly wild hair lifting and bouncing in the breeze with her movement, which was full of life, energy and purpose.

As she walked she thought of the wife that had been so rude to her a few days earlier and hoped that she would find her without too much effort.

The paths between the few shops were dusty, there had been very little rain in the last four weeks and definitely none for three and the main track had dried and cracked in some places.

The young woman became aware of some people looking at her as she walked through the village.

"There she is, there's the evil one that dares to walk amongst us. There's the one who did this to me." The screeching accusations came across the dirt track. Most people stopped to look at who was shouting and at who. Most then carried on with what they were doing, not wanting to get caught up in any confrontation.

The young woman turned around, her rotation slow and deliberate, her arms lifted away from the sides of her body, static energy filling them, ready to defend herself or pounce on any aggressor that might threaten her.

She looked the wife straight in the eyes when she about twenty yards away, shouting her intimidations, her gaze penetrating, stopping the next words from leaving the wife's mouth, causing her to hesitate and then to look around for support or backup from anyone else close by or that she might know.

The young woman walked directly towards this widow, her smile wide and falsely sincere yet her heart and mind filled with the remainder of her intention.

"I can give you something for that," she said, indicating with her right hand, in a soft and directed wave at the wife's scarred face.

"I won't take anything from you,....you ......" The wife hesitated again, first from the fear of making an accusation and secondly from the control being exerted by the young woman's eyes.

"This is not from me, this has been left by your husband, after he left me. He asked me, no he pleaded with me that I should help you. Let me help you, it's what he wanted."

Her voice was calm and soft, her tone was constant, urging the wife to consider but there was no hint of desperation or persuasion, just a reiteration of her husbands wishes.

"What have you done to him? He hasn't come back since he went to see you three days ago, where is he, what have you done with him?"

"What could I do against such a big man?" She looked innocent and vulnerable as she asked the question, "Come let me help you. If you don't trust me, take this home and try it, your husband left it for you. He was desperate that I should give you something for those."

She motioned again towards the scars on the wife's face with her right hand as she then held out her left, having taken out a small earthen jar from her apron's left pocket.

"What's in it?"

The young woman removed the fabric cover to show the wife a grey, black powder which when she held it under her nose, the wife could smell, smoke, heather, wild herbs and something that seemed to envelope and bind the smells together, something she recognised but nothing she had ever experienced as a scent from anything like this pot puri concoction.

"Mix this with boiling water, all of it and drink every drop."

The young woman put it into the wife's right hand and removed hers before the wife could react. The wife held the jar and looked at the contents.

"It's from your husband. It's what your husband would have wanted. Trust me!....your husband did."

The young woman turned and walked away.

Back at her house, the wife cautiously followed the instructions she had been given. She still wondered where her husband had gone, why he hadn't returned but despite her misgivings and concerns, she felt strangely compelled to drink the concoction and felt unrealistically calm at her husbands disappearance.

The powder mixed into a thick drink, tasting a bit like a barbecue broth. She drank every last drop and sat down. Her head muzzy as if she had been drinking.

John suddenly gripped the top of the pew in front. He needed to get himself realigned and steady. His head had started spinning. The knuckles on his hands had turned white from the pressure with which he held the top of the pew. He squinted his eyes and starred at his hands, all with the purpose of stopping the church and his head from jumping and rotating in a mis match of balance and reality.

The husband's pain streamed into his body. He felt remorse, anger, sensations of amputation as his fingers and wrists physically turned bright red. He felt as if all his blood had rushed to his two hands. His grip continued, his head retracted down between his two shoulders, like a tortoise recoiling into his shell. Both his arms were rigid, their effort and strain causing the pew in front to creek as he pushed against it, his exertion

causing opposing forces between the retaining floor bolts, the timber joints and his strength.

JJ turned around to look at The Minister, not knowing that it was John sitting behind him. He had felt the pew move slightly and had become aware of someone's hands on the back of the seat where he was sitting.

John's face was grey, his side molars clamped together to try and control the sensations he was experiencing.

He could see the husband and knew the story, its start and outcome. He twisted in his seat, trying to regain the reality of his church and this service. He saw the young woman, he could feel her fear and now could feel pressure on his chest. His logic questioned if this was a heart attack but his logic was swept aside as his mind saw the young woman being held down by the husband.

JJ watched, not speaking for about ten seconds from turning and seeing The Minister behind him, his association to John being The Minister being hindered by the absence of his dog collar and the presence of a beige shirt and jazzy yellow tie. His mind and tongue caught up to appreciating that this was John Rowlands and he was experiencing something unpleasant.

JJ had swivelled virtually one hundred and eighty degree turn to face John, his body and legs rotated to different degrees, controlled by the design of the pew, his black leather jacket croaking as he twisted. He moved his head from side to side and up to down, to try and get a focused image through his black square rimmed by focal glasses.

John's head shuddered between his shoulders, his eyes compelled to look at the changing grain, the pew drawing him through the story.

He could see a woman etched in flecks and lines, the depth of the varnish hinting at the wife, on her knees.

The wife was hysterical. She had woken up the next day, the taste of the potion still lingering in her mouth and her mind had reacted and jumped into insanity as she first looked at her hands, then her face and finally her body underneath her clothing; all of which was now covered with black curly hair about half an inch long.

It obscured her features. Her eyes were frozen with just one expression, fear. Her mind spun in confusion, the shock of her seeing herself had taken her human ability to co ordinate her limbs and she fell about the inside of the small room, knocking over chairs, the table as she wheeled and whirled in a kneeling, crawling, clawing lather of perspiration. Her head pumped, engorging her face and obscured features, the blood forced to this part of her body, crushing any reasoning and her hope of being healed, her brain unable to bring any control. Now all she was capable of was basic primeval survival.

She pushed open the front door, screaming like a baying dog, half crawling, half kneeling, then falling onto her back, her arms and feet thrashing around to get a grip on anything that would help her to her feet.

John saw this, he felt her desperation, her fear. He felt JJ 's hands on his. They felt cold, the affect sent cooling relief along the same nerves that made him feel his hands were on fire. His wound was now more obvious, the white bandage showing the spread of blood beneath and JJ was aware of it now, his eyes questioning John as he gently tried to break into his ministers world.

"John!.....Rev....." He hissed softly from the back of his throat, trying to be discreet and affective in getting John's attention. It didn't work.

John saw the wife running mindlessly towards the river, her body uncoordinated, her hands tearing at the curly hair now flattened to her arms by the rain, rather than in unison with her legs and feet which were irregular in their stride. She stumbled into the water, still tearing at her arms to remove her deformity. Her feet became cut and bruised as the stones dug and sliced the soft unprotected skin of her soles but she was unaware of the injuries occurring below the surface, her mind was to preoccupied with her unnatural transformation.

He saw her pick up a stone from under the surface and slash at her arms, attempting in her derangement to remove the hair, her skin being cleaved off in jagged chunks as the sharp edge of the stone opened up wound after wound along both her forearms as she swapped the stone between her hands.

Her writhing and stumbling took her further in to the centre of the river, the rush of water foaming up against her chest, the push and pressure of the current, the swell and froth reaching up to her face as it pushed hard against her body, her arms now splashing against the surface of the water, stopping the stone from reaching her skin with any meaningful contact as her mind had not worked out the need for her arms to be lifted up above the surface of the river.

She turned her attention to her neck but the water again was an absorbent barrier to her slashing as it formed a collar of bubbles and foam swirling around her chin and face, the froth becoming one with her tears, her vision blurring white. The rapidly moving chill of the river on her face, hit her brain with a refreshing numbness. She dropped the stone and bent down to retrieve it, taking an unconscious deep breath before she crouched down under the surface. Mixed in with the gushing and bubbling of water she heard uncontrollable laughter from the bank. John saw the wife fumbling around on the river bed trying to find that particular stone she had dropped, as she picked up and tried to focus within the swirl of current defined by the movement of the underwater plant life, each stone in her search. He felt his own legs become light as he felt the buoyancy of the river lift the wife's feet from off the river bed and the start of her amalgamation into the direction of the current below the surface. John's head felt weightless and chilled, the wife's tumbling and struggle to regain balance and contact with the river bed, devouring the oxygen from her last breath as her body strained to extract every last second of life from her besieged lungs. John twisted and jerked in his seat, still holding onto the back of the pew in front, his body fighting with the transmitted current, his face reddening as he held his breath.

He felt the young woman's exhilaration at watching her second victim disappear. He felt the transformation of his body from rotating, bouncing, undulating beneath the surface as the wife's encounter ebbed and his body, still cold and wet, felt still as if he was lying horizontally. He turned his head to look up at the ceiling, his eyes rotating with his perceived change of alignment. John knew the young woman lay on the bank laughing, lying in the rain, her left foot draped over the bank enjoying the rush of water against her toes and ankle. Now his foot, fingers and hand changed from hot to cold, chilled by the rain and water the young woman had laid in for an hour and his mind could see this.

"Rev.......Rev......John." JJ shook John's forearms as he became more concerned by his ministers head and eyes rolling. John saw a crowd of people form within the back of the pew. They disappeared back into the timber, his eyes staring at their dissemination, his mind trying to hold their images and then John felt a conglomeration of other impressions and senses.

"John what's wrong?" JJ was now kneeling on his pew and he pulled on John's forearm to get a response. John's eyes fought against moving their vision to take in anything other than the pew.

The Lay Preacher continued with her service, now aware of the congregations leanings towards the centre of the church and the attention that someone was attracting. She could not see the persons face, just the balding back of a chunky, fair haired man's head, in front kneeling on the pew and facing the person behind. It was obvious to her that he was trying to help someone in the seat behind, and his effort or self consciousness or both showed on his red blemished neck.

John reciprocated JJ 's hold on his arms, his own arms and hand turning up to grip JJ's forearms, his eyes flicking between the pew, its hold and JJ's eyes.

The tension in his arms and grip relaxed, in conjunction with a long wine soaked breath out, his concentration broken.

JJ smelt the intoxication and shrunk back on his haunches, still holding onto John's arms, his face couldn't hide the surprise of smelling John's breath. He looked around the rest of the congregation, partly for support, partly to see if anyone else had realised what he thought, that their minister was drunk. He didn't want them to know.

"Come on John, let's go outside to get some air." He gripped John's arm and pulled him upwards as he rose up onto his knees.

John mirrored JJ's movements, rising to his feet, crouching, as they made their way to the end of their row of pews and into the side isles, making their way to the front door.

"She drowned JJ, she drowned." JJ looked at John as he confirmed the outcome of John's vision.

"Did you see as well? How do you know?"

JJ looked uncomfortable "The Lay Preacher and you!"

JJ continued, still trying to keep his voice low. "Don't you remember? Are you that drunk? God John, you stink of drink, It's not like you. Is it your birthday or something?"

JJ's voice sounded like a throaty growl. "Where is that river?"

The two men's expressions reflected back to each other's face, the same bewildered look, questioning each other.

The Lay Preacher watched them as they walked up the right side isle. She over heard JJ's comment about drowning and felt it related to her service, as if she had failed. Her words hesitated, her mind started to wander, her tongue fell over itself: she tried to gather herself and regain her concentration to complete her service, hoping her assessor, where ever he was had seen the best in her. Inside she felt destroyed.

CHAPTER 21

"I don't think John's feeling too good!" Elaine looked concerned as JJ helped John into the hallway.

"What's happened? John you look dreadful."

John looked back with a scowl, unseen by JJ but felt by Elaine, his response to her observation.

"Thank you JJ." John placed his left hand on JJ's right arm and then started to walk up the stairs.

"You need to get that hand sorted out, he needs to sort that hand out Elaine, it's bleeding." Both Elaine and John looked at his right hand. The bandage had now almost totally turned red.

"You'll have to go to the doctors tomorrow, that's not getting any better."

John's hand was burning again. He turned and looked back down the stairs at his wife, his scowl harder and more unloving than his first. This time JJ saw his expression. It was one that he had never seen on John Rowlands face before, not once within the time he had been The Minister at their church.

JJ felt very uncomfortable. He looked at Elaine who returned his look, she felt embarrassed, both thinking that John's alcohol indulgence had taken his normal personality.

"Thank you JJ, see you soon."

"No problem."

Elaine watched JJ drive off and heard their bedroom door close. Then she heard the door lock.

CHAPTER 22.

John did not hear Elaine banging on the bedroom door, calling his name, nor Rachel shouting Daddy.

Elaine slept in with Rachel, as she and Rachel gave up trying to get John to wake and open the door. Her sleeping with Rachel reassured their youngest that there was nothing to be frightened of and that "Dad was fine, just tired." Elaine was not convinced.

Elaine's conviction was further weakened when John did not appear from their bedroom all of the next day. She knew he was suffering but didn't know the cause. She certainly knew it wasn't the wine from yesterday. While he had indulged, they were not Puritans. They enjoyed a glass of wine and more on the occasions their responsibilities allowed them to break free of his dog collar.

The three children's concern about their father grew through the day in correlation to their ages. Rachel was the first up on Monday morning banging on the bedroom door but John did not hear her.

He didn't hear either of them when Rebecca joined her younger sister and both knocked on the door calling to John.

"Dad will be fine Rach." Elaine had prompted Rebecca to give Rachel a cuddle and to say something to calm her. She had not slept very well and had woken throughout the night, waking mum to ask if dad would be ok. Elaine felt drained when she got up in the morning to make breakfast ready for school.

Paul didn't think too much about the morning, mornings were not his best time of day but even he started to bang on the door when he came home after rugby training at school, when at six in the evening, he thought dad would be up and around.

All any of them heard in response was John saying, "Go away darlings, I'm fine. I'm just tired."

John was fighting with the dreams he was having throughout the remainder of Sunday evening and Monday.

When he got up Tuesday morning, he was oblivious to the fact that it was Tuesday, oblivious to the fact Monday had disappeared with him in bed.

"I really fancy some bacon and eggs, some sausage, toast, anyone want the same?" John walked into the kitchen, his hair greasy from the best part of two days in bed, a big relaxed smile on his face and with an attitude and disposition that conveyed normality. There was no hint of recollection to the last two days.

Rachel ran up to him and gripped around his lower back as hard as she could hug.

"I missed you daddy." John bent down and swept Rachel up into his arms, hugging his youngest firmly, feeling the fragility of her young body. He nuzzled her neck with his nose and mouth and then blew a raspberry on her neck. Rachel giggled

and squirmed as her fathers lips vibrated on her neck.

"I love you daddy, I don't like you being bad, I don't like feeling bad." She twiddled the longer hair at the back of his head as she said it. She loved twiddling with his hair and he liked it as well.

John hugged his daughter even tighter. He kissed her on her forehead, a long, firm, loving kiss.

Rebecca came up to her father and gave him a hug, hugging Rachel at the same time.

"Are you feeling better dad?" Paul asked as he started to walk out of the kitchen door to go for the bus for school.

"What do you mean better?" His question was innocent.

He turned his attention away from Paul and back to Rachel who he was still holding. He squeezed her even tighter.

Elaine cooked the breakfast he asked for and avoided asking any questions, she just watched him, her concern subdued during the chit chat of conversation. He wiped the marks and crumbs off the pine farm house style table and then did the washing up.

The bed he had slept in behind the locked door told a different story to his smiling arrival in the kitchen.

Elaine slumped against the wall at the sight of their bed, her mind recapping the events of the last two days, trying to find

some continuity or reason for her husbands behaviour. She sighed and the slightest of tears glazed across her eyes.

CHAPTER 23

John showered and walked to the church, kissing Elaine as he left home. His mind was calm and he felt happy. It was a sunny October day and he enjoyed the change of colour in the leaves along the tree lined streets. He felt like he was seeing it for the first time.

"How are you feeling Rev? Heard you had a bit of a turn on Sunday."

John stopped on the steps up to the church and turned to answer Mal. "I'm fine Mal, it's a beautiful day. How are you anyway, how's you wrist?"

"I'll live, don't know if my customers will, I'm a bit slow serving them. Some might die of starvation while they're waiting."

"But you're ok overall?"

His voice elongated his answer as it trailed off in volume. "Yeeeeesss" He waived as he turned back towards his fish shop, thinking about his wrist again and the memory of last week and how he got hurt.

John walked around to the side entrance, entered his office and sat down ready to review what was on his desk and to plan.

He looked at the clock, 12.30, he had been there two and a half hours. He looked down at his desk. What had he done?, opened a few letters; hardly anything. He wondered to himself what had he been doing.

John wandered into the church still contemplating his lost morning. He loved the church, its feel, the high ceilings, ornate plaster coving and angelic freezes, the wooden and wrought iron crucifix of Christ on the front wall.

A ministers calling was more than a church, the building, a place to worship but this building had history. It had been the alter to thousands of marriages, thousands of christenings, the commitment of parents to God that their child would be raised within the belief and teachings of Christianity. It had seen thousands of funerals, absorbed the grief of a million people at the loss of their loved ones, seen the departure and aided the commitment of the souls of people who had lived a full life and had surrounded the distraught and inconsolable parents of infants, when the tiny coffins of their beloved child had been laid at the alter before the cross, with whatever minister at that time, trying to find the words to give consolation and justification to God's decision to take an innocent child.

He walked down the aisle and absorbed its history, feeling the life and death of those before him. As he looked around he relished in his belief. He felt the love of his God fill his body.

As John ambled around the church, his now troublesome, aching, throbbing hand reached into his consciousness again, reminding him that "this splinter that would work itself out" to paraphrase Martin, was still deep into the fleshy area of his right thumb.

"What does he know," he thought to himself, feeling his own irritation and annoyance growing as his wound again dominated his senses.

He started to think how Jesus must have felt when his wounds would have strained with his weight as they held him on his cross with those jagged nails, hammered through his hands and he questioned his own pain. John rubbed the palms of his hands alternatively with his thumbs as he thought about Calvary.

John saw the crowd surging and weaving within themselves, each person looking at and shouting with the other as their minds and intentions congealed. They pushed and punched their captive when they got close enough to reach, each eager to make contact, their pack instinct overtaking their free minds and will. The larger men were able to push to the centre of the crowd, catapulting and throwing their victim between  themselves, not always catching the human being who's arms and legs flailed and grasped when in the air, trying to gain their balance.

The crowd's venom and excitement grew with their prisoner becoming more disorientated and weakened as the bruises and cuts grew in number. When he was dropped, there was someone there to grab hold and lift or throw him to the next waiting hand or fist, pulling him across the floor, the stones unforgiving. There was a growing enjoyment as more and more of the crowd became blooded, like a fox hunter on their first hunt, the crowd becoming more frenzied the closer they got to the tree.

John found himself following and becoming part of the crowd as he felt himself infected by their essence. He followed their path, his mind taking in everything that was happening around him as he made his way through the pews, along these enclosed pathways. There wasn't a clear view to the centre of the crowd but John could visualise the victim becoming more frightened. His breathing became gaspy, the anxiety of what was to come affecting his lungs.

As he walked up and down between the pews, John twisted and turned, looking and reacting to the crowd he now felt part of, following the throng. The volume of chants and jeering reached a crescendo as the mob came closer to their destination.

John stumbled, his right foot catching in the strap of a child's handbag left from Sunday's service, his left unknowingly already standing on the strap. His left knee caught the edge of the pew's seat as he grabbed the back of the front pew with his right hand, his left hand slamming down hard on the edge of the seat itself as he tried to stop himself falling full length down in between the wooden seating.

"What on earth?" The words came out through angry teeth as the pain from his knee cap momentarily took his concentration. He rubbed his knee as he adjusted himself, now kneeling on his right knee, his left leg extended. He didn't see the bag despite his surprise and stumble, he was back with the crowd after only a second or so.

He was becoming more agitated the closer he felt they were getting to the where this now callous, revengeful mass were dragging their pray. The urge to push to the centre rose up in him, he felt he had to try and do something.

His thoughts about his saviour's crucifixion, the pain, the humiliation this man had to endure from people which, only a few days before had welcomed and cheered him into Jerusalem; were now running riot.

The feeling of panic and anxiety filled his intention. John was lost, his emotions reacting and infusing with his senses. There was a deep need within him to do something to save this captive, his compassion rising as he heard the sounds of injury and pain, his hearing heightened, dissecting all the noise and commotion from the crowd and hearing the one person that mattered. Strange!

John's eyes focused to the centre, his vision penetrating passed jostling, fist shaking avengers, most convinced in their righteousness, the others being convinced by being part of the pack, swayed by the overall energy and aggression being screamed by the most vocal.

The Minister looked for the hill and the three crosses that were as integral to his beliefs as Jesus being the son of God. He began to wonder who he was being so concerned about.

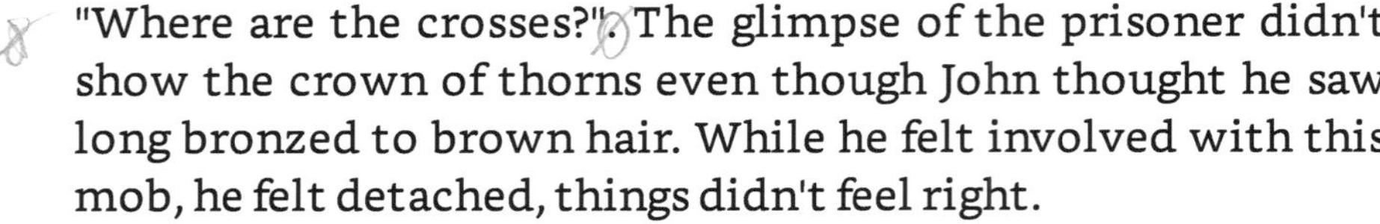

"Where are the crosses?". The glimpse of the prisoner didn't show the crown of thorns even though John thought he saw long bronzed to brown hair. While he felt involved with this mob, he felt detached, things didn't feel right.

If he had a chance he would try to save Jesus from what was to come, who wouldn't?, but if he did, the very fact he wasn't crucified would change the perception of Christian belief.

He strained to get close enough to where he could do something but there was no way he could achieve what his mind was urging him to do, his brain picking out the compulsion to act, divorcing this from his concern with the history of his faith.

The gentleness of this Minister was being overpowered by rising determination. John felt himself slinking and ghosting past the other vigilantes, easing himself closer to the centre of this escalating turmoil.

"You have been accused and found disgraced before God. Your crimes against your fellow man are unspeakable. I find you guilty and by the word of God spoken directly to me as his Earthly voice, your soul will be tested before it can enter Heaven by the grace of our Lord or be damned to eternal banishment to the underworld of Satan."

John looked for the man who's voice carried over the the bedlam of the crowd, which on hearing his condemnation, drew the attention of every person screaming at the captive and to each other. The anger in their voices increased on hearing his authority, their eagerness to succeed sweating through every pore, their faces and bodies wet with the perspiration generated from their excitement and efforts in wanting to be close enough to the captive to exact their own satisfaction; wanting to increase the memory of this day and their part in it, for stories to come.

"Our Lord God has laid out the way for our lives and the paths of righteousness that we as his servants should follow. You have chosen your own path and you shall be damned for it."

The voice came from somewhere beyond his vision. John felt he was getting closer. His head weaved and twisted as he tried to look around the others in the crowd. His thoughts were rapid, one following another. Where was this man? Was he a priest? Was he an executioner ? Where was the hill? Where are the crosses? Was history wrong ? Should he stop himself from doing something? Was doing nothing the right thing to do? Should he interfere, change history, change religion?

"Tie her to that tree, bind her tight."

"Her?" John questioned his hearing, "her?" His brain felt on fire, his head pounding, trying to rationalise what to do within the situation and now "her!" This added to his confusion and compounded the strange feeling he had felt moments earlier.

"Who is this?" His uncertainty about the religious implications now changed his questions to moral ones.

He could now see clearly five larger men working in unison around a tree, two obviously in front of the captive, pinning "her" to the tree while the other three threaded and tied the rope around the tree, her wrists and ankles.

John could still not see her face but now a clearer glimpse of long, thick, flying curly blond hair, lifting and whipping violently from her struggling, silhouetting from behind her captors, the wind gusting, causing the sudden, strained move-

ment of the trees to drown out some of the crowds volume.

He felt himself pushing forward.

"Oh Lord our God, as your faithful disciple and your voice on Earth to the people I serve in your name, this demon witch before you stands accused of satanic powers, of curses and spells, murder and mutilation. We look to your guidance and direction to exact justice or mercy in your name."

John being used to standing in front of people preaching, could feel the growing self importance within the oratory. He was yet to spot whoever was making these pronouncements but he could sense he was increasingly enjoying the event and the position it gave him. As each condemnation escalated the excitement of the mob, the words were announced with more emphasis, more performance, more indulgence.

"Bind her tightly. Give her no chance to cast any spells." These words had more aggression than previous announcements.

John saw the five men double check the ropes, pulling on her restraints, testing their strength.

He weaved past a few more in an effort to get closer. "No you must stop this, this is wrong, this is wrong, untie her."

Eyes looked at him in contempt and surprise. John felt the centre of attention and felt immensely self conscious and uncomfortable. He could now see the young woman. She was pulling and straining on the ropes. Her eyes darted in direction to her captors, each getting a gaze for a second or so, the menace of her stare making each who caught her eye feel threatened.

John's mind was trying to readjust to the confusion that his expectations had convinced him, he was involved in. "The hill, so it didn't happen on a hill! That's why there's no hill." He started to disseminate his situation and what was about to happen.

His head shuddered with the impact of a fist to his right cheek. He felt himself falling backwards from the impact.

Another punch, to the back of his head, propelling him forward, his body and skull reacting against each other as they were now moving in different directions. He instinctively raised his arms up to protect his head though he still couldn't see where the punches were coming from and from who.

"*There's one of her followers, take him as well. Let our Lord pass judgement on both their souls.*"

John felt panic, his arms were waiving furiously, trying to ward off any more punches around his head as if he was trying to swat away hundreds of bees. His fell forward and backwards trying to regain some sort of balance. His knees caps hurt as they took the weight of his oscillating body.

He felt more pain reach his brain, transmitted from his left eye socket, then his right ear. John couldn't see where these blows were coming from but his torso was being snapped in one direction, then the other.

His thoughts momentarily returned to the young woman. "Leave her alone, let her go." He screamed this out, his own pain adding to the urgency of his demand. He caught sight of her eyes, the anger disappearing briefly as she turned to look at him, her defiance turning to thanks.

John could taste blood, his tongue first licking the droplet off his top lip, followed by his bottom lip cupping over his upper lip, the warmth of his body liquid seeping between his lips into his mouth.

Mr. Evans had come into the church looking for John and had not seen him at first as he was expecting to see his minister in the pulpit or standing somewhere in the church or pews but it had been forty seconds or so before he connected the sounds he was hearing to the location of John.

He stood there for a second or so looking at hands whacking at the air, just hands and forearms visible above the tops of the pews, frantic in their movement, accompanied with grunts and squeals. Mike Evans didn't understand. He moved towards the hands he could see, still not expecting to see John where he was, on his knees, between the pews.

As Mike walked closer, through alternating sunlight and shade formations created by the arched windows and the thick stones walls between, feeling instant warmth, then chill and warmth again from the encroaching sunshine, he switched between confusion and concerned.

"Rev! Rev!....John," his calling didn't enter John's ears. "John what's wrong?" His concern increased even though he still hadn't walked to a position to see his kneeling minister.

"John, is that you?" Mike Evans called again to the whirling hands and arms.

John's head now came into view, a stream of blood running down his face, a vertical cut on the right of his forehead, visible to Mike Evans as John's head was fully rotated as humanly possible, looking over his left shoulder.

Mike's mouth opened about to say, something....but all that came out were little hisses of exclamation, confirming his confusion.

His forehead furrowed. His gaze changed from inquisitive to mesmerised as he watched the kneeling minister thrashing around between the seats. As he watched John, he began to feel there was almost some purpose to what he was doing. John was violently swinging forwards and backwards, switching from side to side, his torsos rotating, his head switching direction, working in unison with his arms and hands.

John tried to parry and push away the fists that he saw being aimed at him. The expressions on the faces of the people closest to him in the crowd, showed immense annoyance, anger; directed at him for his intervention. No matter how he tried, how quick he moved away from the punches, he couldn't seem to avoid being struck.

He felt a sharp, hard impact on his left cheek, his head recoiled, jarring his neck as it reacted. His hands tried to parry the blow but it had made contact with his face before his defence could be affective. He felt the warmth of his own blood on his cheek increase until it felt hot; John wiping his face with the back of his hand. There was no time.

The next punch caught him on his right temple, again hard, even solid on impact, unforgiving. He felt dazed but he tried to focus. He knew he must not fall over or people could start kicking him. He could see the ferocity of the mob in their faces. His head pulsed from his temple.

John kept his hands up in front of his face as much as he could but he had never had to do anything like this. He had never been involved in a fight so he was very awkward and ineffective.

He turned and twisted in different directions, at different angles as he tried to avoid being punched and to avoid eye to eye contact in an effort to reduce his presence as he now began to realise that his protests to the young woman's bondage was to bring the worst for him.

Mike saw John smash his face against the arm of the pew, his left cheek splitting open instantly as it made contact with the edge of the wood, his face bouncing backwards. He was spinning but his movements were not controlled by anticipation but governed by reaction.

The other side of his head hit the pew in front, John trying to fend off another punch as the right side of his head hit the back of the pew in front. The eyes of the man who hit him were glaring at him, victorious satisfaction evident on his face.

John's face was now covered with blood, running freely from the cut on his forehead and left cheek. He continued to thrash around on his knees, his body and hands reacting to the crowd attacking him, his face being split open from the pews, the wood consciously and deliberately cutting open John's face, exacting punishment on this Holy man.

His face more than anything made repeated contact with the pews, swellings and bruisings appearing within seconds, cuts opening, though not on every contact but the bruises, wields and swellings distorted his features with every punch. The blood which flowed profusely over his skin, running into his beard, was being splattered and sprayed over the encompassing pews. His dog collar turned red as the blood soaked into the material, his features becoming obscured by this and his face swelling.

Mike broke free of his surprise and confusion and moved towards John, his thought now, to help. The blood flow increased and became a red curtain over John's face. The pews immediately surrounding John were becoming more discoloured with blood.

Mike Evans' mind was logical, ordered. He was trying to work out the situation like an arithmetical conundrum but the irrationality of what he was seeing unnerved him. Mike could feel illogical fear building up as he approached John. The closer he got the more he sensed and his fear grew proportionately. He started to put his glasses on then put them back into their small fabric case and back into his black car coat's right pocket.

"John what on earth is happening? What are you doing? Your face!" Mike tried to catch John's still flailing hands. He managed to get a grip of his forearms and then slipped his grasp down to John's wrists for more control and strength. Mike started shaking like an agitated puppet as he tried to hold onto and steady John who was still trying to fend off his attackers, Mike's own movements being overpowered by John's possessed defence.

"John!, John! it's me Mike, Mike Evans. Look at me. Look at me." His voice grew louder with his anxiousness to break through to John.

The Minister continued to defend himself from phantom punches, his reality transmitted across bodily boundaries. Mike Evans tried to gain eye contact with John. He felt his grip tightening around the wrists of this humble man who was still kneeling on the floor. As his grip tightened and his voice became louder, Mike exerted more strength to stop John from thrashing around. John started to look up towards his parishioner; looking through and past Mike to the others still in this malicious crowd.

Mike saw John's eyes change, his expression became lost, the spark of life faded before Mike's eyes; he saw his minister's energy ebb from his face, his eyes looked for mercy, his bloodied, gashed, swollen face begged for it.

Mike's vision caught the sight of blood smears and splatters over the back of the pew in front and the seat of the pew behind between which, John was kneeling.

He shuddered at the sight and the effect it created on the wood. The compulsion to look almost instantly overtook him, combining an unexpected morbid interest with revulsion. His accountant's mentality had never coped with illness very well, its unexpectedness wasn't ordered enough for him, you had to react, to compensate; you couldn't plan.

The blood dribbled down the grain on the rear of the backrest and the life hidden within its history gripped the ordered mind of this un impulsive man.

Mike tried to pull John to his feet, their wills and intentions repelling each other. Mike's bewilderment dominating his compassion and the stained wood exercised its own influence. He started to feel angry more than concerned and his grip on John's wrists tightened.

"Light the wood and let the fire forged from the soul of the fallen one, put his pupil to the test. Should she live then Lucifer himself holds her hand to protect her. Should she feel the redemption of the flame, then let the mercy of our Lord take her to his side and save her soul from eternal damnation."

Mike looked at John as he didn't see John's mouth move, yet he heard these words as clearly as if John had spoken them. This "really wasn't normal" and he felt increasingly confused and frightened. He felt his clinical revulsion changing to moral condemnation as he sensed an icy shiver down his spine within the building heat of his exertion, in trying to control John.

"How could .... you....YOU do this?" Mike's emotions exploded. "This is just a young girl. What are you doing, what are you all doing?"

Their conflicting reactions resulted in a struggle between Mike trying to subdue John's defending and now John trying to avoid even more physical harm from this now predatory parishioner.

"You can't do this!. This is wrong! What are you doing? What are you all doing?" Mike started shouting at John.

Mike became aware of the past though his mind could not understand the present. He ran his left hand down the back of the pew, the blood skating under his fingers and palm, making it sticky, congealing on his left hand. He flexed his fingers as if trying to wipe off the red glue like bonding.

Mike resumed his grip, again still holding firmly onto the wrists of His minister, trying to control John's reaction but John continued to fight, his fight now encompassing Mike Evans with Mike being drawn into the Ministers reality.

"You can't do this. Are you serious? What has she done?" Mike Evans felt the intent of the crowd precipitate through his body, oozing initially through his palms, filling his chest, gripping his heart.

The two men danced with aggression, their movements now reflecting and reacting to each other, the history of the pews binding them together, in conflicting movement and intention.

Mike saw the tinder wood light at the base of the tree, plumes of smoke misting in front of the woman who's outline he could see. This outline remained static, rigid, conveying a possessed determination, a defiance and it entered his own psyche; a determination to overcome and succeed and this now became directed towards John.

His own movements and grip became stronger, his eyes unknowingly, unconsciously became focused on the back of the pew in front of where John was kneeling.

Mike's eyes followed a large globule of John's blood track down the back of the pew, it seemingly following the line of varnished grain. It sculptured the outline of a head and neck, the hint of a shoulder and an arm, strained, strong. Mike felt the life within the pew and his understanding grew. The efforts of restraint and defiance between the two men escalated, confusion became superseded by testosterone.

"What about the baby? Did you kill the baby as well?"

John looked up, almost as a pause within their struggle, with a puzzled look at the mention of the baby. He stared away from Mike as he continued to struggle against Mike's grip and his imaginary apparitional attackers, his body and arms seeming to be of another person in relation to his mind, his thoughts concentrating to find within his memory any awareness of a baby but he couldn't find any, not relating to this woman but he did find one; a baby that had been Mike's baby.

He looked back at Mike, his expression changed to one of sympathy.

CHAPTER 24

"I'm sorry, this just doesn't seem to make sense from what the two of you have said, you said this man was being dragged to a tree, you saw it as well but it was a woman."

"It was always a woman."

"It wasn't always a woman, well not to me."

"So where did the man go?"

"There was never a man there."

"But he said there was a man there, being dragged and then burnt on a tree."

"Well there wasn't, it was a woman the whole time."

Mike tried to be rational as he answered and corrected the twenty three year old police officer who had responded to the call a frantic Beryl Mortimer had made, having come into the church to do the flowers for tomorrow's christening service and found a bloody faced Minister kneeing between the pews with Mr. Evans appearing to be punching him relentlessly screaming, "What have you done with the baby?"

Beryl had tried to interrupt their confrontation but her surprised screams to the two men had not registered her presence, as she lurched and rotated towards and away from them almost at the same time; her mind in instant turmoil at such an unexpected sight. Her heart had palpitated after she rushed to the office to phone for the police and ambulance and she had become extremely flustered as to which one to phone first.

She had partly collapsed on the floor after going back into the church to the two still struggling men and shouting at them to stop from the other side of the pew in which there were both corralled. It was only when she dropped to her knees that they became aware of her and their confrontation subsided.

The one paramedic attended her or at least tried to in between her talking, relating what she had seen and what she thought, her agitated, erratic movements getting in the way of his attention.

His partner thought initially that he had picked the easier patient but his patience was being strained when trying to calm the minister and attend to his wounds; who was now shaking involuntarily in shock, while trying to speak to the police officer who was attempting at the same time, to make a coherent thread of the story he was being told by both men.

After twenty five minutes of medical attention and police questioning, both police officer and paramedics were now exchanging looks of aggravation between themselves, their respect for each other's profession conveying empathy at each other's dilemma and the underlying tension within the vestry; neither outwardly acknowledging they were interfering with the work of the other.

The first to relent was the police officer, who eventually concluded from the partially contradictory stories each man had related that there was no criminal action to pursue and that trying to present a logical report about two men seeing a woman being burnt on a tree in a forest from inside the church was not the best decision for his career progression. He left the paramedics to get on with their job.

The paramedic attending to John smiled and raised a hand to the leaving officer, relieved that he now had a patient who was becoming more relaxed by not having to answer questions at the same time as he was trying to patch him up.

"You need to go to casualty and have some X-rays so that we know there's no serious damage. Have you got someone who can take you?"

John looked blank, his expression emotionless but direct to the paramedic.

"I will be taking him. Is he alright? Mike, what on earth happened? Beryl phoned me to say you had attacked John. That can't be right. Did you?"

"There's no evidence on his hands that indicates he has caused the injuries on.....I assume..... your husband's face? The cuts and bruises look like they were from your husband bashing his face on the pews in the church." The paramedic naturally answered the question Elaine asked when she rushed into the vestry.

She glanced down at him for a second before returning her gaze at Mike Evans and her husband who both sat side by side in front of the kneeling paramedic, now closing up his medical bag.

Elaine's next comment evaporated with Mrs. Evans piling in through the door, her concern for her husband and his reported behaviour and attack on The Minister igniting her emotions. Her face was thunder, her mind spaghetti, a total mish mosh of electrical impulses but ultimately ready to condemn her husband, having already been told of his beating of the Reverend by Mrs. Mortimer who felt she had to phone her, after she had phoned Elaine, her own medical treatment finishing far quicker than John Rowlands, giving her time to ring around.

"What the hell have you done? Elaine, John, I am so sorry. I never thought he would bring his sort of nonsense here." Liz spun around the room trying to take everyone in, looking for injury, her own face, a natural English pale rose complexion, red and perspiring, her short cut blond bob, swishing like the head of a mop as she jaggedly changed direction, her blue eyes open as wide as they would allow her as the urgency and embarrassment of the situation controlled her thoughts.

Mike Evans looked up at his wife, his expression exposing surprise......and menace.

CHAPTER 25

"The X-rays show he has two fractured cheek bones and there is significant swelling to the right side of his cranium....sorry the right side of his forehead. My advice, he must rest following the treatment we'll give him here. He'll need to be on an intravenous drip over night to reduce the risk of his brain swelling. It's just precautionary, so don't worry unduly. Is there anything you want to ask me?"

Elaine looked at the exceptionally tall, blond haired doctor who had just given her the summary of John's condition. He was Australian or a New Zealander, she could never tell the difference between the accents. Her mind was in a fog as it recapped on what he had just said to her and the whole of the events at the church that afternoon. Elaine looked at his stethoscope swinging across his chest from side to side while he tidied some papers on his desk as he gave her his synopsis of John's condition and treatment.

She had followed the paramedics back to the hospital as they wanted to have John checked out and taken in overnight, just in case.

"So he's got to stay in over night, is that right?

"Yes."

"And tomorrow?"

"Let's see when tomorrow comes."

CHAPTER 26

"Where's daddy?" Rachel's innocent question as her mum walked through the front door, injected a new confusion into her already stomach churning thoughts, her brain inadvertently creating a feeling of nausea throughout her whole body as she tried to work out and make sense of the afternoon, this time with what and how she should tell her children.

Elaine put her right arm around Rachel and squeezed her shoulders against her own body, her warmth conveying reassurance to the cold numbness her own body had descended to.

"Daddy's not going to be home tonight, he's not feeling very well so he's having a night in the hospital."

"Are there doctors looking after him? Do you think he would like to have Pooh to sleep with tonight, I'll go and get him." Rachel started walking up the stairs to go to her bedroom.

Elaine watched her youngest daughter stomp up the stairs purposefully to get Pooh Bear. Out of the three she was the most like John, ready to share and thoughtful to others. Her long black straight waist length hair swung across the width of her back as she pushed herself up each step, her body weight switching from side to side.

"That's really lovely of you darling but I'm sure dad would want you to keep Pooh with you but I'll tell him you were going to let him have Pooh tonight and that will mean just as much to him."

Rachel turned and came back down the stairs, her brown eyes with a glaze of tears across them and went back into another hug with her mum. Elaine gave her a lingering kiss to the top of her head, her black hair feeling soft between her lips.

Rachel watched her mum going to get her dad's clean Simpsons pyjama shorts and top, the ones Rachel "had got for him" last Christmas from his wardrobe, a large stand alone four door mahogany monster that dominated the one wall of her parents bedroom; the wardrobe where she sat amongst the clothes thinking she would find Narnia, while her dad read The Lion, The Witch and The Wardrobe to her through the doors, to heighten her excitement.

When they moved into The Manse, most of the furniture came with the house. A vicars life within the Methodist Church was certainly not extravagant or luxurious. While they had some of their own things, most of the furniture was inherited, from minister to minister and family to family. On occasions this customary practice created real frustration with the inherent family moving into their new home, to find worn out or uncomfortable furniture, heating or plumbing that didn't work properly and despite "Christianity" and the underlying teaching of love and treating people fairly, the financial aspects of providing a ministers salary very often didn't stretch to providing money for the luxury of comfortable furniture or a house with fully functional facilities.

Ministers often had to fight for these things and when they did they ran the risk of being seen as materialistic.

Elaine collected John's pyjamas and toiletries and went back to the hospital, reassuring Rachel as she left that dad would be fine and home very soon.

"Look after Rachel please Paul until I get back."

"Where are you going? What's for tea? What's wrong with Rachel?"

"Hospital, nothing and nothing, just look after Rachel until I get back."

Paul looked questioningly at his mother as she tumbled out of the ageing wooden red front door, her hands juggling the bag of John's things as she opening the door, trying to hug Rachel again as she did, while trying to waive and point at Paul to emphasise the urgency and importance of her instruction, without wanting to sound in a panic or wanting to upset Rachel or say anything that would prompt Paul to ask even more untimely questions.

Paul watched his mother drive off and then turned and looked at Rachel as he ran his hands through his straight black hair. "Do you want my speciality, beans of toast?"

Rachel smiled as she gave him a fun punch in his left side.

CHAPTER 27

The ward felt just as busy at 11am as it had done the day before at 7.30. when Elaine had left John the night before.

"How is John Rowlands?" Elaine asked the young male nurse on the reception desk of ward D7.

"He had a good night's sleep and then he was telling me this morning about the baby that was drowned and that he had to bury. I felt so sorry for him as well as that little baby, he was so emotional about it and the fact that it only happened yesterday, and now he's in here! That's a rough twenty four hours in anyone's book, especially with the father punching John at the end of the service. That really is rough."

The male nurse put his pen down and lent on the desk as he looked directly at Elaine, another patients concerned relative, his demeanour conveying a genuine feeling that he cared about her husband. She instantly felt he was her friend but still resisted her immediate reaction to correct what he had just said.

Her mind went to seven years ago and their previous placement in a small village in Worcestershire and the three year old that fell into the pond when feeding the ducks with his nan. John had conducted that service with dignity and compassion, despite the fact that it had been so upsetting for everyone present, including John, who Elaine remembers, related the death of that little boy to "what if it had been Rebecca"; at that time their youngest child who had been eight. Luckily throughout his ministry and their life together, that funeral had been the only one John had to conduct for a child younger than seventeen and it had a strong affect on him. He had become even more protective and sentimental over their children, trying to remember each and every event their children experienced.

"Shall I take you to his room?" His question brought Elaine back to the reception desk.

"Yes, let's go and see if he's getting better." She felt her comment was a bit optimistic given the circumstances and knew it must have sounded so, the instant she heard her own words.

The nurse smiled and drew her towards him and John's room as he walked down the ward's corridor with his left hand extended towards Elaine.

"John, your wife is here." Charge Nurse Michael James walked through the open door to look at the empty bed. He turned to look at Elaine. He must be in the toilet, I'll go and check."

"He's not in the toilet but give me a minute and I'll have a little wander to see if I can find out where he is. Does he smoke?" Elaine gasped her next breath, a slight anxiousness within her surprise at Michael walking back into the room.

"Uh no."

"So it's unlikely that he's slipped outside for a puff. Give me a couple of minutes."

Michael left feeling very confident at finding John Rowlands.

Elaine looked at the water jug and the next twenty minutes disappeared between daydreams, speculation and blankness; her tiredness switching her mind through various levels of awareness as she sat on the bed, holding her brown handbag's handle with both hands looking........... at that jug of water on the bedside locker. She imagined the little boy drowning and she felt herself holding her breath.

She caught sight of her reflection in the mirror on the wall and stared, now taking a breath as she noticed her reddened complexion; hoping her reflection would materialise into something different to what she was seeing. Elaine sighed as she twisted the handles of her brown handbag, ringing out her frustration and tiredness through the leather. "Oh lord, look at my hair!" She ran her fingers through her black wavy shoulder length hair, which she hadn't washed for two days. She had always had naturally greasy hair which now at forty four looked the hair of a younger woman but she liked to wash it every day.

John loved the wave and life in her hair and she now felt that she would disappoint him when he saw her appearance. The last two days had been "a rush" and abnormal to say the least and Elaine wondered why in their so normal and loving life "this" was happening. She looked at herself from different angles by moving her head around, looking through her right blue eye at her reflection and then through her left green eye. Her reflection didn't look any different regardless of which eye she predominantly looked through.

She switched her head from side to side as she studied her features "oh Geebee," she said to herself, using John's pet name for her, on account of her one green eye and one blue eye; which "when you put them together" John had said on their third date twenty three years ago, "they make Geebee."

That was the real start of their relationship as he made her self consciousness of her mis matched eyes almost totally disappear with the tender way he made reference to them for the first time on that third date, with him christening her jokingly with his special name, accompanied by the most wonderful loving hug. From that moment she had felt secure and their courtship had developed very quickly.

She rubbed herself with both hands as if to erase the laughter lines around her eyes, pulling the skin behind her cheeks back towards her ears, tightening her features. She saw the twenty one year old that had become hidden behind twenty three years and three children. Her legs were still shapely and she appreciated their lasting with a youthfulness to the age she was now as she rotated her feet and watched her calf muscles flex in the mirror. Her mind jumped back to her school days and all the sport she had taken part in and put their firmness down to their development during her youth when she competed and played netball, hockey, athletics and everything that she could possibly have got involved in during her teens. She loved sport then and loved it now and managed to play badminton twice a week for a league club but given a chance and a lack of responsibilities, would be doing more. Her mind imagined some "what if's" as it focused on the water jug.

"Would you like a cup of tea?; Mrs Rowlands.... would you like a cup of tea?"

"What's wrong ?, where's John?" Her mind came back to total focus on hearing Michael's question.

"Uhh I don't know, we don't know. I've asked around and gone to other wards and to the concourse and no one has seen him."

Elaine felt her anxiety rise "You've lost John?" Her agitation made the young nurse feel awkward at his admission that a patient had been lost.

Her drive back home was frantic, her mind whirling as it had the night before, her thoughts regurgitating the distress of yesterday but now with added nausea that anticipation injected with speculation created.

"John, John, are you here?" Elaine flew in through the front door, spinning along the passageway towards the kitchen, calling to upstairs, her head rotating in the opposite direction to her body's arc, trying to cover every inch of the house in order to find John.

"John where are you?" Her voice now had risen to three quarters of its maximum volume, the strain had anyone been listening, would have been obvious.

Elaine's eyes looked skywards.......................nothing!

CHAPTER 28

"How long does this all last then butt? We need to wet the babies head after this."

The father's striped silver and grey tie was bulging in a big ungracious knot and didn't go with the dark brown and purple paisley shirt and black jacket. He had a little, yet fat round head, with flattened down greasy black hair which certainly didn't look like he had washed it for this special occasion. He looked down on Mr. Evans who at five foot seven hated looking up to someone five foot nine and some slob, with greasy hair.

"This must mean a lot to you," he thought sarcastically, "you've even gone to the trouble of not washing your hair for this special occasion. I washed mine this morning, it was easy, just some water and shampoo." He touched his own brown hair and caught a glimpse of his reflection in one of the newly replaced vestibule windows. "Try and be nice," he thought but was finding it difficult as he had taken an instant dislike to the father.

Mike was about to move but hesitated as he saw his reflection fade as if a veil had been drapped across the glass. He stared at the misted up windows, unaware of the similar occurence on the day the pews were delivered. He wiped his forefinger across the glass, expecting it to leave a trace of transparency. It remained misted. He looked at his finger and then back at the glass, his brain questioning what he was trying to analyse; logic ?

His attention was brought back to the father. He now also noticed that the jacket was a different black to the father's trousers but what instantly irritated him was the rush to get the Christening service over before it had even begun, just to get to the pub or club or wherever for where "the head wetting ceremony" was to take place.

He watched the Christening party shuffle past him, the dark haired and very recently birth giving mother holding the baby girl to be committed to God, with curly black hair and dark brown eyes, dressed in an exceptionally frilly white dress; her mother oozing love at holding her first child, her own excitement at her first ever Christening and it being for her own first born, swelling her emotions and trepidation. Her actions appeared erratic, her attention quickly switching from one person to the next, as each one of the party shifted position within the group, all eager to look at and touch the baby while talking to the mother at the same time, on their way into the church.

Mike Evans watched their confusion in looking at each other in an effort to know what to do next, despite his gestures and instructions to "please go down to the front pews," they all entered through the left side, inner porch doors into the church and their hesitation to walk to the front pews, drew them together as a flock.

After about a minute or so of repetition, Mike started to feel less than Christian. He rubbed his fingertips with frustration into the sockets of his eyes and enjoyed the gentle pressure sensation he felt on his blue eyes underneath, like scratching an itch.

"For pity sake, you only have to walk to a seat, I've told you where it is, so why are you all standing in the same spot. I bet you lot haven't been in a church since you were Christened, if ever!" His thoughts drew in assumptions and added speculation, conclusions.......condemnation.

The elation of the event bonded everyone together, their expressions and emotions exchanging within the glances and the looks each gave and received from each other. The whole group moved down the left aisle, looking for a space in the completely vacant pews, confused as to where they should sit. No one wanted to go to the front, to be on show; everyone wanted the anonymity of the small crowd that were there to celebrate.

The move towards the centre pews was unanimous, a congealed thought between twenty three separate minds and all sat within four rows of each other, clustered in an erratic circle to the centre of the church.

Mike Evans walked down the same aisle towards the front of the church, his thoughts no more understanding to their awkwardness. His mind looked for the reassurance that John Rowlands would turn up to conduct this christening rather than he being put in the position as Lay Preacher to carry out the ceremony, for the bewildered ingrates that had just entered "his" church. As he walked deeper into the church, towards the crucifix on the front wall, he told himself to exercise patience and compassion. He turned his head to look at the baby still being held by her mother. He smiled and made eye contact with the mother who glanced up and smiled back, her excitement still evident on her face. His thoughts were still looking for the minister to be the answer to the anxiety he was feeling.

When he arrived at the front of the church, he knew he felt less than confident, given the emotions he was aware of and the conflict that he knew he was in, with the feelings and demeanour he should be conveying to the christening party. He rubbed the flat of his hands down either side of his head, his fingers pushing through his hair, coming together as they reached the back of his neck. Mike smiled as his hands pulled down the back of his neck. He looked at the twenty or so people. His glasses felt a little uncomfortable on the bridge of his nose. He lifted them off and rubbed his nose where they were resting. Mike looked out again at the christening party and tried to maintain his smile.

"Mum, Dad, everyone, sorry I wasn't here to greet you on this very special day for you and for Christine. I'm sorry about my appearance, I had a bit of an accident but I hope that won't spoil things for today; after all, today is about Christine and you Mark and Tina and of course all of the rest of you, Christine's family, your friends, all of who will have a place in Christine's life and who will I'm sure, help Christine to have a happy upbringing with God and love in her life." John's words and beckoning gestures instantly conveyed reassurance, command, love and authority from behind the communion rail that divided the front of the church to the alter and pulpit, the deep blue carpet that lay throughout the church, divided by the light oak rail and spindles.

Mike Evans heard the slight slur in his voice and immediately put it down to whatever pain killing drugs the hospital would have given him. He felt his own anxiety demolished at the sound of John's voice from behind him, whether affected or not and a warmth of reassurance and calmness permeated his body at feeling John' s right hand on his right shoulder.

"Thank you Mike for meeting everyone, let's get things going, I feel a thirst coming on."

"What?" Mike thought, turning in surprise to face John at hearing his last comment.

"You've got to wet the baby's head as well as the cross of baptism water, isn't that right everyone." John turned his question to the small congregation after Mike's questioning look.

Mike wasn't sure if this was the real Reverend John Rowlands or a clever way to endear himself to these people, all too eager "to get it down their necks."

"That's right Rev, the first round is on you!" The baby's father called out on hearing a suggestion he agreed with, come from an unexpected ally, from a minister.

"Uuhh!" The left elbow from his wife on his right side was matched at the same time with an elbow from his own mother on his left side, both feeling sharp and meaningful as they made contact with his ribs.

"Sshh." Both women issued the same admonishment. "Show some respect. You can't say that to a minister."

"Why not? He seems a good bloke." The correction eluded his intelligence, he felt the laughter from the others in the christening party substantiated his humour. He caught the smile on John's face and this added to his confidence.

"The first hymn, one which seems to be a favourite at most christenings, All Things Bright and Beautiful." John smiled at the party and turned towards Mike Evans who had retreated to the front wall, just right of the crucifix above him. Mike saw John lift his eyes to look at the figurine of Jesus. The expression on John's face was not one Mike had seen during the few other christenings when he had aided John, nor during any of the other church ceremonies that John had conducted. It was a look the conveyed impatience, annoyance. It was a look that disappeared as he turned towards the Christening congregation.

The organist started the introduction by playing the melody of the first two lines while everyone stood up and adjusted themselves ready to sing.

Mike dropped his head as he heard what he considered yet another feeble attempt from a group of people who hadn't been inside a church most probably since their own wedding or christening. He tried to push some volume into the hymn, to encourage them to sing with more conviction, to enjoy the opportunity to sing in this special service for this little girl. He glanced up, at least six people were just staring at the order of service in their hands, making no effort to join in.

He watched Tina cradling her baby in the crook of her right arm, holding the order of service with her right hand, singing boisterously to her daughter while rubbing her tummy with her left hand. Mike saw every part of this young mother trying to infuse the memory of this occasion into the mind of this infant by wanting her to react to all the attention she was receiving, to enjoy it as much as she was.

Mike then watched the father. He was one of the people not singing, just looking blankly at the order of service rather than the words on the page, his head twitching and moving in a way that wanted to convey participation without making any effort.

"What a waste of time this was going to be," he thought to himself. "This bloke won't make any attempt to raise his daughter with any sort of belief in Jesus or God. He would probably have difficulty making the connection between Jesus and God." He caught himself thinking these thoughts and just for one moment wondered if he had thought or spoken them out aloud. He didn't need to look at the words of All Things, having sung them thousands of times and this thought brought him back to a more conscious awareness of where he was.

He corrected his first thought about the father. He was not staring at the words but the back of the pew which he was holding, now rubbing it gently with his left hand.

Mark was running his hand side to side along the top of the back rest, watching the wood slip into or emerge from the V shape formed by his thumb, finger and the palm of his hand He looked entranced, like a small boy watching a magician slipping a length of rope through his hands about to transform it or make it disappear.

The hymn finished and the party all sat down, most relieved at reaching the end of the fifth chorus after five verses.

Tina's mother had been reminded of going to chapel with her own grandmother some forty years ago when she was six and singing this hymn. The memory rekindled everything her grandmother had been to her. She looked around at the church and her memories of sitting next to her grandmother enveloped her with a warmth that she had forgotten and she felt the surge of love for her nan fill her. She visualised her sitting next to her and she felt guilty at forgetting the affection and love that she had had for her nan, the bond, the cuddles they had shared and now she wanted to do the same for her first granddaughter. "Why had she stopped coming to church?" This had meant so much when she was a little girl and right up to the time when Tina had been christened in this very church and she now felt that she wanted to do the same with her own grand daughter.

Elizabeth Webb joined Tina in rubbing the baby's tummy, their two hands joined by a third, that of Mark's mother who had lent in across Mark from his left to join the mix of fingers scurrying around the lace of the christening dress, just to make sure she was not left out and that HER granddaughter would remember she was there as well.

Mark looked down for a second at all the hands on his daughter.

"Come on grans, sit back and let the Minister get on with it." His whisper was well intentioned but not quiet enough not to be heard by John who had walked over to the font.

"The life of this child is a precious thing. It is something to be enjoyed, shared, nurtured, protected, loved. Loved with any intensity that would out blaze the fires of hell itself. This child should be loved with a passion greater than the passion through which she was conceived. She should command your every attention and your unfaltering support, no matter what.

Her life is a gift, a gift that not everyone is fortunate to receive. As she grows, it is for you to teach her and to show her the love that Jesus Christ our Lord has for her and that you have for her, so that in and throughout her life, the love you bring to this alter and the commitment that you are making today, before God and before all your family and friends, stays foremost in her mind and in her life. She should see the love you have for each other and for her, made partially through this commitment and your own dedication of her here today, to be given a Christian upbringing and through the way you live your own lives with Jesus within your hearts and those same Christian principals which take you through each day of your lives together."

John's words made people feel uneasy and elated at the same time. The passion and command with which he delivered this "preparation" to the parents and Godparents, just before inviting them to join him at the font, made people realise that this was more than a prequel to the after service drink and buffet.

Mark continued to stroke the top of the pew in front as he partly listened to the minister. His attention wained at the part where John mentioned teaching her about Jesus.

"He's not such a good bloke after all. They're all the same! As soon as you're in church they start working on you, talking about Jesus. Why can't they just do the service and let us get on with our lives. If I wanted to learn about Jesus I'd read a book or something. There must be a book on him somewhere!"

John looked directly at Mark as if he had heard his thoughts as words spoken directly to his face.

The Reverend felt a ripple of despair. His immediate thought losing its sincerity. His expression was completely missed by Mark who's natural smile had transformed into a rigid grin. Tina did however notice the narrowing of the baptising ministers eyes and felt momentarily awkward.

John held out his hand towards the young mother as she and Mark arrived facing him at the font.

She watched as he smoothed her baby's right cheek with the back of his right index finger.

Tina noticed the angry, red discolouration and open wound on his right thumb where it became part of the palm of his hand. There was a sense of relief that it wasn't bleeding but her concerns rose. "What if it did? His hand could bleed onto Christine or her christening dress."

Her thoughts were stopped. "Who else should be standing here with the parents?"

Tina and Mark turned around to beckon the other hesitant godparents who were still deciding whether they should be walking out to the front or whether they should be sitting down.

John inwardly sighed even more, his reverence still not fully restored after Mark's thoughts as he watched six of the party walk towards him, huddled together as they shuffled forward, each one happy when one of the others slipped in front, their positions changing continuously as they moved down the isle, each person politely encouraging the other to go to the front, to be the first.

John watched them stumbling and tripping over each others feet, enjoying the weaving and twisting of their bodies as they recoiled or withdrew from the lead; a spaghetti of arms and hands, waiving, back pushing, pointing and felt a stifled laugh

leave his mouth as his amusement at this flock of godparents momentarily over took his self control.

Tina noticed his snigger and the smiling, fleeting sinister expression that passed across his face as he watched them come to the front of the church. She felt uneasy again. Tina looked at Mark but he had not noticed the minister's face which had started to laugh out aloud at the stumbling shambles of friends and relatives, their self consciousness at trying to be correct, contributing to the meandering calamity.

"Well we certainly have a mixture here for Christine!, don't we Christine?" John's comments came across with humorous edge and were accompanied by his open arms welcoming, encouraging the party to stand next to Mark and Tina, his gestures and persona completely different from ten seconds before. Tina noticed the difference.

"What are all your names. It is lovely to see so many people wanting to be godparents to this beautiful little girl." The back of his index finger again stroked Christine's cheek, the sweep of his nail tickling her right temple as it past on its way to tracking across her forehead, its speed slowing against her skin, his smile widening, Tina's attention becoming more focused on the minister, his euphoria evident, his facial expression beaming from underneath his reddened, swollen injuries of yesterday.

She turned to look at Mark but her parents were already shouting out their names to John.

"Matthew and Sylvia," shouted Matthew. "We're James and Beth."

"Tina's my sister," said Beth.

"I'm Veronica, Tina has been my best friend since we were four and we always said that we would be each other's best friend forever and when we got older that we would be each other's godmother when the time came. I haven't got any children yet, Tina's the lucky one, I haven't even got a boy friend at the moment, well I have, well I mean I've got a boy friend but not a husband, not yet anyway, silly me, he couldn't come today, so I'm really happy to be here and to be a Godmother. When do I get to hold the baby or should I pour water over her head? Will she cry. Do all the babies you christen cry? Is the water cold? I.."

Her next comment was stopped by John putting his right hand on her left shoulder. "All in good time. It's just nice to have you here and I'm sure Tina.....and Mark are both happy that you are so eager."

John's smile helped his right hand momentarily control Veronica's excitement. He looked warmly at this bubbly, young, blond long haired godparent, her bright blue eyes full of life. Her smiled encompassed her whole face as she flicked her attention between the other members of the christening party, her hair swinging vigorously over the top of the collar of her aqua marine coloured dress.

"And who are you?" John said smiling at the red haired man in a long, dark charcoal grey coat who had ended up standing behind Veronica at the back of the group.

Everyone looked around to where John was looking, over Veronica's left shoulder but their focus was on Veronica. Veronica continued with her bombardment of information and questions, puzzled for a second as to why The Minister asked her who she was, when she had just told him. She just carried on.

"I know.... I talk too much, I try not to but I just do!"

Veronica's re engagement took John's attention away from the red haired man and his eyes returned to looking back at this excited godmother to be.

"Christine looks absolutely beautiful Tina, doesn't she everyone! What a fantastic dress. Is it new or has it been handed down through the family? Hang on, your mum dressed you in that dress for your christening. There's a picture of you on her kitchen dresser, next to the one of you and me on our first day at school. I'm right aren't I Sylvia?"

Sylvia smiled and nodded, her prematurely forty six year old long and curly greying hair bouncing, she looked at Veronica, still a little uncertain if she was allowed to say anything to anyone within this ceremony.

Tina's left hand reached out and squeezed her friends right wrist, her love transmitting through her grip, the squeeze being tender, her expression, her eyes calming the excitement her friend couldn't contain.

The man with the red hair moved slightly behind Veronica, catching John's eye again, his eyes focused on John. There was a glint of mischief as his expression said, "will we ever shut this woman up!"

John smiled, the direction of his smile made a few of the christening party turn to look in its direction; no recipient.

Christine stirred in Tina's cradling right arm, her legs stretched, her toes pointed, her hands outstretched, palms facing outwards as if she was pushing herself away from something, trying to bury herself deeper into the crook of her mothers arm.

Tina's uncle Arnold, her mother's brother watched the group of mostly his relations and Veronica, who he had seen growing up with his niece, gesticulating and chatting with the minister at the font. He couldn't catch everything that was being said as his hearing had got a lot worse in recent years. Still only sixty six and young for his age, just like his sister who was two years younger; the paper production factory and its noise over thirty five years had had its affect on this sense.

He glanced down at the back of the seat in front of him as he tried to analyse the group activity. Arnold wanted to be a part of everything within his family and was often the person who organised family do's.

His eyes, like others within the last two weeks were being drawn to the life permeating within the polished grain. The clarity of the voices from the front dimmed to a gentle kerfuffle as his concentration was captured by the pew. Arnold became aware of his right index finger tracing the swirls, his mind now seeing what he thought was a baby's crib, a small box like shape within the back of the pew, its association being influenced by the ongoing events.

Mary his wife, started to look at what he was doing, she too becoming distracted from the front of the church to where his finger was now caressing. She watched his finger for about thirty seconds and then looked up at him. "What are you doing. You should be watching what is going on out there, not wiggling your finger around the back of a seat! You should have worn your blue suit, it fits you better since you put on weight."

Arnold looked briefly at his wife as he smoothed his stomach through his buttoned up green tweed sports jacket. Mary rubbed the side of his head, just above his left ear, disturbing his well combed jet black hair, still without any signs of ageing, which often drew out Mary's mock envy. Arnold twitched his head away from her interfering fingers. She knew he hated having his hair messed up when he was out of the house. Arnold like it regimentally styled. He reviewed his fingers previous movements. "Can you see the picture of a baby's crib in the back ....of this seat, as you put it? Look here!" His finger drew around the shape as he saw it, its repeated action trying to draw Mary's eye to experience the picture he could see.

"It's the back of a church pew, you clown not a Picasso." Mary tried to keep her voice low. She sounded hissy as she jibbed at her husband.

"Look here, look, can't you see. There's the baby's crib and look, these bits look like bits of people standing by the crib." His finger moved with an urgency around the grain, his nail emphasising the outline of his vision.

"It"s the back of a church pew, I've told you! Now pay attention to what's happening out front rather than at the end of your finger." Mary glanced a look down as she flicked his fingering hand with her right hand, like giving a naughty school boy a clip. Arnold would always try to wind her up over things and Mary just thought that this was just another of those occasions.

"Besides, that doesn't look anything like that, if anything, that bit there looks like an axe blade and that bit there, looks like a basket for the head, see and here," her own fingers flicked all over the panelling as if to point out and correct him. "This bit here, see the swirly point and this a long coat,......all this bit looks like ..... like the Grim Reaper, oooohhhhh, can you see, look, nothing like a crib, look here, look."

Mary had become in an instant, as eager to explain the images she saw within these shapes and to correct her husband's misguidance. She didn't know she was seeing different images. The pews were deceitful.

"What! Where? It looks nothing like that! Where's that bit going?" He pushed her hand to one side so that he could point out the bit that he could see.

Mary pinched the back of his right thigh through his brown trousers. She was now feeling a bit mischievous and their marriage and courtship from when they first met fifty years ago, had always been one of teasing and playfulness, each trying to out do the other, each playing pranks or telling stories to wind each other up.

"Ouch!" Arnold reacted vigorously by gripping the back of his leg. Her pinch was unexpectedly harder than Mary intended.

"Shuuuush." Mary directed Arnold with her eyes to look back to the front of the church and to behave, even though she had been the cause of that disturbance.

A few of the christening party looked around when they heard uncle Arnold wince. Mary stood there smiling innocently back at Tina, Mark and Sylvia her sister in law as she casually brushed her coat and then flicked her eyes towards Arnold, raising her eyebrows and shaking her head ever so slightly, discreetly, to convey Arnold's misbehaviour.

Sylvia looked Mary up and down, taking in her pale green linen twin set and brown overcoat, giving her a joking, scolding look of admonishment.

The three relatives smiled. Sylvia laughed gently and wagged her finger playfully at her sister in law. All too often, she would gang up with Mary to tease her brother Arnold. They had been friends for years and all enjoyed the banter.

This occasion, now, felt happy, relaxed. Even though there was a group of seven at the font and sixteen still in the pews, it all felt as if everyone was involved.

"May I direct you all to follow the order of service and to respond.....with God's help we will, during the course of the commitment and prayers. We are here today Father, in your presence, to commit the life of this new born baby, to a life, to be lived in your name and to a life lived as a Christian, through the love and sacrifice made by your son Jesus Christ, our saviour. It is through his own teachings that we know children should be shown and encouraged to live a life as Jesus taught his followers and disciples during his time here on Earth."

John looked up at the immediate group and glanced to the remainder of the party in the pews. He raised his own order of service slightly to motion their response. His mouth opened and he hesitated as he drew the first and distinctly mumbled, "With God's help we will," out of both groups.

He glanced around very quickly, more so to reassure everyone that they were doing it correctly and that they should be more confident the next time.

The tall man behind Veronica shifted from side to side, slight smooth movements. It looked like he had not said anything during the response but John couldn't be certain as he had fleetingly tried to look at everyone during that first response.

"Father, we pray that you protect this innocent child, so that she may grow within her family." John paused ever so slightly to look at Mark and Tina, his smile comforting at first, the parents reacting to his warmth but both noticed his eyes changed their expression while his smile remained unaltered; his eyes urging compliance, "and that your parents will love and protect you from harm and evil."

His second pause and look indicated the second response. "With God's help we will."

There was more volume and commitment, more clarity from both groups.

"Father we pray for this child's parents, that they may know and feel your heavenly love and that they teach their child to live with your love in her heart."

Everyone bar one, John saw responded, "with God's help we will."

"At last," Mike Evans thought. He deliberately held his breath as he was conscious that if he let it go it would be heard as a huge sigh in that few seconds of silence which followed the response. Mike continued to smile and be discreet to the rear of John and let the air flow out through touching teeth as John continued with the service.

John looked up and again caught sight of the slowly, gently oscillating man in the very dark grey to black coat as he now noted, standing behind Veronica and now noticed the hat he was wearing which obscured most of his face and long red hair. John instantly questioned himself as whether he had been wearing it when he first noticed him. He couldn't remember but felt more convinced he had not participated in the second response and now knew he did not do so in the third.

"We pray to Jesus Christ our saviour, who died for us on the cross and who's love for children was borne by the words when he said suffer not the little children to come unto me; we pray now for the eternal soul of this infant and in who's name she is christened." John held out his arms to Tina, motioning her to pass him the baby.

Mike Evans looked on, wondering why John had left the printed order of service and was to his mind, improvising! He felt a little uncomfortable as this left the order of things and Mike liked order in everything. His whole character revolved around control. Mike had become an accountant after considering the meaning of numbers. They were right or wrong. There was one right answer, no interpretation as to was this a better answer than that one because there was only one answer.

Tina looked at Veronica quizzically as she had been following the order of service passionately, so as to get the most out this experience as possible, to remember for Christine. Both saw the digression and this made Tina hold back momentarily. Her look said "Should I do it?"

Tina looked at Mark for reassurance but he hadn't been following the printed order but had kept looking at The Minister who kept talking about God and Jesus all the time. "Why is Jesus so flipping important?" he thought to himself. He found this really annoying the longer it went on.

John saw out of the corner of his eye, the red haired man move from directly behind Veronica and out to the side and away from the group slightly. He thought that he probably wanted a better view.

"With God's help we will...with God's .... with God's help we will ....we will." John lead the response but the party had lost it cohesion, confused as the words he had just spoken were not on the sheets they were following.

John remained standing with his arms outstretched in front of him, the long open cuffs of his cassock hanging more like the sleeves associated to that of a Shaolin monk. He liked wearing this cassock as its movement looked dramatic and he consciously used that movement on times for theatrical affect.

Arnold looked at the end of the finger he had been using to point around the pew. It had turned a dark red. Mary frowned questioningly as he held it up in front of her eyes. She pushed his hand to one side so that she could see what was happening out the front. She got a tissue of of her pocket and gave it to Arnold. "Here!"

"Ta but why is it red?" Arnold sniffed the end of his finger. "It smells like blood."

"Blood! How can it be blood? Have you cut yourself playing with that seat?"

Arnold's face squinted with an accompanying expression which conveyed to Mary how stupid he thought her comment was.

"Well? Have you? I don't believe you, you've just got to fiddle with things. That's what's important, out there," but Mary still rubbed the back of pew where she had seen the axe a couple of minutes before to see if her finger went red as well.

"It's not coming off very easily. I'm sure it is blood. It smells like blood." Arnold was still distracted and showed Mary the end of his finger again.

"Will you stop fussing with your stupid finger." Mary looked down again at the back of the pew, more so to reassure herself that there couldn't be blood on the back of the pew and that she was right to be scolding Arnold. The grain again hinted at the basket she had seen earlier but this time there were some features, the illusion of an eye, the side of a forehead, some hair. It had some familiarity about it. She looked back to the front and then down again to the pew. The grain maintained its image and she looked with more purpose to try and fathom out why these extra images felt familiar.

Tina stepped forward to pass Christine to the outstretched arms of the waiting minister. John's smile was still beaming. As Tina lay Christine into John's arm, the baby tried catching hold of everything that came within her fingers grasp. She wriggled. Her twisting and turning could not find a way out from John's hold. Her tiny feet pointed her white knitted boots from her effort, her hands and arms outstretched, pushing now by comparison to clutching.

John looked up from the baby to her parents, his look also taking in and registering the five other members of the christening party. The red haired man had moved away from Veronica. John shifted slightly to look around Mark but he couldn't see this sixth member of the party.

Christine's gurgling brought John's attention back to the baby he was holding. Cradled now in his left arm, he stroked her cheek again with his right index finger. The baby now fully awake looked at the finger, then towards the hand and then followed on upwards to look in the direction of John's smiling face.

"Doesn't she look gorgeous... Oops sorry." Veronica capped her mouth with her right hand, thinking she had spoken out of turn. John took her excitement. "Yes she does!" He looked back to his order of service.

"We pray for the family and friends of this child, that they should love and cherish her as they watch her grow. We pray that they will be there, for her and for Tina and Mark, to lend support and comfort, help and guidance in the years ahead."

John glanced up and around, still no red haired man. "With God's help we will." There was enthusiasm with this last response as all in the party now felt confident as a result of the repetition and the fact most had realised it was the last time they had to say anything.

Arnold had licked the tissue and had rubbed his finger through most of the prayers, looking over to Mary's order of service when he needed to respond. Despite his finger, he had given some attention to the font and the handing of his new niece to the vicar. He wondered how this minister had so many facial injuries. It wasn't the usual thing you would expect to see.

John whirled around, his cassock splaying out with the speed of his rotation, lifting the still gurgling baby upwards and over his head, offering her to the crucifix on the wall at the front of the church.

"Behold a new life, a life filled with innocence, given to her parents by your grace."

Everyone was startled.

Tina instinctively stepped forward, hands rising as if to take the pass of a rugby ball.

Mark continued to look at The Minister thinking frustratingly to himself, "what's this all about now. Surely there's not more ceremony. Just get to the part where you give her her name, then we can go."

Mathew and Sylvia instantly mirrored their daughter's action and jerked forward towards the font, a mixture of support and reaction.

Mike Evans' eyes and mouth opened simultaneously, "what is John doing? He's never done this before." His thoughts formed the features on his face.

Tina caught sight of Mike's reaction.

"Eeee, is this exciting. I hope my baby's christening is like this." Tina felt Veronica grip her left elbow. She looked back at Veronica. Veronica again capped her mouth as her brain caught up to her verbal reaction.

Veronica's comment instantly diluted Tina's initial panic and she felt a sigh of relief ripple through her body.

Further back in the pews there were mixed levels of reaction to John's offering of Christine to Jesus. Most thought that this was how a christening should be. The presentation of an innocent soul to God, before an alter, to a crucifix, a big bible, in fact anything "holy."

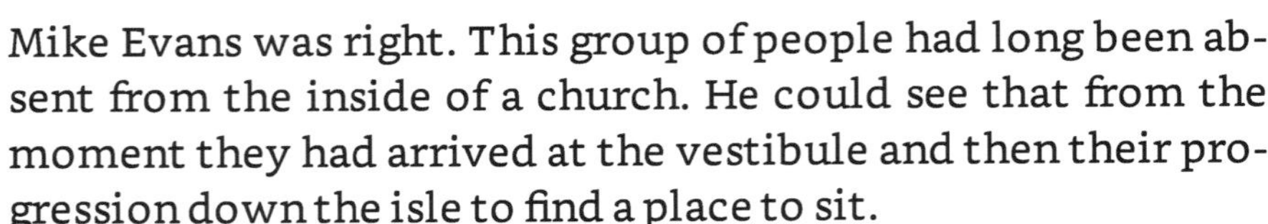

Mike Evans was right. This group of people had long been absent from the inside of a church. He could see that from the moment they had arrived at the vestibule and then their progression down the isle to find a place to sit.

Mary and Arnold he saw, in that fraction of a second, when people's reactions were animated to John's unexpected and out of character uplifting of this innocent infant to the front wall and the effigy of Christ; were the most visible.

Mary had sat down, covering her mouth and cheeks with both hands. Her heart felt in her mouth. She had never seen any

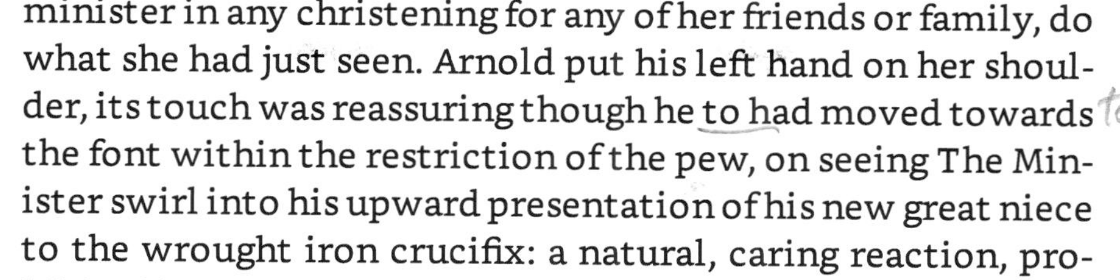

minister in any christening for any of her friends or family, do what she had just seen. Arnold put his left hand on her shoulder, its touch was reassuring though he to had moved towards the font within the restriction of the pew, on seeing The Minister swirl into his upward presentation of his new great niece to the wrought iron crucifix: a natural, caring reaction, prohibited by the physical barrier of the back of the pew in front.

In a few seconds there was restraint. John continued with his unconventional committal of the baby he was holding to his beloved God as he stood erect, meaningful; the tiny white frilly dress clad baby, apparently unstressed, being held some seven to eight feet above the floor, facing a tortured, gnarled, irregular, impressionistic sculpture of The Son of God.

"Father in heaven, this child is the future for this world and of this family, gathered here today, to show their love and support, as we christen this innocent, beautiful little girl. She is the start of life, to continue the life of this family, to be part of this family, to share and learn of its history and to become to others that will follow her, history, that they to will learn from and follow, in the same way that she will learn, in the years ahead of her."

Veronica squeezed Tina's elbow again. "This is the best christening I've been to." Tina felt more relaxed by the fact that her best friend thought this was normal. Tina looked directly at Veronica and then thought, "this is the only christening you've ever been to!" Her own disbelief started to rise again, as quickly as it had just fallen.

John turned to face the parents and godparents standing immediately before him. "You are all, you will be all, accountable for the external soul of this child that I show now to our Lord and Saviour." His eyes made contact with the Mark and Tina and then with all five others standing at the font. He looked around for the red haired man who was still missing.

"This is one for the photo album," Arnold said to Mary who had remained sitting down with Arnold's hand still on her shoulder.

"What if he drops the baby? Oh God Arnold, what if he drops the baby!"

"He won't, I'm sure he does this every week. It's unusual I admit but you've got to be fair, he has made you think that all this is important."

Arnold's fingers massaged his wife's shoulder. She looked up at him as he took a quick photo with their digital camera. Her hands lowered to rest on the top of the pew in front.

Mary's eyes caught sight of the panelling which had lured her attention minutes before. The image was still evident. Her mind instantly reformed the picture of the basket and the previous fashioning of features became enhanced very quickly. She could see the same side of this face and Mary now saw this as the face of a woman. The features were soft and rounded. The grain meandered the shape of her cheek bone. The eye and eye brows, the shape of the socket within the face, this fundamental feature of a persons face, now so clear to her, a young girl, with long wispy hair.

"Ooh!" Mary jumped, her attention back to The Minister who had reassumed his theatrical offering.

"This child's soul is so precious, so special to You, our Father in Heaven and to all within The Church here today. Let her be able to see the beauty of your love, your Earth, The Earth that you created for Adam the first man and for Eve." John swooped around the floor space in front of the alter, the crucifix looking down on the transported baby, John swapping her from above his head, held with both hands, his arms at full extent; to cradling her back in his arms. He repeated this movement 4 times as he spoke, the sound of his heavy cassock and gapping sleeves swishing with his energy.

Mike saw the anxiety on Tina's face. He moved forward slightly with the partial thought he should grab hold of John to calm him but he stopped himself, his own quandary rising as he thought of yesterday. He didn't want a repeat of anything like that, especially with a baby involved.

John came back to stand at the font. He looked triumphant.

The gurgles from the baby brought everyone's heads to look into the crook of John's left arm. There were relieved laughs and sighs. Tina tickled her daughter's tummy.

John looked up from the baby. The red haired man was standing right next to him, his face within inches from John's face. There was a slight trickle of blood on the side of John's forehead which had leaked out from under the bandage, forced out by John's exertion.

The red haired man pointed to it, his face expressionless but mostly obscured from John's direct sight by his outstretched hand which was right in front of his face. He said nothing to help John know what he was pointing at.

John stood there for a second, his senses trying to establish what was being pointed out to him. He felt a slight pulsing from the area covered by the bandage and the warmth of his own blood on his skin.

"Hold your God daughter for one second," he said, handing the baby to Veronica.

"Ooh is it all done? Am I a godmother now. I can't believe it! I'm your godmother."

"Not quite yet," John said as he turned away to wipe the blood away with his handkerchief, slipping a finger under the hospital dressing slightly to hopefully stop any further trickle from coming out from underneath the bandage.

The red haired man swayed back to allow John to turn away from the group. John smiled at Mike and wondered in that second of eye contact, why Mike looked poised to do something.

John turned back and held out his arms to receive the baby back from Veronica.

"Who are going to be this beautiful little girl's godparents........apart from I know, Veronica." John held out his right hand towards Veronica in a way that instructed her not to say anything.

The group laughed. "It's the two of us and mum and dad as well." James the six foot two husband of Beth spoke up as he gestured towards Veronica, himself, Matthew and Sylvia

"And what about...?" John stopped his question as he caught sight of the silent red haired man sit down next to Mary. Arnold looked down towards his wife as she adjusted her seating position a little, so she would be comfortable to see the wetting of the baby's head.

John immediately thought that he had made the mistake of assuming that man was going to be a godparent as well.

"We come into this life with nothing, nothing but the love of our parents for giving us life. Our lives should be filled with love and as we grow, so should the love we receive from our parents and godparents who are here today, to witness this christening and to commit themselves with the bring up of the little girl.

It is your duty specifically to ensure as her godparents, that she is introduced to the teachings of the church and to be brought up with a belief and understanding of God and of his son Jesus Christ."

"Thank God they've got to do that bit," Mark thought to himself.

John stopped looking around at the group and stared at Mark. Mark looked directly back and felt on this occasion his thoughts must have been conveyed. He tugged on the bottom of both sides of his jacket as if to emphasise that he had had his say and to portray he was comfortable with the situation.

"I'll certainly do that! Do I bring her here every Sunday, to Sunday school. What time does it start?"

Everyone in the church looked at Veronica and laughed, including a small almost cynical smile from the red haired man next to Mary.

"I'm sure you will but it's a bit soon for Sunday school but when the time comes, we would love to see both of you here, in fact, we would love to see all of you here, including you Mark." John's laughed response tailed off and turned to an eyebrow lifted look at Mark.

"I call upon these persons present and in the sight of God, to witness the Christening of this baby girl, into the family of the church and into the family stood before your alter. May they love you, protect you, cherish you, teach you and be there for you throughout your life and through their lives."

John turned a full circle holding the baby high again. Only Mike wondered, "what on earth is he doing. These aren't the right words and all this offering; it feels more like a pagan sacrifice than a christening."

He felt himself subconsciously move forward.

"I christen you Claudia, Elsbeth, in the name of The Father, The Son and The Holy Spirit." John touched her head with the water from the font. It trickled down her nose and left cheek.

Tina and Mark gripped each other's hand tightly. They had been mouthing her names to themselves as John was speaking. How could he have got her names wrong? How could he christen her with the wrong names? They looked at each other, their disbelief distilled into anger.

"Oohhh, you picked different names." Veronica virtually took Claudia out of John's arms "Hello Claudia, I'm Veronica your new godmother. This is Sylvia......." Veronica was bouncing Claudia in her left arm as she started to show her to the other dumb struck godparents.

"Won't you have to change her name on the birth certificate now she's been christened?"

"We haven't changed her name. It's Christine Elizabeth Mary not Claudia .....Elbert or whatever he said." Tina's previous anxiety with John's theatrics had fermented long enough with the five seconds of feeling angry and upset at hearing Christine being christened Claudia and she exploded.

"What on earth are you doing? You just christened my baby with the wrong names. What the hell is going on? Did you know about this?" She looked at Mike who had started to make his way to the font, his mouth open with surprise and shock. He had known the selected names from seeing them in the church diary in the office before the christening party and John's arrival.

In the six steps it took him to arrive at John's side everyone of the party were all talking, asking questions and then accusing all at once.

Some of those standing in the pews had started to make their way to the front of the church. Mary remained seated. John's eye still caught a glimpse of the red haired man who was now standing next to Mary, bend down as if to say something in her ear so that she would hear it above the commotion at the font.

"Have you seen enough? I think it's time to leave here. Come."

Mary looked up as she felt a hand touch her head.

John saw the faintest glint of silver as the red haired man turned by the side of Mary.

CHAPTER 29

Mal walked over from his chip shop on seeing the ambulance parked up for ten minutes in front of the church. As he crossed the road, he watched the paramedics carry the trolley down the steps with the help of some other men. Obviously they had been in the church and as it wasn't a funeral, as there would have been hearse where the ambulance was parked; he thought either wedding or christening.

As he got closer he could see most of the other people following and congregating around the trolley were crying. The body was covered by a blanket so he couldn't tell if was a man or a woman.

He caught sight of John and his facial injuries. "What happened to you? Have you been in a car accident? Are you ok? What's happening here?"

"Give me a moment Mal."John ran his hand partway along Mal's forearm both as a sign of reassurance and as a way of stopping Mal from asking further questions.

The ambulance doors were closed by the two paramedics. "We'll take the body to the Royal. I'm really sorry, there was nothing we could have done, more than we did inside."

"Are you sure it's what you said, a brain haemorrhage?"

"Well as far as we can be. There will be a postmortem, probably, unless her medical records indicate something that we don't know about at this stage but a brain haemorrhage like that when they go that quick, it's like.....it's like having your head cut off. Your brain loses all contact instantly with the rest of your body. In one way I think it's the best way to go, quick, no suffering, it's just harder on the people who are left. Do you think her husband will want to come in the ambulance with her?"

"I'll go and ask him but I think it's best personally if he stays with his family." John walked back up the steps, acutely conscience of the crying members of this family, their looks towards him, their grief evident and completely unexpected considering they should be leaving to wet the baby's head and the entire occasion should have been one of elation and celebration.

He walked back down the left isle to where Tina, Sylvia, Veronica and Beth were sitting. Tina was holding Christine who had fallen asleep. Between them and through their own tears and sobbing, they were trying to console Arnold, who was gripping onto the edges of the pew in an effort to carry himself through to his next breath.

"Excuse me Arnold, the paramedics are asking if you want to ride with Mary in the ambulance."

"Oh no Arnold, you stay with us. There's nothing you,....there's nothing anyone of us can do." Sylvia put her arms back around her brother and the sobbing women and Arnold cried more uncontrollably.

"I'll tell the paramedics."John turned slowly to go back out to the paramedics, aware that every sound, every movement he made would aggravate them.

"No you won't. You've done enough damage today. You've spoilt my first grand daughter's christening, my daughter is beside herself because of it and now this."

Sylvia's aggression toward John was understandable to John, who said nothing. Her tone changed to a so softly spoken but forceful, loving encouragement. "Come on Arnold let's go, come on, come on." Sylvia repeated herself as she gently tried to prize Arnold up off the pew he was still crushing with his gripping hands.

Beth took his other arm and mirrored what her mother was doing to her uncle. He watched them walk slowly along the right isle to go out of the church.

John walked into the row of pews where Arnold and Mary had been sitting and sat down.

Mike Evans walked back in from outside where he had been standing with the other men on the steps after helping with the trolley and sat in the pew in front of John. He turned backwards from where he was sitting and put his hand on the back of John's bowing neck. A few silent moments passed.

"I didn't get the names wrong Mike, those were the names she gave me."

"John what can I say. I heard you christen the baby Claudia Elsbeth."

John looked up with a dejected, lost look as Arnold walked slowly into his line of sight.

"Sorry reverend, Mary's left her hand bag here in the seat somewhere." Arnold had remembered that he had moved it when he went back to see why she was still sitting down, when everyone else in their christening party had surrounded the font after John had christened their new born with the wrong name.

He was still crying but had insisted when he remembered her handbag outside that he was going to go back and get it, for her. He sat down where Mary had sat, now next to John and paused, consciously trying to take in within his numbness, the last essence of his wife from the last place she had been with him.

John and Mike said nothing, they felt his grief, his loss and just watched, their own Christian compassion had encompassed them and as much as their belief taught of a spiritual afterlife, they both felt helpless to say anything that would provide any consolation. Their hesitation to even breathe and disturb his thoughts made their silence sound like thunder between them. Arnold was totally unaware of their awkwardness.

Arnold again gripped the front edge of the seat with both hands, his sobbing continued and developed into an uncontrollable torrent of tears, his shoulders and head appearing almost to bounce as he shuddered with every breath that left his screwed up, salt water soaked face. His eyes were crushed shut as his body reacted to the inconsolable loss that his heart was feeling but still the tears found a way between his eye lids. He felt as if all of his strength had left his body, he was spinning, his mind reeling to gain control, to be able to sense where he was, which way up even he was facing. Arnold felt like he was underwater, weightless and flowing. His mind saw the fleeting glances of a river bank and the face of a woman caught against the rocks of a river bed. He heard laughter. His body, his arms, his legs felt as if they had become foam. He had no substance and he felt that he could do nothing but collapse on the floor as he slid off the shiny pew, catching the bottom of his spine on the hard edge of the seat, his sports jacket pulling up at the back as he did so, offering no protection to his back. He screeched a yell of shock as the bottom of his spine jarred against the edge of the seat. His derangement was pounded by every recollection his brain could find and sent every memory, every occasion, every holiday, every tease, every kiss they had shared.

Their vividness was malicious as if his mind had purposely and specifically opened up its entirety in an instant, displaying fifty years of memories and emotions all at once and sent them to torture Arnold; too much too quickly for any conscious and considerate reflection.

John and Mike sat in silence as they exchanged looks between each other which asked if they should help him up. They stayed seated, their hands gesturing some help if Arnold needed it but he was now kneeling between the seats, his right cheek pressed against the back of the pew in front, looking away from them both.

Arnold saw their wedding day, he felt the same excitement in his heart as he had felt on that day forty six years ago, Mary's beautiful black hair framing her face from underneath her white veil. He saw their honeymoon night, the passion that fulfilled them when they made love completely for the first time. He felt the helplessness of not being able to console her following the death of her mother and then her father six months later. Arnold felt her presence pass through him with the memory of their long unbreakable hug, where they felt every breath and heart beat of the other as they held one another so, so tight, ten years ago when the doctor told them that she had cancer, a cancer which she overcame. He felt her tearful joy filled kisses on his lips and cheeks, on the day their daughter was born and again two years later with their son: he could taste the saltiness on his lips now without realising his own tears were enhancing the memory of when they were kissing each of over and over again as they relished the ecstasy of their new borns. He saw their family, their growing and the love and the happiness they had, the caravan holiday where it rained non stop for a week in Tenby, the weddings of their son and daughter and the sadness of watching them move away and the consolation they gave each other for the combined loss that adulthood had given their children.

Her teasing, cheeky effervescent spirit filled him as each memory rushed through his mind and his mind deliberately tried to hold it there, living and reliving each sensation, trying to think and hold every thought and feeling at once not to let Mary leave him. He felt guilty when a new memory took over, taking away the last one and the fact he couldn't think of them all at the same time. He saw himself holding her hand on the way into church today and felt the expectation of the family get together after the service. Arnold gripped the seat harder, his subconscious mind telling him that the harder he gripped, the more he concentrated, the more memories he could conjure from the depths of his life, the greater the chance would be that when he opened his eyes, when he had control, Mary would be there to walk out of the church with him; that these memories were the life substance of his wife and as he still had these, he still had her.

His heart saw her face smiling at him. He whispered, pleaded, his voice talking in sobs, trying with all the distress his emotions concentrated on his vocal chords to get his words out so that she would hear him but his voice was being robbed of any volume. "I love you Mary, I love you so very very much. Why did you have to leave me, I'm nothing without you. You have given me such a beautiful life. How am I going to live without you? You are beautiful. You shouldn't be the first to go, I'm the old one, that's what you always said, you're the old one. We still got so much we want to do. We still got to see our grandchildren grow up. You promised Emma that you would be there for her wedding. You never break your promises. I love you so very very very much Mary. I love you so very very much. I love you so much."

His voice trailed off into despair as Arnold sobbed and choked his thoughts and love out aloud to his wife. He traced his finger around the pictures he could see within the wood. "You were right my love, I can see what you could see now, this bit does look like the reapers blade and this......."

He continued to rub the pew with his finger tips and now followed the story the grain was telling him. The silhouette and hints of a woman's cheek bones took form as he rubbed his tear filled eyes, his crying blurring the clarity of the pew.

".......and this," his voice broke, disappearing between hopelessness and pleading as he pressed his fingers harder against the wood, caressing, feeling the smoothness of the varnish, the pew cruelly reminding him of how Mary's body felt when she was young and svelte, drawing his thoughts and recollections from his past, the grain changing its shape and appearance to present another outline of a memory from their lives; its final and lasting formation holding his attention and crushing his heart, "and this. ....it looks like you......my darling Mary, it looks like you; how are you there?, you should be with me, ...you should be with me....me....meeee."

John and Mike couldn't hold back their own tears, his grief and love so evident, that at that instant they both wondered how any human could ever continue living with such loss, such obvious emptiness. They both sat there with tears streaming down their faces, both trying not to make a sound to draw any attention to themselves, their bottom lips quivering as they tried to stifle their loss of control as they watched this sorrowful man's soul collapse in front of them. John and Mike felt Mary through Arnold, his emotions passing through them, his sensations filling their bodies creating new memories for them, Mary and Arnold's lives implanted like an instant story, their own minds seeing the same occasions and making comparisons to their own lives, their own memories, their own celebrations and sadnesses and feeling the same feelings as if Mary had been their own wife and they had lost her today. They both saw their lives ahead as lonely after substituting their own wives deaths for Mary and each sensed the other was somehow feeling and thinking the same things, their sympathy for Arnold being superseded by their empathy.

John wondered why God would pick such a time to take any soul.

Arnold picked the handbag up from underneath the pew and held it as if Mary were the bag itself, his tenderness oozing through his bewilderment, Arnold waiting almost to give the bag to Mary. He wiped at his tears and stared at the back of the pew, his mind willing Mary to speak to him, his disbelief of her dying hadn't become logical within his mind.

"She was right. It does look more like a woman's face here." His finger traced around the outline of the image as he saw it. Arnold played with the image for about a minute while Mike and John tried wiping their eyes and looked on in silence, respecting his last moments.

"Strange thing, Mary's got a picture of us from years ago and this bit looks like Mary in the picture." Arnold foraged in her bag to where he knew she carried "their" picture. It had been taken on their second date by a passer by they had asked on the beach.

Arnold looked at the photo which Mary had laminated and put into a small aluminium frame. It went with her everywhere.

He held it in his left hand and drew around the image in the pew with his right index finger again. "See! There's her eye, her cheek and she had long black hair in those days and the wind had blown it across her face like this bit here, she was beautiful, she still is beautiful."

Arnold looked at the end of his index finger expecting to see the last traces of red that he hadn't been able to get off with the tissue. His finger tip was completely clean.

CHAPTER 30

"Have a look at this paper Martin, that's the church where we fitted those pews two weeks ago!" Paul put the paper down on the workbench where Martin was standing along with the cup of tea he had made.

Martin started to read the small article that accompanied the picture but Paul told him the story as he was reading.

"That's odd really, don't you think?"

"What, for someone to die in a church?"

"No, not that, for it to make the local paper, with a picture as well!"

"Suppose so." Paul shrugged his shoulders and walked off not thinking any more of it.

Martin drank his tea and studied the picture and read the article a second time.

"I'll give the minister a ring, to ask him about payment," he thought to himself.

Elaine Rowlands answered the phone as she had popped into the church, to do some of the paperwork John had to do there. She had put her foot down and made him take a few days off from doing anything, as she had become more concerned about his health and his state of mind.

"It's nice of you to ask about John. There have been some odd things happening, if I'm honest. It's weird. He seems the same in general and then something happens which is totally out of character for John. He was in hospital five days ago after some sort of fit or something and then the other day he came home after a christening when that poor woman died and he was telling us all about her life and her husband and what they had done and where they had been. He went on and on for ages and he'd never met her before but then what was even more weird, Mike Evans went home and told his wife the same story, the same things. She rang me because she was worried because she said, Mike went on and on and on about the christening and then the life of this woman and her husband and everything, things he wouldn't possibly know unless he knew her or her husband, which he didn't, nor did John but it was the same stuff. How could they have done that?"

The question made Elaine realise that she had gabbled out the answer to Martin's question about John and more. It made her aware of the stress she had inside.

"That sounds uumm....odd, the both of them telling the same story, yeh I suppose so. So what do you think?" Martin sensed her need to tell someone something.

"I don't know what to think. John is always interested in people and is used to listening to their troubles but not Mike, not in that way but they didn't talk to him like that, so they say, they just sat with him and .....waited, so I just don't know."

Martin looked up at Paul who had stood leaning in the doorway, waiting to ask Martin something and had ended up listening to Elaine's conversation as Martin spoke to her on speaker phone.

"Oooooooo," gesticulated Paul as he waived his fingers, imitating a ghost....."spooky". Paul left the office, "when you've finished, no rush,"

"Sorry Mrs Rowlands, someone wanted to ask me a question." Martin wondered if she had heard Paul's "spooky" comment, even tough he had more or less mouthed it.

"That's ok, I didn't know anyone was with you." Martin was instantly relieved. This woman he thought, didn't need any more things going through her mind than were already going through it at the moment.

"Where are you at the moment?" Martin asked, "you sound like you are in an aircraft hanger!"

"I'm sitting in the church on these lovely new pews you've made for us because I was in here doing the flowers for tomorrow amongst other things."

Martin looked at his cluttered office, the lever arch files on the filling cabinets, the three stacked trays on his desk, his picture of Ann next to them, the paperwork in piles on his desk and on the floor behind his chair and he looked around and pictured the ordered church as he listened to Elaine and mentally compared his organised clutter. He rubbed his fingers lovingly across the surface of Ann's picture and looked at the film of saw dust on his fingertips. His factory was dusty and these quiet few seconds of interaction and reflection made him think he should do something to improve the general environment.

"Look, you obviously got things to do, I'll call up on Monday if I may to collect the cheque."

"Yes, of course you can. I'll make sure it's ready for you. What time do you think you'll come up?"

"Don't know at the moment." He looked at his red covered A4 diary as he was speaking, there was very little of any urgency written in for Monday itself. "Tell you what, say ten...ish." He wiped more saw dust off the pages of the diary.

"Ok fine, thanks for ringing."

Martin wrote the appointment in his diary and then looked thoughtful at the page. "10 am Elaine Rowlands cheque" and reflected on why he offered to call up Monday, rather than ask her to send the cheque which had been the purpose of the phone call. Calling up would take up a whole morning, time which would have been better spent doing other things, especially as some of the boys had come that Saturday morning to try and get an order finished for next week.

Elaine sat with the cordless phone on her lap, the bunch of flowers which she was about to arrange when she answered the phone to Martin to one side. Her thoughts were now full of Mary's death, John "mis" christening, Mike telling the same story as John; John's injuries. She sat back in the pew, her whole body relaxed with her sigh. She sat still, pondering, wondering, "what was happening?" and "why?", her thoughts devoid of any meaningful structure.

She took in a deep breath and readied herself to standing up and carrying on with the things she had to do.

"Oh that's all I need now." She looked despairingly at the flowers she had picked up. All Elaine had in her hands were stems and leaves. All the flower heads were on the pew next to her, liked they had been picked off. She slumped forward, her elbows on her knees, the flowers stems dangling between her legs. "Thud, thud," hers ears picked up the sound of her head banging on the top of the pew in front before she sensed the contact with the wood.

She stopped and stared at the wooden back of the pew in front, as if she had an epiphany. Her mind now tried to put the events 
she was telling Martin about in a chronological order. It cris crossed over the last two weeks or so, moving one event before another or back again so that everything was in the right

order as far as she could be certain. She started to think about completely unrelated events or comments made by people and analysed they had nothing to do with things, that she was just becoming paranoid; while the main things that had happened kept getting selected into the chronology she was compiling and her conclusions were always the same.

Elaine froze for a second as her conclusion started to sink in. She jumped to her feet as if avoiding a bucket of water being thrown at where she was sitting and she turned and glared down at the seat, with the look she gave her children should they dare to defy her. A look which scolded and threatened trouble if they did.

In the seconds that followed, Elaine still found it difficult to accept her own thoughts and tried again to think of a different conclusion, insane and mad as logic made it. She couldn't believe herself, believe that this was even a possibility.

"Elaine." She spun around to the sound of her name which was spoken softly, directly but almost sounding like a question, as if the person was unsure who he was speaking to.

A red haired man stood at the end of the row of pews.

CHAPTER 31

JJ and Beryl Mortimer arrived outside the church at the same time from different directions, both with the same intention of giving Elaine a hand in preparing the church for tomorrow's service and to do anything else they could to help, John, Elaine, whoever, whatever. They greeted each other lovingly with a hug and looked up at the sunny blue autumn sky. "What a beautiful day Beryl!"

They found Elaine sitting in the new pews in the centre section of the church, where Beryl and JJ usually sat, bits of flowers and leaves scattered all around her but all the flower heads in one spot to the side of her. She looked different. She didn't have the composure that usually accompanied her. As they got closer, they could see she was shivering. "Elaine are you alright? What's wrong?"

Elaine made no response, no indication that she had even heard Beryl speak to her.

"The church wasn't that cold to make you shiver," JJ thought to himself and the blue woollen jumper Elaine was wearing, while not thick, would have been warm enough for working inside the church.

Beryl sat down beside her, brushing away the white and yellow rose head debris next to Elaine and her brown jeans, which formed a stark contrast to Beryl in a pink dress, who took hold of both her hands. There was still no indication from Elaine that Beryl was there.

Elaine started to shake more, her legs and thighs quivering, small erratic jagged jerks. Beryl held her hands tighter to convey her presence. Elaine's upper body and arms seemed to be out of unison with her lower self.

"She's quaking Beryl not shivering. I saw men do this in the war, when they were so scared they thought they were going to die. She looks in shock. Elaine. Elaine."

JJ put his hand on her shoulders and gave her a gentle push as he lent over from the pew in front. "She's not with us B, we need to get her into the office or somewhere. Help me get her on her feet." JJ went into the pew where the two women were sitting and eased Elaine up from under her arm pits with Beryl helping from her side, giving JJ the extra lift he needed as he tried to stretch around the back of Elaine to reach her furthest arm.

"Drink this tea, Elaine, drink this tea." Beryl spoke softly almost not to wake Elaine out of the trance she appeared to be in, for fear of adding damage to her already disturbing condition.

Elaine took the cup and sipped, flicking a glance at Beryl. JJ brought in two more cups and they sat with Elaine and watched as she sipped her own tea and gradually came back to a coherent and lucid state. They both looked around the small church office, the photo copier, the fax, the computer. They both looked at each other and wondered at why a church really needed an office? They could not remember offices in churches years ago.

"That was a lovely cup of tea, thank you Beryl. Right I'd better get on with the flowers. How long have you two been here?" Elaine got up to go back into the church.

"No, no," said JJ, "I'm taking you home, Beryl and me will do the rest of what has to be done here."

Elaine went to protest but JJ held her arm which stopped her saying anything. "No, you're going home, now."

"Ok, I can tell John about the red haired man who was in church."

Beryl and JJ looked at each other. "What did he look like?" They both asked more or less at the same time.

Elaine looked back blank. "I.......I don't know, uh red hair.......uh I don't know." Elaine look disturbed by not being able to answer.

CHAPTER 32.

Sunday had a strange feel in a few homes that morning in preparation to go to morning service.

John wasn't as relaxed as normal as his ordered days of rest by Elaine meant that he had not prepared the service in his usual way and was going to use a sermon he had used for another church some months earlier.

Elaine had mentioned the red haired man but had no recollection of her state when doing so, only that this man had been in the church. This was playing on John's mind as well as his lack of preparation. He to was struggling to remember what his face looked like. All he could remember was he was tall and his red hair. He could feel his brain almost pulsing as it strained to recall this man's features.

JJ and Beryl, Mike and his wife, Haley and Alister who didn't go last week, all had thoughts and unusual concerns about the forthcoming service.

"Come and sit with us Elaine, how are you feeling? How's John as well?" Elaine didn't get the chance to answer. Beryl guided her along the isle to her usual place.

Despite the lack of preparation for this particular service, the hymn selection fitted in with the theme of John's sermon.

John looked around from the pulpit at the eighty or so congregation and then looked down to his notes.

He looked back at the congregation, this time specifically

at Elaine. She returned his look. John took in JJ, Beryl, Mike and Liz Evans, Alister and Haley, all sitting, grouped around Elaine; all sitting in the new pews in the centre section of the church. Elaine usually sat in the left side seating section, closer to the pulpit.

John started his sermon. He looked at his hand and his notes, even now, partly expecting to see blood, they were both clear. He looked around the church as he spoke. There was the usual mix of people looking directly at him and those fidgeting with sweets or looking at the floor. The group around Elaine were all looking at him. He continued with his sermon.

As John spoke, he sensed after about five minutes Elaine's group and their attention waning. He glanced down at his wife. She was no longer looking up at him, in fact none of that section of the congregation were; they were all looking downwards and ahead. John continued with his sermon though now he was glancing more frequently at Elaine, to reassure himself that she was alright. His glances started to dart around to other members of the church. Everyone else looked no different.

John started to feel the palm of his right hand twinge, the twinge turning into a warm then burning sensation. As he spoke he started rubbing and massaging his hand with more vigour as the burning sensation intensified.

Elizabeth Evans looked either side of herself, expecting to see the woman who had whispered "Elizabeth" but there was only space either side of her and to Mike's right. Mike glanced at her as she twisted herself to find who was trying to attract her attention. Her motion had virtually stopped when she heard her name again and she repeated her scanning of the same spaces with naive expectation of seeing her caller.

Her animation annoyed Mike instantly. "Sit still, what's

wrong?"

"Someone is calling me!" She whispered quietly.

"Who, I didn't hear anyone." Mike was impatient instantly. "Just sit still for God's sake."

Elizabeth pulled her brown hip length coat forward defiantly to adjust it and to transmit her own annoyance with her husband. She stared forward and contemplated.

Mike gave her a slight sideways glance and felt smug at watching her sit rigid, obeying his instructions.

Elizabeth was unaware that she was looking at the back of the pew in front. She sat, her eyes transfixed to the wood, not looking, not seeing the pew as anything other than an obstruction to her looking back into her own past and how she had ended up with a husband and a life with Mike.

Her awareness of the church service had disappeared as her mind concentrated on speculation. When she heard her name being called again, she felt that she was in the same world, her mind connecting with the caller.

She sat staring but her stare transformed into a penetrating look of recognition as the caller made contact and drew her to where she wanted Liz to be.

"Lizzy." She tensed. No one called her that and she had not let anyone call her Lizzy since her mother died twenty two years ago, not even Mike when they first got together and love was fresh. Her mind jumped to recall how her mother's voice sounded. Was this her mother speaking to her after all these years?

She became aware that now she was looking at the back of the pew and exploring the patterns with her eyes. Only the grain knew where it was going and Liz followed unknowingly within her mind's meanderings.

She saw herself as a young nineteen year old, the year her mother died.

"I was nineteen.................still am!" The callers voice was clearly a young woman's, Lizzy felt it instantly now and their bond was formed. "We share the same name, JJ saw me, the first day."

Lizzy thought back to that first service after the pews were installed and her recollection of their teasing Mike. The coincidence of JJ naming the image "Beth" and now her being contacted by a namesake made her very uneasy as she made the connection. She moved again in her seat as the trepidation moved through her body. Lizzy started to feel more and more anxious and it made her fidgety. She looked around her not thinking she would see anyone other than the usual Sunday worshippers. Her agitation annoyed Mike. "I've told you once, sit still". Mike spoke quietly and angrily under his breath, from the back of his mouth, through stiff, unmoving teeth. He punched her thigh with a short discreet jab to make his point, something he had never done openly here before. She felt the dead leg bruising directly and deliberately on her thigh muscle, radiate from its point of impact and go along her leg. The ache gave her a slightly nauseous feeling. Her eyes glared at the back of the seat as she sat defiantly, tolerating another attack.

"We can stop this, I can stop this, I am with you now and you........you are with me." The illogic of this conversation with an unknown, what she was unbelievably hearing unnerved her more than any reassurance from this unseen ally towards sorting her life out with Mike.

Their contact continued, Lizzy deliberately sitting still so as not to receive another bruise and used her eyes as much as she could to look around her, her head and body still from movement.

"Think of JJ, he could help you........or I can do it all, just will it, just think it, it can happen. Here Lizzy, look here where JJ found me." The voice sounded hollow, as if the person were speaking to Lizzy through a long length of pipe or tubing, the sound of each word arriving within Lizzy's ears in order but at different speeds and volume, the message not losing its purpose but the emphasis of each word becoming distorted by the time it reached her.

Lizzy surreptitiously took a quick look, this time looking at the pew back directly in front of her, partly frightened to see any image of "Beth" there and partly frightened that she wouldn't, which would mean she was just hearing voices from nowhere or no one. At least if Beth were there she would have a tangibly insanity to this conversation.

She saw as well within that momentary glance an older man, the oak's formation hinting at age within his face. She could see his left eye and cheek bone and a look of dominance emerged. Underneath she saw the lines of a young woman's torso, her shoulders and arms appearing to strain against.....she couldn't see what; the image conveyed resistance, sinews, muscle.

"We are the stronger, never forget that. He may punch but you can control him and you know how; you just have to know that you can."

"I know!" Liz answered out aloud, her mind totally swamped by deception.

Mike again breathed out a short exasperated sigh full of aggression and again punched Liz sharply on the same spot on her thigh knowing it would add even more pain from this bruised muscle. Liz ignored its affect and Mike wondered at her indifference as he looked piously back up towards John, in a way to convey his total concentration to the sermon and no digression with any other distraction.

She saw herself at nineteen meeting Mike and the recollection of feeling safe warmed her for a moment; that feeling which drew her vulnerability towards his ordered, methodical, dominance. They had married eighteen months later, much against her father's wishes as he hadn't liked Mike for those reasons. Liz felt guilty at the recollection of her mother not being there.

"She was.............. she was there.........she saw you wearing her blue garter and the pink three tiered wedding cake. She has never left you and she agreed with your father, she doesn't like Mike either." Beth's voice brought waves of daughter, mother love in a flood of recollections and gratefulness of being told her mother was there, with the proof to go with the regret she had carried all these years, at her mother not being at her wedding. Her eyes filled with tears as the emotion flooded her body, her arms flopping to her sides, momentarily weakened as she listened to Beth.

Liz felt a warmth surround her and the thought of her pink snuggle blanket came to mind, cuddled up with mum and dad on their settee.

"They took me from my parents. I watched as they held mum on the ground and tied my father up and they dragged me away and why?.....because I fell in love with a man three years older who accused me of being a witch because why?.......because I wouldn't let him control me and I wouldn't have sex with him. That's it. I would have married him but he just wanted to have me and I wouldn't. I've seen things change over three hundred odd years but then things were so different." There was real bitterness and sadness within her story.

Liz gripped the top of the pew as if in agreement and as a result of the surprise at what she was experiencing.

"What's wrong now. Is it too much to ask that you keep still in church. You're like a fidgeting child....sit still." Mike said it as if talking to a dog.

Lizzy looked around at him, her eyes riveted to his with a direct defiance he had never seen before and this time he felt threatened and shuffled in his seat.

John looked at Elizabeth and smiled.

"Lizzy, you can change things." She heard the nineteen year old spirit's last instruction and watched the effigy disappear from the back of the pew.

Liz shuddered as the feeling of ice drew her human warmth out of her body and through her arms and hands that were still holding on to the top of the pew.

Her last impression of that torso was seeing the tension that had been evident within the swirls and knots disappear into flowing lines of grain.

JJ had been watching Elizabeth from behind and wondered at her movements at first as she usually sat so still during the sermon.

He became enthralled with her head which made the slightest of turns and twitches as if she was following something. He lent forward eventually to casually look over her shoulder and his eyes instantly saw the same apparition of Beth, the woman's face he and Elizabeth had teased Mike about last week.

"There you are." he thought to himself and glanced at Elizabeth and then Mike to see if there was any hint that they were seeing what he was. Mike was looking up towards John in the pulpit but Elizabeth, "well maybe," JJ thought to himself.

He felt like he wanted to say "Beth is back" to Elizabeth, partly to annoy Mike again but caught and stopped himself from saying anything. He just continued to look at the image, listening to John in the background.

His memory went unexpectedly to his wife and the dejection and loss he felt when he had come home to find she had left him, replayed through his mind for a second or so, enough to bring tears to his eyes and a nauseous feeling to his throat.

JJ stopped himself from touching Liz on her shoulder as his emotion and friendship for her swelled up inside him, his recollection of how caring and patient she had been with him as he came to terms with his wife leaving.

He thought of their little cuddles and hugs, shared between two close friends as she helped him move on with life and then looked at the materialising Beth in the pew, her presence growing stronger within JJ's perception.

"You should come for me then." JJ looked at Liz, startled by hearing her voice. He replayed that last two seconds, to see her mouth moving but there was no hint that Liz had said anything. JJ's hand lifted again as if to give her a gentle shake on her shoulder but again he stopped himself on realising he had not seen her say anything.

Beth's image formed more clearly as JJ stared at the backrest.

"We could have had a nice life together, we like each other, we're friends, not like Mike."

JJ looked again but still no hint that Liz had said a word.

"It's not too late. Once Mike is out of the way we could be together."

JJ sat up straight and gripped either side of his legs, still looking intently at the back of the pew in front.

"How?" He said it quietly but out aloud.

Liz's head twitched slightly to her left on hearing JJ's voice. This brought an element of self consciousness to JJ. He mouthed the question the second time oblivious to the rational of what he was doing.

JJ looked at the back of Mike's head and saw his rounded face, his features. With or without his steel framed glasses, he had brown condescending eyes that looked down on you. He hated his general expression. JJ had never seen Mike the slightest bit unshaven and his brown hair was always methodically combed with a regimented left side parting. He pictured it gaunt and bloodied, cut off at the neck, irregular flaps of flesh hanging where it had been hacked off his body and finally rammed down on a spike of wood. The image and thought distorted his face with a gruesome satisfaction as he looked at and then listed in his mind, his labelling of his friend's husband: this pompous, self opinionated, correcting, tedious knit picking, bullying hypocrite. Beth was right, he and Liz should be together but this obnoxious bastard that he had tolerated and been polite to over so many years deserved no better than the thoughts that were going through his mind.

"How could I possibly get away with it, how could I do it, with what?" He found himself mouthing the thoughts to the pew in front.

"We can do it, all you have to do is think it strong enough and we can do it. We can do anything you want. Do you want us to help you?"

Beth's image was fully formed to JJ's vision. He looked at her eyes and saw her devilment as he listened to her invitations to deal with Mike.

JJ sounded cautiously inquisitive, not quite believing he was asking. His voice was just above a whisper. "Who is we? Do you mean just you and me, you, me and Liz...who do you mean.

How many is we?"

Beth's voice sounded distant, enticing JJ to listen harder. Her words did not reassure him, his spine bristled. He rubbed his arms. "We are many. All of us are here. We are always with you. We can come and watch all of you sleep. We can see your dreams, we can be your dreams."

JJ started to feel increasingly uneasy, like he had little or no control with what his mind was about to think.

Beth's voice drew back his attention. "Do you want us to help you?"

He hesitated slightly. "Yes, that's what he deserves for how he is to you Beth. You deserve better. Yes that's what needs to happen." He confirmed his imaginings.

JJ clenched the seat front even harder as his mind started willing for Mike's elimination, his distinction between Liz and Beth had disappeared as he looked at what was now like a carved etching of Liz's face in the back of the pew.

"We can do it when he's painting the church, you don't even need to be here, he's starting tomorrow."

"How do you know that?" JJ was now part of this mirage.

Beth's voice remained soft. "I told you, we are here."

"Yes you're right, he's offered to paint the wall behind the crucifix, to freshen it up."

He touched Liz gently on the neck as he conversed with "Beth" and she half turned her head towards him but it was enough to see the smile on her face.

He looked back at Beth and her image had changed, the twists and knots suggested an elongated skull with the curve of deep eye sockets and something long and bent underneath.

JJ's attention was drawn to Mike as he straightened his back as he sat up, his two hands rubbing around the circumference of his neck, easing the tension he had began to feel.

He smiled to himself and looked back up at John as his preaching came back into his hearing.

John paused for a second to add emphasis to the point he was making and gave the faintest of smiles to JJ, just a hint from his lips at recognition as he looked down from the pulpit.

John's eyes went back to Elaine but then he caught sight of the red haired man sitting directly behind Haley. Beside him sat a young woman with long curly wild hair, partly obscured by Haley. In the light he couldn't tell if she was blond or more red haired. The red haired man was leaning forward so that his face and chin were almost leaning over Haley's left shoulder. Haley seemed to be completely oblivious to his intrusive presence.

He watched Elaine sit forward slightly and her right arm extend out to the back of the pew in front, in fact all of the group looked like they were drawing on the back of the pew in front of them.

John started to find it really difficult to concentrate. He started to fall over his words and went back over a few sentences, to repeat himself, looking at his notes to do so.

Elaine looked now, like she was whispering to JJ and Mike who were both leaning forward, apparently saying something to Beryl. He watched Elaine get up and turn to look for, for who? He watched as she passed herself in front of Beryl's legs. She was trying to get to Haley.

Haley looked up as The Ministers Wife made a direct line for her.

"They want the baby!" Elaine moved towards Haley along the

pews as her thoughts raised her level of panic for Haley.

Haley sat back and grasped Alister's hand. They had still not told anyone about the baby but as Elaine called her warning as she moved towards her, she felt everyone immediately around her knew their secret.

She sensed the presence of something by her left cheek. Haley turned to look as she gave a second glance towards Elaine who was almost in front of her.

The red haired man's face was right next to hers. He was leaning even further forward, his left arm hanging over the back rest of the pew Haley was sitting on.

Haley screamed a quick, surprised screech. Elaine saw his face so close to Haley's, their cheeks almost touching when she turned in his direction. Elaine pulled Haley to her feet and away from the red haired man, Haley's body acting as a temporary screen blocking Elaine's view of him.

From the pulpit John lost sight of the red head man and curly haired woman as Elaine and Haley stood in the way of his line of sight.

Elaine hugged Haley protectively. "You have to stop coming to this church, they want your baby." Her voice was soft and forceful. John saw Elaine turn Haley around as if to show her something and he could see Haley's and Alister's confusion.

As their bodies parted, John could see empty pews behind Haley and Elaine.

Haley looked panicked as she looked at Elaine and then the empty pews again. She tried to sit down but Elaine held her arm and then grabbed Alister, pulling him closer to Haley.

"You've got to leave now, take her home Alister." Elaine looked frightened. There was urgency in her voice.

Everyone was looking at the three standing in the pews. Alister and especially Haley were red faced with embarrassment and both wondered why they were being put on show by Elaine.

John had stopped his sermon. His right hand sending pulsing, sharp, burning sensations up his right arm. His hand felt it was going to melt. He gripped it with his other hand.

John spoke to his wife. "Elaine what's wrong?" His tone urged for her answer.

"They've got to leave. Alister please take her home, please." Elaine ushered and shuffled the two along to the end of the pew, their speed hindered by the lack of leg room for the three of them to walk normally. She squeezed their shoulders as she guided them, trying to convey a calmness to which they would respond without questions but any impression of calmness was robbed by the awkwardness and restriction the lack of space created as they bumped and stumbled against each other.

Their embarrassment grew as they walked up the centre isle to leave, Elaine still pushing them gently with her arms around them, ensuring they couldn't turn around.

"It's alright everyone, there's nothing to be concerned about, they just have to leave!"

Elaine's announcement made them blush even more as if they were being expelled for some unholy transgression.

Everyone watched the three walk out into the vestibule. "I tell you what everyone, let's finish earlier for dinner." John hurriedly gave the benediction and invited everyone to leave early. He walked down from the pulpit and asked casually if the group sitting around Elaine would stay behind for a couple of minutes.

The rest of the congregation left with John waiving them goodbye from the front of the church rather than going into the vestibule to say goodbye personally and Elaine's group hung around as John asked.

"We'll be with you now," he said to his three children, "you wait for us by the front doors."

"We're alright here dad, what was mum doing with Haley?" Rachel asked.

Elaine came back in from the front door and joined John where the others were standing in the pews.

The three children were still looking at their dad and now looked at their mother.

"Please....kids, go out into the vestibule." John's expression and voice conveyed his determination that they agree to do what he was asking them to do. He didn't want them to hear what he was going to say.

John stood with them and looked around the group of remaining adults. He kept rubbing his hand, his whole palm bright red, the pain evident on his face. "I don't know how to start what I am about to say, because it may sound like I'm being stupid, paranoid, insane even, I don't know but I may need your help but don't know at this moment why and for what!"

He held his burning hand up to stop any questions and the tears of pain started to well up inside his eyes as he spoke, the pain increasing the more he moved towards confronting this quandary.

"What were you all doing while you were sitting down while I was giving the sermon?" John looked around encouragingly, inviting someone to be the first to speak.

His right hand seared with another surge of pain. He gripped it violently as if to crush it into submission. "This bloody splinter. It's been in my hand now since the pews were delivered. It must be really infected, it's absolutely killing now, it feels like it's on fire. So what were you doing during the sermon, Mike?"

John's voice rose with annoyance and subdued deliberately as he asked Mike again, trying to keep his voice calm despite the intense irritation he was feeling. He was aware of not wanting to sound aggressive in asking, nor wanting to promote defensive feelings for when they answered.

"To be honest John, I was listening to you but I started looking at," he hesitated as he felt it would make him look stupid.

"What Mike?, just tell me!"

Mike was still hesitant and very self conscious at answering John's question. "Well..... at the pictures I could see in the wood, you know in the grain, the shapes in the wood. I think I saw trees and a field or something, I wasn't paying that much attention.....it was just shapes I suppose, so I can't really remember, I was listening to you."

Elaine took hold of her husbands arm. There was a glimmer of recollection to her encounter yesterday.

"I was doing that as well John, as well as listening to you. I could see pictures in the back of the pew. I've got to be honest, I even started tracing them with my finger." JJ volunteered his answer to John's question without being asked. He didn't mention anything about Mike despite and guiltily, remembering everything.

"And me!, I could see a bit of what looked like a house and then a bit of.....of a crib."

"Why do you think it was a crib Beryl? I thought that bit was just a box." said JJ, now remembering he had seen something like that early on.

"Didn't you see there was something hanging over the crib, like a baby's play thing, something like that!"

"I could see that as well Beryl." Elizabeth Evans joined in the conversation, I was doing the same thing."

"But Beryl and JJ were in the row behind you, weren't they Liz!", Elaine said as she leant over the row of pews to look at the back of the seat, to see if she could see this same image as JJ and Beryl had seen on the back of the pew that had given them its images.

Elaine let out a high pitched squeal of pain as her right hand gripped the top of the pew at the start of its support to her, just as she was about to lean over to look at the back of the pew. Her left hand got diverted from its intended position next to her right on top of the pew as she reacted and her left hand grasped her right. Their absence from her manoeuvre caused Elaine to loose her balance and she fell to the side and along the pew. She couldn't break the hold of her clutching hands to reach out and try and stop her fall and although it happened so quickly, she counted every single millisecond as if each were a minute of time. She felt her body weight shift forward and watched the top edge of the waiting pew get closer millimetre by millimetre as her face accelerated towards the solid carved edge. She saw every year of growth within the seat, every swirl, ripple, the smallest mark from polishing, the machine routing of the timber to give its sculptured shape. Her brain took in the every fact of the pew as if it were conducting an in depth forensic study.

Elaine's head jarred back violently as the top of the pew back unavoidably chopped into her cheek bone, slicing its way along and through her face, blood gushing instantly over the sharp edge and down the back of the pew. The impact forced her lower jaw to dislocate on the left side, her upper and lower teeth catching the other set in ways not possible when her jaw was secure, teeth being splintered and cracked as they experienced unnatural contact. She felt like she was looking inside her own face and mouth, her brain now sending images of the damage her face and teeth were receiving from the sensations her face and skull were sending; her nerve impulses, burning, crushing, pounding.

Elaine rolled onto her back, her momentum and weight rotating her body. Her hands reached out instinctively, now breaking free from clutching each other. Mike caught a glimpse of the palm of her right hand as he and John rushed vainly to try and save her from falling. Her left hand whipped across her body as the back edge of the pew in front made violent contact with her upper arm, causing instant bruising.

Hers arms remained limply outstretched in front of her as she hit the floor between the two pews, the area where people's legs and feet would normally rest appearing now as a devouring mouth swallowing its prey, her face covered with blood, splashes of blood spitting out in an erratic spray.

Eager, straining hands reached down and paused for a fraction of a second as Elaine's injuries registered within the brains of her would be rescuers.

Elaine felt herself being pulled and lifted, her awareness numb to definition. There was no singular combined action only concerned, panicked reaction as she sensed her arms, body, her clothing being touched, pulled, lifted by an uncounted number of hands, in an effort to help her.

She heard the voices of one of her children, filter in through her hearing, Rachel's high pitched voice screaming, "mummy mummy" as she saw her mother disappear from view, from the back of the church where she sat with Paul and Rebecca waiting to go home.

The sounds of concern and surprise, muffled and stifled at first became more distinct as the bubble of shock and pain started to evaporate around her consciousness, her mind seeking to re establish equilibrium. She heard the anxiety in her friends and family's voices as her name Elaine and title "mum" were repeated over and over. She heard the painful reactions of her friends trying to lift her out of the crevice between the seats, unaware initially of the scalding, skin blistering reaction each one of them received when they touched any part of her body or clothing.

Elaine grasped at the pews in an effort to help free herself from the devouring hollow of the foot space between the pews; the edge of the seat higher than her head, conveying to her subconscious that she would remain trapped, swallowed by this void. Her blood had made the polished wood even more slippery. She felt the same sizzling sensation she had felt moments earlier, when she put her right hand on the pew. Her hand retracted as she screamed, joining the cacophony of effort, cries of pain and exclamations her senses were now identifying.

She caught sight of her alluded reflection within the shine of the pews as she got helped first to her feet in a squatting position with her right arm lying along the seat as she faced the back rest. The darkness of her reflected blackened hair deepening the colour of its image within the wood, its volume swollen, looking like it was standing on end, stiffened and moulded by her blood when it had poured out of her face and run to the back of her neck and onto her lower scalp and down its strands.

Her memory jumped back to meeting the red haired man yesterday and her panic started to increase as the blocked out images of their meeting returned. Beryl's voice came to the forefront of her attention. Elaine could hear her breathing, it was gasping in between her speaking. "Is she alright? Oh dear Lord, look at her face."

Elaine felt as if Beryl was drowning. Beryl was struggling to get air herself while she attempted to help the others get Elaine up out of the pews. Elaine's own hands were burning as she frantically tried to help those helping her and get herself back onto her feet.

Mike Evans managed to get his hands under Elaine's arm pits to lift her weight up as if he were a fork lift. Elaine saw the beatings he gave Elizabeth when she didn't do things in the correct order. She heard him grimace with the effort of lifting her and she knew his hands were burning. She felt his effort and sensed the scowl of effort on his face from behind her. Mike's OCD had helped him as an accountant, the method of doing things, the exactness of numbers but his rational cracked quickly, his irrational overtaking his own logic and his Christianity very often, when faced with non numeric life.

Elizabeth's fear transmitted into Elaine through the grip she had on Elaine's right arm and the contact Mike had with Elaine and through the contact his right knee had on the pew for the added strength he needed to lift Elaine. Mike Evans was so aware of his dark grey suit trousers, soaked with blood.

John saw Elaine's thoughts, the red haired man yesterday with her. John to, saw Elizabeth's future confrontation when she and Mike were to get back to their home this day, Mike's schizophrenia at his ruined suit, Elizabeth's inability to rectify the damage, to get the blood out; to do what he thought his wife should be able to do.

Beryl saw Elizabeth's tears as she stood toe to toe with Mike screaming at him in their kitchen in her own defence because his suit was ruined by that "stupid, clumsy woman." The premonition confirmed Mike's chauvinism and exposed his secret that he had been able to keep hidden by the fear he created.

Mike felt Beryl's relief when her husband passed away, the feeling of guilt and freedom conflicting in her mind as she looked forward to an unrestricted life because of her husband's lost use of his legs.

John felt JJ's bitterness towards God, at his own wife leaving their marriage many years before. He felt resentful sometimes at coming to church, to praise and worship, doing it on times out of duty and habit rather than for the love of church and its beliefs. One of these beliefs was the commitment of a man and woman in marriage, before God, for better for worse, till death do them part. JJ sometimes blamed God for his wife's leaving. John saw JJ's younger self come home to find her note and his subsequent discovery that she had left on the hope that once separated, a man she worked with, would take his chance with her and start a new life together. He hadn't and she lost her life with JJ and her hoped for future; she and JJ divorced.

Elaine tried to speak but her mumble was indecipherable, her dislocated jaw more painful now when she tried to use it, her gashed face, the blood still pumping freely out of the cut. Her cheek had already swollen to twice its normal size.

John got his clean handkerchief out and pressed it gently and quickly against the cut. "Ooh Elaine, Elaine, you're going to be alright, you're going to be alright." His words were meant to be soothing but didn't convince himself and Elaine's lack of reaction told John he hadn't been heard or that she hadn't been convinced by his attempted reassurance.

His wife was now standing with support from himself and Mike. John looked at Mike.

"Mummy, Mum, dad uuhhh." Rachel saw all her mother's blood.

"Mmmmm, eerrrr," Elaine made noises and motioned with her eyes to get Rachel away from this group of people, away from her. She didn't want Rachel upset, she didn't want Rachel anywhere near these pews.

John still felt and saw her every thought. So did everyone else. Confusion, pain, gave way to embarrassment, anger, exposure, condemnation, judgement.

Everyone had seen aspects of everyone else, aspects that had been unknown.

The red haired man had told Elaine yesterday that he would show her the truth and the truth had devastated her.

Her visions yesterday, without the others there absorbing, transmitting, contributing to her meeting the truth of not just the lives of these people surrounding her now but of the truth that now lay, uninvited within their church, had frozen her to shut down. Her mind had been unable to cope, its reason, its logic destroyed by unbelievable realisation. She had managed today to fight against this fear, her recollection, the derision she had faced from the red head man yesterday, his instant unexplainable disappearance from her side as he mocked her and Christian faith. She had needed to get Haley out of the church as her mind started to unravel the confusion.

"We should get out, let's get out, I...we need to think, I've got to get you to hospital." John looked at Elaine, his awareness enhanced as he started to usher the group out of the pews, his one arm around Elaine, the other outstretched, shepherding them towards the main front doors.

"We've got to take mummy to hospital." Rachel was beginning to sob as she ran back to Paul and Rebecca who had stayed waiting by the front doors of the church for their parents. It was only when the group got closer that it began to dawn on them that something had really happened. They both looked up from their smart phones. "What's happened to mum?" Paul asked.

John ushered them out in the same sweeping movement of his arm. He said nothing, his eyes said everything, conveying different states of emotion to his three children. All Rachel saw were the tear glazed eyes of her father and that started her crying as it made her feel really sad for him and for her mum. Paul and Rebecca appreciated the damage to their mother's face and they stared in disjointed shock, confused at how their mum had suffered such an injury, in church.

Outside, Mike looked at his hands, there were tiny blisters all over his palms and fingers. He stood there silent just looking, drawing unsought attention to himself. The others looked at Mike's hands and then their own. Everyone had the same sort of blisters and everyone's hands felt tender, like they had put their hands into hot coals.

CHAPTER 33

Martin Williams arrived at the church on Monday morning, expecting to meet a congenial John or Elaine. Instead he was greeted by a very abrupt, agitated Mike Evans.

Mike was still trying to make sense of yesterday and the more he thought and tried to apply sense and order, the more frustrated and aggressive he felt. His grey suit was in the bin, there had been no saving it. In fact given the amount of blood all over it, he didn't feel like he would want to wear it again despite Liz's efforts to clean it when they got back and despite the huge argument they had about her incompetence to do anything properly. Even his physical encouragement to correct her shortcomings had failed to gain an improvement in her cleaning abilities and her upper arms had his punch marks to prove it.

The final straw to a really bad day was she was fifteen minutes late at serving dinner. She really was useless.

Mike's mind was cluttered and this was unacceptable. When Martin walked in the office, he was more or less ordered to sit down. Mike stood there in working clothes, clearly painting something in a rich blue colour, judging by the splashes on his new, disposal paper overalls.

"I thought The Reverend or Mrs Rowlands would have been here this morning," Martin said casually, "where are they?"

"I don't know exactly at this precise moment. Hopefully she is out of hospital. I know they did emergency plastic surgery on her face last night and John told me when I spoke to him at 9.12 last night they were happy with the operation. They have also reset her jaw but sorting her teeth out will have to be done by a dentist."

The matter of fact statement conveyed Mike Evans' impatience at having to take time in giving an explanation, took Martin's full attention immediately. He felt concern for Mrs Rowlands.

"Hospital? What happened? She was fine the other day when I was speaking to her." Mike was about to say something when the office door opened and Elaine walked in followed by John who had picked her up from hospital about an hour earlier. They had decided to go to the church as they knew Martin was coming to collect his cheque and despite wanting to go back home and rest, they felt they had to make the effort and take the opportunity to talk to Martin.

Elaine's face was heavily bandaged on her left cheek and he could see beyond the covering that the left side of her face especially was badly swollen and bruised. He looked then at John who followed Elaine in through the office door, still with a bandage on his forehead and bruising and cuts all over his face.

His surprise was impulsive and natural. "What on earth has happened to you two?" He started to stand up, partially out of respect to greet Elaine and John and partially to offer Elaine his seat.

"I'm fine," she said through firm inanimate lips, her voice almost projecting like a ventriloquist.

Mike handed Martin his cheque at the same time as he was about to stand. The result of both made him sit back down, staring at Elaine.

John and Elaine sat in other chairs, the four momentarily

looking at each other, Martin wondering what they were going to say to him, the other three wondering the same, what were they going to say to him.

After a few questioning looks, John moved himself forward on his seat and looked even more awkward as he tried to structure what he was about to say.

Martin leant forward, as if to encourage him, waiting to hear what he had to say.

"Uuhh, this is going to sound......odd ....but since we've had the new pews, there have been some really strange things happening and ....well.....I, we, are not sure what to do."

John talked his way through the last two weeks or so, as best he could remember, helped by Elaine who forced herself to speak when the appropriate time came, backing up John.

Martin listened, interested at first at the stories he was hearing, his interest changing into skepticism, to disbelief.

He thought as he listened, that he should have asked them to send this cheque, that by coming up to the church and now with what he was hearing, John was going to get to the point where everything was his fault.

John stopped talking, Martin's attention was now diverted back to Elaine's face, "and this is what happened to you yesterday? And this is the last thing to have happened? I, I......I can't believe it, do you really believe it, do you expect me to believe it, seriously in this day and age, you're talking about...... about possession, aren't you? Aren't you?" His comments and questions clearly showed his confusion.

Martin thought the more he heard and the more he thought about what he was hearing, the more incredulous the whole situation. He really wished he had asked them to send his cheque. He could see this blowing up into something! He didn't get to thinking what the something was, just that he didn't want to be a part of something.....barmy.

"Martin, it is hard to believe but after yesterday, when we all saw the same things at the same time, we've come to believe it, what ever "it" is, haven't we?" John looked around for moral support. Elaine was as vocal as her jaw would allow her to be and sort of growled a yes out from the back of her throat. She sounded slightly demonic. Mike was more hesitant at confirming his agreement to what had been seen by everyone. He had seen things about other members of the congregation but had "it" exposed him to the them, what person he was when he was at home? He eventually nodded a half hearted acknowledgement so as to appear to agree while his logic told him this was impossible.

Martin sounded confused. "Yes but, yes, you've told me all that but I still can't...." His voice trailed off as he sat back to the rear of the red vinyl chair, his mind more confused by the fact that these were rational people giving him irrational stories, stories that intimated possession or something similar.

"Martin, explain to me how I know about Ann, how I know about her cancer, the horse with black plumes pulling her coffin, the champagne?"

Martin went stiff. How did this minister know about that? He had not talked to John about his wife or her death. He felt a tear well up in his eye. Martin looked sadly at John at hearing about his past with his beautiful Ann being brought up in the same conversation as all this possession nonsense but his logic stopped him from getting angry or retaliating. Instead it told him it had to be true. This was a minister, not a fair ground clairvoyant trying to guess your life to convince you they were genuine so that you would pay them more money. This man was a man of God, supposedly a good man. So was his wife, they were all Christians.

"Ok, let's say I believe what you are saying but let's be honest, it's hard to." Martin still did not want to openly admit to agreeing with his own thoughts. "What can I possibly do?"

"There's only a fews things I can think of as a starting point, to find out where the wood came from. Do you know? Will you have records?, or....., or to take the pews out."

Martin didn't correct John at this point "it's timber" he thought to himself, "a wood is where you walk through and here it comes, the start of the lead up to asking for discount or money back!"

Martin put on a big smile to convey his willingness to oblige in trying to help them out. His smile didn't feel completely natural, even to himself. "I'll have records where the timber came from. Why you want to know that, I don't really see. You've got the pews now, so taking these out and paying for new ones again, is I would have thought, a waste of money but of course I'll look for you and I'll let you know."

Martin felt he handled this brooding situation very tactfully, innocently conveying that there would be no discount or money back and that their decisions could cost them even more. He stood up as he was saying this, putting the cheque into his wallet as he did so.

He continued with his smile though it started to feel even more forced as he thought, "Great! Now I've got to do more work for a job that's finished, that's all I need. Why didn't I ask them to send this cheque. I wouldn't be doing this now!"

CHAPTER 34

Martin arrived back at his workshop still annoyed with himself for somehow getting involved with "this holy quest" as he named it, while driving back.

"Ok" he thought to himself, taking a deep breath and a moment to think where best to start looking for the records of the timber supplier he had bought from for "the church job" as it has been referred to.

It took him about three hours, allowing for interruptions but he found the yellow delivery note which listed a consignment number, batch numbers and quantities. For Martin at least, he felt satisfied that he had found as much as he could.

He phoned his supplier and asked for Jimmy, who had spent time with him when he had picked out the timber he wanted.

Martin paused when the young clerk told him they didn't have a Jimmy working there and then asked why he wanted to know where the cut timber had come from.

"Hello, are you still there?" The manager wondered if he had been cut off while Martin sat and thought through various answers, none of which included anything remotely like the right reason.

"It will take me a couple of days I would guess, to go back through our records but yes, I'll do it for you Martin. In fairness, I know you buy quite a lot of timber from us."

Martin thought of ringing Reverend Rowlands back but then

thought better of it, as the less contact, the less of a chance they could mention anything more to do with the cheque or money. it would only take a couple of days to get the information. He left the office and went to the bank.

At the church that afternoon after taking Elaine home, John locked the doors leading into the church and printed off a few signs from the office computer, CHURCH LOCKED FOR MAINTENANCE.

He stood by the vestibule doorway, looking into the darkened church. It had been a heavy overcast day and the early November nights had little light to send in through the arched windows. He could make out the shapes of things as his eyes adjusted to the light as he was about to shut and lock this door. The first few rows looked uneven as if there were people leaning forward on them or in them. The nerves down his spine went cold, causing him to shudder. He closed the door quickly. He was not ready to do anything yet. In fact he didn't know what to do or even if he had to do anything.

Despite his requests of Martin and the events of yesterday, in fact despite the last couple of weeks, he still doubted the sanity of events. Surely demonic possession was not in his small town church. John stopped in the short corridor between the church and the office, standing outside the vestry, his right hand leaning on the door frame. He thought he heard noises from inside the church but he didn't open the door again to check.

CHAPTER 35

Martin recognised John's voice when he answered the phone four days later. "I've found out where the timber was cut." Martin went straight into conversation.

"That's great, let me get a pen and take down the details."

John took down everything Martin told him. The felling company that had cut down the tree. The ordnance survey reference of the wood and the grid references of areas felled.

The wood was an area of the Forest of Dean and had predominantly been undertaken by a government order to cut down diseased elm trees. The area was then replanted as a decision had been made by the powers to be, to cut down all trees and replant completely.

John was busy looking on the internet for the names of listed churches in the area when Mike came in.

"I've got the location of where the wood was sourced for our pews."

"Oh, that's good! What do you think that is going to tell us?"

"At the moment Mike, I don't know, I really don't know but I've got to do something, even if this information ends up eliminating things."

"And then what?" Mike was looking for a constructed, thought out answer not something airy fairy.

John turned on Mike with unexpected venom "For Christ sake

I don't know. All I know is that in the last two weeks Elaine's ended up in hospital, I've been in hospital, no thanks to you I might add, we have both seen red haired" ......he paused, trying to find the right words to describe their sightings.........."g-hosts,......... someone's died in a christening of all things and you're asking me for the bottom line. Stick to doing the church accounts."

Mike was taken aback, shocked into silence for a few moments. He had never seen John react like that even in heated meetings, not in the five years he had been at this church but it was the comment about sticking to the accounts that got under his skin.

"And another thing, Christians don't abuse their wives, so I suggest you start to think if you are a Christian or just some Philistine thug who thinks five hymns and a sermon gets them a get out of jail ticket. Think on Mike because we've all learnt what you are really like, so perhaps whatever "it" is, isn't bad, isn't evil but is a good thing. Look how Jesus was seen by others, he was seen as a threat, evil, something bad, different because of what he did, ...miracles. If we saw a miracle now, ninety nine percent of us wouldn't believe it. We would put it down to conjuring, a magicians trick on TV. We would explain it away with science rather than believe it was a miracle. Miracles don't happen any more but I need to find out if we are in the middle of a miracle or it's something else, so you decide what you are going to do."

Mike's aggression had risen at the "accounts" comment but John's tirade had pinned him verbally in the corner. He had not been able to get a word in and now "his secret" was being thrown in his face by this opinionated minister that had only been at this, no his church for five years. Now he was telling him how he should behave and how he should treat his wife. His job was to mix into the church and how the people lived there, not to come along and try and change everything with ideas of his own. The only difference was he wore a dog collar.

Mike's eyes glared with anger, his head vibrating with rage as he stared and approached John, putting his face closer to his. Mike was three to four inches shorter than John so looked up at John as he gripped his left arm.

"She is my wife and I'll treat her as I see fit. I don't need you or anyone telling me different. If you want to quote things at me, remember Eve was taken out of Adam's rib, she came second, that's the order of things."

John pulled his arm free and pushed Mike away with his other hand.

"How you see fit is not fit enough, think on Mike."

John left Mike tamping in the room. He was not going to let This Minister get one up on him. He had been coming to this church for forty years. Mike looked at the sign on the door, CHURCH LOCKED FOR MAINTENANCE. He took the key out of the key cabinet and stormed back into the church and looked at the blue, quarter painted wall he had started the day Martin had come for the cheque. Mike had stopped painting after Martin had arrived and by the time he, John and Elaine left, Mike had thought it pointless to continue as he had to be somewhere else by one o'clock.

Mike stared at the wall, going over and over the conversation, the accusations. His thoughts came out aloud. "Stuff it! I'll do this in my time considering it's my time and I'm not getting paid."

He turned around and turned the lights off.

"Not long now." Mike heard the whispered threat come from deeper inside the church. He turned around, surprised at hearing any voice as he knew he was the only person within the church. There was a movement of a black coated figure he just caught sight of, right down the back of the church towards the street entrance doors and the glint of something silver or metal. It looked like John in his cassock.

"John is that you? John!" There was no answer. Mike watched his breath start to cloud into grey vapour from his mouth as he spoke. He rubbed his fingers together and he felt the warmth of their friction.

Mike turned around and left the church "Stay in here then if that's you. I've had enough of you." He locked the door and cocked his right ear back towards the door as he thought he caught the same voice again, "not long now!"

CHAPTER 36

John's three and a half day visit to The Forest of Dean had been hectic and disturbing.

As he drove back home, his thoughts relived the last seventy two hours or so. Once he had thought about the three pub meals he had enjoyed, one alone, one with the The Reverend Michael Andrews who had been the previous minister co incidentally at his church and the third with both Father James and Michael Andrews, though Father James didn't eat or drink anything: his thoughts went over and over the findings and the stories he had heard from the locals in the pub and elsewhere. He tried at first to recall his conversation with Michael Andrews in every chronological detail as they had talked together. John visualised the sixty five year old minister as he looked at him over square bifocal glasses, running his fingers through his thick white curly hair, clasping his hands together on the top of his head as he tried to make sense of the confusion and threats that came with John's thoughts, threats if what he was hearing were true, to people he had been with and ministered for seven years before John's arrival as his successor.

Both Father James and The Reverend Michael Andrews had been really helpful in digging out old parish records from powdering cardboard boxes in the old archives and storage areas of the three churches they ministered in, working separately with John over different days.

The two Ministers on his first night had sat and listened with the same disbelieving looks as John felt, while he told them of the events in his church, his suspicions and his lack of faith at the thought his suspicions may turn out to be true and then not knowing what to do, to overcome whatever he had to face. Father James had been the most subdued out of the two, sitting quietly for the most part with his head lowered, listening below his tilted hat, strangely never looking John directly in the face, even when he spoke. On reflection now, John could not think of one occasion where they actually looked directly at one another during a conversation. He started to wonder if he was now imagining that Father James had kept his face away from being seen deliberately or that he was unusually shy or just strangely furtive.

He turned his lights on as the afternoon's light faded, the heavy grey clouds darkening the trees in the forest he was driving through, making the light eerie despite only being 3 o'clock.

John's thoughts were mixed. He felt a feeling of satisfaction that he had found out from the information Martin had provided, where the timber had come from, where the actual trees had been cut. He had subsequently met Father James from St Christopher's Church at the felling site after they had met first in the pub with Michael Andrews, who John had initially contacted through The Methodist Church Directory before going to The Forest of Dean. John had been contacted after a note had been unexpectedly left for him at the pub's bar, which acted as the accommodation's reception, by this unknown Father James, before his arrival. The note had said "I will meet you at 7.30 in the bar. I can help. Father James." John had been uneasy and puzzled by the directness of the note from someone he didn't know but thought that Michael Andrews may have contacted him about his visit but hadn't brought it up in conversation and now wished he had, especially as now during his recollections, it dawned on him that the note arrived even before Michael Andrews knew why John was going there.

When they had stood next to the new saplings that had been planted to rejuvenate the forest, John had felt uneasy and wondered as he talked, if he was imagining things and if the events at his church were just a mixture of unfortunate and unrelated circumstances. Father James had stood in inanimate silence, listening and his lack of questions and interaction had made John feel that he wasn't listening or perhaps not interested.

The car that overtook him brought his attention back to the road and his speedometer. Forty six in a fifty, that wasn't unduly slow.

Strange he thought, even in this day and age good old fashioned parish records, yellowed pieces of paper, many of them brittle with age, had provided the answers.

Claudia Elsbeth, the name jumped off the page when he painstakingly looked through the oldest book he had ever touched. 1612 she had been born, the 14th of May and then on the next page, the record of her death 29th July 1613. John saw other names, with dates, lives of babies and children, lives that had been shorter than five years and it made him realise how lucky he was to be living now where life expectancy and child mortality were so much longer. He thought and felt the sadness of every parent who's child had not lived, the dates raising his emotional attachment to the names on the page and in most instances the reason for their death, small pox, plague, plague, measles, plague. Only Claudia Elsbeth had "witches spawn" written in the right hand column and he couldn't get those words out of his minds eye.

"Baaaaaap." The horn of the oncoming car made him jump and jerk his car to the left of the white line. He gripped the steering wheel rigidly, his arms locked straight as he gathered his concentration again by staring at the road ahead and then released his held breath with a long sigh of relief and refocused on driving on his side of the road.

His thoughts soon returned. The second night in the pub, he enjoyed the novelty of being alone with a meal and then a few pints of hand pulled real ale which had given him the opportunity to move around asking other drinkers and diners about the forest felling. It turned out to have been about four years ago. Three men who regularly drank at the pub and with who he eventually ended up having a pint or two, had loads of stories about people, the villages, superstitions and had been really interesting company.

The one man Dean, named after the forest so he said, used to have a burger van until two years ago. He would go around the various tourist spots and lay buys and had gone for the two weeks of tree cutting to the felling site.

"Nasty accident there as well. One bloke killed, the other with his leg virtually cut off. Chain saw accident when they were cutting The Witches Oak down. Spooky really, that it happened on that tree!"

John had found his stories of the witches oak fascinating, enhanced he felt by Dean's gruff, throaty sounding voice. He felt like he was listening to a cuddly pirate spinning a yarn over a tankard of ale. Dean he thought must have sampled too many of his own burgers. His two friends Jonny and Herbert "HB" for short, adding in extra detail and other versions or tales with every pint.

He listened with boyish innocence at their stories and banter. It was clear that they were the best of friends and given that they were the same age as they had all been through school together, they looked in different age bands and this along with their significant differences in height gave them the opportunity to rib each other on every occasion they could.

Dean was about five foot five with thick black hair and looked about thirty although he was probably two stone overweight for his height. Jonny was taller about five foot eleven and looked sixty five to seventy, his face heavily worn and tanned from working predominantly out in the Far East for twenty five years; only his bald head was completely smooth and wrinkle free, which as John discretely studied him, seemed to be a mis matched head to face, given his exposure to so much sun. For middle age he looked haggard and tired. There looked to be about a twenty year age gap, which changed at the top of his forehead. He learnt from the banter that Jonny thought shaving his head to raise money for charity had made him look younger as his hair had gone prematurely grey following the unexpected death of his mother ten years ago.

HB was a colossus at six foot seven and about twenty three stone of fair haired, fit, muscular, bespectacled sharp dressing MAN. John speculated through the story telling about HB as now in his mid forties like the other two, what he would have been like when he was in his prime. He was still an extraordinarily good looking, out of the ordinary, softly spoken but confident man and he stood out from the crowd in every way possible, not least by the thousand pound brown calf leather Armani jacket and Calvin Kline red trousers and shoes, that Dean and Jonny teased him about.

"See, he comes out to a pub with his best mates, looking like some posey clothes peg while we are here, happy in our jeans and sweaters."

John wondered at one point if they were taking the micky and making things up, as they had about a dozen different stories that went with the history of this tree.

The tree was also called Robin's Tree, after Robin Hood. As kids when these three were kids, children were allowed to go and play in the woods and they played at being Robin Hood.

They had been friends since infants school. The tree had also been referred by some over its four hundred year history as The HangingTree, as one of its branches had been used to hang people. "You could still see the marks where the ropes were tied around the branch," HB said.

"That's probably from ropes used as swings," Dean corrected.

"Yeh but," HB continued, "people were killed on that tree by all accounts, not for years now though, not for about two hundred odd years, perhaps longer. I think a highwayman was the last killed on that tree, well apart from the two lumberjacks four years ago. My gran used to tell me stories about witches being tied up and burned on that tree or stories about having their heads cut off and things like that."

Jonny agreed, "Yeh your gran used to tell us those stories when she was making cakes."

HB related a summarised story of the killing of the first witch, "Claudia she was known as."
Reverend John felt very uncomfortable at hearing Claudia's name. "This woman was burnt as a witch after she apparently killed a husband and wife, not that they ever found the wife and there wasn't much of the husband left either so the story goes but she was tied to The Witching Tree and with the good old fashioned justice of those days would either die in the fires they built around the tree or if she survived.....because she was a witch, which was a bit unlikely I think considering she was being burnt alive, she would be allowed to live." HB sounded so comically cynical, "but I reckon she would be killed anyway, good options aye?"

John had never heard stories of witches being burnt alive and if they survived, being allowed to live but he went with the flow of the story.

Dean liked telling the story of the twin sisters who had been tied together on both sides of the tree, their backs against the trunk so that they had as little contact as possible with each other in their last agonising moments of life. John remember how he spoke about them. "You can imagine can't you, them two trussed up, their fingers and hands searching behind them, trying to touch or grip each other either for comfort and support or so they could together, once they had got to hold each others hands, summoning up demons from Hell to save them."

The other two glanced looks at John as Dean was talking, as if to say, "He's off on one again." There was a slight sexual inference to Lesbian in how he referred to the two sisters with theatrical drama in his voice when he talked about demons. His friends widened their eyes at John as they took synchronised mouthfuls of beer, letting their friend tell his story.

John felt as if Dean had told this same "twins" story on countless occasions before, as he hardly paused for breath. He tried to look for embellishments as he enjoyed Dean's rhetoric.

"The two sisters used to live in the old hamlet which this village is built on. You can still see some of the old wall, well not the wall but the mounds that cover the old walls. Some have got signs on. Have you seen those?" Dean didn't wait for an answer. John didn't attempt to give one. "The story goes that they both fell in love with the same man, lucky man aye." His eyes glinted with diverted imagination. "These twins were identical apart from the fact that one had black hair and one had brown hair, perhaps blond but anyway because they were so close and they both knew the other also loved this bloke, they decided that the one with brown hair should die it black, that way they looked completely identical, like they were the same person. They took it in turns to see this lucky bugger and made a pact that they would pretend to be the same one he was seeing on every occasion. They told him that the blond sister had gone to visit relatives in the next village so he wouldn't catch on to what they were doing."

Jonny chipped in. "I can't see what they hoped to get by doing this. They both couldn't end up with this fella, they must have realised that, even in those days."

"You always say that, every time I tell this story." Dean held his glass midway between the table and his mouth and looked at his friend with an emphasised, quizzical, impatient look at hearing the same logical interruption again.

"Yes I know but we know the end of the story, don't we," Dean said with a mocking scalding tone as he answered Jonny and then looked at HB and Reverend John.

"Anyway this went on for months, so the story goes and the other thing about this is, because they were identical twins, they could sense and feel what the other one of them was feeling. Now we know about things like that now but then, that sort of thing would make them witches and that's what happened.

There was another woman who wanted this bloke,...... that sort of thing never happens to me!" Dean digressed from the story as he interjected an aside comment. "This other woman bumped into one of these twins in town when she and this bloke were together and I suppose, in trying to get him interested in her, started teasing this twin and tried to put her down and then without warning scrammed her face.

The other twin felt this...she knew what had happened...well so the story goes and the following day went looking for this other woman.

When this woman saw this other twin and the fact she didn't have any marks on her face, this was her chance wasn't it? She started shouting witch at her, as if she had healed her face with magic. The thing is," John remembered Dean gripping his arm towards the end of his story......."the thing is, because the second twin had dyed her hair, even though the village knew these girls, now they looked the same, I mean identical and with this jealous bitch shouting "witch" every second and saying she had used magic to heal her face, remember she didn't have any scram marks, so those stupid people like flipping sheep all ended up taking these two twins to be burnt.......to The Witching Tree."

"Yeh, but what about the twin with the scrammed face. They must have seen those on the other twin and known she was the one this woman had gone for, not the other one, the one without any scram marks."

Dean looked open mouthed in comic frustration at Jonny and shook his head very slightly, staring at John and HB alternately.

"Thud." John didn't see the pot hole in the road but the jolt shook the car like it had been hit by anti aircraft fire which again stopped his memory and his laughing slightly to himself in the car at this recollection and brought his attention back to looking more closely at the road.

The Reverend Michael Andrews had talked a bit about local superstitions and stories after listening to The Reverend John's story, while they both looked through parish records on John's second afternoon buy they didn't provide much information. However it was the older Catholic Church that had the oldest records and Father James had seamed more affable at spending significantly more time with John.

He also knew of these same stories that Dean and HB had told, in some sort of fashion "but then he would," concluded John, living in the same community and going to the same pubs and things. That didn't make the stories true only that they have been told over years and years to frighten and entertain the minds of children and tourist, stories of witchcraft and witches, of hangings and burning.

What did convince John that they must be more than just stories were the entries he found in these older parish records with Father James. Over a period spanning almost one hundred and fifty years there were entries against the recorded deaths of twenty three people, twenty two women and one man.The entries read various reasons some repeated, some unique, "witch", "devil worshiper"..." witch" "witch" "satanic retribution" "demonic execution" ...."warlock".

They had found reference to some of these deaths in other stored documents, references to a "Tree of Judgment", "God's Oak", "The Witching Tree" and both ministers he felt, had become engrossed with the unexpected excitement of finding as much detail about the reasons for the deaths of those twenty three from within these forgotten records.

Their excitement momentarily overshadowed the reason why John was looking as their reading and investigation took on a life of its own. As one piece of detail was found by one, the next connection, reference or inference was written down by the other, the link stronger or weaker than the last, their interpretation discussed over John's third pub meal, to try and maintain consistency and accuracy.

Father James had been very helpful and had conveyed an unprompted eagerness as John thought to find and piece together the next bit of their investigation. In fact he had been very insightful in making connections and links. John felt lucky to have met him on his first day. He thought at first he might be a bit guarded, Catholic to Methodist but he was far from that. A very tall man with his "catholic" priests hat pulled right down his head. John felt he must be very shy as Father James mostly seemed to avoid eye contact, keeping his gaze low and speaking in a quiet but purposeful voice. John had felt compelled to listen.

John had all of these papers photocopied in his brief case, reworked by them both into a chronological list over their last meal meeting together.

On top of the list and the "first witch to be burned", Claudia. The second death which had a reference as a sacrifice to God, "witches spawn" Claudia Elsbeth. The dates had shown she was just fourteen months old. He squeezed the steering wheel between his hands as if he were kneading dough and the same shiver of cold came over him as he remembered that same feeling on reading that child's name for the first time from those old records; the same name as he mistakenly christened baby Christine some days before. The coincidence had chilled him, bringing the memory of his last christening back with a vengeance. He could see himself staring at that name, first in disbelief and then consciously trying to dismiss the event as coincidence but his own logic refused to let him believe it was just coincidence. He had gone rigid at the table where those records had been laid open for inspection and when Father James had asked him on that occasion what was wrong and had he found something, John had glossed over his reaction and findings with a reference to what he was thinking about having to eat at the pub that night. John thought on how he had been aware of Father James staring at him and how he had purposely avoided looking back at him, in case Father James had become more involved with that precise part of John's findings at that moment. He felt as awkward and uneasy now in the car as he had then.

John recalled his second thoughts then. "How could anyone take the life of an innocent child, a child that could barely walk and think she was a witch?" He again saw Father James' stare intensify as he continued to avoid eye contact, to avoid discovery. The vision of that moment was disturbing and had made him feel dishonest by not telling Father James his findings and their connection to his own actions when he had been asked.

Father James had said nothing more but his transfixed gaze on John had made John feel self conscious to the extent that he eventually blushed with embarrassment.

He felt his face now with his left hand and glanced in the mirror, he could feel and see even in the poor light within his car that he was blushing again. Adjusting his seating position didn't help diminish his solitary self consciousness. His thoughts returned to trying to clarify some logic.

John's conclusion, however real or accurate to the history as it was lived and recorded by the old parish records was that this tree had existed and had been used as an object in the purging and persecution of witches. Whether the twenty three souls taken had been witches and were guilty of witchcraft or simply accused of being a witch, neither John or this old Catholic priest, John thought would know, only that now they knew, this tree was now in John's church as pews.

John's near excitement during the records investigation changed to dread on reaching the conclusion.

As a minister, he had preached about the forces of good and evil, The Devil, God, Jesus; belief and sacrifice, faith. John had never been involved with anything paranormal, any exorcism, anything ghostly even. Throughout every thought that went through and returned to go through his mind again and again, was the underlying fear that he didn't know what to do and even if he did come up with an idea, that he wouldn't have the courage needed to go through with things. He drove and prayed at the same time, praying for guidance, for enlightenment, for anything, for a miracle; that when he got back home there would be different pews in the church, that there would not be any possession, no spirits within the pews.

Father James' words of comfort and direction had been so welcome, even inspiring when he sat with John as they finished listing their findings on John's last day just before leaving to go home. Now in the car alone, the further John drove away from Father James, the weaker his belief in himself, in God became. How was he going to defeat these spirits? At least Father James had encountered spirits or ghosts or as he said, "something" during his ministry.

He told a story where he had been asked to go to a house where things were flying around the room and as he told John "I was scared." However, John even when listening didn't feel convinced. He felt it would be difficult for anything to scare Father James judging by his tone of speech in whatever he said. John felt threatened by his definite, firm tone.

"Make no mistake about it I was frightened. I couldn't believe it at first either but these poor people had lived in the house for a couple of years in the next village and things had started happening after the death of her mother in law."

John went through the story in his mind looking to find the self belief he felt when he heard it from Father James but the words that made the most impact and now when thinking, gave John the greatest comfort, were when Father James' frozen cold hand took his hand and said, "John.... remember, we teach people and lead people to believe in God, in a spirit, a force, something intangible, something based on faith and while you and I believe in the life of Jesus, that he actually lived, we still teach people he is The Son of God, the son of a spirit, a force. If we believe in God's existence we have to believe in The Devil, in evil and evil spirits. So when you meet evil, an evil spirit, an evil witch, let that be the confirmation that God exists, as a spirit, as a person in Jesus, as a sign of good. Use that! The greater the threat, the greater the evil, the greater God can be, the more you can use him, the greater your belief should be."

He looked at himself in the mirror and saw his facial injuries were healing noticeably and that gave him momentary consolation until Elaine's injuries came back to mind. She had phoned him that morning to say she had an appointment with the dentist later that day and that she was feeling a lot better having rested for much of the time he had been away. Paul and Rebecca had done nearly everything she would have done. John's thoughts were fully brought back to his driving as he heard the screech of his tyres as he floored the brake pedal.

CHAPTER 37

Elaine was worrying, her stomach churning, she had a feeling that she was going to be sick any second. She breathed deeply. It was five hours ago since John phoned her, telling her he was going to be late and not to worry but with everything that had been going on, her imagination was working overtime.

She looked out of the window when she eventually heard the squeaking of the car ramp as the recovery vehicle lowered John's damaged car onto the road outside their home.

Rachel had been sent to bed at the normal time as tomorrow was a school day. Paul and Rebecca were out and Elaine had not phoned them to worry them. What could they do?

Elaine hugged her husband with a hug that conveyed every moment of their marriage. He felt her love energise him, calm and reassure him, strengthen and support him. He felt protected. "Are you alright? Have you found out all that you need to?"

John was hesitant, almost reluctant, his own feelings of inadequacy surrounded his reply. "Yes I have, ...I think. Father James was very, very helpful, I'll go through things with you tomorrow and then......and then, I don't know the and then yet, I just don't know what to do."

John pondered as his new found knowledge refilled his thoughts with the awareness that now he knew the past, he had to do something for the future.

They walked into the lounge still partly hugging each other.

"How big was the deer you hit?"

John tried to answer Elaine in a way that put sense in his answer as the surprise of his accident jumped back into his thinking. "It was pretty big, I don't know where it came from, it was just there all of a sudden, right in the middle of the road, with, ...with a man next to him, well I think a man. I swerved. I saw a man's shape. I missed the man, thank God but when I got out there wasn't any man around, just the deer on the road."

"Is it dead? What sort of man?"

"I don't know, the vet came out and gave it some injections and loaded it with some of the police into his trailer, while I waited for the car to be sorted. It's made a heck of a mess to the bonnet and given the age of our car that may be a write off as well. I'll worry about that again, that's the least of our worries at the moment darling. Come on, let's have a glass of wine." John didn't pass any further comment on the man.

CHAPTER 38

John did not sleep well at all, despite the four glasses of wine. His mind would not switch off. It went over and over the last three weeks, now mixing in this new found information but not with any organised thought. When he did wake up, he felt like he hadn't been to sleep at all, his mind still going over the same things.

For some reason later that morning, he rang Martin to tell him what he had found out. John was not looking for Martin's help or comment, he just felt he should do it.

As Martin listened, partially wondering what any of this really had to do with him, he thought back to his visit to the timber suppliers and the three hours he had spent there hand picking with one of the staff, each piece of seasoned oak, ready for making these pews. He had not purchased any other timber that day and had gone with the intention as always of getting the best, for his own reputation and for his customers satisfaction.

He recalled how he had looked over various lengths three or four times, checking for any imperfections, any warping as he talked to a very helpful ginger, long haired but shy, brow dipping rep who never looked directly at him as they talked, called Jim or Jimmy, about this nice job he had picked up to make new pews for a church and how he picked up a splinter when rubbing the wood, as he inspected the life within the grain. The splinter, one of thousands over his years of being a carpenter had drawn a small drop of blood and he had thought nothing of this daily hazard as he wiped it off the seasoned timber.

Martin continued to listen but started to wonder as John finished talking, how much of the decision to select the timber had been his. The call ended and Martin's interest disappeared after some five pondering minutes as he turned to his in tray to look for the next order.

John left for the church. He had a feeling of foreboding and inadequacy. As he walked, he thought and his thoughts and confidence became more uncertain as if the high blustering wind was sweeping away his resolution from within his mind as it forced itself against his face and head with a biting chill. "Well at least it's not raining but I should have worn a bobble hat. My ears are freezing." He smiled momentarily at his own thoughts about the weather. When he got about half way, he turned around and walked back home.

"I still don't know what to do," he said to a surprised Elaine, as he walked in through the back door. He looked more agitated. "Perhaps we should just have the pews taken out, that might be the answer.....the easiest way." John had left without saying a word to his wife as he didn't want to worry her or to put her at risk, which was now quite contradictory given how he walked back into their house and what he now suggested.

"You were going to tell me what you had found out but you nipped out without saying a word." Elaine emphasised the You's in her telling off. "How can I help you if you don't talk to me. Now ,.....sit down, show me what you have found out, so we can think this through together." He knew from her tone that she was not happy and was serious in her order.

John got the papers out and spread them out on the kitchen table, moving the two cups of tea Elaine had quickly made after he had come back in.

"Ok, so what's the final conclusion?" Elaine jumped right to the end of where this conversation would eventually lead.

John looked startled. His answer conveyed his own incredulous understanding of his findings. "The conclusion is we have pews in the church made from a tree that was used to sacrifice witches. It was also used to hang people."

"So?"

"So!, so that's it. We've got a tree on which people were killed, ...in our church."

"And you think......?"

"Look!" John said very slowly and with determined, controlled patience. These are all the names of the people accused and killed as witches, well, we assume all the names if you take the parish records to be complete. The first witch to be killed on this tree was called Claudia, the second was Claudia Elsbeth, she was fourteen months old, a witch at fourteen months, can you believe it?"

"And this was Claudia's daughter I suppose, cos they used to name children after the parents years ago."

"No the parish records show her to be the daughter of Claudia's brother James and here look, two days after the recorded death of Claudia Elsbeth, James is tried and killed as a "witch" or more accurately a "warlock" because that's what it says here." John pointed to his own hand writing next to the name James on the photocopy of one of the old parish records.

We also found this. We can only assume this was written after the death of Claudia Elsbeth. It's not addressed to anyone but it's on the same paper back at the church, so it seems it was written at the same time. It says that a baby girl was saved from a life of demonic slavery, that her soul was saved and sacrificed in the name of God. There's something else here that

Father James found. This James was also accused of teaching witchcraft, like a leader but in those days, once someone was accused of being a witch, they were more or less dead anyway cos if you survived the trials of burning or drowning you were still killed as a witch; you couldn't win!

It's the name of the baby Claudia Elsbeth, that's the name I used the other week in the christening, why would I have picked that?, why would I have known that ....that obscure combination of names?"

John went on through the list of names, the reasons for their deaths.

"But you still haven't said what you eventually think!"

"I think, Father James thinks," John paused and reflected on his conversation with Father James, "that this tree, our pews, have the spirits of these witches in them. Whether they were witches or not, whether you believe in witches and magic or not, these people were killed as witches, in the name of God. I don't believe in magic, I don't believe in witches but I do believe in evil and the basis that it can come in different forms. You can bet your life that these "witches", these people, used herbs and things like that and because that was different; ignorant, uneducated people in those days accused them of witchcraft. That's not flying around on broomsticks with pointed hats, black cats, twitching your nose like Samantha in Bewitched but they were killed for nothing, they were possibly, probably all innocent of proper witchcraft; basically they were, ...killed in the name of God, killed for nothing but ignorance, that's the truth of it."

Elaine's voice rose in pitch, in correlation with her surprise and her anticipation. "And you think their spirits are trapped, trapped in the wood, the pews now, ...somehow?"

John's answer came with head rubbing, twitching, hesitated,

confused delivery. "I don't know, I think it..... then when I think it, I think ....how stupid it sounds but I've got no other explanation for it, have you? If they were witches, even some of them, even just Claudia and the rest were innocent, think how they would have felt at being killed in God's name, how they would have felt towards God, their anger, their fear, their desperation. I really don't know what to do. This is not some Hollywood film, some Tom Cruise, Mel Gibson, action film. We are a small country side town, real people. None of us in our lives have ever met or will meet anything like this, even if only part of this is remotely true or possible. This sort of thing doesn't exist, it's only in films, in books, not in real life and it's,............" John hesitated even more as he tried to think straight, to be logical, ..."they are in our church and ....I............ I've got to do something about it ....and I'm scared Elaine, I'm scared for me, for you, for our kids for everyone in the church."

John's uneasiness and his conflict with his rational was evident on his face, throughout his whole body and the feelings it conveyed transferred easily and uncomfortably to Elaine. She had hoped that her realisation from last week when she had sustained her own injuries were misguided. She'd wanted John's conclusion to be telling her something completely different, she was willing for a happier conclusion and now she felt her stomach churn with swelling anxiety.

"I came back today, I turned around and came back because I couldn't face going into the church alone. Do I bless the pews because I didn't the first time we used them, do I exorcise them because I've never done that either.

I preach about God and belief but the truth is I've never had to do anything out of the ordinary which puts any of it to the test."

Elaine put her hand on his arm and squeezed it, her voice

filled with support. "Why did you become a minister, do you remember? I'll tell you why, to make a difference. Do you remember?" She urged his memory........ "We talked when you first said you felt called to be a minister; because you.....YOU wanted to make a difference to this world. You've been a minister for twenty years and I'm certain YOU HAVE made a difference to so many peoples lives. This is just something different, something,.....yes bigger but if you are right, if it is what you say it is, then we have to face it, we have to believe."

John stared affectionately at Elaine, his mind trying to establish a sense to things. "Do you know what I think?" John still didn't sound definite, I think we should hold a service where we both bless the pews and..........and I suppose, exorcise the pews by reading all these names out, to release them from their possession, so that they can move on, to ......to ask for their forgiveness of.....God.....of God?.....because of God, because of others ignorant faith in God.........is that right? What do you think?"

"Possession?" Elaine blundered out the word and felt her comment, her question, her confirmation just compounded her confusion despite the conversation they were having and despite her own experiences, her own earlier unaccepted, denied realisations. Do you see the people in the congregation willingly come to an exorcism, for want of a phrase, most of them come to look good in everyone else's eyes. You saw Mike and how he beats Liz," Elaine paused, "and how do we know about that now; we've never known about it before, not until the pews arrived. In fact we know more about some people now, than we ever did before." Elaine's expression changed as an enlightened idea, came into her mind.

"Put them to the test!"

"What?" John sat back in surprise. Elaine, despite her beliefs and marriage to John, had never advocated confrontation, testing, in the way she was now suggesting. She believed in giving support to people so that they should never feel helpless or alone but now, this suggestion almost seemed aggressive to John.

"Put them to the test. Jesus was always testing people, so tell them the problem and then invite them to come and pray and to help you overcome the problem."

"Do you honestly see them doing that?"

"What have you got to lose, I'll be with you." John took her hand and looked directly into her eyes, trying to assess her train of thought, her commitment, the reality of what she had just suggested.

CHAPTER 39

That Saturday afternoon John, Elaine, JJ, Beryl, Mike and Elisabeth Evans all turned up at the church following John's phone call to them asking if they could meet him and Elaine.

"Are you serious? You want us to fight spirits in "the pews", to conduct some sort of exorcism, for God's sake John, where are you coming from. You sound like some bloody nutter!"

Mike Evans reaction was less than supportive when John explained his recent trip and what he believed he had found out. To think there could be anything this intangible to Mike was unthinkable. John and Elaine looked closely as he protested the sanity of what he had just heard. While his reaction was emotive, his emotions didn't quite match his reaction. John and Elaine exchanged looks, both sensing something was not quite right as he made his protests.

Beryl and JJ instantly agreed to be at both services tomorrow, to speak in support of John if needed, when he asked for his congregation's support in blessing these pews and to have a special prayer meeting during the evening service, with the aim of freeing any spirits and bringing the next lease of life to these pews for their work in God's world, to be glorified for those who worshiped.

"And will you be able to help us tomorrow Liz?" John asked Mike's wife. Liz instinctively looked at Mike, especially after his earlier protests.

Mike looked at Liz, daring her to defy him, to say or do anything that didn't comply to his order . "She feels the same as me John, this is just superstitious nonsense. I have never heard such.........such crap from anyone, especially a minister."

Mike became incensed immediately at John asking "his" wife for "her" support. He had always decided what they did within the church community.

Liz's voice was unfaltering. Every word she said came over with a slow positive determination. Everyone in the vestry knew she had made up her own mind.

"You can count on my support John. I'll do whatever you want me to do. If what you say is right and I think it is, especially after what we all experienced last Sunday, then we all have to take a stand. How can we call ourselves Christians if we don't help John, if we let you face, ...whatever alone. Sometimes you have to take the hard option and that's what I'm doing."

She turned to Mike with a new look in her eyes, "I don't expect anything from you ever again, you spineless runt."

Mike coloured up both from embarrassment and anger. He watched his wife walk out the rear door of the vestry and walk out along the rear passageway towards the church kitchen. There was a different persona about her presence.

He stormed off through the other door that led into the church, slamming the door behind him to ensure there was a barrier between himself and the others but he knew his control had walked out of the door with Elizabeth.

Mike sat there for a couple of hours, in no rush to leave and go back home or to go back into any other part of the building where he might meet John or anyone else for that matter. He stared at the light streams coming in through the semi opened shutters and in through a few of the stained glassed panes and became absorbed by the tints and colours and the misting affect they created with the dust that was hanging in the air.

"You just don't realise how much dust is floating around," he thought to himself. "You'd think this place is pretty clean." He found himself starting to assess the volume of dust mist he could see but stopped himself before his mind started to make complicated calculations to get to an answer.

The old pew he had decided to sit in, in the far left corner of the church creaked as he moved around, crossing one leg over the other and then swapping; his slow, erratic uncomfortableness mirroring the changes in his mind as his brain pondered and reflected on his situation, "that wife of his," this unbelievable bloody stupid garbage he was being asked to believe.

He adjusted his seating position, placing both feet firmly on the floor and bent forward, his elbows on his knees, his head bowed down as far as space and his back would allow and his mind regurgitated the same thoughts over and over. His position remained unchanged and his breathing slowed to just above sleep, his closed eyes helping to subdue his anger and focus on his thought repetition.

The silence of the church accepted the muted rumble of the traffic passing outside which added another dimension to the solitude he was enjoying. It filtered through the oak doors and on through the vestibule, through its closed inner doors, diluted of volume, creating a fabric to the silence, giving it substance, a silence you could almost touch, a sensation surrounding Mike, a silence which had feeling.

The wood warmed up underneath his bottom and thighs. It radiated against his legs as he shifted his position slightly while remaining in the same position and Mike became aware of its warmth as his legs and bottom touched the surface of the seat, each time he made an adjustment his seating position, no matter how minor or slight.

His ears subconsciously picked up the sound of creaks around him. At first they added to his feeling of solitude, making it thick, a texture to his isolation.

He looked down at his own thighs and deliberately sat rigid, his eyes transfixed to his own legs and the seat of the pew, ensuring that he wasn't moving. Mike shallowed his breathing, controlling the rise of his chest as he took in long, slow, streams of air through his nostrils. His eyes now open and fully awake out of his earlier absorbed contemplations, glanced around again slowly, not lifting his head, their direction aiming his focus and directing his hearing to where he could hear the movement from within the other pews around the church. He held himself still, counting almost each creak and tweak, each groan of wood the church pews were making, the sound they made as people moved around on them, the wood living and responding to the weight they supported; yet he knew he was alone, the sounds of life trying to deceive his logic.

His right hand involuntarily came to touch his right cheek and he held it there, feeling the heat his face was feeling, as if he was close to and looking directly into a raging fire. He could sense his skin burning and he looked at the perspiration now on his hand from his face. His throat felt hot but as he breathed out in short puffs to relieve the burning sensation, his breath clouded in plumes of iced speckles, floating in front of his face. Mike stared and felt the ambiguity and it confused him.

He sat purposely static and listened again to the sound of the pews, wondering what he was listening to. The church was empty apart from him. Mike raised his head tentatively up over the top of the back of the pew in front and looked around the church. The sound of wood moving, squeaking, groaning seemed to surround him. Mike became aware of the sound of the traffic passing on the main road outside and put the sounds of the pews down to the vibration of the traffic. "Bloody stupid garbage. What are you going to do?" Mike looked around in the now darkened church and asked a rhetorical question to himself. "This is just bloody stupid. John's lost it. All this crap about possession, it's just the vibration of the traffic outside that's causing all this." Mike looked around in the now completely unlit and darkened church and felt reassured that his mind had established the answer, the logical, explainable answer.

He looked around the church again, his eyes straining to focus with the lack of light. The sounds of the pews held his concentration, drawing his hearing to their points of origins, each movement emitting its own variation of sound, the wood talking. Mike stood still and stared into the darkened body of the church, its shadows changing Mike's vision of the church he knew so well; its textures eluding clarification. "Time to go home to that stupid wife of mine. Let's hope dinner is ready." Mike spoke out aloud to himself as he walked to the front of the church and out through the door leading into the vestry. He stopped and turned to look back into the church before leaving "I never knew these seats were so noisy. They say wood is a living thing but I never knew they were affected by the traffic as much as this!" His thoughts ended as he walked through into the vestry and closed the door behind him. The noises in the church stopped the moment he closed the door. Mike didn't hear the church resume its pure silence.

CHAPTER 40

The looks that the other members of the congregation gave each other on hearing John talk about the origin of the pews displayed the same disbelief as JJ, Beryl and the Evans' yesterday.

Some felt horror at the thought that there were pews in their church which had been made from a tree used for execution purposes. How could such a thing happen? Didn't anyone check for this sort of thing? Some people with little to do, had nothing better to say, than to immediately look to throw blame on someone for not checking on things. They stifled their outrage, sitting there feeling indignant at being unknowingly put in this situation.

Others listened with interest with no deeper thought than that was then, this is now and the pews are just pieces of wood.

Some had their morbid interest awakened, their minds creating questions, wanting to know more. How many people died? How did they die? Why were they killed? Where and when did this happen?

John had taken the precaution of taping off the rows of pews where he and Elaine had been hurt on "those occasions." He hoped at this stage that this was the only area where the "witching tree pews" were within the church. As he cordoned off the pews before the start of service, he had felt a mixture of being threatened, as if now he knew about their origin, the pews were not going to hold back and be discreet about things anymore: his other feeling was one of insecurity. Even in his own church, where he felt his belief and strength should be at their strongest, he felt completely inadequate. He wondered how far their influence could reach.

His new knowledge had given him the chance as he thought back over the previous weeks, to clarify in his own mind, that people had only been affected within this particular section of seating to his understanding and he really hoped he was right and that their influence did not extend to beyond where they were bolted to the floor. John could not convince himself and here he was now, telling the congregation and now asking them, if they felt they could come to the evening service with the special intention of blessing and cleansing the pews, that their unity and faith were needed for this purpose.

John asked for a show of hands, more so for his own reassurance than to make people commit in front of others, where they could see others raising their hands and would not want to be seen as unresponsive.

John glanced around as he announced the number of the first hymn and continued to look around more than usual during its singing, for tell tale signs of unusual behaviour. His mind breathed a very discreet sigh of relief to himself as he watched everyone sit down.

"Let us pray."

"Let us pray." A female voice hinted an echo of his words around him. John gripped the sides of the bible on the pulpit lectern.

"Go on, start your pray." The voice was sarcastic, taunting and just above a whisper.

John looked around himself, his body and legs hidden from the congregation's view behind the pulpit. He could see nothing around him, just space.

"Father in heaven......"

Trevor Davies felt a shudder as John started his prayer. He looked around to see if the inner vestibule doors were still open as he had never found sitting in the back of the church cold before but he felt chilled.

He always sat on his own, preferring not to be distracted by sitting with others so that he could fully concentrate on every part of the service, whoever the minister was. He had missed the last few weeks having been away on holiday. Trevor had noticed the difference in shade and age of the new pews by comparison to the old ones which hadn't needed replacing and wondered why there were some to the front and centre which had tape on both of their sides, stopping anyone from using them.

At forty three he had been diagnosed twice with cancer since the age of twenty nine and had come through the ordeals with treatment and with the help of a local support group. One member of that group, Vivian, was a strong believer and told Trevor that she prayed for him every day. That had influenced his thinking into whether there was a God or not and while he was still uncertain, he wanted to concentrate during each service to assess and analysis the likelihood. If nothing else, the principles of the Christian faith whether there was a God or not, were good rules to live by.

This was a far departure from the young, aggressive eighteen year old he had become when Mary, his girlfriend of the same age, had been killed in a car accident, in a car they had both been passengers in. He had never forgiven himself for jokingly jumping into the rear seat she was getting into. It was only after his first diagnosis at twenty nine, did his reactive anger start to dissipate and his demeanour started to change to a more calm nature.

His attendance this morning drew another name sake spirit towards him.

"Mary would be here now if it hadn't been for you!" Trevor took his eyes off John and darted looks around himself, wondering where the voice had come from.

"What! What are you talking about?. He instantly on hearing the accusation reacted and the remorse hit him, upsetting him instantly as his memories of that day barged their way past John's prayer.

There was no one close to him. He sat alone in the centre of the rear row of pews on the left side of the church with three clear rows in front of him; the nearest person being two rows in front on the right hand side of the centre isle.

Trevor looked around a second time, reassured that no one had said anything to him and then looked back towards John. His stare was hijacked by a young lady standing in the line of taped off pews looking back towards him.

This time he watched her speak to him, her voice soft, clear. "Trevor, we know you have lost someone, lost Mary, we have all lost someone."

Trevor forced himself into the backrest, a reaction to the surprise of seeing her standing where she was and talking to him, along with the anger and indignity he felt at being accused of Mary's death by this stranger, someone he didn't even recognise as being part of the usual congregation.

He looked at everyone else in a glance. No one seemed to be aware she was standing there during the prayers, not even John who continued with what to him would be the back of someone standing up, while everyone remained seated with their heads bowed. Trevor could see that he was the only person to react to her presence.

His focus and attention were sucked towards her, his awareness of being part of the congregation swept to one side as he just looked at her gaze transfixed on

him. His mind started to analyse her clothing, trying to date it but its appearance and hers were fluid. The dark blue, scooped neck, long sleeve dress she was wearing seemed to shrivel in front of his eyes with holes appearing all over the fabric, exposing her skin underneath which quickly turned from flesh colour to charcoal blackened mounds, smeared with bubbling blood. Her hair changed from being long, black and straight to long, blond and curly. She dipped her head for a few seconds, hiding her face, raising it again to be someone different, someone familiar.

Trevor gripped the seat either side of his legs, his back unable to press any harder into the back of the seat. He could see nothing else in the church other than Mary his eighteen year old dead girlfriend standing in front of him. He watched afraid to move or speak as the blue blackened dress transformed into the black cotton jeans, yellow V necked T shirt and black leather bolero jacket Mary had been wearing the day of the car crash.

He sat ridged, a tear in his right eye about to swell and roll over his lower eyelid as he watched her lips move to speak to him again, her voice still the voice of the young woman.

"My name was Mary Jones as well and I was killed because of someone else, someone who thought they were just having a joke. They just joked they thought I was a witch but that wasn't a joke when I lived and someone who didn't like me overheard them and I was taken and then tried by the towns people and hung......

hung almost like your Mary."

Trevor saw the car accident as if he were still on that same journey. He felt the jerk of his seat belt against his chest and watched the belt around Mary yank out of the faulty rear right side receiver, the loop of the belt springing back and go each side of her body as she jerked forward in the seat, the steel clip catching in her throat, breaking her neck as the inertia snapped the belt tight. It was a freak accident, a combination of highly unlikely coincidences but Trevor could never forgive himself. He thought time and time again why didn't they swap seats or Mary could have moved to the centre seat when she had trouble clipping in the belt, thinking after a few attempts that it was secure.

He heard her voice change as she spoke until it was Mary's voice he was hearing. The tear ran down his right cheek and his lips started to quiver as the unreal realisation that his Mary was standing in front of him. Trevor stood up, enticed by the apparition of his beautiful girlfriend and slowly started to reach out towards her with his right hand.

From the pulpit, John could see Trevor standing, his right arm extending towards the front of the church. He was the only person on their feet. John's eyes flew around the church as he continued with the prayer, looking for something, anything that would explain why Trevor was standing.

"Father in heaven, we believe in life external and ever

lasting, sitting at your right hand, where time has no meaning and love is everything. Let us cherish the time we have here on this Earth and with your help to our understanding, let us live our lives with each other, with our hearts filled with your heavenly love."

Mary's voice became apparent to John. He lifted his head up quickly to look around the church again and saw Mary instantly, standing facing him from where Trevor had been looking at the transforming apparition. "I would have liked to have lived longer than I did, to have shared my love and life with Trevor. Where was God when he allowed me to die because of a freak accident?" John heard two different women's voices. The first Trevor's Mary, the other he had heard when she had repeated him at the start of the prayers when she said "Let us pray." It changed as she was speaking, becoming a little deeper and sounding a little older. "Where was God in the hearts of those who took me from my family and hung me."

John hesitated and stumbled while he tried to continue his prayer as he watched Mary change to Mary, their images and clothing morphing between each spirit. Within seconds of watching the distortions their effigy had disappeared.

Trevor had watched his girlfriend fade in front of his eyes. She had not altered from looking at him despite the fact that John was seeing something different from the front of the church. Her face was the last of her to effervesce, her look towards Trevor, a smile of under

standing and forgiveness. It took Trevor's heart with it.

The spirit of the witch Mary spoke again to Trevor, her voice ethereal yet subdued, conveying authority. "Tell him. Tell John. Tell him God is never where he should be, where he can help you, help us, when we need him most. Prayers are a waste of time, he never answers and we are the ones who suffer."

The emotion generated by the vision, resurrected the old Trevor and his long subdued aggression started to rise. His head throbbed with thoughts about how Mary could have stayed with him, now that he had seen her again, only twenty five feet in front of where he was sitting. He looked up at John and the words of his prayer repeated themselves in his mind as he thought back to the time of her appearance. "Father in heaven, we believe in life external and everlasting, sitting at your right hand, where time has no meaning and love is everything. Let us cherish the time we have here on this Earth and with your help to our understanding, let us live our lives with each other, with our hearts filled with your heavenly love."

Trevor was now shaking with erupting anger, subdued over the best part of twenty years of guilt and grief. "Tell him!" Mary's voice gave him direction.

Trevor looked up at John who was trying to regain his composure and continue with the prayer. "We have learnt....sorry-..been taught that your grace...I mean your love...."

Trevor was still standing. "This is a load of bloody bollocks. What are you trying to say. Eternal life is better than real life? I'm not bloody bothered about eternal frigging life, I wanted life with Mary. Don't stand there spouting crap about eternity when I haven't lived my life in the way I wanted to, with Mary."

"That's it tell him." Then his Mary's voice followed. "Yes tell him."

Trevor's whole body was vibrating, energised with uncontrollable rage at the second loss of his girlfriend.

"This is you and your bloody God. Why should we come here and listen to you spout on about love and compassion when God himself couldn't show me compassion. What loving God kills a eighteen year old girl for nothing." His voice screamed ...."for nothing."

John stopped his prayer and by now, all members of the congregation had turned around to look at Trevor and his uncharacteristic outburst. He had already considered intervention and he tried to gather himself within the disruption of the prayers and his service.

The voice of the entrapped Mary spoke again. "What can you do to save your Mary? What can God do?....nothing!"

Trevor started to become physically violent. He started to kick the pews in front of him, back kicking with his heels, the pew he was sitting on. Everyone looked as tounded at him, John walking down from the pulpit. He knew this was unnatural. "Trevor, please Trevor, there's no need to be like this. I know it's not you. Come on, come on, come with me outside, come on....." John walked into the row of pews while Trevor kept on kicking out, front and back. "Come on with me." John held out his right hand. "Come on Trevor, let's go outside."

Unbelievably and thankfully to John, Trevor took his hand and followed John out of the church. John paused at the doors and turned back. Sing the next two hymns, one after the other and I'll be back soon.

There was a general murmur of "what was happening" as the organist started playing Love Divine and the congregation, despite their uncertainty started singing. John walked back in at the end of This Little light of Mine, without Trevor. As he walked down the isle, back towards the pulpit, passed the taped off seats, he saw and heard Mary, the convicted witch appear within the line of pews, her body and clothing burnt, bubbled and bloodied. "Carry on...............John."

He paused mid step, looking towards her and the empty space around her in the pews. John could feel his body shudder momentarily at her intimidation. He glanced at the people sitting behind her and it was obvious they could not see her. He looked back at Mary. She had disappeared for a second time.

John continued to walk back to the pulpit, his mind racing with what he was going to try and do in the evening service, what might happen having just seen the embodiment of Mary, Trevor's reaction and he still had this service to get through. He caught sight of Elaine looking back at him as he walked down the isle. She looked extremely worried.

He walked slowly, head bowed, looking at the floor, back up into the pulpit, his steps deliberate and soft, his mind telling him to be quiet so as not to prompt any more "incidents." John's self doubts were mounting rapidly. His eyes caught a glimpse of dusty old black shoes and trousers, the tails of a long black coat standing where he would stand in the pulpit. He looked up and it was like a shadow had been lost by the switching on of a light, the blackness disappeared. He stood in the pulpit facing the congregation and then down at the open bible and the single strand of red hair on the right hand page.

The mix of expressions on the faces looking back at him, helped John to decide to speed up proceedings and change the conventional order of service. "Let's sing 315 as you all seem to be in good voice judging by the last two hymns." There were a few smiles and ripples of laughter and the next hymn went without problem. John watched people sit down, ready for his sermon, except a whole line of people that remained standing in the taped off pews, their heads bowed, their faces obscured. Virtually within the instant that he saw them and looked at Elaine and back, the pews were empty.

He looked down at the bible to gird himself. "Inspire them John, so that you get their support, their faith."

The woman's voice was different again, another voice.

He could feel the vibrations down his arms, his nerves burning. "Help me Father!" His own silent pray went heavenwards as he took a deep breath and swallowed to clear his throat.

"Pick someone John." A different woman's voice seemed to come from behind him. He spun around to look at the wall behind him, no one. He felt instantly sick. This was not the answer he wanted to his prayer.

He spoke quietly, discreetly through clamped lips. "What? Who are you?"

Two voices came to him from all directions. "You know about us.......from the witching tree."

"Us!" John's mind frantically sifted through thoughts to try and make sense of these new voices. "I know about you?" He felt more confused.

"Pick someone.....from here." The voices spoke in harmony. "You know about us. Dean told you how we were burnt for being witches in the forest."

John spun back around to face the congregation. He tried to control his expression by putting on a smile. He didn't want to pre empt tonights service by exposing their presence during this service. Elaine could see it was false.

The voices became impatient. "Pick someone John or we will take Elaine. Pick someone who is worthless to you

by comparison."

John started quivering as he heard their threats and turned the pages of the bible as if looking for new scriptures to read, to deflect from this interruption to his continuance. He now knew they were the twin sisters Dean had told him about in the pub, in the Forest of Dean. He tried to control himself so as not to spook the congregation as he needed as many of them that would turn up for the evening service. His desperation forced sweat from his forehead. He felt weak at the knees and held onto the lectern for support. His mind tried not to think of anyone but it found Simon Dyke, an apologetic, shy, hesitant twenty six year old parishioner who came every week and sat mostly, at the very back of the church on John's left side. Despite years of trying to get him to talk more than "hello, yes" or "no," John for all his ideology had never taken to him. He tried to make excuses in his mind for how Simon was but deep down he thought he was spineless, someone who needed a kick up his ass to stand up for himself in the real world; perhaps an attitude left over from his rugby days. Fight.

"Simon it is then." The twins voices harmonised. "Carry on with the rest of your service. Inspire them." Their goading froze John, his face transfixed towards his church, his wife and children, his congregation.

"Simon, John has sent us to you." Simon felt the hairs on the back on his neck freeze. He felt the unexplained warmth on either side of his body despite feeling cold inside. The hair around both sides of his head ruffled as the twins caressed him. He looked around bewildered for the source of the breeze that must be filtering into the church, catching his head and then at John who was now continuing with his service, seemingly oblivious.

The twins spoke as one, their voices complimenting each other in musical unison. "Simon, have you ever been with two girls at the same time?" Their memories of each of their individual experiences with the man they had loved, conglomerated into a euphoria of emotions, transmitted into the essence of Simon.

Simon's mind felt disturbed and he started to move agitatedly on the pew as he tried to work out and understand what was happening. The twins took total control and dominated him. A wave of calmness washed over his body and he lulled forward, his elbows on his knees, giving the impression of praying.

He saw and felt their existence as they transgressed through his brain and body, his sexual awakening now so badly mis timed and intense within someone who had never even kissed a girl.

"Leave.......leave with us. We are coming with you."

Simon slithered to the side isle and crouched down and around the back through the front doors, the twins directing him, their influence undiminished. He walked, still hunched over to disguise his erection. He stopped himself suddenly as his stooped vision took in the black trousers, shoes and long legs of someone standing in his way in the vestibule. He looked up, partly to apologise for almost walking into the person. Simon felt self conscious about himself. The face of who he now saw, as a very tall man was obscured for the most behind the tilted wide brim of the black hat he was wearing. He could just see the front of his chin and the ragged tousle of red hair hanging forward as he looked down on Simon.

His voice came down to Simon, calm, firm, an instruction. "See you tonight. Don't be late. Don't miss out."

Simon was often late which is why he always sat alone at the back, virtually mirroring Trevor's position on the other side of the centre isle. "Ye...yes....I'll be here."

He tried to straighten himself as he turned to move towards the door, the red haired man moved to one side, his voice again calm and authoritative. "You two stay here for now. You will see Simon again tonight."

Simon felt a ripple through his body as the twins stayed in the church while he bundled out the front door into the cold autumn morning. He turned to get a look at the man who been in the vestibule. It was empty.

John's sermon, the last hymn and the benediction was a haze to him. He had gone through the motions, his mind distracted in looking for any other incidents which would warn the congregation of what he feared they might encounter in the evening service. He caught sight of Simon leaving, his thoughts for a second wondering if anything had happened to him but then dismissing them easily, without concern.

At the end of the service he faced a mixture of reactions and questions as virtually each person from the congregation stopped to speak to him as they left the church. Some gave their excuses as to why they wouldn't be able to make that evening. Others asked specifically about Trevor, reassured by John that he had been calmed outside on the church steps before going home, promising John he would be in the service that night; John virtually telling him to take some time out and come back in a few weeks, not really wanting his presence in this evening service. John felt an overall feeling of support, peppered with a little trepidation from most people.

He felt more and more guilty as each person left unaware of the red haired man he and Elaine had seen or the common experience the small group had shared the week before. As he walked home alone wanting to think, oblivious to the driving rain which started after he waved Elaine off in the car, hands stuffed deep into his pockets, he pondered over what he had told them, what he had not told them, their questions and comments as they left for their Sunday dinners. They only knew half the story of the wood's past, not of the recent happenings, not even the row of twenty odd or so people he had estimated in thinking back, who stood in the cordoned off pews that morning. He wondered if so many people would have said they would come that evening if they knew of the most recent incidents attached to the pews.

John felt like he was deceiving them. A moment later a contradictory thought. "What they don't know can't harm them!" justified his deceit. "It was for their own good." He didn't want them to worry. He didn't trust in their strength of faith as he was questioning his own.

CHAPTER 41

Sunday dinner and the afternoon was pensive. No wine just long silences and understanding looks between John and Elaine, only answering questions or responding to their three children when they needed to. John sat alone in his study for hours and then made sure he was at the church earlier than the door stewards for the evening service, so that he was prepared in the vestry before the service and could concentrate on greeting everyone, just as he had said goodbye that morning.

Mike Evans was one of the stewards rostered for that night and he still thought this was a "bloody stupid idea" and he told John again, when he joined him at the front doors.

The rain had not stopped all day and looking out, down the steps and at Mal's closed fish shop across the road, reminded him of the day the pews were delivered. The light from the lamp posts caught the heavy drops as they fell and gave them a luminosity, making them more vivid to John and Mike as they looked out towards the people arriving, wrapped up in rain coats and umbrellas.

Paul Morgan the other steward arrived with his wife Maxine. She went and sat next to Liz while Paul stayed near the front door. The three men started to greet the evening worshipers, their minds each with different thoughts. John and Mike while doing the same greeting, felt more assured and frustrated respectively, as each person arrived. Mike's annoyance grew. His face did not look welcoming as his emotions governed its muscles. He did not want to be there for this "cleansing" service and had argued with Liz when they had got home after yesterday's meeting and again after this morning's service. He felt differently towards John since the accountant comment. John felt more confident as the numbers of the congregation grew.

Paul at twenty nine and quirky looking by conventional standards, was thinking about the Sunday night sex he and Maxine had after going to the pub for a few drinks and was wondering which option they should try tonight. At five foot eight, he always looked taller given his very slight build and this was accentuated by the fact that he mostly wore tight fitting clothes. He also wore his light brown hair spiked to make himself look taller.

As they greeted and exchanged pleasantries and comments about the torrential rain, none of them had noticed Liz and Maxine get up and move to sit in the two rows of pews that John had taped off for the morning service.

"Come on Maxine, let's go and sit in the naughty seats," Liz said, "after all, that's where Mike and myself usually sit." She led the long brown haired, brown eyed, slightly Chinese looking Maxine down to the front pews, pulling the tape off to allow them access. As Liz sat down, the feeling of defiance and rebellion she had felt against Mike as he pointed earlier to a row of pews in the right seating section, grew stronger.

"Sit there tonight," he had said. It was in one of the rows furthest away from their usual seats.

As they adjusted their dresses, their knees touching as they sat down, Liz felt Maxine's libido. It drew her attention to her curvy body within the tight blue pencil dress underneath her open, dark blue raincoat, in a way she had never noticed over the years she had known her within the church. She turned towards Maxine, running her right hand sensually along the top of the pew in front, the grain now somehow, distinguishable to her touch despite its smoothness and varnish. Liz repeated the action a few times, consciously letting the pressure she used with her fingers and thumb rise and fall as the wood slipped between; the sensation of the grain tantalising her as she sensed Maxine and Paul, the pew making its connection between the two women.

Liz leant in towards Maxine and whispered like a teenage schoolgirl. "Do you have sex every Sunday night, after going to the pub?"

Maxine flinched in surprise."Who told you about that?", she hesitated and almost blushed demurely but then let her sensuality ooze out to answer, the real Maxine exposing behind closed doors. Her voice almost growled with expectation. "Yes we do actually. It starts the week off with a bang." She sounded out of breath as if she had just had the anticipated sex. Maxine stopped herself, her surprise remained high at the fact that she answered Liz without intention. The two giggled, trying to keep their laughter suppressed below the volume of the softly playing organ. The two women suddenly felt connected. Maxine felt she knew Liz and Mike. She rubbed her wrists to relieve what she felt was pressure. Liz pulled her coat cuffs down so that they covered her thumb where it joined the palm of her hand.

Jeff and Jean James arrived at the church sharing a big red golf umbrella. Both in their late forties, trim and generally tanned, both golf players and relatively fit as they played about four to five times a week, having taken early retirement when they came into their inheritance money, when respective sets of parents died within two years of each other, two years ago.

Beryl had been their Sunday school teacher when they were teenagers. They had been some of the people more intrigued by the occult part of the John's story. As a school science teacher, while he believed in God, the story of the six day creation was not an option. Jean had been the science lab assistant at the same school and they both often experimented with each other in the store rooms before they got married in their mid twenties. They had one daughter who was now twenty three and had tried for more children but that just wasn't to be.

There was a similarity about their appearance, more like brother and sister, tall, fair haired, blue eyes; they were the sort of couple that people had said, had grown to look more like each other over the years they had known Jeff and Jean.

They had spent a bit more time with John when leaving the morning service and had asked how many people had been killed on the tree, had their deaths all been the same, was it just for witchcraft; they looked for a deeper dimension from within these pews. They felt that they had decided to come tonight out of interest, out of a curiosity as to what else John might say about the past. They sat down in the second row of pews behind Liz and Maxine. For them, they deliberately switched from their usual spot which was in the old pews. They looked questioningly at the seat and the back of the pew in front, their excitement heightened by knowing now, something of their origin. With so much free time on their hands, they read and researched different subjects which came up to "get into them" and had spent Sunday afternoon scanning some occult, devil worship type of books, just for background knowledge. The organ music slipped into the background of their attention as they looked at the wood formation, the grain quickly caught their willing imaginations.

They looked at each other with insightful recognition, their memories taken as one, fused by their expectations. Jean rubbed her hands up and down her thighs as she felt the tingles of excitement running through her body. In the pre service wait they became enveloped within their own bubble, oblivious to the other members arriving or already sitting around them.

"Do you remember the other weeks service, with that woman lay preacher in the evening, I forget her name, when John was taken ill?" Jean whispered to Jeff through the left side of her mouth.

"Yes, what about her?"

"Do you remember what the sermon was about?"

Jeff's mouth started to answer but no sound came out and he paused before continuing..... "no, I don't."

Jean looked puzzled as she couldn't remember either. "No nor me. That's strange for us, don't you think?"

Jeff squeezed her knee, there was instant recollection as they and the pew made combined contact.

Jeff remembered his thoughts as of that Sunday but they were not thoughts, they were instructions. He rubbed the back of his fingers against the pew in front, like he was stroking a pet. "Yes we have done those things all week." His mind spoke to the pews as if he was in a conversation. Jean looked at him, hearing everything he was thinking, her head nodding slightly in agreement, to reassure, they had followed their directions.

Jean sounded apologetic when her thoughts entered the conversation. "We've made up six different pots but we haven't had chance to try any of them yet. We were going to, just to see if we had done things right, when Harry and Sheryl called around for a cup of coffee in the week to talk about the golf holiday we're arranging together."

Jean stopped herself from continuing as she started to feel self conscious, as if she were too effervescent, especially when Jeff looked at her with a look to take control of her tongue. In those momentary glances within those few seconds, their contact with each other and the pew revealed the hesitation they had felt and exercised during that coffee visit. They saw themselves deliberating in the kitchen as the coffee percolated about adding one or other of the potions, their minds temporarily infected with out of character jealousy and envy which overtook their usual good humoured banter with their friends, about the fact that Harry and Sheryl just seemed to beat them in whatever combination of golf they played.

Jeff and Jean shuffled a little uncomfortably as if caught out, their minds recalling those deliberations and their private conversation in the kitchen as they plated up the Bourbon biscuits. "I'm fed up with Harry winning every time we play. I'm more than fed up, I'm sick of it. Sick of listening to his gloating, his boasts, his crap. He generally only wins on the last ball but then I get his offer of lessons. I want to show him some lessons. Let's give them this one."

"We don't know what it can do yet, we need to know. Let's wait. We can plan this better. Let's do this when we're on holiday and we can blame the food." Jean recalled her scheming logic of that Friday afternoon. "No! We can't do this to friends, can we? Not just because they beat us." Her mind contradicted itself as she held one of the Tupperware potion pots. She stood transfixed with it, holding it in front of her, taking the pot and Jeff into her one encapsulating look within their kitchen.

The hissing from the percolator brought their attention back to the process of making the coffee. Jean sat in the pew and imitated the percolator's sound, her and Jeff's memory of two days ago giving them both a feeling of unnatural embarrassment for being undecided, uncommitted and they didn't know why.

They looked at the man and woman who were now sitting down either side of them and gave small acknowledging smiles to both, their smiles were not reciprocated. They recognised their faces as being the two new people who had sat down next to them very recently, during that woman lay preacher's service. They hadn't said anything or made any gesture to Jeff and Jean then and had disappeared suddenly when the lay preachers sermon ended abruptly as a result of John's collapse and JJ helping him out of the church. They were still wearing the same heavy black, old fashioned Partisan style clothes, with thick brown scarves and Jeff had thought for that reason, they must have been farmers, even though he had thought it odd that they had come to church dressed in such a way.

They became seized into the past the moment the man and woman, put one hand each, on Jeff and Jean's leg. The back of the pew conveyed the outline of trees and hills, the amalgamation of this illusion drawing them both back to living three years ago.

Their own emotions became the emotions of the husband and wife, their feelings pleading for the release of their daughter as she was dragged to The Witching Tree. Jean felt the woman's despair at trying to get to her nineteen year old, jet black haired daughter screaming for mercy, as she tried to claw her way through the lynch party to get hold of her child, their finger tips just making the briefest of contact and then being pulled away from each other so they could not get hold of each other's hands. Jean in that moment felt the heat from the child's fingers as if she had touched burning coal, the intensity of their contact replaying the desperation of the mother and her daughter Beth to hold each other, for protection and safety. Her face winced with the shock.

Jeff imagined he was struggling with the people dragging his daughter to her unjustified death. He moved around agitated in his seat, his reactions controlled and subdued by the increase in pressure on his leg by the woman sitting next to him. The gruesome image of his daughter's legs jumping and jerking as the rope cut into her skin with her neck taking the whole weight of her body brought tears to his eyes, his paternal love erupting in a second by the transference of grief and then in the next moment, the memory of seeing his wife hanging next to his daughter, the crowds delirium and vengefulness fulfilled for that day, with the freeing of two souls in God's name. Jeff and Jean were being controlled, exposed to memories and emotions in sustainable doses, injecting recollections and feelings to work in conjunction with their logical scientific minds.

Jeff's imagination stood looking at their two bodies, hanging, his misappropriated loss and emptiness causing him to grip Jean's hand tighter than need be, the tears welling up in his eyes. There was no stopping his emotional dam from bursting, his mind deceivingly convinced his own daughter had been hanged. His body and head felt like he was swirling, being drawn down through the vortex of a whirl pool. The carnage the pews exerted on his feelings, thoughts and memories were incomprehensible to sanity. His head dropped, weighed down by the feeling of grief that his own cherished daughter had instantly been taken from him. He lolled around in the pew, his skeleton and muscles providing little support, causing his head and shoulders to sway from side to side as he tried to find some bodily strength to hold himself still. His memory brought back vivid recollections of her life, like a strobe light exposing the picture of a photograph within that brief moment of flash. He saw her birth and then the first birthday card at the age of three she had written to him, the squiggly, jagged writing "I love you daddy" still precious twenty years later and her card still in his bedside cabinet, along with every other card she had given him. He remembered her first steps and then later, her running out of school into his arms, her excitement at seeing her dad picking her up uncontainable as she gave him a huge kiss on his cheek. Jeff touched his own body, feeling the recollection of her hug as she kissed him. His heart relished every thought that his memory recollected and he was conscious now of the feeling of gratitude that he had felt for being lucky enough to have their daughter years ago and the gratitude that he in pray, had sent to God for blessing them with such a beautiful child. He twisted his lips and clamped his teeth to keep control. He started weeping quietly to himself, trying to disguise his loss of control as his tears covered his face, running down under his chin and onto his neck. Jean let go of his hand and lovingly squeezed and rubbed the back of his neck for comfort as Jeff wiped his face with both hands, not lifting his head as he tried to remain hidden. She took hold of his wet hand and rubbed it with her thumb and then jumped at having her ring hand unexpectedly crushed by Jeff's sudden grip. The reason for the six pots now become totally clear to them both, their mixture of berries, mushrooms, flower petals, stems, roots; combined and concocted from old forgotten recipes to bring death and demise to anyone unfortunate enough to be given an unknowing sample. Jean and Jeff had been infiltrated a second time and had taken another unconscious step to conversion.

Jeff felt the exhilaration of this shabbily clothed man as he mixed the same amalgamations to avenge the deaths of his wife and daughter so long ago in the past. He sat still next to Jean and felt the intoxication of beer fog his mind, like he had just left the pub but he could see this man's actions of that night, with no loss of clarity or memory.

There had been no rush on his part throughout that night, months later after the malicious, meaningless execution of his wife and daughter, when he had gone into the village tavern, amongst the murderers who had killed his Marian and Beth. There had been the silent exchange of looks as he walked in, between himself and every other man who he recognised as part of that witching mob. Some looked frightened, some embarrassed and some looked back at him with devout piety, assured in their rightfulness. The still grieving husband and father sat deliberately to the centre of the short wooden bar top, so that every man who came to buy a drink had to be in close proximity to where he was and this gave him the chance to engage in conversation. There was no anger, no threat in his approach, just the casualness of a man having some ale.

After about an hour and a half, he was invited by the ten or eleven men he had spoken to earlier buying drinks, to come and join them. He watched as their inebriation grew and carefully and surreptitiously dropped his concoctions into their drinks. The longer the evening lasted the easier it became. The more he pretended to be drunk, putting his hands over their tankards by deliberate mistake to take "his drink", so that he could tip his revengeful mixture into their ales, the elation of his retribution grew. He sat and laughed out loud within the crowd, buying a round of drinks, endearing himself. Jeff touched his own head at the feeling someone was playfully ruffling his hair and Jean could see with this, the group of men, back slapping and head rubbing the black haired, thirty something year old father, with beer driven affection. They had become oblivious to their delusional and unholy crime and treated the husband like a long lost friend, the ale thinking for them. Jeff could feel the excitement of revenge and it appealed to the non logical, emotional side of his brain; sweeping him into a dimension of unreality and history. In these moments of Jeff's integration, he had become that father and his emotions were being torn with the same feelings as if his arms and legs were being separated by four apposing horses, ripping his body and limbs into four quarters.

The night breeze lay a chill on his face and body and the smell of the trees came into his nostrils. His jacket was undone and open and he pulled it around his chest to keep out the cold. Jean took his right hand again and rubbed it. She felt a lot warmer than he did and her hands transmitted her body heat. Jean felt his temperature dropping as she saw the memory of the husband walking through the wood to the witching tree after leaving the tavern. The man in black increased the pressure he was exerting on Jean's leg, almost as an acknowledgement of her support and love for Jeff, in the same way his wife had loved him. Jean had lost all contact to the music in the church and her vision was the same as Jeff's, The Witching Tree. They watched with their stolen minds as the desolated father sat down close to the tree and just looked at where his beloved wife and daughter had been hanged. Jeff eased himself onto the left side of his bottom, putting his right hand under his right buttock, bringing his hand back out from underneath him and then rubbing his fingers against each other and the palm of his hand, feeling the dampness from the dew on the grass from the night time air. The seat of his trousers were wet.

The husband sat crying as he desperately willed God for the return of his wife and daughter, draining the last drop of ale he had carried from the tavern, throwing the earthenware canteen against the tree. The sky was clear and the moon's light, illuminated the witching tree and those that surrounded it within the clearing. There was a cold, still, blue monochrome beauty to the scene, had the father been there to appreciate the isolation and quiet of a midnight walk. Jeff looked at Jean and spoke softly, just loud enough for her to hear him over the organ music. His words were filled with the love and sincerity of person apologising to a loved one on their death bed, where partners in those last desperate moments together are swamped with the panic of their imminent passing, their emotions and their realisation that life is about to end and that there will be no second chance to say anything or to hold and feel each others love again. Jeff and Jean sensed the flailing urgency to reaffirm undying love and promises before being separated and passing onto the next life. He felt as if he was wanting to make good for all his inadequacies that had brought any sadness or remorse to the life they had shared together, that human combination when in marriage, had only seen and looked for love and happiness and this drew the very essence of being human, to its exposure. His voice cracked with the torrent of remorse and confusion, from the emotions he was feeling "I'm sorry.... I couldn't save you or our beautiful Beth, there were too many of them holding me down. I couldn't move, I tried but I just wasn't strong enough and I should have been. I let you down. I promised you I would look after you and I promised you I would never let anything hurt our baby, our beautiful baby girl and I did. I let you both down. I'm sorry, I'm so sorry. I can't let anything happen like that again, I can't. I've got to protect her Jean and you."

Jeff's face continued with its contortions as his tried to restrict these historic emotions infiltrating his own. He had been shown the entrapped souls of this small, loving family and they had exposed him to an overwhelming comparison of his own emotions within his life, struggling to cope with their grief and deaths, while now their memories making him fearful for his own wife and daughter. Jeff looked directly into the eyes of the woman sitting next to him with a resolute, defiant look; his mind his own for a second or so as he swore a self thought oath of protection for Jean and his own daughter, the new knowledge of these potions adding to his determination for their future.

The black clothed man next to Jean touched her leg again which prompted her into putting her left hand on Jeff's right knee, mirroring the woman in black, still with her hand on his left leg. They saw the father slump from sitting on the grass to rolling onto his side and then his back, after taking the full mixture of concoctions he had dispensed more individually, to the witch hunting mob he had deceived in the tavern earlier.

Jeff's voice remained soft and fragile as the father's spirit continued to relive his death.

"None of them darlings, will ever be able to do the same thing again as they did to you, never again my darlings."

Jeff eyes and nose were still watering and he rubbed them with the back of his left hand. His clothes felt damp and chill against his body. The woman sitting next to him took his hand with hers. It was icy and all of the heat he had absorbed from Jean's touch moments earlier was sucked out of his body. He could feel it drain up through his chest, along his arm and out through his hand into the hand of the female worshipper in black. She didn't look at him but sat still as if listening attentively to the sermon, in a service which hadn't even started.

The tastes that then passed across his tongue made him retch slightly and Jean started to lick her lips with an expression that shouted disgust at the flavours that she could taste in her own mouth. Jeff gripped her right hand and both held each other hands tight as they saw the calm suicide of the father as he prayed to be reunited with his departed loved ones. He was a withered mixture of inebriated, distraught, guilt ridden corpse, yet to die and all he could hear in answer to his pray was the sound of God sniggering within the blustering breeze through the trees. He looked at the tree canopy and branches swaying between moonlight and moon shadow as the wind injected animation. Jeff's face had drained of colour and his complexion had become as grey as the night sky he and Jean were seeing within their mutual vision. Jean desperately squeezed his hand again as she saw the life of the father fading, not wanting Jeff to follow in his wake. The woman glanced at her. She gripped his thigh just above his knee as she brought him back to the present, calming his and Jean's growing and conflicting sensations of victory over the mob, inconsolable mourning for the murdered family and the father's last seconds within his final suicide.

The change of tune from the organ to one with a more uplifting melody, finally returned them back to the evening service. They both had a smile for each other which, had anyone been looking at them with any interest, would have been seen as a look of someone who knew something you didn't. The only two people who looked at them, were the man and woman sitting next to them and they smiled, remaining silent.

Donna and Peter Phillips had stood behind Jeff and Jean, waiting to see an opportunity to slip through some sort of gap if one opened up between John, the stewards and Jeff and Jean. By comparison Donna and Peter didn't question much, they were here tonight because John asked for as many people to come as possible. Peter in his mid thirties and a year older than Donna, worked on the railways doing track maintenance. It was hard work and often unsocial where he would work through the night. At five foot ten, his bulk made him look bigger than he was and the work had made him very strong physically, despite his appearance looking a bit overweight. For him, it was a job where he was told what to do and supervised. He didn't have to think too much or take responsibility and this in its own course had weakened his mental strength.

Donna had a part time job in Mal's fish shop. She was equally introverted so for her "salt and vinegar, open or wrapped, it's nice out or that's a lovely piece of fish," was an engaging conversation. Her brown hair was just as greasy for this evening services as it was on the days she worked at Mal's, only then it was tied back. She always put this down to the frying of the chips. When she wasn't working she let it hang down and its greasy straightness accentuated her five foot six height as it gave her the appearance of being malnourished, her body pencil like, as it clung to her shoulders, back and chest. They managed to slip through a gap and smiled shyly at John and Paul, their eyes more focused on the floor than towards the three men greeting them in the porch. They sat at the back of the church in silence with empty thoughts and just waited for the start of the service.

John and the stewards continued to greet the evening congregation.

"Hello, I didn't think I'd see you so soon."

"Excuse me John we need some more hymn books." Paul politely interrupted John's greeting. "Oh sorry, look, speak to you after. Lovely to see you again and you." John looked at the man accompanying the young woman.

Barbara arrived still wearing her black PVC mac. She put her see through bubble umbrella into the holder and walked down the right isle, the rain still running down the length of her coat. Her hips twitched the PVC invitingly as Paul watched the charisma of her coat, his mind sparked into thinking what he and Maxine could do in their bedroom later that night. "Uumm definitely a PVC night."

Barbara literally slipped into her seat, the water on her mac making contact with the polished seat, acting like a skate on ice. She caught her balance and centred her bottom to the seat. She sat there quietly, looking around with her eyes only, her head more or less static. Barbara rarely missed a service and had felt compelled to come to this service after John's morning talk.

Her thoughts started to blacken as she listened to the organ.

"That's not the way to think Barbara," she thought to herself, "you've never thought like that about people. Why now? People are not looking at you like that. I'm not a nutter nor a prostitute." Her face grimaced as these strange thoughts started to filter across her brain.

"Cut it out. I'm not having it." She said it out aloud to herself, as if to stop someone different from leading her mind astray. She had never thought badly of people and she started to stare with a self assured intensity at the crucifix. Her posture altered and conveyed defiance. She crossed her arms across her chest and held them with tension.

"Do you still take drugs?" Her mind took in the question and she turned her head slowly, looking to her left and right at the empty seats next to her. "Don't go there,"she responded. Barbara's defiance grew as she made her response slowly and decisively, speaking again quietly out aloud to herself and to the question. Her eyes widened and her memories of her early twenties rekindled one by one. Barbara started to smile as some of those memories brought sentimental emotions about friends she had known forty years ago.

She shifted in her seat a little, her coat squeaking slightly on the wood. Her thoughts started to picture the friends she had shared her hippy days with, the music festivals, the changes in fashion and her smile widened as she recalled and relished the changes she had enjoyed as a young woman in the then rapidly changing, liberated society.

"What about those men, those lovers?" Barbara again turned her head and looked at empty seats beside her.

"Do you think I care? I didn't care then and I certainly don't care now after all this time. I've done nothing I regret and there's nothing you can say that makes me feel bad."

Barbara stopped herself as it dawned on her that she was speaking aloud to herself and answering who? She again looked surreptitiously around her at the other members of the congregation who were already seated and those who were still coming in, to see if anyone of them were taunting her. No one made any eye contact with Barbara with any conviction that convinced her that it was anyone there in the church. There were just fleeting glances of acknowledgement between Barbara and those around her.

She settled herself and looked back up at the crucifix and thought of the reasons why she started coming to church those forty years ago. Her memories interwove with her intentions to support John and the reason for coming this evening. Barbara started to rock very slowly back and forth in her seat giving animation to her confusion and her memories congealed with her present well meant intentions as they gathered momentum from a trickle into a stampede of thoughts and emotions from her younger life. She sat, quietly rocking and her past became her reality.

John started to walk to the front of the church when they felt everyone had arrived by six o'clock, looking up at the wrought iron effigy as he entered the main part of the church. His confidence had grown .....slightly ....and had surged when Elaine arrived. She had told their three children to stay at home this night which had made them happier than if they had to go to church a second time that day. The morning was ok but they didn't like evening services much and most of the time Paul and Rebecca still had homework to finish.

John had taken one step past the back row of pews, hearing, knowing the muffled clattering to his right hand side was Simon subsiding into his seat, virtually late again and then every light in the church went out, complete darkness. The organ stopped. John's heart stopped as the instant darkness and silence surrounded him. His chaotic speculations burst into action. Were the pews aware? Were they going to fight back? Was he strong enough? His mind spewed questions. He looked around, fright tightening his chest.

"There's a power cut. Everywhere is out." Mike called in from the porch as he stood about to close the outer doors.

John felt himself relax, his relief pumped through his body. He re started his walk down the isle, his left hand swinging from the top of one pew to the next in front, acting as a guideline but it made him think about his insecurity. He stopped momentarily and sniffed as the scent of lavender made itself known. The darkness obscured the flowers right down at the front of the church and his head moved slowly from side to side as he tried to remember if there were any lavender in the two large arrangements behind the communion rail. After so many years of flowers and their involvement with weddings, funerals and generally every service, his knowledge had developed on what flower was what; even though he still found associating their fragrances to a specific bloom difficult. John did however know what lavender looked and smelt like and he could not remember seeing any within those two displays. His heart missed a beat and he touched his chest with his right hand, aware of its spontaneous irregularity.

"We'll get some candles, stay sitting everyone for the moment, we don't want anyone falling over in the dark." He tried to sound casual and in control but his heart felt like it was drumming in his ears, the sound of it pumping in his chest was as clear as if he were listening to it through a stethoscope.

As John past the new pews where Elaine had been hurt, his right hand burnt with pain. He instinctively reacted and clutched it with his left hand. "Ooowwe," his reaction drew everyone's focus on him. Why should that happen now. The nurses had got the splinter out when he had taken Elaine to hospital.

John and the stewards brought candles out of the vestry having found them by using the torch on Paul's mobile phone. As they walked back into church with John and Mike holding a lit candle each, both carrying another five or so more candles, it created an ethereal atmosphere as the candle light illuminated John and Mike's features as they held the candles out in front of their faces. Paul followed with his mobile shining the torch light down onto the floor. Their small procession was reminiscent of the three wise men.

Mike placed his lit candle into the candle stick to the right of the crucifix and then moved the candle stick to the front of the communion rail.

"This bloody service should be cancelled here and now, no light just candles and not as many as we need. It's going to be too dark to see the hymn books and the organ doesn't work. Why doesn't John listen, or think." Mike had again suggested that they cancel the service while they were in the vestry looking for candles but John just seemed adamant to continue. Mike was feeling less than Christian again. "He's annoying me more and more."
His thoughts continued to deteriorate towards the minister as he lit the other candles and then pushed them into the various candlesticks at the front of the church. He watched John and Paul doing the same and the light grew as did the murmurs of approval from the congregation.

As more candles lit, the light from them concentrated in the area immediately in front of Jesus's effigy on the cross and the communion rail. The crucifix seemed to dance with the flickering of the fifteen candle flames, the light grey wrought iron picking up shards of light and reflecting tiny reddened and orange sparkles. As the three men looked at the cross, caught by the reflections, their own shadows were cast back towards the congregation, creating areas of deeper darkness, robbing those seated of what little light there was.

John turned to face the congregation, hearing as he did so, the closing of one of the inner doors at the back of the church. He strained to see who it was but he could just about hear them. The combination of candlelight and his eyes refused to allow him to see their two faces only the blackened shape of their bodies as they sat discreetly in the rear rows.

Alister and Haley hadn't been at that morning service but felt they should be there for this service.

"Look everyone, I think with this temporary hitch or I hope temporary, we will continue by candlelight but because this was not planned as a candlelit service, we have not got as many candles as we normally have so I think it would be a good idea if we could all move to the front and bunch up and if we then move the candle holders closer to you, we will all be able to see a bit better. If you've got mobile phones with torches that could help for singing the hymns."

John turned to look at the cross, the orange red shimmering gave a strange life to the figure which represented a symbol of their faith. In the darkness of the church, its reflection of the candle illumination hinted at being on fire.

Everyone moved forward to seats closer to the front. There was the usual reluctance when people are asked to move from where they have chosen to sit. While people re selected their next seat, John, Paul and Mike moved the candles to the front and sides of the now herded congregation.

John returned to the front of the church and went to walk up into the pulpit, stopping himself in mid step, saying out aloud, "No John, you won't be able to see anything from up there, that's why we've got the candles."

He appreciated the ripple of laughter as he turned around and faced everyone as he walked back to the communion rail.

He looked at the clustered group and now realised that there were parishioners sitting in the pews that he had cordoned off for the morning service. All of the first ten rows of the centre isle were more or less full. The thought of "I wished it looked like this every week" went through his mind. He took a moment to look at the seated congregation. The light from the candles now played with the features of these people looking back at him, waiting for the service to start.

Some, were just unrecognisable to his eyes, the candlelight

not reaching where they were sitting with enough strength to light up their faces. The shadows from the shoulders and heads of others sitting around them casting distorting black shadows which robbed their distinction.

John thought for one second of asking people to move out of the rows with the new pews but then thought of the disruption and reluctance there would be from the people in the row on having to move again. He heard what he thought was a whisper of encouragement from someone facing him. It was an odd thing to say, "what next my lover?"

He couldn't have heard it right. "Yes you're right" he replied, "what next! Well we've had the rain, wind, power cuts. All we need now is plague and famine and we've got an apocalyptic problem." There was another ripple of laughter. This time it made him feel uneasy as apposed to reassured, as he remembered the significance of why they were there and perhaps for him, the inappropriateness of the comment he had just made, given what he was intending or hoping to do.

His heart was still at full power as he put his right hand on his chest again and took a slow, deliberate deep breath in an attempt to exercise control over his own body. "God, don't let me have a heart attack here." The prayer left him while he held his breath.

John wondered if it was his imagination but there seemed to be more people now they were sitting together than he remembered entering the church or that had been sitting around the church before the lights went out. He caught a glimpse of a young man who he thought was Alister. The silhouette he could just about see sitting next to him, if it was, must be Haley. Where one was the other would be. His concern for Haley and her baby went irrationally to yellow alert. He looked around for Elaine but heard again one of the congregation call out softly "what next......a mother." He didn't understand the significance of "mother" but put it down to someone being sarcastically impatient and it distracted his attention from Haley. John hesitated again from continuing and then worryingly wondered if he was being taunted. He thought again of the significance of "mother" from this quiet prompt and thought again of Haley and then of Elaine and her frantic herding of Haley and Alister out of the church. He squeezed his chest above his heart, feeling its pressure through his skin and clothing.

"Yes right, the first hymn was going to be," he turned to look at the list of hymns, "well it's written up there but none of us can see it so I'm going to change things slightly considering the circumstances and we'll attempt 269, God's little light will shine." This time the laughter was jocular, everyone seeing the funny side of John's joke. Their laughter encouraged him and as they sang the first hymn without the organ, he started to think of his prayer, the cleansing and blessing. His new found intermittent strength left as quickly as it arrived and by the last verse he was feeling sick with worry.

He looked up from his hymn book, he could feel his heart beating faster, the rhythm distinct within his ears. John looked around, sure in his own mind that everyone else must hear it. He had never felt so anxious, not last week when Elaine was hurt, not when any of the three children were born. John prayed an instant "help me pray." Why were there some people still standing? Everyone knew it was custom to sit down after the end of a hymn, except the last hymn before the benediction. The unusualness and enormity of what he was leading to, faltered his conviction.

Elaine, JJ and Beryl saw John go static. They all saw his face freeze. The candle light played with his fixed features, appearing to move his face, changing his expression as the erratic flickering made the shape and form of the shadows on his skin bend and jump for consistency. His eyes reflected a disbelief as he stared above their heads to something above where they were sitting. All three sensed John....they felt his heart within their minds. They turned around in unison to look at what ever had stopped him in his tracks. Some others did the same, prompted by his pause and looked around when they saw and heard the others turn, to look behind them. They saw nothing but other seated members of the church.

Elaine felt John's trepidation. She knew this service was worrying him. She cleared her throat as a sign for him to continue, hoping he would pick up on her voice. He looked towards her, returning his vision to the congregation. There was no one standing now, just rows of heads and shoulders, some with hinted facial features, some with none, just bowed heads or faces hidden by the shadows cast by others. Elaine saw the movement of someone out of the corner of her left eye, someone standing in the shadow of the pulpit. She didn't recall seeing Paul or Mike move to one side. Elaine looked around to see if she could see where they had sat.

The candlelight gave the pews a new persona. Without natural light or the overhead electric lights to lighten the wood, the pews looked dark, sinister. Small sections on the backs of the pews became dimly illuminated for a couple of seconds or so as people shifted their seating positions slightly, the smallest movements of their bodies producing gaps and cracks through which the struggling light would dart and strike the pew.

The wood lightened in ever changing shapes and sizes, the dance of the oak coming to the attention of some worshipers quicker than others, depending on where they were sitting in relation to the candle holders. The sudden changes started to hold their eyes, their minds seeing different things within the momentary glimpses when they saw the oak highlighted. The darkness heightened their thoughts in those split seconds.

Everyone was making contact with everyone else in some way. Shoulders touching shoulders, touching arms, thighs touching thighs, legs stretched out, feet touching the pew in front. The contact gave everyone unknown unity and the pews unknown access to their imaginations. Only Simon still sat segregated from anyone else's direct contact in a pew on his own. He felt his hair move again, like masses of fingers running through his light brown locks. After an afternoon of self gratification, Simon had been drawn back to the evening service not knowing why. He had no recollection of the morning's experience although he felt there had been something odd about the morning.

The twins voices were still in harmony. They sounded enticing and cheeky. Simon was instantly drawn back to them by their invitation.

"It's nice to have you back with us. We've missed you Simon. Come with us again. We can stay with you this time."

Liz became more conscious of the warmth from Maxine's thigh as they waited for John to speak. She imagined the after church drink and then saw them in their bedroom. Liz compared their adventurousness to her strictly ordered life, order in every way. She rubbed her wrists at the thought of the tourniquets and the once a month regimented, disturbed sex. Maxine rubbed her wrists as well, Liz's feeling of frustration and entrapment tightening her chest as she breathed.

As with others before in earlier services the grain called again to Jeff and Jean. They sat watching it form pictures, their minds seeing the same things, more history come to life, their conscious minds combatted their imagination with the logical questioning of why and how they could see this.

The pew sensed their inquisitiveness and was eager to recruit two other believers. Jean felt the binding on her wrists and ankles and saw the face of Claudia emerge in the form of wisps and swirls, the grain manipulating her thoughts. Jeff looked at Jean, the candlelight not providing clarity, she looked like someone different, her features distorted and emphasised in an unusual manner. Jeff compared her face to the image he saw in the wood before him, there were similarities. His logic tried to squash his imagination and put it down to the lack of light and subconscious suggestion. He took a second look, the similarity remained. The shapes within the grain remained unchanged.

"Dear Lord, our Father in Heaven, we come here before you tonight to pray and confess our continued love for you and your only son Jesus Christ our Lord."

The start of John's prayer disturbed the integration that had moved between the congregation. Some looked up at John, others continued to look at the dappling of light hitting the pews, their thoughts held, their ears numb to John's words.

John saw a shadow move to his right, by the pulpit. He turned his head slightly to get a better look at who was standing there. The shadows hid the answer.

"Father, you have taught us to love one another, your commandments tell us to love one another as we love ourselves, yet two thousand years after the sacrifice of your only son, we still fail you and you still continue to love us."

As he spoke, John was feeling the contradiction of sanctity and fright. The shadow had unnerved him even more and he was already struggling.

Elaine could hear the hesitation, the lack of authority in his voice, it sounded like he was looking for reassurance, for someone to shout out their approval.

"We .....we are ....here tonight, to ask your blessing on ....the new pews that we have brought into your house, to continue your

glory."

Peter Phillips looked at Donna. "What?" He whispered, she leant in. "What's wrong?" She whispered back.

"Nothing's wrong, you said something to me! Didn't you?"

"No, I didn't say anything."

John continued, still sounding unsure by comparison to usual services and stopped their exchange.

"You Dear Lord ....have made all things in this world for us, your children, from the air that we breathe ....to the ground that we walk on, that ......that we are buried in, the same ground which grows the many riches and food which sustain our lives."

Elaine felt there was more positiveness in his voice as he entered the main body of this prayer, a prayer she had heard yesterday afternoon after he had prepared it.

John turned to look up at the cross, his hands outstretched to the side. The candles cast conflicting shadows on the crucifix wall as they lit the back of John from different directions. John and the flowing sleeves of his cassock formed bat like silhouettes.

"Ooooohhh I've seen him do this before, he's really good. He swooshes around like he's praying to the four corners of the world. I think he's ever so dramatic. I wanted you to see him as you missed him at the christening. I want him for our wedding. I think he'll be really good, you feel like you're involved rather than just someone sitting here. What do you think? We've just got to make sure he gets our names right. Mind you if he does say the wrong name we can always correct him because we sign the register afterwards. I think Tina had to change Christine's name to Claudia Elsbeth. I'm not sure really now, I'll have to check. Mary love her, died at the wrong time, not that it was her fault. I know she didn't mean to do it but it stopped the party afterwards, well you couldn't have a party then but I didn't get to speak to Tina. I thought afterwards it was a funny thing to do, to change her name at the christening. I know she's my best friend and I'm a godmother now, so I'll have to make sure Christine, no, Claudia comes to church when she's older, that's what this minister said. I'm responsible for her Christian something or other, anyway she's got to come to church when she's older. That's why I'm here now, I've got to find out what to do. He remembered me. I didn't think he would even though it was only a two weeks ago. I'll have to find out what Christine's real name is. Stupid though it sounds, there was so much crying and shouting and everything I didn't get chance to talk to Tina at all, all the family were there at the ambulance and everything, that bit was really sad, I loved Mary, we all did. Claudia is lovely, I like Claudia it's different but I'm not too sure about Elsbeth. It's a bit old I think, in fact I've never heard the name. Ooh here he goes again."

Veronica whispered her gushing to Richard sitting next to her as she watched John with child like excitement, turn back to face the congregation, his cassock swirling gently, the shadows exaggerating the flare of the sleeves and stole on the front wall.

"Whoosh, he's like Zoro. I wonder if we could have a candlelit wedding ceremony. It looks really pretty. I think it needs more candles though. What do you think?"

Veronica just about contained her enthralment and stopped herself from standing up as she pulled her right hand back from making a full and dramatic "Z" sword swish on the back of the pew in front; her left hand flicking out to the side to complete her sword fighting stance, almost hitting Richard in the face as she did.

Richard had leant in to his girl friend to listen to her excited whispering. He had fallen in love with her life and energy but repeatedly said to friends that her mouth could run a power station. He looked at her with a fixed, glazed smile, debating if he should try and answer any one of her questions. Richard thought as he squeezed her left thigh and said nothing. "Marriage!...........mmm?"

"From this ground grew the trees from which these new pews are made".

John looked up, there were people standing again. The shadow by the pulpit seemed closer, larger, even darker. John's mind jumped to the thought that some candles had gone out. His glances confirmed they were all still lit.

His right hand still raised, outstretched had started throbbing. He lowered it hoping it would stop, the lack of blood reaching his hand being the cause.

"What do you mean what next my lover? What are you talking about?" Peter Phillips asked Donna.

"What?" Donna looked totally puzzled. Peter pushed his whisper to the limit before his voice gained depth and volume. "You said what next my lover, what are you talking about?"

There was an uneasiness in his question, a feeling of effrontery. His body language looked jittery and Donna now felt this. It suddenly clicked with her, his defensiveness when he said, "what are you talking about?" Although he whispered it, he said it the same way as he had done when she found out six years ago that he was having a bit of a fling with a woman he'd been seeing in the food distribution company he worked for then. Donna had found out about it by accident when she'd emptied a pair overalls for washing and found a serviette from the cafeteria with a mobile number on it. She had used his mobile to phone it when he was in the shower and hung up when a woman answered, "what's up lover?" and then giggled.

Donna followed him that night and spied on them while they

"canoodled" in a quiet corner of a pub miles from home. Peter denied everything even after Donna had given him a chance to confess the following morning. The short video on her mobile made him change his story and that was the end of her trust in him.

She had felt betrayed. They had been married for five years from their early twenties but their plans to have children around about thirty went out the window after tests revealed Donna was infertile. The sex and passion stopped not long after the results. She felt guilty at enjoying what came naturally but which now would not produce an end result. Donna withdrew into herself as it was all "her fault."

Donna could see his new woman laughing uncontrollably and she knew it was about her, the things Peter was telling her, about how she was, her character, her shyness. She knew he hadn't been shy, not with his first affair but now walked around with a subdued, invisible persona; not wanting to draw attention to himself. He wanted to stay under her radar and everyone else's. He had become falsely mundane and she now saw through his tactic.

Peter could not keep eye contact with Donna. Her looking into his eyes went beyond his blue irises. It reached into his secrets and extracted them, giving them shape and form. "So this one has got black shoulder length hair, brown eyes and oh yes, thirty six inch legs and you love it when she wraps them around you. I told you what I would do to you if you ever cheated on me again, didn't I? Do you remember?"

Donna's voice was not Donna's even though her words made him remember exactly what she said she would do if he ever did anything like that again. She growled her whisper through sealed teeth, her own brown eyes were wide, angry and fixed on him the whole time. Donna did not blink once throughout this confrontation. There was no hint of any shyness.

The light from the candles was not enough to light her eyes in the way that they glowed. Peter felt his groin burn. He looked down and focused his eyesight between his legs with the faint thought this was going to help and sat, pushing his hands down onto his legs, forcing both onto the pew to try and control what he was feeling. He had an infection once and remembered weeing was like passing volcanic lava and this is what his entire genitalia felt like now. He ground his teeth tight, his lips clamped against each other not to let out any embarrassing sounds.

Donna could see even in this light, his face had turned bright red with the effort he was exerting to remain in control. She smiled a wicked grimacing smile and he heard her words in his mind "that's good enough for you", as clear as he had heard "what next my lover."

She watched him as he began to convulse, gentle almost casual heaves, his cheeks puffing out, his mouth unable to open to expel any air or sound. Donna turned her head to one side as she enjoyed his predicament. Peter felt his tongue moving around inside, searching for whatever was making him feel as if something had been stuffed into his mouth against his will. His mouth tasted bloody and salty at the same time, his tongue uncontrollably looked for where he must have bit the inside of his lip or cheek.

Beryl felt Peter rocking against her left arm, his convulsion unknown to her even though she was sitting right beside him.

"You have given us free will, free will to love you and to love fellow mankind, their failings, their success, their lives. Even non believers will look to blame you for our failings yet you are without blame."

Beryl listened to the next line of John's prayer and her own remorse flooded back into her thoughts. For all her belief and the years of Sunday school work, she could never forgive herself for the unwanted relief she felt when her husband Frank had passed away. She had watched him deteriorate over years of constricting Parkinson's disease which had taken the controlled use of his legs first and then had worked up through his body.

Frank had believed in God as much as Beryl and their lives had been blessed with two children and a house full of love. Despite the fact she was seventy six, she was to others, full of life and enthusiasm but her spark had been slowly and grotesquely bludgeoned out of her day by day as she saw her God loving husband, her children loving husband, HER loving husband, grow worse over a seven year period until he died two days after her seventieth birthday.

She remembered the family meal, her children and grand children, the presents, the hugs and the kisses she received, the love that permeated from every pore of those around her, for her on that day and the absence of any real attention Frank received by comparison. She felt as guilty now thinking about it as she had done on that day for enjoying it. The tears welled up in her eyes as she remembered two of her grandchildren, Michael and Philip both eleven, standing in front of Frank, staring at him, watching him twist and wriggle, shake and jerk. They tried to copy him but they couldn't copy his unco-ordination. They gigged and jumped around mimicking his demise until their mum came and edged them away gently. Beryl remembered his eyes just about following their walking away. She remembered the games of cowboys and indians he had played with these two when he was chief babysitter. Beryl saw Frank crawling down the hallway with the two boys, in cowboy hats and guns, to creep up on Indians or riding the arms of their lounge chairs like horses and their shrieks of enjoyment, the fact that both of them even wet themselves at different times when they had got so excited by the story and the game he had created, a special world between grand father and grand child. She remembered them saying "come on gran-dad, get up and play with us. You always used to play with us" and then one of then saying, "I think mum is right, he is going to die soon." Beryl remembered looking at Frank and seeing the frustration and the sadness at not be able to even say, "I still love you two cowboys the best. You are the best part-ners a cowboy could have," something he used to say to them during every game. She remembered the tears oozing out of his eyes as he managed one final glance up at his grand chil-dren as they left to go and play in the garden of the pub. She saw the final destruction of his will to live as he heard them say "he's no fun anymore." His shaking and twitching stopped as he watched them leave. She remembered wiping his nose, to maintain his dignity and the final look in his eye that ex-pressed the emotion or intention "I'm sorry, just let me die." Her heart filled with love for her memories of the life they had shared together and now six years on, through every guilt rid-dled day, she wanted the same, to be with Frank.

JJ squeezed her hand. He could feel her sadness, it was as real to him as Beryl. He remember the funeral service held by Michael Andrews the previous minister. It had been an un-usually warm March morning and there had been daffodils everywhere in the cemetery.

She felt JJ telling her, "I don't want you to go." Their friendship had been so close to a marriage as her marriage to Frank would allow. JJ had carried a torch for her since they met fifty five years ago.

"Lord,"

John stopped. The people standing all raised their bowed heads, breaking their appearance of praying. The erratic can-dle light did not give his eyes enough light to let him see any of their features. The church felt cold. Even wearing his cassock he felt the coldness rise from his feet, through his legs and body. He thought about the central heating and the fact that without electric, the boiler would have switched off but "the church wouldn't have chilled this quickly, would it?"

Elaine watched his hesitation continue, glancing to her right and left. Everyone was seated appearing attentive, looking at him or with their heads bowed in prayer.

Elaine stood up to show her encouragement. John saw her rise to stand besides one of those already standing. Her face was obvious to him, even by candlelight but he still couldn't see who she was standing next to.

"Lord, you gave us free will but our choices do not always please you. The previous use for the tree from which the wood was taken to make these pews, was for the taking of life, in the name of justice, in your name."

John felt Elaine's support as he focused back on the prayer, his mind seeing the words written down on the page as he progressed through it. For him remembering the prayer as best he could made saying it more meaningful, more natural and in this light, remembering it took away the distraction of trying to read and focus on a badly lit page. He was going to save that effort, now because of this power cut, for reading out the list of victims.

He turned slowly to face the crucifix to continue with the next part of his prayer. Looking straight back down at him was the red haired man, his face so close to John's that he couldn't focus on his face and take in all his features, his own shadow from the candles providing a veil of darkness absorbing parts of this figure. He felt his body heat evaporating, the rising chill devouring his body and now a numbness around his face and in his brain.

John recoiled, stepping back against the base of the communion rail. He looked down at his foot and instantly back towards the red haired man. John eyes focused on the now unobstructed crucifix. His heart looked for strength. He prayed for a sign. To everyone else in the church it looked like he had just stumbled for a second, perhaps his cassock had caught on the communion rail as he turned.

He shuddered, a mixture of the coldness again as he had felt a few moments ago and surprised fear took precedent over his other senses. He looked around, only Elaine was standing. His mind felt toyed with. "What was happening here? Why were these people standing up then sitting and up again? Where was this red head man who had been standing with his face in his?"

He took a few steps towards the crucifix wall, his shadow shrinking the closer he got. The fear he was trying to control, still made him feel like he wanted to urinate. John tried to pull his lower stomach in, in a conscious effort to try and control this highly untimely urge. With each slow, purposeful step he regained more conviction to continue with his prayer while his brain was searching for that fleeting vision of the red haired man's face, his obscured, distorted features snap shot and taken into the depths of his recollections.

His mind was working on a number of levels simultaneously and he could feel his conviction being stifled by his own uncertainty.

He turned around to face the congregation.

"Father......"

A look of dumb struck horror stopped John from saying anything more. As he said the word, his brain established an impossible photofit with this red haired man. John felt that he had met this man, somewhere, there was a familiarity, not that he had felt it when he had first turned around. He concentrated on that instant face to face, a few seconds ago and visualised himself over and over, turning and looking up at his face, trying to put clarity where there had been obscurity. The hat he wore. It looked like an old papal style as far as he had registered its shape.

He couldn't believe his own conclusion as this percolated to the top of his thoughts and now commanded his entire concentration. His mind analysed, refuted, accepted, rejected, questioned what it was telling him. His thoughts changed randomly and his feelings followed suit. In those few seconds where he stood before the congregation John went through the spectrum of disbelief, fear, insecurity, determination, inadequacy, weakness.

Elaine caught his eye as she raised her hand to attract his attention and he gathered these thoughts as best he could, looking around his parishioners as they waited for his leadership. He took a deep breath, the sound of his heart still clearly thundering in his ears, his blood pressure exerting a swelling, pulsating feeling in his head, his bladder hot, feeling it was about to burst.

"Father we come before you now for your blessings and for your forgiveness to those who misused that tree, this wood and that with your blessing and your forgiveness, the past remains in the past and the future becomes ours to enjoy and for others who follow us, worshipping your glory and that they will be able to do so without fear, within the sanctity and the protection of this church."

John felt his heart fluttering, the pulsing pressure in his head seemed to ease the more he spoke. With each word he felt more commanding, more like a minister leading with spiritual certainty yet he still felt the fragility of his confidence, like it would be ripped out of his mind at any time. He felt so vulnerable, so weak. As he spoke, he prayed, silent quick prayers of his own intermixed with the prayer that he was leading; "God please help me, God please be with me." He didn't feel he was getting any support.

"Please, could everyone stand and respond with God's help we will."

He felt a sudden surge of security as everyone stood, to be on the same level as himself, joining again some who he saw were already standing as he raised his eyes to look at the congregation.

The lighting from the candles changed as the standing bodies blocked the frail beams from moving as freely as the did when they were sitting down. The front of the church became darker and as the herded worshipers stood, they seemed to congeal into one body, only defined by the differences in height between their heads and shoulders.

Mike Evans thoughts were taken back into the church on the day he and John argued, taken now by the feeling of cold that touched his body. He remembered storming into the church and how it felt unusually cold but had put the sensation down to his anger and the sweat pumping out of his body by their confrontation, being cooled by the church's heating not being on, the chill of that large worshipping room had felt less that welcoming in darkness.

His feelings and thoughts had been far from Godly on that occasion as well. He had stayed sitting in the darkness of the church for nearly two hours, long after John and Elaine had left, brooding about the whole affair, trying to organise his own thoughts. He had imagined himself holding John's throat with one hand, pushing him back against a wall, like the school bully he had been, as he had been unusually tall in his junior school years and had eventually began his retaliation on the other kids who had teased him for being so tall and thin and had enjoyed the feeling of power it gave him and the fear he generated.

His talking to himself had been interrupted when he had seen the movement of what looked like a man and a woman at the front of the church. The man from his outline was very tall. Mike had estimated about six foot five, about a foot and a half taller than the person who he assumed was a woman, standing next to him. The man he remembered wore a wide brim hat, which he had spotted when he had looked down at the woman after he had answered his question.

"Is the minister here?"

"No." Mike had said but as he put the hymn book down that he had been holding and got up to ask them if he could be of help or take a message, in that brief moment of distraction, when he looked up the pair had gone.

"Bloody ignorant people," he had thought, "probably more non church going pagans that want a church wedding so she can wear a white dress and have nice photos!" He had sat back down and continued with his brooding. He had not heard the woman's giggle and the word "him."

His indignation grew again, standing next to Liz and the fact that they were now in this ridiculous service because of her, because she dared to defy him. When they got home, he was going to show her who was boss. He put his hand in his jacket pocket and felt a couple of lengths of thin nylon rope that he carried with him on most occasions. Mike twiddled with them for a few seconds, feeling them justified his intentions, enjoying the sense of superiority these thin pieces of restraint gave him.

He rubbed his neck with both hands. "I need a massage or something," he thought to himself, "my neck is killing me. Yeh, I need a good massage." Liz looked at him from the side and relished the thought of breaking his neck, "that would solve your problems, wouldn't it darling," she thought sarcastically to herself.

Haley looked to where she sensed Liz's bondage and thought back briefly to her tying Alister to their bed a couple of weeks ago but with some stockings. In the darkness of the the church and because they sat in the back row on the end, one of the furthest seating positions away from the light, a feeling of dominance came over her again and she gently rubbed Alister between his legs, the naughtiness and inappropriateness of her actions heightening the excitement.

Alister jumped slightly at her unexpectedness but then reciprocated by gently rubbing her left buttock and then giving it a good long squeeze. The firmness of her bottom exciting him more. She squeezed him harder.

Maxine felt the sexual power from Haley. She didn't need to turn around and look, she knew what Haley was doing. Her mind jumped on ahead to the pub and afterwards. Perhaps she should chat to Haley after the service. Haley's mind answered, now with an eagerness to find out about Maxine's role plays. Maxine turned around and looked directly and knowingly at Haley, her expression mostly hidden by the darkness but clear and understood by Haley.

Haley rubbed her tummy gently with her other hand and Alister noticed.

"Are you Ok?" Haley smiled she was.

John held the paper with the list of names out in front of him trying to catch the light from the candles so that he could read them. He adjusted his glasses.

Most people stood, holding onto the top of the pew in front and those who weren't, pressed closely against someone who was.

Jeff and Jean felt their excitement grow and they felt it between themselves and from others. Jeff's hands rubbed and squeezed the pew as he held it, listening to John, both of their minds now totally open to the suggestion of its history. The reduced lighting darkened the appearance of the wood even more and the elevated angle didn't allow Jeff or Jean who was about half a foot or so shorter to see any of the grain itself within the pew. They did feel its presence and started to see Claudia. They both began to feel warm, hot even as they empathised with her experience of the flames. They started to feel agitated but their logic combatted history with the present. Both started to enjoy the revelation.

"Father, we commend the names of the following, to be blessed by you, that their eternal souls be free from torment, that their lives as we believe now, were so wrongfully taken in your name, through ignorance, through superstition, be sanctified and glorified so that their spirits are free to move on and join you in heaven."

John held out his arms towards the congregation beckoning their participation "With God's help we will."

The murmur came back at him through the twilight, lacking any conviction or enthusiasm. His previous brief feeling of security, their strength in numbers instantly took a nose dive.

"They are just going through the motions," he thought to himself.

"Of course they are. Did you really expect anything different?"

John wheeled around to this familiar voice. He felt the clutch of death grip his chest like being immersed in ice water, where the cold stops your lungs from functioning. He automatically took sharp, short staccato breaths as the naturalness of being able to breathe was taken from him. He smelt a strange smell which churned his stomach. He smelt smoke mixed with other odours he had not come across before and again, another waft of lavender.

His cassock again whirled around him, his legs in that moment becoming visible as the heavy church robe lifted. He looked within the darkness like a child's spinning top, his legs and feet like the tops pivotal pointer, his cassock flaring.

The red haired man stood behind him, directly below the crucifix, his head bowed with the brim of his hat obscuring his face, only strands of his red hair were visible hanging down to his shoulders from underneath his hat. The candle light failed to illuminate anything else on this man. Everything else was black, his presence swallowed by John's shadow.

"Oh wow, there are two of them this time Richard! I didn't see him there, he must have been standing really still. I wonder if this other one will be as good as him? Come on Zoro."

Veronica swished her arm discreetly in a "Z" action as she kept it pointing to the floor. She didn't want to make the same mistake a second time. She was entranced with this new experience and urged John on.

Elaine heard her excited whisper to Richard, as her inexperience of church hadn't let her gauge how loud a whisper should be, so that it is only heard by the person sitting next to you.

Elaine turned around to where she heard this voice come from, her concern more about what she heard rather than for hearing it.

"Oops sorry. I'm new here, sorry. I'll try to be quiet but I never seem to be, sorry, sorry!"

Veronica pushed out a whispered apology to Elaine and looked around quickly, motioning her apology to the other six or seven people she registered, who had turned their heads to look at the name of "Zoro".

"Marriage?" Richard thought again.

Elaine turned back to look at John and who ever else this new girl could see. She concentrated and saw the faintest outline of a tall man standing under the effigy of Christ which hadn't been apparent to her before, his shape a darker shade of black within the shadows.

John heard Veronica's whisper and it made him smile briefly, her naturalness and innocence finding its way into his turmoil. The words of Father James somehow came to mind. "If we believe in God's existence, we have to believe in The Devil, in evil spirits."

These words had given him inspiration when Father James spoke them and he remembered his car journey back and how he felt his strength of belief ebb away the further he drove away from this preacher. John wished he was with him now to give him the strength he lacked.

He felt the vibrations of fear through his body and the thoughts about his congregation returned. "If they didn't have the conviction to believe, to make him believe their commitment to this prayer, what hope was there of cleansing these pews, or releasing the spirits he was praying for. Weren't they listening to the words of his prayer. Was it all just habit?"

"They won't help you, they never do!" The red haired man again merged with the darkness, disappearing as he spoke. Veronica concentrated, her eyes trying to penetrate the gloom to follow this second minister's movements.

"Father," he stopped again, his second exchange with this man, building recognition and more confusion on his first thoughts. His voice had a strength to it and it continued to sound like someone he knew.

"Father, bless the souls of Claudia Tanner, Claudia Elsbeth Morgan and James Morgan. Let us pray for their souls so that they may come to sit with you in glory, that they may at last be free from the

curse of false accusation and condemnation to hell."

He said this as he half turned to look behind him and stared at the embodiment of shadows the red haired man conjured with. There was an almost petrified defiance in his voice. The red hair man became apparent again to John. He stood still and silent, his head still bowed, as if he was assessing, thinking, scrutinising this faltering minister.

John turned back to face everyone again his hands outstretched, beckoning the interjection of response. His voice had more urgency in it as he tried to overcome the fear that was making him shake and create a feeling where he could hopefully convey the need for the response to be heart felt and meaningful, that this prayer mattered.

"With God's help we will." There was little difference in this response and he felt his heart slip again. He thought he saw the movement of people sitting down but as he had been concentrating on looking at the next few names to be read out within the poor light, those standing in front of him were only in his peripheral vision.

"I told you they won't help, their belief is lip service to this God of yours. They have never had to face anything to test their belief or to test your God." The voice came again from behind John but this time he didn't turn. He stood, trying to mentally control his quivering, his arms and legs leadened stiff and solid with the coldness of fear running through his entirety.

"You're wrong," he said it out aloud in quaking retaliation more than intention.

"Tell them then, tell them what you really found, tell them about me, tell them I am here in your pathetic building you call a church and watch them run at the thought they have to do anything for their faith." His voice goaded John and its familiarity grew in his consciousness from his subconscious.

Elaine heard John say "you're wrong." So did many others in the silence between his prayer and their response. Her eyes were transfixed on her husband, willing him, praying for his conviction to overwhelm everyone.

His voice had lost all authority, it sounded as frightened as he felt inside, devoid of volume, faltering and shaking on every word.

"Fa...ther, b, bless the , the ... souls of the fo, following, all t,t,t, taken wrongfully in your name."

John paused, his mind quickly considering the next thing he should say, his conflict to keep his flock safe from the truth and hope they would commit to the prayer or to tell them now of these spirits and the pews possession, even possibly of this man in black who was part of the shadows and there speaking to him, no matter how absurd.

"God help me," his thought went heavenwards and was intercepted on the way.

"God won't help you, he can't and if he could, he won't."

"How do you know what I'm thinking, my prayers even?" His own thoughts responded to his tormentor.

"Ask your God that, call it a miracle but miracles don't exist. You're hoping for one here, for their help."

His scorn rocked John's frail and uneasy, dwindling determination. He was about to try and rethink his brief personal prayer, almost feeling as if he was trying to sneak one away, without this stranger knowing but his gathering thoughts were stopped from forming, his mental words crushed. "You may as well ask him to get down off his cross and help, look how close he is, how you worship him there but nothing will happen."

Alister looked at Haley and the curly haired woman who had sat down during John's reading out of the first three names.

"What do you think of the name Claudia?" she asked Haley as she gently and respectfully touched Haley's stomach to indicate her awareness of Haley's baby.

Haley rocked on her bottom and moved slightly away from her, "I think,.... I think, it's a strong name for a girl but I don't, we don't know if it is a girl yet." Haley answered out of politeness but felt her anxiety rise as she answered.

"Trust me Haley, I'm sure it's a girl." The voice was calming but Haley's anxiety didn't disappear. She felt threatened.

"Well if it is, we might keep Claudia as a name in mind." Her voice was a little shaky in answering.

"Oh it's a girl Haley trust me, I'm was never wrong in these matters."

"What do you mean was?" Haley despite her anxiousness, picked up on the past tense of this woman's comment.

"What do you think Dad?" She looked at Alister but her smile lessened as she turned her focus to him and away from Haley.

"Umm yeh, It's as good as any, I suppose, we haven't thought that far ahead yet, it's still early days." Alister tried to keep his eyes on this woman while being aware of the prayers that were still being said.

"My name is Claudia," she emphasised, "and I have, ...sorry had a niece called Claudia Elsbeth. My brother named her after me first as an honour to me and then after his wife Elsbeth". Alister and Haley looked at each other, both experiencing a feeling of déjà vu at hearing these names but their expressions conveyed the same mutual confusion as to why.

John continued with the next few names, continuing his

prayer and deciding on an elaboration, to tell them more of the truth. His voice didn't have any command, it sounded crushed and he felt intimidated. His lung filling breath steadied the quivering in his voice slightly.

"Father, bless the souls of the following, all taken in your name and who's spirits are still within these pews, trapped and unable to come to you and now are within our church. Help us all to pray with the belief that you will help them, that you will free them from an eternity of wandering, that we can with our prayers bring their souls to you.

Jane Williams, burnt as a witch, Mary Jones, burnt as a witch, Elizabeth Jenkins, hung as a witch and her body then burned on the tree from which these pews are made. Marion Jenkins, mother of Elizabeth, hung as a witch and burnt on the same tree, from which the wood has been taken and formed into these pews."

Another younger women now to one side of Jeff, sat down next to the woman in black, as these last few names were called out. Jeff and Jean looked at the man still standing next to Jean, he continued to stare ahead, motionless, until he turned to look directly at Jeff. "You will know what to do." He looked down at Jean and his smile excited her and froze her at the same time. She turned instinctively to look at Jeff for reassurance of his protective presence and when they both turned back to look at the man with the brown scarf and old black clothing next to Jean, only his scarf remained on the seat where he had been sitting. Jeff lent around Jean and picked it up, draping it around his neck. "I'll keep it for him until we see him next!"

As John read the names out he now became aware of people sitting each time he read out a name.

There was a feeling of surprise in the next unconvincing response from the congregation "With God's help we will," a feeling over layered with concern.

John knew what they were thinking. He could feel it and everyone else had their feelings transmitted by the pews. There was confusion, fright, questions, accusations, panic, disbelief as to what they had just heard, penitence by some, "Oh God help me, help us, be with us now if this is true."

Many thought the same at the same time, their thoughts shouting into John's mind.

"What?"

"There are spirits in the church, real spirits?"

"What is this minister trying to do. It's his job to sort out spirits, he's the minister, how could he put us in such a position. I've got to get out, I've got to get out."

The pews exercised their control, spreading beyond where they were bolted, compelling their continued attendance, transmitting their anxieties into John.

John could see from the shifting of the shadowed congregation his words had been heard by most. He could see heads turning, bodies twisting, some, a few looking to get out of the pew but blocked by the general reaction and immobility of their Christian brothers and sisters standing next to them on either side, blocked as well by darkened, motionless figures sitting in the pews. He felt the discarding of faith falling from most of his parishioners as panic and confusion overtook their senses.

"See, do you hear one heart, one person other than Elaine your wife, say that they will pray with you to pray for these souls. It's not their fault, it's not for them to do. That's what they think. You can hear everything else but you can't hear support or help for you. Listen to their lack of conviction."

The man appeared behind John, standing over him, the rim of the tall papal hat tilted down towards John, emphasising their differences in height and exaggerating the height of the red haired man. John felt his presence trying to merge with his own body. His skin tingled with fright and tension, his sinews ridged. The tension transmitted a burning feeling around his skin. He felt uncomfortable with his clothes touching it. His body felt as if it was overheating, like he had severe sun burn, the same feeling as he had when Elaine was injured the previous week. Elaine watched the hinted shape take form behind her husband, the shadow created by the candles lighting John's body, his black cassock with purple stole and elaborate gold beading and crosses softened in their stark contrast by the dim flickering, the area of space immediately behind John the darkest place in the church from which this man materialised out of the blackest shadow.

"Father, we pray for the souls of Lidia Cooper, Jane Fletcher, Jane Potter, all tried and convicted as witches and who's lives were unjustly taken by men in your name."

John's voice still failed to regain a level of authority any where near close to his normal unthreatened Sunday sermons. There was a escalating shake in it as he tried to contain his own terror. The top of his penis burnt with the feeling of wanting to urinate and his bladder fought to hold back his urges as this apparition, now no longer ether became substance. John felt convinced that the brim of his hat was brushing the very ends of his own hair as he stood below the superior height of this metamorphosis. He was now facing for the first time in his life, in his ministry, a spirit, something beyond his experience, something which was now pushing him to question the strength of his belief, the strength of God and the strength of evil.

He watched three more people sit down but couldn't see who they were. He threw his hands forward again towards the confused, rocking congregation; his movement conveyed his quandaries, his voice while louder in this last section of prayer was unable to quell the sudden level of activity. He started to feel he was finally loosing control and going to wet himself, his bladder swelling, the continuing sensation adding to his discomfort and perspiration. He fought hard within his concentration to hold his bladder from disgracing him in front of everyone.

Beryl gave an unexpected added voice to "with God's help we will," as she saw her Frank standing beside her as if he had always been there. She smiled a smile of understanding and reached to take his hand while still holding the top of the pew with her other hand. She sat down as John called out the names of others and asked God for his mercy and for the souls of the dead to be released from their entrapment within the pews.

Beryl looked straight ahead, the final beauty of the grain holding her attention as the dancing light from the candles showed her images and suggestions that reminded her of their wedding day. She saw the lines of the old Rolls Royce they had been "loaned" by Frank's friend who worked in service as a chauffeur and who had been left unattended by the owners while abroad on holiday; its frog eyed headlights emerging from the grain and that image rekindled all her memories of that day. She felt herself holding Frank's hand and said, "I'm so sorry, I feel so guilty, I didn't have enough love, I should have loved you more, I should have had more faith."

"That's why I'm here now B." Beryl's head swooned as if she were seventeen again and had met her Frank for the first time. Those sixty odd years disappeared and this time they were meeting for the first time with a life time of memories. She sensed his hand on her cheek and their love exploded between the divide of life and death.

Her voice choked as she tried to keep control of herself, still appreciating she was in church. "I've missed you so much my darling, I've missed you so much."

His voice oozed love and compassion. "I'm with you everyday B. I'm next to you when you sit on the bed and I watch you cry most nights just before you go to sleep because I know..... you silly B, that you are missing me. You needn't cry, I'm fine and although I am not with you, well in that way, I am and always will be. I know what you are thinking and feeling. That's one of the advantages of being where I am. We were and are soul mates and I know your soul."

Beryl's cheek felt the memory of Frank's touch, the warmth of his fingers against her skin, the one thing he had always done since they met. She could visualise her husband, gently, lovingly, rub the back of his fingers from her chin and up to her left cheek and then open his fingers and cup her face with his whole hand. She had always felt secure with that feeling.

"I hear you talking to me, telling me what you have done that day and I know B because I've never left you. I stood by you at the graveside, did you feel me there?"

Beryl's recollection of that day, the saddest in her life because of its finality drew the tears to her eyes but his presence now brought tears of happiness within her desolation at his death.

"I did and I tried to convince myself that I wasn't being stupid, that you were there but I couldn't see how, I just felt my life had ended."

Beryl bowed her head down between the pews and just let her tears of relief flow down her face. She dabbed herself with a tissue from her pocket and absorbed the feeling of Frank into her for an unexpected yet final time, a feeling that no one would ever believe could be possible. She tried to hold on to that feeling of love and togetherness between them as she watched his image fade into eternity.

The pews transported everyone to the same sensation. They

all felt euphoria flow through their bodies for a second and then felt Beryl's regrets and guilt that she had punished herself with privately everyday since his death. She believed that she had not prayed hard enough in the early stages for God to intervene, to help Frank.

The preacher's voice held John rigid with its tone and intensity. He could feel his aggression as he goaded John with his own psychotic mixture of excitement and derision.

"Do you feel it, her happiness now and her helplessness. Her life of love to her husband and her love and belief in your God and she blames herself for not praying hard enough or soon enough, for Frank not meaning enough for God to do something. Where is God now, I'm here, where is he?" John jumped as he felt his arm being pulled from behind.

"Father" .....his voice disappeared, terror totally dominated.

"Oh God." His mind and his own thoughts about his own safety and Elaine's were panicking. He felt his breathing gasping, he couldn't get any rhythm or control. He tried to swallow but his mouth and throat were now totally dry. John felt as if he was drowning and fighting to get his head above water to take in any breath in order to stay alive. The earlier cold within his body was still there, numbing his torso and now, all around his face. It came from different directions with total inconsistency, like waves of cold river water splashing and gushing all over him as if he were tumbling through rapids, different parts of his face and head being chilled, then relief as another wave froze a different part of his head and face.

He tried to continue his prayer but his own fear had enveloped his concentration, holding it within his mind and not letting him release it into the planned action he had thought would take place, to complete the cleansing of these pews.

John felt his arm being pulled more violently than the first time.

"Finish your prayer, go on finish your prayer." The voice had demanding authority and now conveyed frighteningly paradoxical support to John. The red haired minister continued with his tirade of intimidation.

"You could be sitting next to God and be talking to him face to face and he still wouldn't do anything. Go on waste your breath!"

The preacher looked at the congregation. John stood still, petrified in his attempt to continue with the names and prayer, his hesitation dismissed with a contemptuous, sarcastic intervention by the red head. "Behold the Son of God who died that you might live. Pay him and your own devoted minister heed that he may work in God's name for your salvation."

The words from the tall orator came over John's head with unexpected command for their attention and their support. The spirit stood, his own arms outstretched to the side casting a shadow virtually obscuring the wrought iron crucifix from anyone's sight.

"Eee, this new one's just as good. I didn't expect that. He's like Batman....just cos he's taller." Veronica was enthralled.

John was still shaking involuntarily but these words somehow gripped his fear and held it at bay long enough to obey the command the red haired spectre had given.

The preacher glared at John, his voice bellowing with deep demonic volume. John's body jumped in an uncontrolled reaction. "Finish it, pray to God to help you." John was so confused as it still sounded like support to his action but was said with such derision.

John found himself usurped into continuing with the reading of the list of names, the preacher individually continuing with reading out the remainder of the names and then in unison with John, who was dragged through his petrification to join in. John felt sure he couldn't see the list from where he was standing, menacingly still, behind him, like a ventriloquist controlling his dummy.

The red haired minister changed from speaking out the names of these alleged witches with John and started to speak in John's ear. As John continued with his list, his hands rattling the paper as he shook, he saw the remainder of the congregation standing more still than before the oration. Out of the corner of his left eye, John could see his darkened face, the candlelight failing to highlight his features with any clarity, hindered by John's reluctance, induced by fear, not to look directly at him.

"Your prayers won't make the slightest difference, pray all you want and who do you pray for? For these? For us? Pray for yourself?"

John heard his contempt in every syllable and his voice sounded more familiar with every word. His mind tried to strip away the contempt, which created the distortion within the voice, to a voice within his memory, one he heard which had sounded calm.

Despite the deluge, John couldn't decide if he was being helped or tormented. As he heard these words being spoken with disgust he kept thinking of Father James' guidance. "Where there is evil, The Devil, then there must be God." Surely, here was evil, in his own church with his wife and these God loving people from his congregation.

"God loving?" The words came back at his thought, the instant it was thought. This spirit knew his every thought as he thought it.

"These people aren't God loving, if they were they would be

more committed. Listen to them, they are weak, apathetic. Do you think they could die for God, for love, we will see soon."

This shock of these last words, spurred John to continue to read, now almost trancelike as if he had stepped out from himself. He could hear his own voice but it sounded like someone different, like you hear your own recorded voice, when you can't believe you sound like that but everyone hears your voice exactly the same but it's different to your own ears. Elaine watched, rooted to the spot in her pew, her hands gripping and pressing the top edge of the back of the seat in front as if their contact with the wood were the controls of a TV and she was trying to change what was happening in front of her.

Elaine caught sight of Peter Phillips who was still holding his mouth with a clasped hand, trying not to vomit but still with his shoulders and body jerking with the restrained convulsions which would accompany someone being sick. She saw Donna shaking next to him in what looked like uncontrolled laughter but quiet, discreet; Donna holding onto the top of the pew in front, her arms rigid in trying to keep control and not laugh out loud.

She saw Claudia being tied to the oak tree and the fire started. Her own hands started to feel warm. The intensity grew but she couldn't let go of the back rest. She could feel her body getting hot. Maxine sitting next to her could see the same vision. Everyone could see it. There was an unseen unity but it took them to pain. John felt helpless as he sensed his congregation's swamped confusion, their mixed urges, to leave, to stay, to pray. He felt their feelings of blame towards him for their uncontrollable anxieties.

They watched Claudia as she screamed at them as she was tied to the oak, cursing everyone that was there taking part in her trial, this facade of righteousness. She had avenged her own innocence and virginity and was trialled and burnt as a witch for it; all her previous concoctions which helped people's ailments for which the village had been grateful, now laid before her in her trial, as spells and potions.

"You've seen this!" The preachers voice now subdued yet still disturbingly menacing. The comment made John shudder again as he half turned in reaction towards the voice and then refocused towards the congregation, afraid of what he might confront. He remembered everything from a few weeks ago in an instant. He had lived through her capture and her execution.

"But let me show you what is worse."

John's instant recollection became transferred to his parishioners minds as if they had been part of that trial mob. They felt their bodies burning. He could see the writhing silhouettes as they gripped the pews or touched someone else who had direct contact with a pew. He watched and sensed every death, every moment of suicide begging pain, as everyone of his congregation endured the deaths of every signal individual that had had their life taken on that tree one after the other and would have begged for death themselves if given the chance, to escape the purgatory of living through this service. The consciousness of this service had now disappeared from the congregation's awareness and they were now immersed within the history of the pews, each turn or twist within these seats, leading them through the four hundred year history since Claudia's death.

They felt the father's soul leave his body as the poisonous concoctions drove out the last seconds of his mortal existence and its absorption and acceptance by the witching tree, joining the souls of his wife and daughter Marion and Elizabeth, his desire to be with them stronger than wanting to go to heaven. They felt the tree grow in dominance and become alive with the acceptance of more unjustly sacrificed and murdered women accused of being witches, their last moments of mortality filled with excruciating pain and terror as the rope strangled them or broke their necks or the fires burnt and ate away at their flesh, devouring their bodies within the purging flames of misguided Christianity. The congregation were in two worlds, the past ruling their present and they were subjected to the repeated and similar gruesome deaths twenty three times.

They were all totally silent as if the pain they were experiencing had robbed them of every other audible human response. John could see through the gloom, agonising expressions across the faces he could see with any clarity within the indiscriminate light from the candles but it was like watching people trying to keep their pain or embarrassment a secret from the person standing next to them. They were fighting with themselves. They all looked like they were trying to be discreet even though the agonies he knew they were experiencing were cutting through each one of their bodies.

He watched people holding their eyes, their heads, their chests, their hearts. He could vaguely see women appear to be leaning forward within the pews, as much as the light would allow and hold themselves between their legs and he felt their feelings of Claudia's unwanted penetration and the unnatural sensation made his mind scream. He held his lower abdomen, it felt infiltrated, an unnatural growth within his body, aware of Claudia's face appearing central to his minds eye, as if she were over seeing the torment before him. John watched helplessly as he saw the suffocating reactions of his parishioners gasping for breath, whether from smoke, water or the sensation of a tightening rope around their necks, the delirium flooding across their thoughts. He prayed to God to give them strength.

"Yeeeesss pray for them," the hissed challenge exuded even

more disgust.

The congregation felt the searing heat of the fire burning into Claudia's flesh, long before any flame touched her skin. He watched their conscious bodies react unconsciously to the memory the pews selected to expose them to, the cold of the river, its buoyancy bringing witches back to the surface, their gulps for air, the tightness of the rope becoming more strained, cutting into their throat or wrists depending how cruel their captures had been; as they were pulled to the bank or back up to the bridge when the river confirmed their demonic status or innocence and the dragging to the witching tree for the final part of their trial. John watched them squirm, twist and jerk as their minds tried to get away from the fires they felt were swallowing them from the past. None of them could now move from where they were standing. He smelt the same unfamiliar odour that had made his stomach churn earlier, the feeling of vomiting wheeling up in his throat; his bladder still straining to keep control, the smell he now connected to burning flesh, the pews educating his ignorance as to the possessions and sacrifices these long dead people had endured and which had been accepted by the witching tree.

The agonies endured by all the others accused of being witches and killed, flooded continuously through their bodies. There was no escape, in the same way that the victims couldn't escape. The turmoil at their confusion to the accusations, the pleading of innocence, the despair and grief at being taken from their loved ones. They felt feelings of emptiness and their minds totally distressed with the impending thoughts of extinction and their own bereavement. The love for their relatives, husbands, sons and daughters for their future safety from the mob that within their masses, hid their own individual identities and exacted justices in God's name; tore their hearts open. Their prayers for their own salvation and for the safety of those they loved, pleading for God's intervention, to save them, to make the baying mob come to their senses, so that they would listen to reason, to understand what they were saying, that they were not witches, that they were not possessed. They felt the last ebbs of life leave those sacrificed. They saw the accession of the twenty three human souls and their retreat from their intended destination, their last prayers still unanswered and their evaporation from existence. John's congregation were now within the hollowness of hope, their own lives and prayers feeling worthless as they heard the prayers for help from those who had been about to die. Everyone bar five of the congregation had been exposed to the futility of their prayers and the last conscious curses each victim passed onto the mob and God.

John continued to gasp for breath as the ongoing feeling of drowning held him back from finding oxygen. Some were still gripping their chest or throats as the sensations they were enduring changed.

John heard their thoughts and he felt as if all their individual experiences were being channelled through him with their prayers or fears to God. He felt he could just about stand. His awareness of his own legs, their failing strength on the edge of collapse.

"What are you going to do? Protect them? Let them fall? Leave them? Let God save them....hah," the derision and scorn kept hammering at John's faith. He gasped a breath but it only filled a small percentage of his lung capacity continuing his headiness through the lack of oxygen.

Only five people were spared as to what was happening around them in the pews, their awareness cloaked by their innocence or selected protection. Alister and Haley as they sat next to this Claudia, who they had never met before but felt strangely now, very comfortable with. Veronica and Richard who had come to church for the first time that night for Christine's future benefit and Elaine who had given her husband unquestioning support. All the other church goers felt their horrendous pains subside as quickly as it rose as the red haired man took John to the next stage. They stood, their minds frozen to response, waiting unknowingly, placed into an awake coma, all now aware of John, their minds infused with memories.

"Did God listen to my sister? Did God help her. Did he help my fourteen month old baby daughter Claudia Elsbeth, who she was looking after, when these God loving, God fearing people went into Claudia's house and found MY daughter." John held what little air he had in his lungs, his attention totally focused and suspended on hearing the name Claudia Elsbeth......again.

John could hear his anger grow beyond any insanity he had experienced with each word he heard. The rage within this tall man was transmitting though the exertion he could feel on his arm. It felt like his fingers were going to puncture his skin and rip the triceps muscle off the bottom of his upper arm.

"They did the same to my daughter as they did to Claudia. They tied my daughter who couldn't be guilty of anything to the same tree. It was still hot. I can hear even now, her screams as her skin was burnt against the hot bark. When I got there after preaching the word of our God, your God, in the next village, I pleaded with them, this so called congregation of Christians, to let my daughter go, that she was my daughter and not my sisters."

John felt a change in his tormentors tone. His overwhelming anger now conveyed despair, his words not as clearly defined now that he was talking about his daughter. They sounded slightly slurred like he had lost total control, like someone on the edge of crying and not wanting to be overcome with those upsetting emotions.

"They held me back so I couldn't help and made me watch as they pulled the ropes so tight, pulling her little arms and legs out of their sockets, they let her hang there for penitence. She couldn't stop screaming and crying and I could do nothing,....nothing to help her. Do you know how....how that feels as a father, to watch your child crying with so much pain and you can't even touch her, to let her know you are there. You are a father. How would you feel watching one of your three children crying for you or Elaine in the same sort of pain my little baby was in. Have any of your three children cried for you in such pain that you wanted to die for them so that they wouldn't suffer."

John's eyes stared in terrified anger as he heard the minister refer to his three children, his concern for their safety turning his stomach as his awareness to this ministers knowledge of his family became apparent to his brain. Johns eyes glassed with tears on sensing how he would feel if he were watching his own children. The red head continued, resilient to the emotion his recollection was creating within John's mind.

"I looked at her, her face covered with tears. I watched her looking around, looking around for me, for her mum, she had only just learnt to say mother or father but she looked for us and tried to call for us but she was in such pain, she couldn't do anything but scream with the agony she was in. She was terrified and she wouldn't have known why or what was happening, how could she, she was fourteen months old, all she knew was me, her mother and Claudia. They made me watch but held me where she couldn't see me so she screamed there, wanting me and her mother and she died still wanting us to be there with her. I cried and pleaded with the people who knew me to let her go but they knocked me unconscious and I wasn't even able to hold her as she died. YOUR sort of people did that! Christians. Do you still pray for these?" His hand gestured over the top of John's shoulder.

John heard this repetition in his question and now heard the tears in this still grieving fathers voice. He heard his sniff in between the words and felt unexpected sympathy for his crying.

"I prayed to God, I prayed for him to do something to save my daughter and I would still be praying now and he would still do nothing. Your God is there, thirty feet away from us, with all his believers here. He is every where but no where when you pray for his help.

They relit the fires and I watched and heard her tiny screams turn into one long mum and dad seeking bewildered and excruciating cry which ripped my God loving heart out. I changed my prayers to Lucifer, that if he spared her any more pain, I would renounce my soul and sacrifice the lives of so called Christians in place of all those wrongfully killed on this tree in the name of God. I could sense her beautiful, innocent mind, leave her body and go to this God, your God that did nothing to answer my prayers; saved by The Devil. I knew that I would never be with her again in the afterlife that Jesus taught us about as I would spend eternity in hell for renouncing my soul, but it was worth my soul to save my beautiful little Claudia any more pain. She could barely speak but her penitence and the sacrifice of her soul were necessary to "please God", to ensure she would be allowed into heaven. You tell me what sort of a God does that?"

John remembered from his first illusional experience, the crying of a baby from a house in the forest.

His thoughts transferred to his own children and as much as this situation allowed, he could not help feeling agreement with what he had just heard. His rational from the logic within this preachers story, chipped away another piece of rock on which Peter had built The Church for Christ, from his own religious foundations and his sympathy for this preacher emerged from within the decline of his faith.

The possessed preacher told this part of the tree's history with seething venom, his grip on John's arm vice like throughout, his grief for his daughters disembodiment and his own execution, had converted his previous existence into an entrapped soul within that tree.

"A day later still unable to believe what they had done, I pleaded for my own life without knowing why because without my little Claudia Elsbeth, my life to me meant nothing. They were not going to do anything that day other than to kill anyone who had an association to my sister Claudia. That mindless mob were still frenzied, still drunk with sanctity, still drunk from their celebrations in the tavern. They told me before they started the fire that my soul would be purged of Satan, so that it could enter heaven. There was no sense with them, they had no reason, no proof, nothing only their claim of God's will, their own desire for killing in God's name. By the time they tied me to the same tree, they had beaten me so much that I could hardly walk, they had cudgelled the strength out of me and by then I wanted to die, to be put out of my misery, not for my pain but for not being able to hold my Claudia and be with her. I thought about the last time I held her, the day I left to go to the next village to preach and I could feel her pushing her lips against my face, trying to kiss me. I had just kissed her on the cheek and she was trying to copy me. I can feel the warmth and softness of her wet lips even now on my face just before I left. I can smell my beautiful little baby, here with you and your Christians. I can feel her hair against my skin and I have thought and felt those last loving moments with her every second for four hundred years not to forget her. You know what hell is?; it's not being with your child. Would you agree?

I cursed every last one of them for their ignorance, their stupidly, for their fear. I cursed the tree as God's instrument for the purging of souls and cursed every soul taken in God's name, that it would be freed only by the taking of another Christian soul in its place.

Stupidity??

They went looking for my wife and she was accused of being a witch and they killed her two days later.

So where is our loving God's compassion now. I didn't see it there, I don't see him here, do you?"

John knew he was screaming contempt at him but no one else seemed to hear or react. The preacher's fury did not let up and all that he was saying compounded on John's falling faith. He watched the last of the congregation sit as he terrified, vainly, read the last of the twenty three names out and looked at those still standing. The distinction between both suddenly became clear. His face looked deformed within the struggling candle light as he strained to cope with this dilemma.

"You can't take the lives of any of these people here. They are all innocent. They had nothing to do with the deaths of anyone on that tree. None of them were even born." His voice had so little strength that it didn't even sound as if he was pleading, it sounded exhausted and defeated.

The preacher's anger entered its final realm and he transmitted this through his continued grip on John's arm as the memories of his family and his four hundred years of contempt for God burned every ember of his spirit. John felt he was about to faint as the preachers hold on his muscle intensified. The arctic numbness still dominated his self control, his body felt frozen, his voice had virtually gasped every remaining name, the feeling of drowning still adding to his panic.

The older minister spoke his answer slowly, purposefully with total derision and sarcasm. John felt the end of this trial was about to manifest itself and he feared how.

"It's not me taking their lives, it's God and themselves; their dishonesty to his teaching, to their Christian beliefs and principals.

So I'll ask you again, who do you pray for John? These innocent Christians. Innocent of what? Of wife beating and cruelty, of adultery, of guilt, of impatience, waiting for their husband to die because he was too much bother. You are praying for people who have broken the laws and teachings of Jesus and God of who we both served. You are praying for people that when tested, fail. You pray for people who came tonight so see what they might learn of these pews past, my past, Claudia's past; anything other than the real reason for your prayers to help the souls of those taken in God's name.

Twenty three innocent people died on that tree, The Witching Tree, God's Tree, twenty three innocent people who had done nothing against God.

Show me one innocent heart felt prayer excluding your wife and I'll show you some mercy, more mercy than God would show you and more than he showed me."

John stood motionless, drained, looking at the congregation. His own feeling of cold numbness had eased, as if released on the preachers say so. He still could not see their faces clearly but the number of those standing seemed to fit with the number of people he thought had come to church that night. Despite his throat being totally dry and being afraid that his voice would remain silent, John took as deep a breath as his tight chest would allow and prayed he would be able to speak.

"Father, Dear Lord our eternal Father in Heaven, for the souls of all these poor, wrongly accused people, branded as witches and killed in your name, we pray for forgiveness so that their souls may be free to leave these pews and enter the kingdom of heaven."

He finished his prayer with a total feeling of defeat, that the whole point had been lost, wiped out, with no earthly chance of accomplishment.

John held out his right arm to beacon the response, his left arm too painful even to lift and he heard one loud, eager, enthusiastic voice respond to his call. "With God's help we will."

"I think I'm getting the hang of this!" Veronica whispered to Richard, "oops sorry again, still too loud, sorry, I hope you won't stop me coming here." Veronica put her hand over her mouth and gestured her apology around the congregation, realising that her intended response was still far too loud for a church service.

Very few people turned or reacted to Veronica as she turned to Richard and now conscious of how loud her voice had still been, whispered even quieter so only Richard could hear. "I still prefer the shorter one, the one that did the christening. He did really well this time on all those names. There's something funny about the tall one, he's good but I like the christening minister, that's what I'll call him the christening minster so you know who I'm talking about. What do you think my lover?"

"Well well! Who would have thought that from this group of hypocrites would come a sincere, well meaning innocent voice. I told you not so long ago, the greater the threat, the greater the evil, the greater God can be, the more you can use him."

John heard these words again and his mind rushed back to The Forest of Dean.

"Do you feel you have used Him? Do you feel God was here and that he answered your prayers tonight? I said I might spare them. Did you think I was telling you the truth?"

A still petrified and shaking John turned to face the voice that had been taunting him. The wind from outside blew the lights from all the candles out at the same time as Veronica and Richard opened the front door to slip away unnoticed, Veronica not wanting to have to explain why she didn't know what she should be doing or wanting quite yet, to talk to the either of the two ministers, especially the tall one."He was a bit creepy," she said to Richard on their way out.

The darkness that engulfed the church obscured John and hid the preacher as John caught his breath for courage when he turned to look up into his face, the preacher's figure became one with shadow and John. As Elaine felt her mobility released, she started to move slowly along the pew and towards her husband to give him a hug, though she could not distinguish either. She strained to try and adjust her eyes to the virtual total darkness that had instantly shrouded everyone. John walked past her weakly, saying nothing and went and stood in the vestibule. Elaine stood silently in the row of pews while she waited for John to finish with everyone leaving.

Haley felt a gentle touch on her tummy in the complete blackness that filled the church. "I know there's going to be a girl. Trust me I'm never wrong on these sort of things Haley. Think about that name Claudia, it grows on you."

The woman smiled, a subtle slight smile conveying understanding within the darkness. Haley lowered her eyelids slowly, with the smallest gesture of a nod, acknowledging her intention to consider the name. She gripped Alister's hand.

The three walked out together using the light from Alister's phone. They stood in the door way doing their coats up, contemplating the wet walk home. Both turned as one, to politely say "goodbye" to Claudia but she was no longer standing next to them. They looked down the steps to the pavement and back into the church vestibule in case she had gone back for an umbrella but there was no sign of her. Their synchronised paces splashed down the steps to the street. Haley put her right hand onto her tummy and started to think of girls names. "Rebecca, Shan, ...Claudia...mmm,"

Others followed in the same way. They all left unknowingly

with a different future after that evening, mostly the same as before the service but with new memories and realisations, as if they had been told a story, rather than enduring an experience.

There was an unspoken conclusion that the service had ended even though John had not said any benediction and people left, passing comment that they felt a bit heady, probably from the smell of the candles.

"See you John. Thanks for everything mate. We're leaving now. Good service." Simon was one of the first to pass, his attitude very up beat, a big, relaxed smile filling his face. John look at him almost skip down the steps, a complete difference to his normal persona.

Mike Evans still fiddled with the nylon ropes in his pocket as he walked down the isle but decided as the fresh air cleared his head that he didn't feel up to showing Liz who was boss that night.

John looked penetratingly at Jeff and Jean as they walked into and then out of the vestibule, shaking his hand in passing but without stopping to talk or comment. His expression conveyed satisfaction as they left and he watched as Jeff and Jean held each other's arms, looking directly into one another eyes as if to say "wow", their intrigue had been answered. Their bodies he could see had recovered from their experiences as they walked down the road in the rain without their umbrella; their elation with their new found history was keeping the memory real and they couldn't stop comparing what each other had felt. Their recruitment was successful.

Paul and Maxine left arm in arm also, excited by the forthcoming drink and PVC. Maxine wondered at the possible inclusion of Liz at some time in the future, in the way that a best friend wants to include you because they don't want you to miss out on something wonderful or exciting. She wondered at how she might bring the subject up with Paul and speculated as to what his reaction might be. She giggled, the same young, school girl type of giggle, she had shared with Liz earlier.

Peter and Donna left, Donna walking ahead as Peter followed holding his groin discreetly underneath his rain coat. He had managed somehow and to his relief, to hold the vomit back that he felt he need to expel. His tongue still flicked inside his mouth, searching for whatever was giving him that gagging feeling.

Beryl and JJ left together under JJ's umbrella.

John walked back to the communion rail and sat on it, his head, his eyes looking for Elaine. For the first time ever, he didn't wait by the front doors for everyone to leave. He waved a large general wave to everyone who were still in the church in their mixed stages of readiness to leave.

John looked up from the communion rail, as he watched the last of the congregation leave through the open doors. Elaine picked her way along the emptied pew and made her way to the front of the church. She felt a huge sigh of relief expel from her mouth as she reached her husband. There was a calmness about him which purveyed itself with a lack of animation, like someone shut down when controlled by shock.

John looked at her but said nothing. He didn't speak about the service, didn't ask how she thought it went, it was over. Both were silent. She bent over and kissed him on the top of the head. John accepted it without any noticeable response.

CHAPTER 42

It was Monday morning and the usual school time rush and chaos that surrounded school days was absent and the happiness of an inset day had let everyone get up later that morning and there was a far more relaxed feeling about a 10.30 breakfast.

The phone rang interrupting John who was helping prepare the bacon and eggs and he came back into the kitchen with an almost comedic, yet solemn look on his face.

"Who was that?", Elaine asked, with a sideways look of concern.

"Oh. That was JJ. He's ringing from the church to tell me Mike has had an accident while painting the wall behind the crucifix, remember he offered to do it at the last property meeting and he was half way through doing it.

Look I've got to go. JJ tells me the police and an ambulance are there and he......and they want me to get there as soon as possible."

Elaine stopped chopping the mushrooms. "What! ....What sort of an accident? How are you going to be able to do anything. Is he seriously hurt or what?"

"It's pretty bad according to JJ." He took a quick bite of his toast. "Look, I've got to go. Where are the car keys to your car?"

John continued with a tone so matter a fact. "I thought actually that might have been Elizabeth ringing about Mike!"

Elaine looked at him, her mouth slightly open with astonishment and then repeated her question with more urgency. "What sort of accident, what's happened?"

John's answer was even more impatient. "Elaine, just give me your keys now, I need to go."

She put the knife down from chopping the mushrooms and wiped her hands before getting her car keys out of the black handbag she had taken to the church last night.

John grabbed up the remainder of his slice of toast and mumbled out of his toast filled mouth as he rushed towards the back door. "I'll be back as soon as I can. Leave me some bacon, I'll cook it when I get back."

Elaine picked up the knife again and continued to chop the mushrooms, her knife action more vigorous incorporating her frustration at not getting a clear answer.

John arrived in the church itself within five minutes of leaving home. As he walked in, he took in the two police men standing on some of the chairs they must have got out of the church hall. JJ was standing in between them looking up towards the iron crucifix. The scuff marks on the wall showed where the ladder Mike had been using had slipped sideways across the wall towards Christ's outstretched left hand, the effigy almost indicating now where Mike was empaled. There were two ambulance paramedics, one man standing half way up the repositioned ladder which was on the right of the crucifix, the other a young woman on a smaller extension steps that John knew they had got from the boiler room, to his left.

Between the four of them they were trying to administer drugs and help to a twisted, unconscious Mike Evans. It looked like his body had been threaded in some way between the iron work limbs, body and cross that was the focal point at the front of the church.

JJ looked flustered. He moved towards the front wall, his hands raised in the air offering vague, meaningless help to what was happening fifteen foot above him. He turned away and back again, his arms and intentions oscillating between staying out of things and helping the struggling four uniforms in their efforts to free Mike.

John took the activity in but stopped in his tracks towards the front of the church when he saw Mike interwoven and bleeding from numerous areas of his limp, hanging body.

John shouted out of shock. "Is he alive? Is he breathing? JJ did you find him like this? How on earth did he get like that? He's .....he's twined into the sculpture ......how?"

The four service personnel all glanced around at John without comment and all turned back to trying to unweave Mike from the wrought iron. The two police officers were attempting to lift his weight by pushing against his legs and feet, guided by the directions being given to them by the paramedics who were trying to un thread his arms and eager to get their patient onto the floor.

John watched various streams of blood meandering around and down the wrought iron work and drip onto the chairs the police officers were standing on and the polished floor between the chairs.

JJ reiterated John's questions. "Is he alive? Is he breathing?"

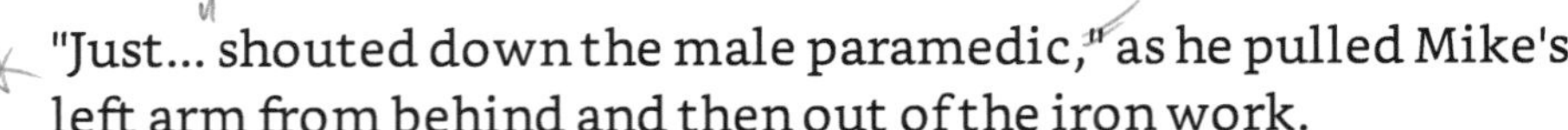

"Just... shouted down the male paramedic, as he pulled Mike's left arm from behind and then out of the iron work.

Mike's body slumped forward with the change of support, his freed left arm swinging lose. The ambulance man managed to grab Mike's arm and put it over his right shoulder, using his own body to step slowly up the next rung of the ladder to lift Mike's weight. The two policemen were then able to untangle both his legs and ankles, both then taking the extra weight by holding his legs.

John watched bemused until his attention was distracted. Despite being nearly eleven o'clock in the morning the church was quite dark. The drab November day outside was over hung with heavy rain clouds and lots of the window shutters were closed. No one had thought to turn the lights on. John wondered at how Mike planned to paint the wall in such poor light.

"Where there is evil." John whirled around, his heart instantly pounding at hearing these words. His eyes shot around the church looking into the crannies, recesses and cracks of the building. He rubbed his eyes under his glasses, his eyesight almost seemed blurred, creating the semblance of shadows and in distinction. He felt threatened.

He held his breath as his eyes searched for the person who had just spoken, inwardly hoping he wouldn't find its source. John rotated three hundred and sixty degrees four times as his mind entered bewilderment on hearing this familiar voice.

"What's wrong John?" JJ called as he watched John rotate in his mind muddle.

John stopped and looked towards JJ and then looked up at the four still struggling to finally release Mike in order to lower him to the floor. His look became a glance, hijacked in time by the movement of a tall man's shadow in front of the five people trying to help Mike.

He followed the shadow as it walked from left to right, from underneath the pulpit and across in front of the six people behind the alter rail. None of the five conscious people noticed what John could see.

That same haunting voice, its resonance, its command chilled John again as it came out of the gloominess and the shadow disappeared. "Where there is The Devil, there is God."

John squinted in the hope of seeing the form but there was just the church, its pews and walls.

"What next my lover?" The woman's voice made him turn and look back towards the entrance doors of the church. There was nothing there but blue carpet and an empty isle.

"I told you where there is The Devil, there is God." John swirled in the direction of the man's voice. This time the voice had form; tall, black, standing still and silent across the far side of the church from John, underneath the first floor gallery and in the poorly lit side isle. The figure stood there, the wide brim Papal hat dipped towards John, the head of the tall figure bowed, obscuring his face.

The recollection of last night froze John as this new encounter brought back those vivid traumas as if they had been buried for years. There had been no discussion, no comment between Elaine and himself after they had left the church. They had sat in silence in the lounge with a bottle of wine, drained. Their belief had been that it was over, the exorcism, the freeing of souls, had brought an unspoken relief to them both but now, back in his church, with Mike still dangling from the symbol of their religion, it hit John with a new feeling of despair as he looked across at this semblance of an embodied silhouette.

He felt himself shivering but his attempt to try and control his involuntary shaking failed to stop his quivering vibrations. His voice shook with uncertainty.

"You told me you would show mercy, that you would spare them if you heard one innocent heart felt pray. You heard that. You said so. So why are you here now? Why this?"

The blackened figure remained static, un intimidated by John's frightened accusations.

John's voice for the briefest of moments gained an unexpected aggression to it. "What do you want?"

The silhouette raised his head, the brim of his hat rising to the horizontal, exposing his eyes underneath. They were lifeless, cold, penetrating, compelling. The instant John saw them he knew who he was facing and his blood ran cold.

His voice now distinct and identifiable with his face, drew John's bodily warmth out of him as his memory flooded every second of recollection of their previous meetings in a barrage of images and discussions.

John acknowledged within a second to himself again, the existence of spirits, life after death and now the unholy spiritual manifestation of physical evil in human form.

The man's face showed no submission, only stark confidence and determination. He looked directly into John's eyes with defiance and arrogance, his face grinning, his smile devoid of any warmth or compassion. He turned towards the front of the church as if to walk out of the church and then paused. He looked back towards John and smiled again but a smile that conveyed confrontation and aggression, his eyes dark in their hollow recesses, angry in their expression. He touched the brim of his hat in mock respect, his grin remained solid.

John took the opportunity to challenge him again. "You told me you would show mercy, that you would spare them. Is this sparing them?" He pointed towards Mike who'd been freed and had been lowered to the floor.

The darkened apparition began to devolve into whisps and vapour as he spoke. "I did show you and them mercy. I didn't say I would spare them. I could have taken twenty three all at once but I didn't. I've taken one....... today, ...him, the one you dislike the most but there are more to follow." He pointed towards Mike with a transparent arm, his blackness disbursing, showing parts of the church behind him which should have been shielded by his presence.

John thought for the first time about last nights service with the specific thought now, that their attempted exorcism, their service to release those souls had failed. His heart sank at the realisation that his church may still be possessed. His own mind almost taunted him with a wave of thoughts. "Oh my God, does this mean every time we hold a service, every time someone comes in, ...no ....comes even near the church that they could be taken. This can't be right! Oh God no, this can't be right."

His mind jumped to the apparition's last comment, "the one I disliked the most?" He still questioned his confusion. "Does he know my feelings, my thoughts."

John remembered how this spirit intercepted his desperate prayers to God during their confrontation in the service. "He can't know what I'm thinking, what I'm feeling, not all the time. He can't."

"Can't I?"

John was staring at the floor as his mind tried to work out the logic or the illogic of what he was thinking, what he was hearing; his eyes wide with fear and defiance. He shuddered and looked back towards his tormentor who contradicted him. His skin bristled as the feeling of violation, the rape of his own soul swept through him.

"Does this mean you are going to use my thoughts, my feelings to select the next sacrifice. Oh God no. I can't be this......your ....your instrument of death. Oh God this can't be, this can't."

His twitching and bodily reactions to his thought process brought amusement to the almost vaporised form. A soft, Satanic giggle floated from the far side of the church, its impact knocking John off balance like he had been hit by a gale force wind. He stepped back with his right leg to steady himself and looked back across the floor to the departed minister.

His voice trembled, his unanswered speculation drawing his human frailty and placing them into his throat conveying his panic. "And how many more innocent people will you take?"

"Twenty one."

"Twenty one?" John repeated the number, his voice shuddered with puzzlement.

"He's the second."

"The second? Who was the first? Tell me .... who was the first?" John paused, his mind straining to think of someone. His question sounded desperate. "The lady .... Mary at the christening?"

John's voice escalated in volume attracting the attention of the five who had lowered Mike's body to the floor, their intense concentration and focus on their task broken at the confirmation of Mike's failed life.

The black apparition sniggered, his laugh hanging in John's ears, infiltrating his body. The second giggle of a woman filtered in harmoniously as if in unison, turning John again as he tried to find her in the church.

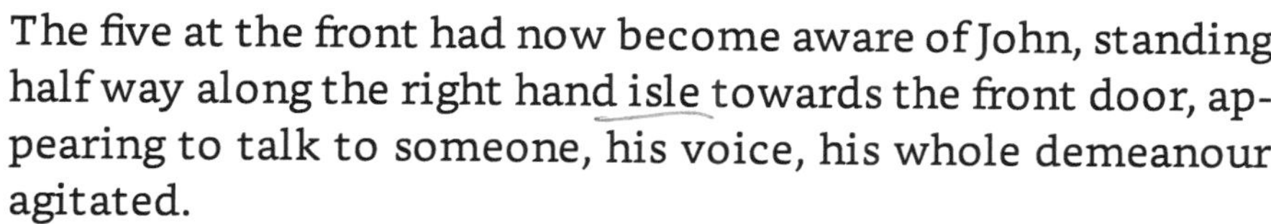

The five at the front had now become aware of John, standing half way along the right hand isle towards the front door, appearing to talk to someone, his voice, his whole demeanour agitated.

"I can't just stand by while you take the lives of these innocent people. I'll fight for them, every single one." His voice regained some of its assurance, its confidence.

The black manifestation smiled a transparent grin that drew

the confidence out of John and smashed it to oblivion. "Do you think you are strong enough John? Stronger than me? Your faith is failing you. I felt it the first time we met. You're floundering within the pages of The Bible, looking for help."

John stood there, unaware that he was shaking as if naked in the snow. He shivered as the red haired man finally disappeared in front of him, the church, its walls and features appearing clearly through his dissipation.

He stood rooted to the floor, trying to make sense of this second encounter. John found himself repeating what the spectre had said, as a way he thought of trying to regain his composure, his thought processes, his confidence. "Where there is evil, where there is The Devil, there must be God."

He became aware of the silence and felt the eyes of the five boring into him. He took a deep breath. As he walked towards them, he felt a calmness return and filter through his body with each slow troubled step. He looked at them watching him walk towards them. John said nothing as he looked down at Mike and leant against the communion rail. JJ watched him adjust himself, looked at his expression as he studied Mike's body, an expression that didn't convey any compassion.

He and JJ tried to answer the questions the policemen asked but both seemed to the officers to be in shock. The paramedics wheeled Mike's body out of the side door of the church having brought the trolley into the church while the police tried to talk with John and JJ.

"Do either of you need a lift home?" the one policeman asked, having decided that their questions were not getting any affective answers.

John and JJ looked blank at each other until John gathered himself to say he had Elaine's car but it would be good if they would take JJ home.

John locked the church up with Mike's blood stained keys after the paramedics had emptied his pockets before they left with his body. John drove home, his mind now re activating into body numbing, mind swamping turmoil, seemingly kick started into thinking as he got closer to home and further away from the church. As he pulled onto the drive behind his own damaged car, he took in a deep breath and locked the car door.

The wooden kitchen door creaked as he slowly walked back into the kitchen and lay Elaine's car keys on the kitchen work tops. Elaine was sitting at the table watching Rachel colour in a Disney Princess colouring book.

John walked to the cooker and turned on the gas ring under the frying pan with the fat in from the bacon he had missed out on earlier. The smell of cooking bacon quickly rose from the pan and he looked at the way the fat melted and threw in the four slices that had been left for him on a plate next to the cooker.

Elaine looked at him expecting him to say something. Eventually and consciously after about forty seconds, she said gently, appreciating that his answer may be upsetting, "Well?"

John took in a long slow sniff of the new cooking slices of bacon and let out a shallow sigh when his lungs had filled. "Bacon! ....It's been such a long time."

Elaine continued to stare at him, waiting for John to say something, thinking his comment was reflecting on the stress of yesterday and his visit to the church that morning.

He walked around the table and hugged Rachel with a hug like she had never felt before. It was a long loving, essence transmitting hug when you want the person you are hugging to feeling how much you love them, how much you want for them, how much you want to protect them and how much you miss them when they are not with you or when you know you will not be with them.

"Well, what on earth has happened? Tell me." Elaine was now more impatient and concerned.

"The ladder slipped and he fell against and .... and into the crucifix." John appeared to hesitate at giving too much detail in front of Rachel. The sharp edges on the sculpture.........".

"What about them. What?" Elaine put down the coffee she was holding. "Is he alright? John, tell me what's happened!" Her voice was exasperated.

John lowered his voice after he kissed Rachel on the forehead, his kiss as firm and lingering as his hug. Elaine thought he was being discreet so that Rachel wouldn't hear. He answered her with no change in his tone, just matter of fact. "Well I think JJ's in shock." He paused, almost with a look of mischievous glee. It reminded Elaine of the look he had that first Sunday morning, when he started to tell the congregation about the fitting of the new pews. "Well there are bits of Mike's skin hanging off the crucifix and blood of course, which I'll have to go back later to clean off where he fell against it."

She gripped the side of the kitchen table. "What!, you can't be serious?" Elaine shrieked and looked at John and couldn't believe his indifference.

"That's a nice hug daddy." Rachel looked up at John and started to twiddle his hair. "Oh look mummy, daddy's hair is getting long. You need to get it cut daddy and it's turning red, look mum, look here!"

Future Publications

Adult

Collared
The Third Incarnation
It's all in the Bag
Possession is Nine Tenths of the Law
My Grandfather Child
New Pews, Eucharist
Damocles Scalpel

Children's

Captain Flash, The Cuddly Horse and his Magic Dreams.

Stories include:
Admiral Rawandsnarl and the Pirate Penguins
Captain Flash and The Frothing Whirlpool.

Grampy's Stories
Ned and Alf, The Giants. The Golden Eagle and
The Indian Minor.

Facebook : Stephen E. Scott

The Second Release : It's all in The Bag

I see this as hopefully "a self help", short 11 month autobiography , when initially after diagnosis, I thought I was going to die. Aside from my wife, daughter, family and friends; the most important thing I wanted to do, was to publish the books I had been writing.

Hopefully, it will help someone or someone they care about, avoid going through, what I went through because it is not just the person diagnosed that "goes through it" but everyone, when a person is told "we're sorry to tell you, you've got cancer."

Your life is too important, read this, don't lose it, live it.

The Third Release : Collared

Some things in life can't be forgotten. As a child, you are innocent unless you are exposed to the deplorable, evil side of human nature. Looking back, you realise that what you have gone through, took away your innocence.

Few people get the chance or are strong enough if that chance comes along, to take revenge on the perpetrator who stole your innocence. Natalie is lucky. She is one of the few............and she has friends.

The Third Novel : The Third Incarnation

If you believe in the immortal soul, reincarnation, heaven, hell, the afterlife; the afterlife of one life is the pre life of the next.

Rebecca's third incarnation with her new parents and sister, is not like her previous existences.

Printed in Poland
by Amazon Fulfillment
Poland Sp. z o.o., Wrocław